WHITE TOPEE

Also by Eve Langley
The Pea-Pickers

ANGUS & ROBERTSON PUBLISHERS

*Unit 4, Eden Park, 31 Waterloo Road,
North Ryde, NSW, Australia 2113;
94 Newton Road, Auckland 1,
New Zealand; and
16 Golden Square, London W1R 4BN,
United Kingdom*

*First published in Australia
by Angus & Robertson Publishers in 1954
This Sirius paperback edition 1989*

Copyright © Eve Langley, 1954

*National Library of Australia
Cataloguing-in-publication data.*

*Langley, Eve, 1908-1974.
  White topee.*

  ISBN 0 207 16283 2.

  I. Title.

A823'.2

Printed in Australia by Griffin Press

WHITE TOPEE

EVE LANGLEY

SIRIUS

INTRODUCTION

In June 1974 the body of Eve Maria Langley was found in her three-roomed hut, 'Iona Lympus', at Katoomba NSW. The date of death was given as somewhere between the 1st and 13th of June. Most details on the Death Certificate were given as 'not known'. The body had lain undisturbed for about a month and the face was gnawed by rats. Only the investigations of the local pensions officer had led to its discovery. The cause of death was determined as: (1) Coronary occlusion (Hours); (2) Atherosclerosis (Years).

The Katoomba hut, and also a blue and yellow gypsy bus, disgorged boxes of mouldering rubbish, all the memorabilia with which Eve Langley shored up her identity. (This "identity" fanned out into a series of roles, fantastic and theatrically costumed. Langley was Oscar Wilde, John Keats, Prince Saltykov, Jesus Christ, Adolf Hitler — anything transcending Eve Langley, mistakenly female, artistically rejected.) There were photographs, old gramophone records, odd packages collected for 'Oscar', carefully wrapped and containing nothing. A battered trunk bore the name 'Oscar Wilde' on one side, 'Eve Langley' on the other. Amongst a collection of empty cat food cans and wine bottles presided her family of dolls and a large teddy-bear.

Already the bush was taking over. In 1984 nothing remained but the abandoned hut and an unmarked ditch of a grave, high on the hill in the Katoomba cemetery.

Few people knew who she was — yet she had seemed, once, to be assured a place as a major Australian novelist. Her early promise is evidenced by a considerable body of poetry, short stories, articles and plays published in literary magazines in Australia and New Zealand. Her champions included Douglas Stewart, Frank Dalby Davison, Norman Lindsay, Hal Porter, Ruth Park, Gloria Rawlinson, Robin Hyde...

She had never stopped writing. She had died with a strong literary reputation, but in eclipse. The Mitchell Library, NSW, holds ten other 'novels' in manuscript form and also an enormous collection of poetry, prose, sketches, other unfinished 'novels' on brown paper, blurred jottings on Weetie boxes. She wrote tirelessly, swiftly, prolifically. Yet to what ultimate purpose? In those unpublished manuscripts Eve Langley emerges as an artist of exceptional calibre, but constantly betrayed into lesser achievement.

Eve Maria Langley (christened Ethel Jane)[1] was born on a cattle station, 'Forbes', near Molong NSW in 1904. Her sister, June Lilian (the model for Blue, Steve's mate in *The Pea-Pickers*), was born a year later and would be her inseparable companion for three decades. Her mother, Mira Langley (nee Davidson) had married Arthur Langley, an itinerant labourer, in 1902 — thereby disinheriting herself from Gippsland family's landholdings. Langley's earliest bushman fantasies were powerfully fed by this female precariousness in the face of a solid bush patriarchy. Arthur Langley died, Mira threw her lot in with an Irishman, Patrick Cullen (whom the girls cordially detested), and the family moved again — briefly to Brunswick, Victoria; and thence to Dandenong.

Langley's formal education was perfunctory. After attending several State schools she took on domestic work, then became a printer's devil at Walker and May's in Melbourne (disguised as a boy). She read voraciously, already intent on fabricating a fabulous mythical ancestry for herself and her family — part Jewish, part Roman, part Greek and part Scythian.[2]

In the 1920s Eve and June (now Steve and Blue) began their sojourn fruit- tea- and pea-picking in Gippsland. The girls were dressed as boys, for which deception they soon ran foul of the local constabulary. They sought to find their true heritage and ancestry. This is the stuff from which *The Pea-Pickers* is fashioned. On one level the novel is sheer gutsy, picaresque adventure, cavalier and episodic, the broadly comic yarn of the storyteller. Yet Langley's descriptions of landscape are already heightened, they are carefully crafted lyric prose. (In later work they would become overwhelming to the detriment of conventional plot and characterisation.)

The reasons behind this public and personal confounding in Eve Langley's writing are complex and disquieting. Some of them are to be found in her inability to define herself as a female artist (on both counts), in her growing fixation with time and immortality and with a golden past seeded with decay at its very inception. And add to this a prose style which exploded the bounds of appropriate literary codes and decorum, deeply offending certain sections of the critical establishment.

Thus the very tone of *White Topee* is muted, wistful, elegiac; it is a protracted, nostalgic, backward-turning meditation . . . In her own words, Langley is 'sick with memory' (*WT,* p. 95). She is immortalising her own past, contemplating a company of ghosts. Two passages on the Australian summer will suffice to show this:

> And joining themselves to that line I saw our own dreams, and the toil we had given out of ourselves through this great ideal summer, the Australian summer that we had shared together and that now was ended. (*WT,* p. 250).

> In those days my mind was foaming over with richness. And a summer like that summer will never come back again. (*WT,* p. 4).

Langley had lived half a century at the time of *White Topee*'s publication. In the novel she is salvaging the responses and ambitions of a girl in her late twenties, a girl racketing around Gippsland masquerading as a boy, a girl dreaming of becoming the poet of Gippsland's fiery past. And the hindsight is both painful and protective:

> . . . she writes incessantly and endlessly about that time as though she had been bewitched like a princess — you know, fallen asleep for a hundred years, bewitched in that era.[3]

In both *The Pea-Pickers* and *White Topee* Langley's two great desires, to be loved and to be famous, collide head on in the pursuit of predictably inappropriate love objects. Macca, the first and last of her blazing golden gods is simply a slow, puzzled, somewhat ironic Gippsland male — but his massive mythic dimensions ignite the entire landscape and obscure any viable domestic image.

At the end of both novels, Langley's protagonist's choice between the demands of life and art is ostensibly solid. Steve chooses splendid isolation, she eschews marriage since marriage implies, for her, creative anaesthesia. But the fault lines are already apparent in *The Pea-Pickers*. Steve's role playing may be light hearted and mockingly undercut; yet the central conflict is clearly delineated as early as p. 3:

> I knew that I was a woman, but I thought I should have been a man. I knew that I was comical — but I thought I was serious and beautiful as well. It was tragic to be only

a comical woman when I longed above all things to be a serious and handsome man.

The third point of my consciousness was a desire for freedom, that is, never to work.

The fourth was a desire, amounting to obsession, to be loved.

The tone in *White Topee* is altered, the charade more strident. Steve is more consciously 'male' in her pursuits, she collects rifles and finally she launches into an extraordinary explanation of her behaviour. (Extraordinary also in the sense that Angus & Robertson should publish it in 1954!) For what Steve describes as an explanation for her behaviour is her own reincarnation as Oscar Wilde, inexplicably cast down as a female baby in a buggy in Manildra, NSW, the child of Mira and Arthur Langley. Given this explanation, it is easy to understand how Langley's later, more erotically graphic and exotic fantasies were not so easily deemed publishable for a general reading public. Hence the massive store of unpublished manuscripts that followed her every move from Victoria.

In 1932 Langley followed June and Mira to New Zealand. She fell in swiftly with the bohemian and artistic circles of Auckland. In 1936 she met Hilary Clark who, subsisting romantically in an old mill, was immediately transmuted into yet another of the golden-haired Apollo figures Macca had inspired. (The males destined to become the objects of Langley's passion always merge into one mythic shape. Yet she would marry Hilary and bear him three children.)

The breakdown of her marriage to Hilary Clark is detailed in the New Zealand manuscripts. Langley, now seriously torn between the demands of motherhood, wifehood and artistic creativity, became increasingly depressed. The role of artist was seen as primarily the province of Hilary and she attempted to put his creative needs before her own, with disastrous results. Her delusions increased and she suffered considerably from pressure from her mother-in-law to conform to a more acceptable stereotype. Her own guilt and her inability to control what she saw as two distinct and mutually exclusive functions grew insupportable.

On 14 August 1942 she was committed by Hilary to Auckland

Mental Hospital, where she was to remain until 6 March 1949. The condition was diagnosed as schizophrenia (for which she would have received Electric Shock Therapy without the benefit of relaxants). She was to be re-committed (again by Hilary) for some months in 1950. On 31 March 1952 the marriage was dissolved by Decree absolute. Langley returned to her life as the isolated poet — living in a boarding house, collecting publishers rejections.

On 16 June 1954 she had her name changed by Deed Poll to Oscar Wilde. All mail now came addressed to 'Oscar'. She specifically requested that Angus & Robertson recognise the change because:

> As Oscar Wilde I can take anything and the rottenest rebuff and disappointment this world holds and remain myself inviolate, free white and twenty-one, with not a care in the world. But as Eve Langley I just collapse at the first blow into a vomiting fainting mass of death.[4]

In 1960 Eve Langley returned permanently to Australia, purchasing the shack 'Iona Lympus' in the Blue Mountains. She continued to write, to plan trips to England and her beloved Greece — to which she managed an abortive visit in 1965, only to be bailed out back to Australia through the auspices of Douglas Stewart and Angus & Robertson. She returned home to her hut, debilitated, starving, clutching what was left of her treasured baggage and the remnants of her doll family. There she would remain for the next nine years, writing, silent, 'not known'.

Despite the obvious dislocation in Eve Langley's development, a thorough assessment of her unpublished work remains to be done. Her achievement remains considerable, the lyric detail and intensity of her prose unique in Australian fiction. But one central problem of her life and work is this falling away from a brilliant beginning. The doubts begin to accrue with *White Topee. Is* it her swan song, uncongenial, bravely published by Angus & Robertson either to bastion her reputation or to provide a peculiar memorial to her talent? Was Langley merely deteriorating into dottiness or taking a new direction, developing a different sort of fiction, already there in the dense, dream landscapes of *The Pea-Pickers*?

Certainly the editors at Angus & Robertson *wanted* to publish the manuscript, and no doubt they were set to perform the same 'agonised midwifery' that Beatrice Davis performed when editing *The Pea-Pickers*[5] — but there were doubts, reservations, apprehensions as attested by their reports:

> This novel pruned and condensed, would certainly be worth publishing. It is written with Eve Langley's characteristic brilliance and originality... But I am afraid that no amount of editing will make it as good as *The Pea-Pickers*.
>
> *White Topees* [original title] has many of the virtues of *The Pea-Pickers*... but somehow there is less of them, particularly of the humour.
>
> I think we should publish it, in a condensed form. With some writers it might be better not to accept a second novel that is very like the first and inferior to it. But in this case we may never see a third, and there are very few writers of Eve Langley's quality — even her second-best quality.[6]

On top of everything else (there were worries about shapelessness, the love affair with Macca seemed to be 'even more unsatisfactory than before', the static, uneventful earthing of the Steve character in a tea plantation, the lack of developed characters: there was 'no-one to share the central space with Steve' and thus 'her introspection... [was] quite unbridled'), there was the problem of the fantastic Oscar Wilde reincarnation sequence towards the novel's end — Langley's own explanation for her male creative powers bonded to a female shape. After much vacillation Langley herself had written to Angus & Robertson:

> Have decided to send over to you a part that is to me, its most important part. But which, being unusual, I thought I would leave out. It is a powerful piece of writing, but since it really is my own recollection of being born, or my 'continuity of being' feeling which I have kept secret for years, I felt shy about sending it to you.
>
> ...it makes me feel so ill, sometimes, as though I had not not been born, but had been found out in the bush, shanghaied, that I cannot bear to think on it for too long.[7]

Her agonies over the passage became exacerbated with delay and debate at Angus & Robertson. In her mind the passage had by now become a full-blown *idée fixe*: it would be the basis of her next 'novel', *Wild Australia*. Consternation then rose to panic as she remonstrated with Angus & Robertson:

> Those who read the Oscar Wilde passages in *White Topees* couldn't undersand how you would refer to them as dubious . . . for Gods sake bring out *White Topees* and leave in the Oscar Wilde part, because its different. Why other writers can write what they like and why I CAN'T, I don't know.[8]

Today, what the editors at Angus & Robertson called 'a strange and fascinating episode' remains as an integral part of the novel; it is odd company in a supposedly naturalistic novel of the 1950s. In 1954, quite predictably, the critics came baying in confused directions: there was simply no formula to contain this latest Langley. Two pronouncements are typical:

> It is impossible to be lukewarm about Eve Langley. Either you lap up her strikingly original prose, or you wonder what the heck she's writing about.[9]

> . . .*White Topee* is more than anything else a poem . . . but much of it is a poem disguised as prose . . . and in reading it one is in the presence of something great amid a rambling eccentricity.[10]

Over and over the unadulterated authorial egoism and lack of plot and structure in the book is bewailed, the fantastic, disturbing qualities of the work continuously dissected, the poetry praised — as a cuckoo in the wrong literary nest. Langley is brilliant, peculiar, radical . . . and indigestible. There is a strong conviction that genius has fumbled badly or perpetrated a mockery, played a silly trick at a respectable *soirée*:

> It is possible — in fact it must be — that we of ordinary common clay just don't penetrate into those magic regions or meet the fabulous people which individuals of exquisite sensibility seem to come across by instinct, even in Australia . . . This reaction may have been caused by the feeling I had, right through this book, that I was being hoaxed, that Eve Langley couldn't possibly be serious.[11]

Yet the very intensity of critical reaction, even the splenetic pique voiced by those most outraged at Langley's performance, highlights the uniqueness, the infuriatingly illegitimate power and revolutionary thrust informing the work. Langley is patently *not* telling a tale — and this creates a defensive literary dyspepsia:

> This is a curious and exasperating book...it may be a novel, it may be a tone poem in language...[It has] a life such as that of a half-broken horse pig-rooting half across a paddock rather than going about its proper business of getting somewhere in particular.
>
> [There is] the difficulty of finding its proper category...the difficulty of finding in it any pattern of image and event which is capable of revealing, on the part of its author, an artistic purpose and plan.
>
> Everything, from seasonal changes to a casual word of encounter, is filtered through the mesh of an over-urgent imagination which relies too exclusively on sense images... Everything is thickened and congealed with the emotions of suggestiveness... There is no characterisation, no developing action, no sense of a way of life in which men engage and in which they may find their own significance.[12]

It is all, superficially, quite fair enough. In *White Topee* Steve goes tea-picking at Jim McLachlan's, pea-picking at Domenic Olivieri's. She refuses Macca's proposal and then bewails her loss. She regrets the passing of an era. She writes to Blue. She records comic episodes amongst the Italian pickers. She chronicles Gippsland's past. She rides off over the Australian Alps with her racehorse Alpini II and her dog Micolo, glancing back nostalgically at Gippsland's ghosts. She writes a lot of poetry. That is all there is to the plot and the cast.

But that is *not* all there is to this extraordinary novel. Steve is intoxicated with a landscape of dreams and images, and hell-bent on immortalising an incandescent Gippsland which fades as she gazes. She is its poet, its chronicler, alone and dedicated. Her central consciousness is thus intensely vulnerable to the fading flares of visual shows and sensations. Her vocation also involves the jettisoning of her female function — hence the embracing of the Oscar Wilde persona. She absorbs landscapes, observes her own role, orchestrates a repeating pattern of haunting and precise sense impressions which cluster, resonate and determine the shape and texture of the novel. *White Topee* is thus the figure of her youth, of a last springtime and summer, the 'last and loveliest' (*WT,* p. 61) she would ever know.

Langley is immortalising a long, doomed season, celebrating and transmuting each detail. Consequently the surface texture of the novel is all blue-dazzle and fizzing silver. It spirals down to a magnetic centre of concentration, to the white topee itself as it revolves outside her hut. The white topee is thus the symbolic vortex of the novel, to which all the other carefully studded gleams and glimpses of the Gippsland lakes and bushland accrue like luminous, palpable confetti:

> The memory of that hut! The poem-saturated place, the golden walls and the dark, the Grecian tea-tree marsh just behind it, with one white topee swirling day and night in all weathers, on a short broken staff of tea-tree. I loved the look of that topee. It was an idol, a god, to me — the great god of the British Empire. I remember the day I set it there.
>
> The ancient days gradually washed it white, and the sun and the moon and the wind gave it a grandeur inexpressible. And this solar helmet spinning and flying on its living axis, gave to my days a gubernatorial nobility. . . The white topee was the eternal symbol of the white man as it swung back and forth under the Australian sun, and coldly and most lonely under the Aurora Australis, the pink and subtly thunderous Aurora Australis, and the blanched craters of the slow-moving moon. (*WT*, p. 153–4).

But it would be too simplistic to read the white topee as merely a figure for imperialism — it is neither limited nor specific. Rather, it represents all that is exotic, nostalgic and transitory in Langley's memoried Gippsland Lakes landscape. More than that, the white topee catalyses the process of creativity, it represents Langley's own unique theory of composition:

> I write books and this [*sic*] books because of continuity of being and an endeavour to relate Time and Space and Objects to myself. . . anything white arouses a great flash of light and sense of immortality in my mind and the white topee of the tea planter whirling in the pole by my hut in the bush, keeps reminding me of something in the East, and an endless stream of stories and past days pour out of it . . . I can only say that the linking up to Time and Space and Objectivity is great fun, and makes one feel

immortal and able to remember. . . such an infinite variety of experiences.[13]

It is all this 'variety of experiences', this lushness of vanishing, hallucinatory landscape that Langley captures in the charged prose of the novel. As Steve in the novel she wears the topee everywhere (she has six of them!). As Eve Langley she would wear it defiantly up and down the streets of Katoomba, exciting considerable interest.

If the topee is the spotlight, then the bush and lakes provide a vast cyclorama, picked out in minutely observed detail, wind, water, lakes, sky and shifting seasons brood over delicately chiselled miniatures. Langley wants 'to cry out everything in one long tumultuous inky shout'. (*WT*, p. 61) Even a printed page of poetry can mesmerise:

> Frail colonial poetry. . .the very italics in which it was printed had the charm of fine wheat. It fell delicately into the mind and sprouted there. (*WT*, p. 16)

Langley's strength lies in a dense superimposition of unpredictable figures, a synaesthetic combination which wires the prose with small shocks. Ferns hump 'like the hard backs of black eagles' (*WT*, p. 74); the bracken has lost 'the furry bouts of youth and [is] furrowed with ribbed lines of leather' (*WT*, p. 145); gums spiral slowly in the sparkling fires of a 'rainy blue air' (*WT*, p. 61); a wattle tosses its mane extravagantly 'a head of soft powdery golden curls stuck out of every dark place — a gigantic theatrical wig of gold above a silver face, for its leaves were like misty coins' (*WT*, p. 62); Kookaburras slice the sky with their 'naked steely laugh' (*WT*, p. 145); hawks balance 'their tawny wings making tilted lights against the blue sky, a syllable formed between the element and the bird' (*WT*, p. 55); gum trees flaunt 'their million leaves. . .like red-lacquered eyes' (*WT*, p. 99), and cut ferns 'exuded musically. . .their clear sap' (*WT*, p. 9). . . And at the centre of all these remembered scenes of her dream district runs Steve's attempt to defeat Time and Transcience, to reclaim and repossess a season that will never come again:

> Now all those days were far away, and in the hut [where she and Macca trysted] I thought, there is silence, desolation, wreckage, coldness and patches of quiet moonlight where there should be music, happy love, strong walls, warmth, and eternally loved faces. Agony

and sorrow stabbed my heart like spears. Yet I knew the real and perfect joy that comes to one who has kept the faith and loved strongly all the past. I am the ghost, the lonely phantom, the familiar spirit that haunts the house of those I loved long ago.

I thought of nothing but Time. Time was my passion. (*WT*, p. 69)

At such moments the narrative focus shifts subtly, it becomes a wistful elegiac lament. Steve, the poet, the preserver, the lone 'bushman' dedicated to self-imposed isolation surveys a more complicated field of conflict. Macca, the golden god, is both temptation and trap. To marry him would be to condemn herself to the constrictions of married female life. This is the dilemma Langley wrestled with throughout her life — even to that last hut in Katoomba.

Thus Steve, in the first proposal scene, rejects Macca relatively painlessly. She is desired and powerful and able to rise to a somewhat melodramatic sacrifice. The assumption of a male persona — she would far rather be Macca's mate and discuss the virtues of Bairnsdale's females — protects her:

> Because, you see, I really didn't want to be loved. Not at all. What I really wanted was to be a man, and free for ever to write and think and dream... I would rather have wandered the earth and written for ever than bothered about love. (*WT*, p. 157)

Later in the novel, rejected rather than rejecting, her resolve weakens. She begs her lover for a blood-red camellia that he is engaged in gathering so as to adorn another woman's dress. Her emotions war, she would be 'purely feminine and want him, and win him' on the one hand; but, determinedly, 'tormentedly virgin' (*WT*, p. 165) on the other hand, she casts her lot back in with 'the past and poetry' (*WT*, p. 163). The distress that results is deep, and uncomfortably close to the doubts that would forever dog Langley herself. Steve may want to be 'six feet in height, with enough strength to lift half a ton', (*WT*, p. 222) and go working in Malaya New Guinea, she may want 'anything, anything rather than be a woman' (*WT*, p. 221–2), she may dream of longing 'to be a man and live in dry yellow glittering gum-leafed gunyahs and labour in pitiless heat' (*WT*, p. 50)...but her female self constantly confronts and confounds her. She is at ease in neither role:

> I had not the reasoning powers of a man, whose summing up of his kind is based on humanity. Mine was based on femininity, and femininity must be fed with emotion and passion, the lesser things bringing pain in the backwash. (*WT*, p. 93)

Consequently the rejection mechanism that Steve employed against Macca offered no real resolution for Langley. She remained embattled against conflicting impulses and beliefs, finding no satisfying solution even in the assumption of the Oscar Wilde persona.

Macca was more, however, than the deified male Langley (or Steve) might have been. He carried within him the weathers and seasons of her beloved Gippsland. He symbolised its 'many pasts' and its passing:

> Macca was to me the symbol of man in the year 1928 in Australia, and that symbol, and man as he was, they were both flying from me... In those days so many were being born that they loaded the young with premature age, and hurried them onward that they might find a place for themselves. Hating change of any sort, I saw Macca and his kind changing before me and new men coming along of another age, and new songs to take the place of those they sang. (*WT*, p. 223)

It is this obsession with reclaiming and immortalising a golden past — fraught as this is with grief over a lost youth, and coloured as it is by the ongoing struggle between male and female energies — that renders the orthodoxies of plot and characterisation an irrelevance in *White Topee*. As late as 1960 Beatrice Davis, Langley's editor at Angus & Robertson attempted to gently nudge Langley towards writing for a wider readership:

> The point is that you, with your genius for poetry and fantasy, are a writer for the few who are capable of appreciating your gifts.[14]

But Eve Langley remained unmoved. Her books, to her, were not fantastic at all — instead they dovetailed unremarkably with her understanding of reality as 'the landscapes of dreams'. She believed that these dreams, if approached with a newer understanding, might well offer at least as much as — if not more than — neat plot and characterisation. Ruth Park offers a final insight:

> I have thought long and seriously about the following comment: she was the sanest, the most stable person I ever knew. She was, I believe, born into the wrong age..[15]

Joy L. Thwaite, Sydney, 1989

NOTES

1. Extract Certificate. Birth registered in NSW, 1 September 1904. Ethel Jane Langley.
2. Hazel de Berg, *Eve Langley* (Tape 49—Cut One, National Library Tape, Canberra, 1964).
3. Hal Porter, cited in "The Shadows are Different: An Appreciation of Eve Langley" (ABC Radio Drama Features, 1975). Transcript p. 14.
4. Eve Langley. *Eve Langley: Restricted Papers (Angus & Robertson Correspondence File: 1941-1968).* Letter to Nan McDonald, 12 April 1954. Mitchell Library. MSS3269.
5. Ruth Park, "Some Notes on my personal association with the writer Eve Langley, in 1940–42, Auckland, New Zealand". Written at Norfolk Island, August 1976, p. 6. Mitchell Library. MSS3128.
6. Readers' Reports on *White Topee*, undated. Mitchell Library. MSS3269.
7. Letter from Eve Langley to Angus & Robertson, 8 December, 1952. Mitchell Library. MSS3269.
8. Letter from Eve Langley to Angus & Robertson, 30 March, 1954. Mitchell Library. MSS3269.
9. Peggy Wright, *News Ltd.,* Adelaide, 29.7.54. Thursday Woman's Magazine, p. 9.
10. *Sydney Morning Herald,* 21.8.54 (no page no. Angus & Robertson photocopy).
11. William Stewart (Angus & Robertson photocopy—paper uncited) 14.7.54.
12. Vincent Buckley, *Voice* (Vol. 4, No. 2) December, 1954, p. 27).
13. Eve Langley, "Biographical Questionnaire" sent to Angus & Robertson, 14 April, 1950. Copy lent by Meg Stewart/Angus & Robertson.
14. Letter from Beatrice Davis to Eve Langley, 7 January, 1960. Mitchell Library. MSS3269.
15. Ruth Park, "Notes", p. 6.

CONTENTS

DOWN CALULU WAY

I

THE Australian sun rose rapidly, blindingly; entered the lonely gully and began to scorch more easily the short dry grass around my hut. I heard the iron on the roof give an uneasy warning note at the sudden heat; I saw the light burn on the heads of the dry bracken. I flung open the door of the baracca, as I called it, and in white cotton pyjamas I stood for coolness on the hard dry dirt outside and stared up the gully.

On my right above lay the sloping hill of the tea paddocks, the largest field, on my left, an uncultivated and high hill of ferns and eucalyptus and dry white logs hidden from sight in the deep undergrowth. The entire place was the property of Jim McLachlan, an island tea-planter who had come from somewhere round Malaya with the intention of growing tea on his Victorian estate. He had a large and beautiful residence on the Lakes, a tennis court rising white and enticing out of a huge olive-green garden of passion fruit. And around the property were two hundred acres planted out with different types of tea-plants, Ceylonese, Indian, Malayan, and Chinese. Right down on the blue edge of the lake stood the offices and tea factory and sheds. About were the numerous more or less luxurious little huts in which he housed his staff. I attended to his mail and to the field books and did all the typing for the company of McLachlan, McMillan and Company. McMillan, a big New South Wales squatter, and a grandson of the McMillan, the explorer who opened up Gippsland, which is now dotted with stony solemn grey cairns to his memory, had shares in the affair. He and McLachlan knew my family well, and so I came to be working on this plantation.

Behind my hut the gully continued, dry and white, with a dark bearded twilight of tea-tree in the middle; beyond that, a spring of scummy water, and beyond that, Fell's Swamp, full of

3

wild duck and turtles. One cannot describe such a gully, for it is in the flesh of those that live in it and partakes of their fears and joys. By association, it had grown beautiful to me. The white earth was keen and dramatic; the sparse grass rich, since I saw no other; and the few bush violets growing in the tea-tree grove had a dewy and classical look; a mysterious purple was embedded in them; a frosty white furry tongue was set in their mouths and caught a little of the morning dew before the deadly sun burnt everything. The chief enchantment, to me, was the wild roar of the wind, far above me, caught in the bracken and bright wild dandelions that whirled on their stalks all day, and did not live long. This wild and desirous wind that rarely reached me came from the sheets of bright blue water, the long and brilliant Gippsland Lakes. Since I could escape it, I loved to hear it. While it wrestled with itself and the bushes on the hill, and the far-off dry wooden farm-houses, I was happy. It held a sound of torment, bewitching, ringing, and sad. On off-days I sat in the shade of the baracca, cleaning my seven rifles and writing interminably majestic prose and blank verse. In those days my mind was foaming over with richness. And a summer like that summer will never come back again.

On working days I rose up and dressed in corded breeches, white shirt and topee, and went "over the top", as we called the great hill between the huts and the main paddock, and down into the offices to lend a hand, or now and then, out into the paddocks to act as overseer. I used to call myself "the overseer" in those days, for I had the driving critical concentration of one of the ancient Egyptian sort, indigenous to the Pyramids around Luxor. I had to see that the sample of leaf picked was large enough—and small enough—and picked at the precisely right stage, and also to see that so many baskets an hour were picked. It makes a lot of difference in the drying if one can get a large amount into the sheds in one go. I was beloved of the Italian and Chinese pickers, who spoke of me most admirably in their several tongues, and told me in effect that I only needed a large whip and the Pyramids at the back of me. We worked a thirty- to twenty-hour week, from Monday to Friday, because of the great heat. On this Saturday late in 1927 I was to visit my friends, Edgar Buccaneer and his wife, who

4

lived in the village and operated their fishing fleet all over the Gippsland Lakes.

My dog Teddy, sleeping in a fish-crate at the foot of a stump, whimpered with a watery sound, as who would not, having slept for long in a crate that had been used to take fish to market? In the lane the racehorse grazed. The day was going to be very hot. I went into my hut and dressed in riding kit, a sleeveless brown silk shirt, breeches, and high boots. I caught the startled Alpini II, saddled him, and with the many graceful wheelings and turnings necessary for the species to open gates, which mine could do with an exquisite cleverness, we set off for the village.

Edgar's wife heard the swooping drum of the racer's hooves as I cantered up the grassy hill to the house, and she came out on the veranda. The Black Serpent, as I called her, was one of the most immortal and marvellous women I have ever known. She had a Kirghiz face, a round brown-red Tartar face, with lined lips curling over her teeth and many creases about her mouth. She shook her hair back from her face with a proud confident gesture when she came forward to greet me.

"Thought you might come today, Steve," she said. "I have been thinking of New Year's Day. Macca is coming down for the regatta, perhaps. He will want to see you. And see you change. Why will you never change, Steve? I mean, when are you going to give up wearing shirts and shorts and topees and khaki slacks around, and dress—well, as you ought to dress?"

I smiled and lit a cigarette, the remarkable blue and gold Polo brand that was being smoked to death in Australia at that time. Every summer punctually I was asked to change my evil ways, and get out of my field clothes and sun helmet into something frilly.

"No," I said, as I watched her slowly making tea and pouring it out in cups with yellow milk from her own cows, and setting out on the table large rough golden buns and a plate of salty butter. "No, I am afraid I cannot change. I know you are dying to get me into a frightfully frilly frock, with a wide hat and silk stockings and Paris heels as high as Eiffel, but, my dear, consider—I shall have to ride home to the plantation on Alpini. Anyhow, McLachlan thinks that feminine clothes look

5

out of place on his plantation. He comes from the saronged islands, and the lava-lava'd tropics. Why affront an old Oxonian with half the gardens of England scattered over a ninon frock? And Macca does not care what I wear. No, I am going to wear, if it is fine, my tropical kit; if it is wet, my Donegal tweeds and the good old Scotch College sweater of cardinal, gold and royal blue, cardinal." I had inherited this from my cousins, who went to Scotch College, the best college in the Southern Hemisphere according to them, as my father had gone before them. "Remember Cicero—'If we are to be real friends, you must love me for myself, not for my clothes.' I do hope you remember Cicero?"

The Black Serpent sighed, and said that she did not.

Impatiently I said then, "After all, it is the essence of the man and the past that I am meeting. It is the poetry we knew together, and the Latin translation we loved doing a few summers ago. All these things must spring into his mind when we meet. And all the old, old Italian songs that we sang together." For my old mate Mackinnon was a great sort of poet in his way, a reddish-haired youth with blue eyes and a dreamy expression. He spoke in ironic tones, but with a real touch of genius, and talked like a long Australian coast-line, lying hot under the showering down of the sun. He was a drover by choice, preferring to bring stock down from Black Mountain and Bogong High Plains rather than to push a pen in an office. Macca was of the old tradition.

"But clothes are important," said the Black Serpent, adding a rushing steam of amber tea to her cup. The gate clicked. "There's Edgar," she said.

Her husband came in, tall, broad-shouldered and stooped. His eyes twinkled bluely and humorously at the sight of me. Flinging his hat over to a chair in the corner, he dragged at his golden moustache and brushed his black hair. For, astonishingly enough, he really had a bright golden moustache and a head of jet-black hair. "Ha! Wilde!" he said. For some reason or other he often called me Wilde. It was a change from "Steve Hart", which most of my friends called me, and which was enough to make bank managers reach for their automatics at the mere sight of me.

Edgar Buccaneer had been along the foreshore inspecting the great mass of nets his crew had piled up and out to dry. We sat talking of the fishing, absently, lazily. I felt completely contented and very dull with the great load of the heat of the long Australian summer morning. I was waiting. After New Year's Day, I promised myself, life would change. A brilliancy would come into me.

"Jess, did you make up those returns for the week?" said Edgar. "The market's gone down again, I hear. So Henderson said this morning. He got a telegram from the agents saying that the market had dropped. The Hendersons are splitting up, too. The old man was saying that Tom would be fishing on his own this year, with a big fleet. He's bought two or three motor trucks and another new car, and he's employing drivers to sell fish in Bruthen and Bairnsdale as well as send it down to the markets. Get rich that way," said Edgar indolently. He had enough himself, but kept the fleet going out of sentiment, and as an interest for his son, Eb. "By the way, Steve, Tom wondered if you would do a bit of selvedging for him this week-end, after you finish up out at the tea-plantation. Soon as you're ready. About twenty or forty fathom to do, if you're willing. He can't get anyone else to do it during the week or the week-end, and now that he's starting out with his own fleet, he wants to get this net fixed up."

"I haven't done any selvedging for ages," I said. "And I *did* want my next few week-ends free, but since Tom's a Melbourne University man, I will, for the sake of the old school tie, help the dear boy out, by a bit of delicate embroidering. The pickers are picking the leaf at the peak now, down on the lake side. Oh, a gorgeous sample. You know——" I was thoroughly Conrad in my love of that sea, that lake, and all the wealth of richness it gave to the luminous and salty soil above and around it— "that wet hill just above the lake near Leonard Fell's is the best possible place, to my mind, for growing tea. Jim McLachlan says its over-rich and will dry it out in time. But you get a wonderful quality in the leaf, an instinct for purple or a reddish, shellish blend. And the leaves glitter in the sun some days and are perfumed splendidly. McLachlan says that the Chinese variety does best there."

"McLachlan knows how to grow tea all right," said Edgar.

"By the way, I promised Leonardo della Vergine that I'd go down during the week-end and attend to his accounts generally.

7

I don't know how I'm to do Tom Henderson's selvedging at the one and same time."

Edgar began to laugh at the name of Leonardo, an Italian tea-planter farther down the lakes at Calulu. "Ha, ha, reminds me! Saw him going into Bairnsdale on the *Gippsland* the other day, wearing a big grey hat high up on two hairs on his head."

"I can imagine."

"Yes, he tried to get it off to wave good-bye to one of his cobbers on the jetty, you know, and it stuck. The boat was almost out of sight when the hat came off with a bang you could hear from here to Wood's Point."

"Go on! Now you're stretching it."

"What, the hat? My oath, someone ought to have stretched it!"

"I suppose you're getting ready for the regatta on New Year's Day?" I asked, remembering the coming down of Macca.

"Yes, getting the old double-barrel ready for the event, you know." Edgar was the regatta starter every year, and had held that office for over twenty years.

Since I had promised to selvedge the net for Tom Henderson, it was assumed that I should stay for the week-end at the Buccaneer's. Next morning, Eb, the son of the house, a big fair viking of a youth, a splendid shot with a rifle, a genius at tennis, and the best duck-shooter around Gippsland, brought the long, white, fairy, silent nets up to the house. He hammered a nail into the wall, strung an end of the net on it and, giving me a threaded netting needle, left me to it with the heavily swaying mesh. Up and down the wide veranda overlooking the sea I paced, peacefully, slowly, calmly, like a Greek peripatetic philosopher. On the opposite veranda Eb was doing the same. A wide cool veranda, of the island-bungalow sort, went right round the house. We Greeks kept at it. I chanted lines from the *Aeneid* while I worked and Eb sang island songs of a Hawaiian nature. Every so often tea and cakes were brought out to us, and we were content. When we had finished our forty fathom or so each we went down to collect five guineas apiece from Tom Henderson. He was a startlingly individual looking person, with a magnificent head of the most beautiful fair hair I had ever seen, and a small fair moustache. He had a heavy Oxford accent, but most Melbourne University men of the twenties had. As we sat smoking on his veranda he said, "I may be able to give you some more work soon."

"By Jove," I said, "I'm about booked up. I'm out working in Jim McLachlan's office, and next week-end I have to go down and help Leonardo della Vergine out with his books."

"Well, I'm stuck, really, Steve. And frightfully busy myself, getting my new fleet out. And I only want a big dinghy I've got turned over, and scraped, de-barnacled, and careened generally. I'll give you a tenner for the job, if you'll take it on. You and Eb could do it together. It wants a coat of priming and fresh paint. If you're interested you could drop in and let me know."

We regarded Tom solemnly and guardedly.

"Hang it all, though," said Eb, "the Gippsland Tennis Championships are coming off soon! I don't know . . . really . . ."

"Ah, yes, of course, there's your tennis, Eb," said Tom.

"And when I think of you, old boy, whacking away towards the silver cup on the courts in Bairnsdale while Steve and I scratch the insects off that liner of yours . . . I don't know." Eb looked heatedly at the Melbourne University man.

"Well, Steve doesn't play tennis as much as you, really, Eb," said Tom.

"Oh, Steve plays pretty regularly."

I said hastily that I didn't at all care for the game, not in such torrid heat. Anyhow, at home, our tennis court was stuck right under the mulberry-trees in our front garden, and I was sick of it.

"Well then," said Eb, "you can take on the careening for Tom."

"Please do, Steve," implored Tom. And I agreed.

So, late on Sunday night I cantered off home to the baracca and, opening the door, went in. A letter from Blue, my sister, lay on the bed, and I decided to answer it next day, which was a holiday. Ah, there was a sensual delight in writing letters in that hut. The earth round about was so arid, so bare, that the thoughts flowing from me were received by it, greedily, it seemed. Musics floated through it, and images to the point of ecstasy were there. I heard the flowing of flutes and the imprint of delicate feet lay in the dust of the earthern floor. Ferns were growing up round the door, and when cut in half they exuded musically, I thought, their clear sap. And I was alone. Yes, that was better than anything. Deluded by the charm of poetry and prose, I sat alone, musing on the sorrow and genius of my life, breathing out egotism and breathing it in again, untempered by any man's cool judgment, fevered and intoxicated by my imaginings, so I lived from day to day.

Dear Blue,

Dreamily and terribly hot are the days; as dazed as the dream of a man making a long road in Algiers; and in the heat's centre, myself, the jewel, breathing out the genius of the universe, and longing as of old to be loved, to be famous and to be loved. But not to be loved by man. To be loved of a race. To be a god, and find a race that might love me. In this country, as in the Bible, it is eternal summer, and beautiful is the garment of summer on the brown body of Australia. I gather unto me the gold and the silver and the peculiar treasures of the kings of the summer; and I seek eternally for the blue fish-pools in Heshbon by the gate of Bath-rabbim; the dark gate of Bath-rabbim; and for that tower of Lebanon which looketh towards Damascus. Ah, my God, the antiquity of that gaze, returning look for look of the sun and the moon, those two sharp and silent swords that rise from the city of Damascus and pierce with a slowness, like age, the body of heaven.

Man comes into the fields at dawn; yea, he is steeped in the wines of sorrow and troubled by the storms of great love. I am the ruler of the fields, and when I sorrow, a deadness comes upon them, and upon the liberated green gem of the sea, that which spills its brilliancy on the envious earth. My arm is a great rock wherein are lions; they that come forth to prey on the brown summers and white winters of my body; they that burn up the pleasant places and at evening, return to sleep between the rocks.

I say, Blue, speaking of lions, what about sending up that Francotte ·44 of mine? I miss that cadet rifle dreadfully these days. Please send it up by rail at once with the big box of bullets. It always reminds me of the French Army in its turbulent periods between 1880 and 1903; and when the small blue smoke drifts slowly out of the obtuse little barrel, I think of Algeria and the Foreign Legion. It was a very popular rifle with quite a number of Arab tribes years ago. But the rear-sight was bad for desert warfare on account of the poorness of the metal put into it. I wish to heaven I could buy an elephant–gun, though, really, with the exception of myself, there are no elephants in this country; but if ever you come across a fellow with an elephant-gun, heavy bore, to sell, my dear Blue, please write and tell me at once. I should love to hear the roar of it up against my ear once more.

There was a faint roar from somewhere up the hill. I went out into the sun, which fell on me eagerly and clung to the sutures of my head. And there was the tea-planter from Calulu, the worthy Leonardo della Vergine, standing or clinging rather to the wire fence, in his pepper-and-salt suit. Always I imagined that this gentleman was some relative of the great Leonardo da Vinci, for whenever I spoke to him, saying, "Leonardo", up in my mind rose the gigantic artist of Rome in all his genius and glory and a massive white marble frame was about him.

"*Steva*," he cried, faintly, far off, "*come va?*"

"*Bene, grazie, Leonardo della Vergine*," I howled, "*E voi? Come state?*"

"*O, non ce male. Con perm esso . . . io vengo?*"

"Yes, righto; come on down."

Down shambled Leonardo, under the weight of a heavy bag. This he set at my feet, and with a fertile smile attempted to raise his hat. As Edgar Buccaneer had said, it was too small. He tugged at it fiercely with one hand, for a minute, while murmuring grace-fully his pleasure on beholding me.

"You are more beautiful than of old, Steva." He bowed and, raising both hands to the hat, tugged violently.

"*Ma che*, no," I said modestly, pretending not to notice the Lao-coon-like struggle going on before me. "You, yourself, look younger and fresher." It was true. His struggle with the hat was rejuven-ating him, minute by minute.

Seizing on a false sense of weakening in the head-covering, he said, working it off his ears a little, "How do you do?" But the hat let him down; he was now almost on the ground with it,

11

struggling with little inane courtesies and salutations, while he applied everything short of a can-opener to rid himself of the choking grip.

"Here," I exclaimed, "sit down on this hollow log!"

He sat and, planting my knee in the small of his back, I grasped the hat and tore it off with a harsh screech of torn lining and sweat band. As it flung him off the log with the force of a shanghai, Leonardo was not to be cheated.

"Thank you, Steva," he shrieked. "How do you do?"

"Very well, thank you, Leonardo," I said politely, and handed him his hat as he lay in the dust alongside the hollow log. "But what have you come for in this heat?"

"I come for bring few greens for you, Steva, and some *vino*." Leonardo was a prosperous person, but not excessively proud. "Where your sister Blue?"

"She has yielded to Venus, she has gone over to Hymen."

"What? She go for work for this man? I think might be she work for me."

"Ah no, Hymen has picked for her a lover, one golden as the oil in thy heavy frying-pans, one red-lipped as the tomatoes thou didst fry for her in old days, one strong and provoking as the wines that stand in thy windy halls, one sharp-witted as thy barb-wire fence. She is, in short, to be married."

"Merried? To *un' amore*?"

"True, O bringer of grins and greens."

"Long time I waited for not see you, Steva, and die in my heart."

"Ah well, that's far more romantic than dying in your boots."

"*Steva, io non capisco*. Long time I remember you when you come for my plice with Peppino. Where gone Peppino, now?"

"Down the line somewhere, working."

"You think come back Metung in Primavera?"

"Who knows?"

"Long time I think of day when you eat and sing in my house. I want good for you to come and work my plice this year. *Coi libbri dei conti e la machina per scrivere. Io ho perduto molto moneta senza di voi, Steva. Non posso fa niente senza la comptabilita per fare le ricevute.*"

"Ah, Leonardo, I knew those red-lined ledgers of thine would

12

need attention again soon. I shall come down in December next year and attend to them."

Leonardo fell to the earth in despair. *"Mia cara, la moneta . . . molti affari bisogna . . . l'aritmetica; la matematica, non posso far. Tutto questo e per voi; voi siete abile, Steva; io non lo sono."*

I bowed gracefully in the face of this torrent of compliments to my book-keeping, and said again, "I'll come down next December. *Non possoprima."*

"Per sicuro? Not possible before that?"

"No! With an assurance as pure as your Italian, Leonardo. *Addio."*

Leonardo went roaring homeward in his car to plan a charming and complicated menu for next December. As for me, I had to finish Blue's letter and then go down to Jim McLachlan's house to pick up half a dozen torches he was giving me for no reason at all, save that he didn't want them himself.

I walked down the dry grass hill to where the great white house of the tea-planter stood amidst a wealth of tropical fruits and flowers against the sea. White frangipanni, papaw and jacaranda, and lantanas and the frozen snow tiger that the tropical orchid is, and all the maddening and saddening fruits and flowers that the tropics produce to lure us far from home, all these haunted one on coming near Jim McLachlan's home. Jim, having just finished a game of tennis, was lying back in a coarse white hammock near a small table laden with whisky decanter and softly sizzling syphon. His handsome face, moody under the luxurious blaze of his auburn hair, lit up a little at the sight of me.

"Hullo, Steve," he said. "I did hope you would come along. Do have a drink," and in his ineffably charming way he poured out a small whisky for me and shot the soda-water down into it strongly so that it foamed and made the day suddenly cool. While I drank and smoked Jim was fishing away under a decorative cretonne couch. Drawing out a white fine canvas box, strapped and buckled and plastered with labels from London to Singapore, from Tokyo to Melbourne, and everywhere else, he undid it, and lugged out a small topee, strapped and pugareed. "It's far too small for me, Steve, and I thought you'd like it. I know you have about half a dozen already, but you might like this one. It's quite a lovely thing."

And really, as topees go, it was. It had an air about it. I don't know how many Eastern mornings that topee reminded me of, and of the most terrific middays. And one always looked from that topee down, down, reflectively on the sharp, fine, impeccably laundered tropical kit beneath, the white straight wide trousers and white kid shoes; and the weight of the brazen sun was heavy above, and the faint, far dark leaves of some fragile Japanese bush waved in one's mind.

"And you really must take it and wear it, Steve," said Jim persuasively, "for it seems to me to belong to you. Sometimes you look thoroughly Eastern to me—an impassive face, pale and sad, like that of the youngest of the Buddhas. And at other times the thoroughly comic face of some ancient Chinese deity. I think I shall have another whisky." Jim poured himself out yet another, and stared at me, and laughed. He was very fond of me. I had known him for years. His pure and beautiful white face and the fiery flame of red hair tossing and waving over his head, as he sat by the open window, all this was as familiar as a temple of stone to me. "Shall we go and play a set out on the tennis court, Steve? Or would you like a hundred up in the billiard-room? No. You would rather sit here and listen to me talking to you. Have you ever noticed, Steve, that Australia is a difficult country to talk in? After a while one exhausts the surface moisture and dirt and has to go down into deep geological strata to get something into one's talk. Whereas in Europe there is no ceasing. I've a perfectly marvellous idea for a large black-red rose garden, quite out of Baudelaire."

"Oh yes," I said, "that garden so like a bramble at dawn, that has in shadow and legend recaptured the grief of the deepest red carnation. That ineffable sin of time, the unstruck hour, and the brown leaf that lies alone in its *étude* of passion."

I stayed for a long afternoon talking with Jim; we had afternoon tea, and then at last he produced the torches and some books and, laden, I started for home.

On the next day we started work again. I rose early and, dressed in Bedford cords, white shirt, and topee, went over the top and down to the collection of offices at the edge of the lake. These lakes are about one hundred miles in length and stretch from

14

Lakes Entrance up past Nungurner, Calulu, Metung, Cunning hame, Paynesville, and to the large town of Bairnsdale.

There was a small plantation of some special tea growing on a dry and desolate hill overlooking the lake. The leaf was pale blue with the heat; the pickers were already there, their tall baskets, which McLachlan had brought from the Islands with him, lying like mute guitars over their shoulders. The Italians saw me arrive at the door of the office, and shouted out, "Bon giorno, Steva!"

"Bon giorno, tutti," I replied. I unlocked the office door and went in. The cool papers lying on the table deadened one's mind; the black glitter of the typewriter, Babylonian, rich and significant, caught the light from the lake and the sun. And dry tea leaves had drifted in from the ovens over the way and lay about in corners. So I got hold of an old broom and began to sweep the floor before I sat down to the typewriter and Mr McLachlan's correspondence. There was an unwritten agreement between Jim and me that if I tired of the office, the typing, the correspondence, and the balancing of his chaotic accounts, I could go out into the plantation and take over from the Italian overseer for a while, or help feed the leaf into the rotary crushers or the hoppers. This was always delicious to me. I have always so greatly loved the earth. And this particular small plantation I had a great fondness for. A wide blue sky from which at evening the great Ajax and Hector of Troia seemed to lean downward to me, and golden hawks as pallid as Isis screamed above me all day long. Here, standing at the headland, I might think I stood in Egypt, for the sand was thick and heavy on the earth.

A big boat called the Gippsland came down to our wharf and took the consignment of tea away. Over the pale lake the boat moved slowly, blazing with colour; the black smoke she exhaled hung close to her, with a reddish blush in it, as though she were burning inwardly. As small, sharp, and delicate as a jewel, the boat passed below me, bright and fiery, with the heavy cloud of dark smoke clinging and clinging to her funnels. Slow and feverish on the pale-blue lake she passed daily. At four o'clock in the afternoon she returned, pitch-black against the falling sun, her colours lost and the smoke enveloping her still. I knew then that it was time to knock off, lock the office, and go away down to my baracca. But sometimes, after the Cubans had gone, I walked over the great silent paddock alone. Among the squat, broad, shining-leafed tea-bushes I strode, singing "Ambarvalia" and "The Chilterns" and "Ante Aram". That cry:

> *One face, with lips than autumn-lilies tenderer,*
> *And voice more sweet than the far plaint of viols is,*
> *Or the soft moan of any grey-eyed lute-player.*

Or Omar's lines:

> *Myself when young, did eagerly frequent*
> *Doctor and saint and heard great argument.*

Before going home I sometimes made a pot of tea—green tea, usually. I lit the stove in Jim's office if he wasn't there, and the sticks of Australian wood burnt with a sharp fierce smell and a glassy quiver of heat. The sun and earth lay sentient in them. While I ate I read the poetry in old journals. The *Australian Woman's Mirror* was a thing of most awful Greek antiquity to me, but yet older and sadder than the Greeks. Frail colonial poetry I read in it. The very italics in which it was printed had the charm of fine wheat. It fell delicately into the mind and sprouted there. An immense book stood on the shelf by the door; it had a cover like coarse frogskin, and bitten into its back were golden words, enticing words, *The Cities of Etruria*. One opened it and out fell stone sherds and vases and urns and stelae clattering to the earth again. And snatches of old Greek melodies sprang into the air above one's head. On shelves in a locked book-case were a number of volumes on tea-planting and its related branches. No one but McLachlan was allowed access to them, and he valued them above rubies.

When I had shut the office door behind me I stood alone in the paddock, among the hot stones and the dry black soil and the poor crop. Up on the hill a line of gum-trees, young saplings, had been burnt by a chance fire—just scorched to a gold that was bannerlike. Their golden yellow flags, dry and glittering, flew in the sweet wind of the afternoon. My heart began to toil sorrowfully in my breast, and move under a load of love and poetry that was a tribute to my country.

"Ah, Australia, Australia," I murmured. "None other gods!"

16

Riding down to the Tambo River, in the golden haze of the gigantic Australian afternoon, I saw a small, noble-looking cavalcade approaching. In an old cart lay my friend, the Mohammedan, Karta Singh. A slow horse drew him along. Tied to the back of the cart by long horse-hair reins was a wet buggy, covered with weeds. "Salaam, Karta Singh!" I cried, drawing my horse over to him. "What? Have you turned into Little Claus? Are you bringing home chariots from the depths of the river these days? And this fine horse that draws you, is it a river-horse drawn from the marble depths of this ancient Roman river that once, Alph-like, ran through leagues measureless to man? From what temple of chalcedony, plinth of red petra, and door of ruby did you bring this bright and amiable Pegasus? Surely the golden shafts of the race-chariots may be seen upthrust out of Tambo this afternoon, after thou hast raided this stream that once did run from Trans-Jordania down into Antipodes."

"Salaam, Steva!" said Karta morosely. The rich golden and many-jewelled bangle on his strong brown wrist jingled as he pulled in his horse. It is the religious token of the true follower of the Prophet. And the more the bangles, the greater the faith. On feast days Karta wore gemmy necklaces about his throat, too, and the rubies and "sapphires", as he called them—the Shah's fires —struck off harvests of red and blue splendour into one's eyes hurtfully. "*Allah Akbhar, Allah Akbhar*," said Karta Singh. "There is no God but God, and Mohammed is His Prophet." He spoke to the horse, and the equipage, with the slowly dripping buggy behind, stopped and trembled uneasily before me. "No, this is not a river-horse, Steva. I have bad luck . . ."

Just at this moment, Jim McLachlan came thundering along the road in his heavy military-type open car. He saw us, stopped in a cloud of dust, and raised his topee. "Good afternoon, Steve! Salaam, Karta Singh!"

"Salaam, sahib," returned that worthy. "Sahib, I am full of sorrow. Yesterday, as you know, I went far away into a city with my man, he who works for me, Ram Singh, the little old man, the honest one, with the beard like a cloud in the blue moonlit sky, and with long white hair like a woman's, he who takes snuff without my knowledge, and drinks red wine. Yet, since he loves

17

Allah, and is his most faithful servant, I do forgive him. *Allah Akbhar*. There is no God but God . . ."

"And Mohammed is His Prophet," returned Jim.

"In the city did Rammi Singh and I sit to drink. And for long. Might be we are drunk. I not remember." His glazed brown eyes burnt fierily above his black-grey beard, and his turban wobbled worriedly. "Well, we get to the river, the Tambo, and cry out for the punt. Ben, the puntman, he bring the punt over to us. The mare, my good mare, the young one, she walk on, and we sit in the buggy, drinking with Ben the puntman, and while he took us across the Tambo River, he did not take us far enough, but stopped half-way, crying, 'Lo, enough! Are we not there? Is this not the golden bank of Jordan? Therefore move the chariot forward!' And we did, and too soon, for the mare stepped forward and dragged us with her, and we did all fall in the river. All, all of us did bathe in this son of Ganges and weep. Alas, sahib, Ram Singh he get wet, and I get wet too, I, Karta Singh. Thou knowest, sahib, that I am ever dry and do pride myself on my dust, that which I collect from all the roads."

"Ah, Karta Singh," said Jim, "the heart is bereaved at the thought of your sorrows. Who knows, old friend, what may happen when the beer and the beard mingle? Truly in all your Koran there is no remedy for this."

"No, sahib Jim."

"*Infelix qui——*" I began happily in my usual breezy strain.

"You fella Steve," returned Karta Singh, who was a matter-of-fact man, "I do not know what you say half the time, and I must get home before dark with my buggy. Salaam, sahib Steve . . . salaam, sahib Jim."

Shaking the reins with braceleted jingling hands, he moved off in dignity. I, too, departed down the steep hill singing. Jim started up his car. But there was a wild Indian shriek like a wolf's, a rumble of wheels and a rattling of woodwork, as the buggy, slipping from the horsehair reins, rushed down upon me. Carried by the momentum given by its water-sodden weight, it rumbled heavily and swiftly past me downhill, chattering noisily to itself, and leapt with an exultant shout back into the river. Jim lay back in his car, howling with glee. I positively yelled with laughter. On the hill-top Karta Singh stood lamenting, whirling his torn-off

18

turban to the winds of the earth as they passed, and tearing his beard out right and left; and the mighty Australian sunset grew high in haze and glory around him, as the twilight and the night came on.

New Year's Day, the day when I should see my long-lost friend, came sweeping, blue and hot, across the continent. On such a majestic day as that, in such a quality of time that only the gods know, did Jim McLachlan and I go down to the regatta to watch the hundreds of craft drifting up and down in the old familiar waters. We were dressed in white tropical kit, and Jim's auburn hair glittered brilliantly under the white topee. My youthful aunt, Miss Hamilton, the owner of Ensay Station, had her big yacht *Boomerang* riding alongside the wharf, and I went over to pay my dutiful respects to her. She had a crowd of university men and women on board, and spread afternoon tea for us, afterward. She was medievally fond of students, and stood smiling amongst them like some rich green tree in an Italian renaissance painting.

Edgar Buccaneer's big double-barrelled gun roared once, and that meant that the regatta had started. I stood nervously on my aunt's yacht, waiting for Macca's boat to draw in. It came pounding and shimmering alongside. And I saw him. Among all the little red and hot faces that bent over the side, his was the one, the golden one. He saw me and smiled his dewy smile.

"Hullo, Steve."

"Hullo, Macca. Are you getting off for the regatta?"

"No, I'm going down to Lakes Entrance with the girl friend." I saw a pleasant-looking female of some sort by his side and grinned at her.

"Dash it, Macca, I wanted to have a yarn with you," I said. "Not that I've much to tell you, but I've been away up over the Alps since I saw you last, and had a great time. And I thought you might be able to tell me all about your recent travels. Tell you what, though. I've got to take in a mob of store cattle for Billy Creeker tomorrow morning to the Bairnsdale yards. I'll be passing through Lucknow on the way, and I'll call in on you, as I pass."

"Anyone going in with you?"

"Ah well, Jeff Creeker thought he might be able to come and give me a hand with the droving, but I'm not sure. And, Macca,

19

if you have those two volumes of mine of Rupert Brooke, you might get them out for me, and I shall take them back home again."

"Righto, Steve, I'll be expecting you." His boat whistled and in a few minutes he had gone on down to the Lakes.

After the regatta I went up with Jim to his place and we had tea together, his imperturbable Chinese house-boy serving us with cool green salads and fruits and ice-creams, while I watched the red shades of the sherry gliding over my hand. We listened to the radio after tea; the Melbourne and interstate stations spread vast acres of vibrant music across the continent, and the great earth charged it with its own magnificence, in this, the most rich and potent of Australian summers.

I had to go home early because of the droving trip next day. The restless mob of cattle were in the yards above the baracca and kept me awake half the night with their clamour. I thought every time I woke of the unpleasant job of rounding them up in the morning and getting them out of the yards, up the lane and onto the public highway to Bairnsdale, and hoped Jeff Creeker would dash along in the morning and help me with the mob as far as the punt at Swanreach. I should have to go past the punt in any case, and ride along the Tambo down below the hotel, and take them over the bridge and up the road past the blacksmith's and on the Main Highway into Bairnsdale.

In the morning I went over to Jim's place to breakfast. His Chinese cook was busy making hot pancakes, anticipating my early arrival, and I had breakfast before I left to collect the cattle. And I found half a bottle of wine in Jim's luxurious little pantry and drank it all before I rapped on the door of his bedroom. He was lying in bed under a high canopy of mosquito net; his hair shone red through it, and the smoke of his first cigarette rose up. His very beautiful Greek mouth smiled at me; he handed me an official-looking envelope, addressed to "The Clerk of Courts, Bairnsdale".

"Take that in for me, will you, Steve, there's a dear?" he said. "I may want you to go in on my behalf in a couple of months' time to the Clerk of Courts, too, if you don't mind. I've got to go down to Melbourne shortly and shan't be able to be there in Bairnsdale. Could you go?"

"Yes, Mac, anything for you, my love. You look very charming this morning."

"You look thoroughly Australian, Steve." Jim stared at my riding breeches, my khaki shirt, riding boots, and stockwhip. "Utterly Australian. What time do you expect to be back?"

"About ten or eleven tonight, I think. I shall be lucky, starting even as early as this, to get the mob into Bairnsdale by five this evening. Slow going in the heat, you know. Crook cattle, too. All bush stuff—they'll be careering from one side of the road to the other, rushing into open paddocks, going for all the open dams on the road and dashing down all the tracks to Bruthen and Bumberrah, and there are about twenty back tracks to Bruthen and Bumberrah before you get to the Nicholson. I'll have tea at one of the hotels, give the horse a good feed at the stables, and then turn on my heel at about seven at night, and canter all the way home. I think he can do it in about three hours."

"Knock me up when you get back if you want anything, Steve," said Jim.

"Right. Cheerio." And I was away.

I went then up the dry lane and caught the horse, saddled him, and took him along to the mob. At the sight of the cattle a dogged, dazed stare came into his eyes, and I knew that there was an unhappy day ahead for us. Alpini II loved the race-course, the gay crowds, the jockeys brilliant in their silk, the soft tan of racing leather, and the billowing folds of the big saddle-cloths and light racing sheets buckled round his throat. Racing was in his blood, and he had a splendid stride; in springtime he galloped like a god and was as light as a bubble to be astride. But the pedestrian slow, sad, and heavy work of droving saddened him. I can't say I like droving either. To tell you the candid truth, I hate it. It's so dreadfully slow. It has to be.

Jeff Creeker came along riding a solid-looking bay, and said, "Hullo, Steve, me lad! D'ye want a hand out with them? I'll help you out on to the road with them; I'd come into Bairnsdale with you, too, Steve, but I've got to attend to a lot of machinery dad's got hold of." Jeff's father, Billy Creeker, was keen on machinery; his big, neglected property was littered with all types of machines for harvesting and binding and sowing and general farm labour.

Jeff attended to all these, while his father visited. Theirs was a Utopian existence.

Jeff and I got the mob out onto the sandy main road past Creeker's iron gate, and Jeff helped me with them as far as Proust's, gave me a sympathetic farewell, and left me to it. The sun was still below the hills as I took the road with the reluctant, bellowing mob. It struck the lake with a flash of silver, and from then onward, all through the day, it smote white and high and far away on the earth. The road to Bairnsdale is desolate; there was one green place only, a deserted orchard, below it a bridge and a pool of muddy water lying thick and brown. But at Johnsonville, on the blue tidal river, a white crane floated, a far-away flower of a bird crying in the wilderness. On I rode, droving, over red gravel roads, sandy roads, and clay roads, by miles of post-and-rail and wire fences until houses began to come into view. So far the mob of cattle had gone quite smoothly and amiably along.

We were now coming into Lucknow, where Macca lived. I saw the long low house under the shining gum-trees and rode over towards it. Macca's mother had been one of the Svensons from Monaro, an old family who used to help my grandfather with the breeding of Indian Army remounts. He had a big run up on Monaro where he used to take the remounts for grazing, and the Svensons used to help take them up and bring them down again. This house was designed after the Monaro homestead, and was a very pleasant place, with the brilliant scarlet and black and cream Sturt pea growing all over the place, and the large lawns of buffalo grass and the tennis court idle in the sun. Macca had said that he might possibly be going back to his uncle's place up in Black Mountain, a roving sort of cattle station up in the heavily timbered ranges. And young Macca liked to work for his uncle, because he had a very pretty dark daughter. On my way in I had thought of this, and at the cross-roads leading to Bruthen and Black Mountain, I had stopped to carefully examine the white gravel road for the trace of his horse's hooves. It was early in the day; no one had passed. So I galloped up to the gate of the house. Macca came out and stood in the hot sunshine; his red-golden hair shone on his head, the sides of his face, and the backs of his hands, as he raised them to his eyes to shade them from the sun. A short, white-faced, blue-eyed youth, with full lips, a short nose, dreaming lazy eyes and a mild sweet smile.

"Well, Steve," he said, in his stifled way, "are you coming in?"

"No, Macca, I've got the mob of cattle down the road. I just came along to get those two volumes of Rupert Brooke from you."

"Certainly." He disappeared inside the big cool house and brought out, like two white kernels, my books of Rupert Brooke.

"Thank you. I suppose you're going back to Black Mountain in the new year, Macca?"

"I think so, Steve. Otherwise I may be going over into New South Wales, or up to my brother Reg at Mildura." Macca's brother Reg was redder than he, and owned a small place up at Mildura where he grew lexias and raisins and dried them for market. In my imagination I could see his very red head gleaming through the violent dust-storms of Mildura, and I was never keen on that part of Australia.

"Well, so long, Macca."

"So long, Steve."

I wheeled my horse and cantered off down to the waiting mob. By travelling fast I reached Bairnsdale at about three in the afternoon, put them in the dry yards down by the railway station, and went to deliver the letter to the Clerk of Courts at the Courthouse, which is down by the Mitchell River among the leaves and long Australian grasses. I delivered the letter and went to eat at a café before I turned for home. The black horse moved slowly under me through the parched white country, and we came home at last. I was too tired to go up to Jim's place. In those days I used to slay myself with exhaustion. I lived and died of it, and did not care. So in the night I came to the baracca and lay down and slept for hours, until late in the next afternoon.

I crawled down to the office at fallen noon and worked away until sundown to make up for lost time. The men were working over the leaf in the drying shed and Jim was examining the sample. Over the acres of dark romantic bushes rose the horizon-lilac images of the wind, shaped like ancient Greeks. On the next property a great field of wheat blew forward with the yellow fiery dry blush that is the assenting bow of the grain to the heat and the summer winds. And all about the dry limbs of the blue-grey gum-trees near the earth was the intolerable classical glitter of heat, a clear flame burning before a pure god.

Greedily I held on to the days; meticulously I embalmed them within myself. I built up strong years in my cells. I tied myself to eternity with lofty thoughts. And every day the tea-leaf ripened and burnt into darkness in the sheds, or drifted with a desolate singing wind about the floors, or packed in strong white Asiatic cases was taken across the serpent-haunted Lakes down to Melbourne. Up and down the columns of McLachlan's red-lined ledgers I ambled pen in hand, and on the Babylonian typewriter stamped out letters that went all over the world. Yellowly the summer burnt through us all, taking its splendid toll, for the summer in Australia is inescapable, demanding its share of one's immortality. The wheat next door was reaped, leaving the abrupt stubble of dry sun rays burnt and sallow with intense heat in its place. That short, sweet, dry stubble after reaping! And around the edge of the lakes in high golden gum-trees, creamy-throated and splashed with sultry blue hues, the swamp-hawks screamed in the secret Arabian of their aeons. They were so majestically Egyptian in their shining, cowled, jewelled splendour, each day of dreadful heat, and screamed so shrilly as they set lustrous eyes downward looking on the alien face of Australia, that one almost expected to see Horus the Hawk God arise and salute them in solemn and immobile sorrow because of days lost and forgotten and forbidden.

At afternoon-tea time I used to light a fire in the little stove in the office, and make tea, green tea, very chaffy-looking, but quite nice if one added a lot of sugar. And going to the door I cooeed out across the plantation.

"*Coooooo-eeeeeeeee!*"

The men, the pickers, turned and yelled out in Italian, Spanish, Austrian, and every other tongue, "*Bene! Si!*" and so on, and over they came to the office. We ate golden cakes that Jim's cook had made for us. These we kept in tins on shelves above the desk. All our little graceful fragile cups were there and bowls for sugar, cream, and milk. The ceremony "*per versare il te*" was a considerable one, and saturated with Latin ceremony and richness and solemnity. They were great men, poets, all these men. Jim sauntered in, and slung his topee on its peg and, stretching out his

24

long and graceful legs, took the cup of tea I gave to him, and drank away with the thirst of a tired man on a very hot day. He asked for the drying-shed temperature, skimmed through the overseer's report book regarding the processing of the leaf, and commented very favourably on the general work being done. The pickers handed a particularly fine sample of leaf to him and he rejoiced.

"If one could only get this country irrigated," he said, "it would grow the best tea in the world. If these lakes were fresh water, as they were eighty years ago, one could put in an irrigation scheme that would make this place into the best tea-growing district under the sun. I had a soil analysis of this plantation taken soon after I opened it up, and it compared favourably with the best districts in China, where generation after generation of tea crops go back into the ground in the form of humus—and what a flavour they give to that Pekoe! Imagine seven centuries of tea-leaves being under a recent crop! Talk about flavour!" Jim had travelled all through the tea-growing districts of China, and knew what he was talking about. "And most and the best of those crops are grown on lakes like this one, you know, or just above those amber foaming Chinese seas. Of course, in China, they use all sorts of secret potashes and fertilizers that we can't get in Australia. And they are infernally skilled at mixing the same. Their secrets are hundreds of years old. Tell you an amusing thing. Fellow next to me, an Irishman—came down from Oxford the same year as I did, myself—he developed a big plantation next to mine in Hunan. Well, this fellow stuck among his Chinese merchant neighbours, used to watch them desperately, and strive to find out precisely what they used for fertilizer. He had his own English brands of potash and so on, but they didn't seem to fit in with the soil. Too stiff. So, he ran things together a little, and treated the tea field as he thought it should be treated. He opened up the big ditches during fallowing, and filled them with tea waste—slack bushes, waste leaf, and crushed sugar-cane leaf and pulp, and as much sour milk and butter as he could get hold of. Into the ditches he had cartload after cartload slung, and covered up and left to comp. And the result? Amazing! A very good leaf, rich, dark, and pungent, with a most individual flavour, sweet and milky. You could practically drink that tea without

25

adding milk and sugar. Very economical, indeed. The idea caught on, and within a few weeks every tea-grower in the province was slinging everything old about the place into the ditches. Preserved fish a hundred years old and sharks' fins of twenty years' vintage, and even old clothes and books and boots went into mulch in the effort to find a new flavour. I can still distinctly remember the taste of a most honourable Mandarin's boots that were attached to the roots of some of the tea-bushes from the leaves of which I drank to the health of princes and gods. And a Mandarin's boots are strong, and made to last." Jim laughed a lot and drank his tea and ate the cakes, and then went off to play tennis, while we worked on.

At the week-end I took Teddy, my Edwardian terrier, and went to stay down at the Buccaneer's. I took him because there was no food to leave beside him. He seemed unable to catch rabbits. I was unsure what exactly could be his function in life. I thought that by successive try-outs around different localities I might find out. Eb had two fine gun-dogs. Tooloo, an expensive setter, named from a dark arm of land, Tooloo Arm, that ran out into the Lakes, was an old dog, with a massive curled coat, from which all the real spring of youth had gone, but it had an emperorian charm about it, aged though it was. Micolo, a young black and white staghound, was a deerlike animal of great beauty. His coat was white, dappled with saddles of harlequin black; over his spine an immense patch, like a mask, moved; his legs seemed to spray out from his body with dancing grace, and every inch of his being, from the slender and wistful nose to the long heavy slim tail, was mastered, it appeared, by a balance that came from race and birth. He flung himself down on the earth every now and then, with a crash like a chord of music on the black and white keys of the piano. I tied Teddy down the garden by the kennels of these two dogs, Micolo and Tooloo. That night they howled for a long while, and then were suddenly quiet.

Eb said next morning, "The dogs slipped their collars last night, must have been off somewhere. I bet you what you like they were over at Frank Bond's."

"Bond's got a lot of sheep, too," said Edgar, frowning at his son, as he dried his face on the towel in the bathroom. "Eb, you want to be careful. Bond'll be wild if those dogs get at his sheep, you know."

"How can I look after everything?" cried Eb irritably. "I've got to be out with the nets up at the Tambo mouth half the night. I can't do everything. Why don't the girls look after the dogs?"

"They're your dogs!" exclaimed the girls in a vehement waiting chorus, as if they had been expecting this attack. One of them buttered her toast thickly; another rose, went to the stove and, lifting the blue coffee-pot, poured out strong black coffee into which she let fall thick yellow cream.

"He's got to work; he's right; there's no time. You girls! Tie the dogs up, do you hear!" exclaimed their father, combing his black hair and stroking his golden moustache.

When night came the dogs, tied up by the girls and myself, howled in the warm moonlight. In the early morning the trees were dark about the gate, and the wind moved in them, loudly and sweetly; the apple-trees under which the dogs were kennelled came out of the darkness and looked grey and old; they, too, became loud-voiced as the wind reached them. The sky was pink over the sea, but a greenish blue away from the sunrise. The white flowers in the lucerne hedge were dry with the heat of the night; the roosters in the poultry pens leapt up and opened their scarlet wings and crowed in the direction of the other roosters, who answered faintly over the hill. Then, closing their wings with a rattling fierceness, they growled and walked off to pick at a few grains on the earth.

My dog Teddy yawned noisily, curving his red tongue back into the roof of his mouth; a few clear drops fell from it. He was a small, thin, silken-haired terrier; his coat was a soft cream hue and smooth, with curling ends. His brown eyes protruded from the delicate bones of the brow and were large and sad. He sat on his tail and scratched as far under his collar as he could. Then, with his head between his paws, he rent and pulled and dragged at the leather. Micolo and Tooloo, sitting in their kennels, which were warm from the night's sleep, watched him. When he worked the collar off they stared at each other, lowered their eyes boredly and licked their paws. Teddy showed off. He rushed round the apple-trees, open-mouthed, excitedly, picked up rubbish, carried it delicately in his mouth, tossed it in the air, and dragged himself

27

c

along on the ground on his stomach, panting silently. Micolo rose and tossed his head this way and that in his collar. His lean, shining, lizard-like head contracted; the slender curves of his ears assisted him. He raised a blind awkward paw to help himself, pulled back, twisted gracefully, scraped the collar over one ear, shook his head and was free. For Tooloo it was more difficult. His thick curled head held the collar with a worn firm grip. The mark of it was plain on his neck; the dust rose from the small curls as he struggled. He whined mournfully, for the other dogs were dodging behind the apple-trees, down on their haunches with their tails raised and Micolo's wagging heavily and wickedly as he stared at Teddy. Tooloo raised his paw and clawed at the collar, scratching the smooth darkness. It did not shift. So he lay down and rolled away from the chain holding him to the kennel. He rose and leapt away from it, pulled away from it, jerked away from it, but it held. Holding his head down low, he lay back and dragged with his full weight, choked, dragged, twisted—and the collar slid over one ear. With an old, savage yelp he slid to one side, almost on his ear, and the collar fell in front of him.

Swinging together like dancers in a ballet, the three dogs raced down the green paddock and across to Frank Bond's where the sheep were lying. Rushing through a misty purple patch of penny-royal, they came out perfumed, galloped back into it again and rolled together there beautifully, with open laughing mouths. Micolo flung his black and white deerlike body across Tooloo's rich curled back, and snapped at him with sharp, dewy white teeth; his fierce clean breath smoked in the morning air. Teddy, with his silken coat of a desert-like hue, caught Micolo by the throat, and held him, growling deeply; his sad brown eyes glowed. The black and white, the black and the lustrous yellow forms swept, breathing harshly, through a swamp of buttercups, hard yellow flowers that rose swiftly after they had gone.

In Bond's grazing paddock, the sheep were already feeding; dirty white cloud-like shapes, they wandered with their noses to the ground, giving the grass a tug that had a strange talent, an air of savage practice in it. Now and then one looked up, stared with a blind terror at something far away, bleated in a high voice and waited. From the depths of the herd an old patriarchal sonorous voice answered him, deep, wise and hollow, reassuring.

28

Down went the grey curly head again to twist brutally at the short grass. Teddy ran lightly up to the nearest ewe, and appeared to be running and playing alongside it with glances of longing. He was waiting for it to bend its head down with a curving blow at him. Micolo followed him, not planning anything, just ready for whatever happened. The frightened ewe bent its head to butt the little dog. He seized its ear and pulled it down a little. Micolo saw it falling, and with a wild fierce cry of strength leapt forward and sank his teeth in. They struggled on the ground, on the dry and poetic summer earth, a beautiful group, the stout curly ewe with the long white lashes quivering over its large human eyes, staring upward at them. Teddy's cream-gold silk hide blended with the curls, as he lay holding its ear tightly between his teeth and his black lips. Micolo stared down at the sheep with hard brown eyes, brilliant and restless, blinking bewilderedly, impatiently.

Just at that moment Frank Bond came up and fired from two hundred yards, a double barrel full of small shot, and the canine poets departed, peppered, for the perfumed shelter of the penny-royal. Tooloo lay in it for the rest of the day. Micolo ran down to the boatshed on the foreshore and lay in the dark on the nets, above the diamond-bright water there. Teddy, with only a few pellets to his credit, came home and gave the show away. This terminated my visit. I had to go back to the hut, taking Teddy with me. Edgar Buccaneer, after one glance at Teddy's buttocks, and a brief visit from Frank Bond, was ropeable.

"Steve, take that mongrel away from here!" he shouted, pointing to Teddy, his nostrils dilated with fury and his golden moustache stiffened with his anger.

"Mongrel!" I exclaimed. "Not mongrel! Tyson, the Cattle King, made me a present of that dog. Surely to Heaven you haven't the temerity to call anything canine of Tyson's a mongrel!"

"With all due respects to Tyson, you take that dog away from here before any more of Bond's sheep suffer."

I looked for some spot on which to touch him to kindness, but he was implacable and looked away from me. His mouth opened and closed angrily under the hanging viking moustache, as he spoke. For some reason or other Edgar Buccaneer always reminded me of King Menelaus of Sparta.

Edgar moved silently back and forth in his high black fishing boots, with a narrow strip of pure white at their soles and thighs, and his grey trousers fitted into them like Elizabethan pantaloons.

"At once, Steve, at once," he insisted, pointing to the Tysonic Teddy. So I departed with my jewel from the crown of Tyson the Cattle King of Australasia.

From the grey hut, where I sat with my feet on a rug of rabbit-skins, golden, black, red and white, I wrote stiffly to Blue, in a hard masculine way that used to come over me at times.

Dear Blue,

I have been having a bit of trouble with Bond over some sheep. Teddy, Micolo, and Tooloo got at some of his ewes early this morning, and everyone went into a terribly silly stew about it. Bond claimed three quid compensation and got it. They wanted to shoot Teddy at close range, so I said a few words and rode away. Nerves being a bit upset, my specialist advised me a holiday in a quiet place, and an extremely strict dietetic regimen of black coffee and cigarettes. I am therefore back in my baracca on the tea-plantation, living life out. You told me in your last letter that you would like to take Teddy. Is that so? If you'd take him, I'd be glad, but lonely. I hate parting with him, but sheep-maulers are no good to me in sheep country. The freight to Dandenong is small. If you will take the animalo, I will take him into Bairnsdale and put him on board the train. I am rather short of cash, at present. After the disturbance, the new shoes for the racer and a racing pad, I am left with £88 4s. This must see me to Bruthen or Buffalo or South Africa or elsewhere when the last picking is over. Let me advise you never to buy a horse. I could be in Western Australia now on all he's cost me, and after a twenty-mile ride on the racing pad I feel I'm sitting on a steamed pudding. But still, he is a great galloper.

Glad to hear that you're going to Buffalo for the hop-picking. Cut a photo of Porepunkah out of the paper yesterday. I'd send it to you, but can't bear to part with it . . . flinty road, bordered with misty vegetation, and dark trees crawling past a black-smith's shop. Shades of Pricie and the grey cap and old Seldomfed! The whiskers twitch and turn to the north even as I gaze. If you should see a thin-looking bloke on a racer ride in under the bridge at Panlook's in the autumn, don't throw a fit. I have a dream of riding over the Alps some day for the fun of it, and for the sake of old continued Odysseys. *Addio*.

One day, I rode up to Orbost on the Snowy River, to transact some business for Jim McLachlan, and rode home through miles of grey bush, singing. At the punt at Swanreach, I called through the red swirling dust of midday, "Punt-o! punt-o, punt-o!": and with a melancholy clank it was brought across by a dark man with a long ratty moustache. This was Ben Simon, who had shared the bottle and the bath with Karta Singh and Rammi when they sank the cart and the young mare for a battle with the Tambo River.

"What a hot day!" I said to Ben, staring down from my saddle at his swarthy mature face; the long lashes rose from his hard brown eyes as he looked at me, upward.

"Yes, I was in Egypt in the last war, I never felt anything like the heat you get down on these Gippsland rivers. Must have had a long ride. Horse looks tired."

"Yes, been up to Orbost for Jim McLachlan."

"Long ride. Should have gone up in the mail-car as far as Lakes Entrance with Foley, and then caught the other Orbost mail-car. Too far in this heat."

"Ah . . . keeping up the old tradition. We Australians, you know. Never walk or drive cars when we can ride."

"True. Your grandfather, Mr Davidson, was one of the best breeders of remounts for India that they had in Australasia, I heard some one say the other day."

Clank, clank, went the punt chains, ringing out over the warm dark river, and the water seemed sweet on my lips. The smell of river weed and water-moistened wood made me feel an odd love for everything.

"Care for a cup of tea?" said Ben.

Then something Eastern in me arose and loved him, too. For the gift of a cup of tea, on such a day when my horse shone and the river glittered dreamily, reached my heart. His curled black dog barked with loose kind jaws as I followed him into the small

31

hut on the river-bank among the grasses and sunflowers. Old newspapers were scattered everywhere, and ringed with tea stains; old almanacs hung on the wall, and a small fire lay huddled under ashes on the hearth. Ben set a kettle across the bars and, sweeping the newspapers out of a chair, gave it to me.

"Ah, if only I had a job like this," I said admiringly, thinking how smart and yet studious I could make this hut. "Lots of traffic, too. I should sit in this hut all day and work the punt by pressing a button. I'd open a shop, too, and sell lots of soft drinks, and books. I'd write the books myself and illustrate them."

"Ah, you can't press any buttons around here, Steve," said Ben. "It takes a man to handle some of the traffic across here. Sorry I have no milk. Do you mind your tea," said he, setting an enamel mug in front of me, "being black and strong?"

"Ah, no, by the gods, this is good. You don't know how I love to sit here in this hut and drink tea with you. I have an emotion about tea, an ancient feeling about it; I can't resist it. It makes me desire to sing, to tell tales . . . well, it's strange stuff."

"And so you're clerk-typist for Jim McLachlan," said Ben, stirring his tea. "I often take him across in the punt, in that big military car of his. He's a fine fellow, isn't he, McLachlan? By Jove, he's travelled, hasn't he, eh? He was talking to me about Egypt the other day—been further over it than I have been, knows it all off by heart. And you've got a good position with him in his office. But still, of course, one longs for a little active work at times. And you, you say, would like to be able to work this punt. I think, Steve, that it is the hut that attracts you. And the River Tambo. Yes, you would like living on this river. You would like the punt life. One gets the idea of travelling without ever really moving off the water. But the water," said Ben, raising his eyes to mine and fixing them with a shy yearning look, "makes you so thirsty. I can't help it." He stared down at his tea, remembering perhaps the night he and Karta Singh and Rammi Singh had fallen into the river, for it had become a sort of New Year's joke among the people of Metung. "I often think I'll lose my job if the water continues to make me so thirsty. I grow reckless, and when anyone wants me to drink, I'll drink and drink; and then it's all over with me, with my work. I'm lonely, too. I wish I was married. At night it's very lonely along this river.

You say, 'Oh, one sees many people.' That's true, of course, but they soon clear out. Just a bit of a yarn while you're taking them over, but they're shaking their reins impatiently all the time, longing to get home. And the river. Oh, damn the river! The river just drives me to drink."

Ben filled his cup and mine again. I drowsed comfortably in my chair, and the old dog at the door snapped largely at the river flies.

"Yes," said Ben, slapping his knee with his broad hand, shining along the forefinger from the friction of the punt handle. "The way it floats into all sorts of little dry out-of-the-way hollows, the very way it has of surging past so silently, and always with dry land above it—well, you don't know how like a drink of beer that looks. The sort of drink man has been dreaming of since the beginning of thirst, which started with the sun, I suppose. Imagine having a throat dry like this bank, and having as much beer as there's water in the Tambo flowing down it. I watch the water hesitate at a log; there it imitates the talk of men about the bar in the pub down the road. Sometimes I can pick out words here and there. 'Orr, life's horrible, horrible,' says a lot of water caught over a stick, hanging over it with a bit of slime running through it. And then, down in a yellow whirlpool there's a voice gabbling like a man in the D.Ts. One day I heard a lot of bubbles singing out, 'Come down here, we've got beer down here!'"

"Too lonely," I said sympathetically, but I felt afraid of Ben for a moment. Would he leap on me and drag me down with him, under the water, heading for a place where the bubbles cried loudest, "There's beer here, come down here"? I stared at him thoughtfully. "If you were married, it would be better."

"As you say," remarked Ben quietly, "if I had married . . . well, then of course . . ." And his face looked paler, softer, reflective, and he stroked his big brown moustache, but one had a sense that he was acting, that all his life he had been looking for roles, slipping in and out of them through loneliness and emptiness.

"So! I must go now," I said, rising. He helped me to the saddle among the tall sunflowers, and I rode away.

Two days afterwards the overseer came down to my baracca and handed me a letter at twilight; it had been a luminous sort of river twilight, and the grass grew damp and smelt deep, early in the evening, for autumn was coming. The brownish pencilled address had in it something like the thin twigs against the sunset sky. All day they had been hidden, I remembered, or removed from the sky, but now, caused by a mood of the heavens, a nut-brownness and redness, they lay there, tormentingly lovely. On opening the letter, I read in the brown-pencilled writing,

Dear Steve,

When you come over the Swanreach punt next, will you please bring me a sample of tea from the plantation? And will you please tell Mr McLachlan that I should like to buy some tea in bulk from him?

Yours sincerely,

BEN SIMON.

So next day when I set out for Bruthen I carried with me a small sample of tea, green and black, for Ben to decide over. Staring at the white back track, or lifting my glance to the paddocks rusting or golden, with smoke haze rising at the feet of the ranges, so I came to the river.

"Good morning," I said to Ben.

"Good morning," he said to me. "Did you bring along the sample of tea, Steve?"

"Yes, Ben, here it is." I handed over the neat little packet.

"Another hot day," he said, toiling at the chains of the punt. "Where're you off to today, Steve?"

"Bruthen. Jim McLachlan wants me to go over and see Dudley Timmins about two or three ton of sunflower seed that he wants to buy from him, and four or five ton of maize. I've got to look over the sample and take some back to see if it's all right. Dreadful day for a long ride, but I may as well go. By Jove, it's torrid over at Bruthen now, you know, with the bean and sunflower crops in full swing. Terribly over-irrigated little spot, Bruthen, don't you think, Ben? Of course the Tambo runs through it in full flood all the time, full of the Snowy River and all its tributaries, and it's just too tempting for the Bruthen growers. But it's horribly tropical there, some days."

"Ah, it's like that all along the Tambo Valley," said Ben. Alone on the broad river we stood, the olive man with the long dark-brown moustache, toiling subduedly at the handle of the punt, and I, sitting straight and brown-bodied on my slender black horse, with his white starred forehead.

"Thanks," as we reached the opposite bank. "Thanks." And the horse leapt with a wicked cruel eagerness to the turf and, scrambling up the side of the road, left Ben alone to toil back to the hut, the sunflowers, and the dog.

Dry, unhealthy, and accursed was the road to Bruthen; behind evil post-and-rail fences the miserable gum-trees drooped in the heat; tailings from old superficial mining cuts by the roadside were filled with rusty water and red gravel. A fierce desolation spread over everything.

Above Bruthen I halted on a hill that once, it seemed, had been made of gold that had decayed, but a feeling of being wrought and precious stayed with it, and two ancient trees knotted and carved by age and weather gave a value to the hill-top. Below, was a shed of some sort, large, and with a name on it, and a wharf, of all things. Had the river once been here? To see a wharf in the middle of such dryness was tantalizing.

I met Dudley Timmins, cantering up deeply and churningly on the wet black-brown tracks surrounding his crop of sunflowers. They towered high above us, with black seeded faces and golden pollenous hair. Such was their texture and its sentience that I felt as though the huge flowers above were in the palm of my hand. Dudley Timmins was well moulded all over; the flesh on his red-brown cheeks was as even as that on his legs and back. His straight nose, calm blue eyes, and firm full mouth kept the man peacefully to himself. All was regular and level, within and without. His voice was keen, kindly, staccato. I rode round the maize cribs with him, and to the sunflower-seed bins, and looked over the samples therein.

"I shall pack you up some maize and sunflower seed to take over to Mr McLachlan," said Dudley Timmins. "He's in Melbourne, you say, at present? Got a very fine plantation over there. Should be able to grow tea quite successfully in country like this."

The day grew frightfully hot, all at once, and the thick black tropical mud about the feet of our horses smoked and lived hideously between the vivid green stalks of the sunflowers. And a huge black waterspout of cloud came up, rapidly.

"Rain coming," said Dudley Timmins.

"Yes," I replied. "I'll take the samples and get home to Metung at once. I don't want to get caught in the rain over here at Bruthen." So he parcelled up the samples in the big shed, while red-golden-haired young men worked among the maize, raising to the sun and storm their well-shaped arms, and turning to me and from me their heroic heads, vaguely Greek and splendid in toil. And the storm came rapidly on over Bruthen, thickening and quickening under my apprehensive stare.

I set off on my long ride home, and the lightning in the wild black clouds above cracked in bright golden veins across the sky. The premonitory signs of rain are always delicious; there is a morbid pleasure in watching the enormous clouds spoil the blue sky; there is an animal fear that pleases in the ruminative silence of the brooding heavens; and the last wind that blows before the storm breaks has a romance in it only paralleled by that of the first wind of the morning. It comes, it would seem, from original and slightly cruel sources. It means differently. And the first few drops of rain in a dry land are deep and sweet; they smell as sweetly as orchards full of spring blossoms, even in the barren dust. But when the rain sets in pitilessly, mercilessly, it is all a delusion, that which went before.

Bowed under the downpour, in light riding clothes, I kept going until I reached a deserted house that I had noticed on my journey over to Bruthen. The rusty roof and collapsed framework were supported on each side by a glossy green pine-tree. I thrust open the large gate and rode in. A great gust of wind blew a surprising cloud of smoke from the chimney. I hesitated; the storm seemed more reassuring than the unknown person within the house that I had supposed to be deserted. Yet I was soaked through. I dismounted and knocked. No one answered; turning the handle of the door, I looked in. A sinewy tall man with quick-looking limbs and a long, distinctly Russian grey-blue beard stood staring at a red honeycomb of fire burning far into a great pine root. A little to one side stood a high, bony horse, sad and sleepy. The old man stared at me energetically. His face was hard and stubborn, but above that, eager. Very smooth eyes flashed between wrinkled lids, white eyes, clean and moist.

"Good day," he said smoothly. "I saw you go past when it was fine this morning. Now it's wet, and that's how people meet. Put your horse under the veranda; there's plenty of room. Isn't that Alpini II, the one that Callinan of Nowa Nowa used to own? I thought so."

"Yes, that's Alpini II. Rosso, the wealthy Italian merchant in Bairnsdale, bred him. He runs Alpini I, the sire. Both are splendid gallopers. Aren't you 'Lightning'?" I inquired. "Lightning" was a well-known identity around Bruthen, and so was his horse, Cadillac.

"Yes," said the old fellow excitedly, "that's me. I'm Lightning, and this is my horse, Cadillac." He pronounced it Ca*dill*ac. "Amazing animal, Cadillac. Here, come over and warm yourself. And who are you? Aren't you Mr McLachlan's typist? You work in his office, don't you? Yes, I thought so. Everyone knows everyone in Gippsland, don't they? Heaven, what rain! You can't possibly ride home in weather like this. And Metung is eighteen miles off. No, you cannot. We shall see a flood tomorrow in the Tambo."

I stood on the veranda, relishing the sight of the baffled rain. Roaring and sighing, it swept across the lonely bush. Alpini shook his body impatiently. Removing his gear, I tied him up with a halter under the veranda and entered the old house again.

"You'll soon get dry." Lightning thrust a billyful of brown tea among the coals. His boots squeaked as he crouched in front of the fire, toasting a large slice of stale bread. The old horse behind him sighed, and its lower lip, a great pink-lined slab of flesh, trembled pathetically for some time. The old man, as he watched me eating and drinking the hot tea, had a change of mind. He grew reminiscent, and sat down on a half-filled chaff-bag and lit a bent pipe at the fire. We talked away about Victoria and New South Wales.

"How did you get the name of Lightning?" I asked.

"Well, when I was a young fellow I came out from the United States of America . . . that would be in about 1894, to the plains of New South Wales, working as a bore locater. I used a complicated instrument I brought out with me from the States, and I travelled from station to station, divining water for the rich squatters. I wore an Assam suit, Assam silk, a panama hat and good shoes, American shoes. I had an air about me. I had bores spouting out thousands of gallons of water where there wasn't a drop of water suspected. Imagine talking of bores with rain like this falling in front of you!" He looked out of the window at the Gippsland bush and sighed. "Squatters in New South Wales would pay thousands to get a good rain like this. I loved station life. And they called me Lightning because I could locate deep bores so rapidly and bring water to the surface quicker than any man in the State. But I grew old, you know. And, like a lot of men who've come to Australia in early youth, I grew to like the bush so much I couldn't leave it. I've got a beautiful home in the city, but I wouldn't give you twopence for it. I'd rather be wandering about this bush with the old horse, Cadillac. That's the way Australia gets you. Do you find that? It's like the islands, you know. But the bush is worse than the islands. They're small, and you exhaust them quickly, but not this huge and old Australian bush. Never."

The sun came out rapidly all over the earth, and shone in the afternoon with a heavy fierce glare, but the bush, this dry Australian bush, was terrified of the storm and bent away from it. It breathed hastily, crushed, bowed, at its feet, trees flung themselves upon sister and brother trees, and shuddered in terror. The water poured down the uncouth roads, washing them into reptilian shades of gleaming humped backs and sprawling legs. I said good-bye to the old man, and went and saddled my horse and rode off to Metung. I thought to myself, "Ben could never work the punt this afternoon, after that torrential downpour, for the Tambo rises many feet in an hour or so. I'll have to go down to the bridge across the river at Swanreach." It was a much longer ride. The sun had gone in again and fierce showers came thrashing the blue-grey and terrified gum-trees. I was shuddering and wet through when I came to the long shining mud hill at Swanreach, that lead down from the hotel on the hill-top to the wide bridge across the Tambo.

A large shining car left the hotel yard and went past me down the steep hill to the swollen and flooded river. The windows were dim with rain, but someone called out to me loudly from the back seat. Down flew the car to the river, halted on the bank with shrill brakes crying out, attempted to turn, to grip the road, and slid backwards into the running, throbbing river. It bobbed blindly for a moment and then fell gulpingly into the depths. A young man crossing the bridge, shouted loudly. From the hotel several men rushed out, looking blindly about them. The young man shouted again, and pointed to the car. The rest ran down the hill, and a strong, fair young man leapt into the river; he came to the surface after a moment or two, dragging a purple-faced man with him to the bank. It was Macca's father, half drowned, bedraggled.

"And who else was in the car?" the diver cried breathlessly, staring about him and rubbing his wet head with his arm. "Was there anyone else with him?"

"Ben, the puntman, and his dog, I think. Yes, Ben came with him."

"Well, I'll try, but I don't think I can get the door open again. The current's too strong." He threw himself into the river again. We stared absorbedly at the water flowing over the car. The rain fell, the bridge shone grey, and the yellow countryside slanted mutely down to the dark group of men who stood round Macca's father. He wasn't really out to it. The young man rose again, with Ben in tow, and broke towards the bank with strong, clipped strokes, Ben's liberated dog following.

"Got him," he said. "The dog's safe, too." The men gathered round him, praising him, glad of his strength and his life, his force against the forces of the river, and he, too, was glad; he would never forget it; the river had proved him. I rode away just as the doctor came tearing along the road from Metung in his car. And I had an important accident to tell everyone about.

A letter from Blue was waiting for me, begging me to go with her to the Buffalo district again. But for the time being I had lost my desire to go over the Alps.

Knowing my love of Gippsland as you do, and the impassioned and eternal summers here that I feel I cannot leave, I wonder you bother about me at all, Blue. I am sure that I should not love this country so much; I suppose I shall have to suffer for my love of it some day. Love of the earth is really the only

39

evil thing about me. The trouble with you is that you gloss over my careless poetic nature and remember only the romantic companionship. And I am so careless of all things save Art and Literature that I am almost evil. What was it Wilde said in the "Decay of Lying"? Something about there being more terrible things in one cell of the brain than in all the books in the world. Again, since I have quite a time to go working with Jim on the tea, I cannot find time to make a 123-mile trip across the Alps. I am going to stay at the Buccaneers' for a fortnight. I shall be half happy, half sad there, but it will be for the best. However, often like that lonely wanderer through the arid and ancient deserts of Israel I cry in my heart for my people.

Ah, what a house that was! And the Black Serpent, what a constant and various pleasure she was! Voluptuous kindness flowed from her and her fruitfulness glowed over the house.

One misty wet afternoon, Tom Henderson came up to ask me if I would start working for him again. Throughout the next week or two the days were formed of his mind and mine. Long and noble and blazingly Greek in the blue heavens above were the days when I worked for Tom Henderson over his launches and fishing craft. I always saw him as a fair figure twisted about the tall brown masts of his boats, with the intricate halyards slapping his shoulders. Up there in the blue sky, above the blue water, he gleamed against the day with his staring white shirt and glaring ash-blond hair.

The first work he gave me was burning paint off one of his fishing launches, along the foreshore under a giant silver and yellow gum-tree that stood paint-splashed near the water. I started at nine in the morning, the hour when the *Gippsland* hooted as she rounded the point, when she rolled into Metung like a silver dream, her funnels and masts quivering, bells ringing down in her heart and a coloured dew of passengers clinging to her rails. At ten o'clock we had morning tea in the sitting-room, cool, dark, and romantic. The elderly housekeeper brought in delicate cups and cakes, and Tom's mother, Mrs Henderson, poured the tea. She was a frail, exquisite type of woman, gentle and yet firmly authoritative. Being all thoroughly Australian, we were quiet and sat staring at the hot splendour of the Grecian day outside with its foaming-up of white and golden-blue clouds, all churning into the hours. Far down the garden a dozen pairs of Tom's pyjamas fluttered mauve and gold and blue on the line. Sometimes he spoke to us of Queensland, where he had lived for a time. With a few slow, bright words, he made the tropical fruits, picked by the bills of brilliant-winged birds, ripen and fall from the gum-trees round the house.

He told us of the owner of a Melbourne newspaper who lived in a house of most astonishing and secret loveliness not far down the coast from Metung, in a hidden and forbidden Conradesque creek, full of romantic mangroves. Often, cruising far down the shaft of light that we called Silvershot, we were startled by the springing up under our eyes of his huge steam-yacht, the *Mistral*; out from Grecian craggy creeks it came, and from blue swan-haunted shades and tropical silences, a glorious thing, silent as a dream, tall, towering, pure white, with streams of water pouring down its high sides and funnels shaking and spars quivering. No living face, however, did we ever see looking down from it, and no voice did we hear on the *Mistral*. It was a ghostly ship.

After morning tea we went out again and worked until the gong rang hollowly and temple-like, all gold for Angkor Vat, to bring us to lunch. In the dark and perfumed dining-room the silver and napery on the table shone, and Tom Henderson broke chunks of ice into the glasses of sherry; and in peace and coolness, far away from the horrid heat, we ate and drank, and spoke gently and tentatively of the Borthwicks in their big green and white home on the Point, and McMillan in his squatter's bungalow high up on the dry, the sweet and white grassy hill. Ah, Australia, Australia, one cannot have enough of remembering you!

When the careening of the launch was over I cut dark-green tea-tree round on the back beach, loading it on the dinghy and rowing slowly and heavily across the oily calm of the lake, in which thousands of gold bees dreamed and drifted. They crawled on to my lazy oars and buzzed faintly as they recovered and dried in the sunlight. I waited until they were conscious enough to fly. The days were long; there was no hurry. The tea-tree bushes had to be tied with yellow sweet-smelling twine and knotted under big jetties, and round the small private jetties for shrimp bushes. Cool, deep green was the shade round the wet wooden structures, and scorched-looking swallows with blue-black wings almost cut the skin off my face as they whipped startled out of their nests that stuck like sculptured mud wings to the walls. My brown arms, shining with the Italian oil I used to rub into them, grew tired of stretching up to tie shrimp bushes, tired of backwatering and edging the boat's bumbling, rumbling, rubbing, grating side up to the private jetties.

Sometimes Tom would take the motor-boat *Viking* over to Box's Creek to put some bushes on the sticks standing up in the muddy depths there. The sun glared across the dry boards of the broken planks of the jetty that reached out to the boat as I jumped into it, with feet that tried to be curved as the boat was curved. The mysterious dirty box that held the motor amidships stuttered and steamed an oily nauseous steam, and we went up the creek. That creek, mud-floored and mosquito-thick, was salt, green-black and swamp-bush bordered, and quiet. It said, "I must not be disturbed", and we dropped the rattling anchor overboard with slow hands and a look all round, unwilling to annoy the creek.

When the many shrimp bushes were all tied the anchor came up again. I lay back against the tiller. Tom stood up against the mast, and we shook and shuddered homeward in the face of a stiff wind. When we had anchored the motor-boat, I picked up the superb gun Tom had lent me and went off shooting round Kingscote, a big romantic property that belonged to the Misses King. Staring down the coiling silvery barrel of his gun, down its circling and giddy bore, I recalled twilights along the lakeside when I had gone shooting with it lying in the curve of my arm and round my waist the opulent belt of cartridges. Never before had the flowers along the lake loomed so thick and white; great perfumed lilies, seen hastily, endured for a lifetime in my soul as I passed; pine branches, dusty and heavy above the blue and gold water, hung within me heavily for years afterwards, and the hills I climbed springily sent up a protest, damp with night dew, to my nostrils. I felt that I should be sorry when I had to give back the gun. It had brought poetry to me. I had never shot anything with it. Why should I? It is pleasant and princely to go through the bush with the power of life and death under one's hand, and refrain from exercising that power. The timber in the stock was autumnal and deep; the barrel was simply chased like an old jewel, tilted lightly towards the desired prey. I just desired. I couldn't bring the prey down to my feet.

When I had finished my work with Tom Henderson I rode back to the tea-plantation. In my hut I sat down heavily on the fish-crate near the empty fireplace, and for a little relaxation I read the last letter that Blue had received from Peppino, the friend of our pea-picking days. If I find that I am destined for purgatory one of these days I shall ask that some of Peppino's letters be allowed me. For there is a freshness of view, a sense of man's original struggle with the common tongue that restores me to myself, that brings down all things to the beginning.

Mai dear,

Lettle creature I receved yor leter and like wat yow good and I two.

Sorry never weret to you beffor because I beene to Melbourne this crestmas good time when you weret letter tell me you are gon ating gon see your famele.

I wel must conclude Peppino Nicolace scusim dont tim Remember me to Steve to you geve my weret hand yor lettle creature Lettule creature, Peppino.

I send to you me dress,

Erica Post Office,
Victoria.

Let us marvel at Peppino's "dress". He was nobly, magnificently and sufficiently clothed in the Erica Post Office, Victoria. Molyneux could not design better for the crowned heads of Europe. Poiret would be utterly superseded and Schiaparelli cast down, at the mere sight of Peppino's "dress". Peppino was an expert sugar-beet worker, and spent much of his time at Maffra working on the sugar-beet. He had had a lot of experience with tea, as well, and I hoped fervently that he would soon be turning up in Metung and getting a job from Jim McLachlan on the plantation. I could not see enough of him.

Grey clouds were coming over from the sea in a speaking flight, pressing down on me, urging me to write poetry and make delicate water-colour drawings. When the rain came in search of me I shivered and recalled the past. At Kingscote, along the lake's edge,

43

long ago Macca had dug up the marble head of a goddess, Grecian, lost; he had found among the old flowers the book of Grimm's fairytales, and we had eaten limes at dawn under the trees that grew among dead grass and red roses. Ah, who could possibly sit in this lonely hut and hear the rain and not shudder for want of company? With my mind fixed on Kingscote and the dry grasses, the red roses and the friend of my youth, I passed into a state of swift toiling entrancedness, hearing a voice that began gradually within me, my own voice, that of my mind, declaiming poetry, and growing louder and stronger until it died away. What it had said I wrote down vexedly on a sheet of smoked yellow paper, for in the hut everything was smoked, since the fumes swept into the room, as lonely perhaps as myself.

Yes, I will bring thee leaves from trees that toil
Songfully through the winter to embroil
Their heads in tender shades from deep December.
I'll bring thee leaves of grass and I'll remember
Thy lovely favourites, greyer than a hill . . .
The olive leaf, and yet another still . . .
Coveted by lone hearts that leap all night
To wild sad thoughts . . . the thin pine-needles tight
And sourly green within their gummy cells
Shaped by the peaceful mourning of wind-swells.
Leaves that have pressed against the halting moon
And dreamed to death, unheeded, oversoon,
And fruit leaves stabbed by many a wild bird's bill,
Soft struck at midnight by the plover's quill.
I know a gentle close that's held these sweets
For sixty jealous years, spurned by the feet
Of surly seas, and shiny with the spittle
Of galleon snails and pockmarked by the little
Uncertain sweeping footsteps of the rain. . . .
I'll go faint-footed to its head again,
And drag the bending bud leaves from its hair.
They will be sisters to your breasts, they are so fair.
These trembling things, soft shaken by the frore
Sad kisses of the lake upon the sad lips of the shore.

44

Alas, alas, I thought, up on the hill now the rain falls heavily through the fern and the dry white logs that I love will be sodden and slippery. I have no candle tonight. I cannot write further rhymes. What shall I do with the rest of this wild and stormy night? And many moods came on me. "But I, I am calm!" exclaims Herod. Yes, chasuble upon chasuble of ebony and gold shall be set for me, and shall the jewels fall? Staring about the baracca, I thought of tomorrow, and a long day over the accounts. My voluptuous longing for richness, the heritage of my ancestors, made me turn like a pinned serpent, here and there, in search of art, of glory and beauty. No, no, how can I stay here? I rose up and put on a pair of khaki shorts and a raincoat and, pulling a grey tweed cap over my shorn head, I walked out into the night.

Through the night, the bush, the weeping leaves, the growing murmur of bush creeks, I wandered, going towards the school, where Stevenson, the schoolmaster, kept the big gramophone and the records of great singers, to enchant his pupils with daily. The gramophone stood in the darkness, I kept the thought of it before me, all the way. Down the wet hill I walked when I had come out of the bush, and I passed by Oliver Johnson's farm, past that hut where I had sat with Macca one wet night years ago. There had been trappers living in the hut then, and they had made a huge red fire for us, and given us hot cocoa to drink, and had generally treated us as visiting gods. And now up the back track, over little twigs, I went, down to the schoolhouse.

"The schoolmaster's name is Stevenson," I said to myself. "Stevenson . . . Johnson. Only sons. No man can do more than be a son. Why not Stevens-god . . . Stevens-will . . . Stevens-power . . . Stevens-agony? Oh no, it has to be the nearest thing the race can grasp. My son, my son, Absalom! Would God I had died for thee. . . ." And with the ancient king I mourned in the bitterness of my heart.

Listening to the avid gabble of water running from a gargoyle at the corner of the schoolhouse, I opened the door with the key Stevenson had lent me. My wanderings by night amused him; he liked to come into the school in the morning and sense that I had been there, and play over to the scholars the records that I had been playing. "Ah, Steve has been here," he used to say. In the cupboard below the gramophone the records were kept. Such a haunting and enchanting perfume came to one—old, evasive, modern, tormenting. Where, one wondered, had one smelt that odour before? I turned the torch on the cupboard and found Caruso's *"A' Vucchella"*—"To a Little Red Mouth".

The first clamorous tinkling of little bells follows the spinning sound of the needle over the disk, an ancient decayed little sound, a toccata, and the golden hair swinging over the breasts of those women who listened to it, in Browning's Italy. And bell-like, defiant, startling, common almost, the voice of Caruso cries in the dialect of Naples.

> *"Ah, ma chiesta vucchella, c'para na rosella . . ."*

All through that wet night I listened to him, and was haunted by him for days afterward. I found a fine photograph of him and kept it for years. He reminded me of a jewelled lizard, of a great Roman emperor and of the poet Horace. And the name Caruso, does it not mean "to carouse"? Perhaps he had lived in Roman times and in the great villas of the Romans along the sea of Naples had sung all night while they feasted.

The rain ceased and I left the school by the way I came. It was wet all next day. I had very little work to do. I took out a sheet of paper and began a poem on it.

> *Arise, and let me come to you.*
> *I remember everything.*
> *Your bronze eyes . . .*

"No," I said, "I shall write a letter home." While the rain fell mildly after its impulsiveness of the night before I wrote, pausing sometimes to stare out on the wet grass, the tall dead white tree shaking with the wandering heaviness and emptiness peculiar to dead wood, and I saw beyond it the huge upturned root of a fallen giant, with a pool of water below it, where after showers the stock in the gully drank.

It is half-past six, and I have just finished my solitary tea, literally speaking—one cup with eggs and toast and cake to follow. After a long week of terrible furnace heat the sky is overcast, intermittent showers are coming in from the sea, and it is cool in the baracca for the first time since it last rained. Blue, you know well the vast contentment and the happiness that rain gives after great heat. The imagination turns to the all-too-brief cup of delicate black coffee, to eggs—why eggs, I wonder?—to buttered brown toast, oozing richly from every pore, to soft round crumbling biscuits, to wide rich slices of golden fruit cake, smelling of wine and raisins, great damp heavy slices that go down slowly, sensuous stuff.

I will imagine for mine own pleasure that I am sitting with you once more. Mia will be sitting on the soft brocaded hassock by the fire, because Blue likes to be opposite the window; no, she likes to be overlooking the table with its fairly set dishes and silver. The cups are gleaming dully in the shadows, the spoons are curving into them; the ginger jar, sugar bowl, and coffee chest, with brocaded men and crinolined dames and tall ships in the night living immovably on them, mirror the fire. Round plates shine, bisected by shining knives; empty egg shells rest delicately in blue cups; pale flat biscuits slide over their dishes; hot, deep, damp, irresistible English muffins, buttered, melting, hot, exhale a gigantic nostalgia through the room; the damp cake winks richly with soft fruity eyes, imploring to be lessened, golden slice by golden slice. The fire leaps up, the kettle chaunts, blotches of crimson and gold are the flowers in green leaves; the books are there, the night is there, and the wandering rain, and your faces, and I'm home again. I am with my own people. I need not talk if I don't want to. I need not laugh at inanities. Books are touched, are opened, closed, and put aside. Old names recur, hard days are remembered, and easy ones laughed over and richly appreciated. And then, when *we* have finished wandering with our tongues, the old violin wavers into wordless speech, and the white-haired bow says, "Don't you remember? *Non ti ricordi?* Listen, *amico*," it says, "this is *'Bandiera Rosa'*, and you are before the big fire at Buffalo, *ancora*. The big fire before which the Italians are cooking a fragrant tea, and they are trying to follow my strong voice. Racing bridles, sweaters and mufflers and caps are jumbled up on the wide tables; there's a smell of face cream, tobacco, and spaghetti and meat, frying meat, and, *diavolo*, how good it is, the hot fire and the jolly company! And as for you, *amico*,

47

you're not happy—no, you never will be, though I am here, singing my sweetest to make you so. And now the Midnight Waltz, so that you may remember the old orchard at Sarsfield, the fallen red apples lying in the shadows on moonlight nights, and the black resonance of the spinning disk, with the light on it, and the deep armchair in the corner, and a fair face and two most exquisite eyes, long-lashed and eloquent, and your own sick sorrow that was nothing more than imaginative vanity. Yes, the old orchard, and Jim Peterson, your Swedish mate, hooting like a tug-boat in a fog down at the fence. And then the Ettagorah and Gerogery waltzes, brought back from over the border in New South Wales. The train is under you, rocking to the refrain, nearing the border, and a silent girl named Rose is sitting opposite. The plains are greening under the recent rains, and light clouds are mirrored in their own blood, spilt in hollow places about the earth. *Amico,* I am pleasant, and I want to instruct you into seeing and hearing everything, as you should hear my music. If I were not taken up and placed under the warm round chin of the player, and if her fingers didn't guide the bow, I'd be silent, causing you neither grief nor faint happiness. And if you hadn't taken up the violin of life and learnt to waken it into song it would never have played those sad, terrible, and differing harmonies that so bewilder and gladden you."

I have spoken of the Wilsons, who lived at Lucknow, burning, blazing, and unbending Lucknow. I used to call in and see them whenever I passed through. The eldest son, Kelly, owned an old property up in Black Mountain now, and was busy breeding working bullocks for the mills up there; Rita, his sister, was now a fine big girl. They would retail to all the slow gossip of Gippsland.

One evening when I was at the Buccaneer's Kelly Wilson rode up to the gate. A heavy cloudy twilight seemed to hang over the gate, and in its centre, Kelly hung, too, and his mare's head hung . . . everything weighed heavily over the gate. I looked out and saw the pure-bred white Arab drooping towards me and on it sat Kelly Wilson, whom I had seen in old days as a planet, golden-rayed, flushed and dewy and eagle-nosed. Now that the delirium tremens of youth had disappeared I could see him in the dwarfed way we see others when years have passed. He was a short, fair youth with a head of dull golden hair; his large eyes were a harsh bright blue, a mineral blue, and wavered in and out of fair eyelashes. A large Adam's apple in a slight white throat moved aggressively as he talked in a deep, mocking voice with an air of knowing all and knowing it well. A torn yellow-green raincoat bound him away from the weather; it smelt of old showers. He looked at people as though he found in them something ignorant that amused him. The big voice boomed out in harsh defiant words. Everyone in the house looked at him amusedly. The contrast of an enormous head rocking on a short body gave him the appearance of some man of ancient race, and he looked so utterly out of place on the earth that one longed nervously to have him back on board the Arab mare again.

He insisted that I should ride in with him to Lucknow and spend the week-end with him and his mother and sisters; and he stood before the fire talking about his life on Black Mountain until I was ready to go. I caught and saddled my horse in the moonlight, and we rode off down the steep cliff to the main road. The two animals, excited by each other's liveliness, stepped buoyantly over the hard white road. It was a long ride past Brooker's, Proust's, Olsen's, Redenbach's, and down the old back track to the punt on the Tambo. We entered a turn-off near the Nicholson and took the old short-cut through Sarsfield into Lucknow, and came at last to the large house standing off the road, with stockyards round it, full of milling horses. The Wilsons bought up horses and sold them again. It was late; the house was in darkness. We went into the big green kitchen.

"There ought to be some food somewhere," Kelly said, searching in the enormous cupboard that they had brought down by bullock wagon years ago. "You saw the marks of the bullock chains on it, didn't you?" he said as he stooped to take a large apple pie from the shelf. "Ah, yes, you saw them when you were here last, I believe."

When we had eaten the apple pie between us Kelly and I washed our faces and hands in the bathroom—a peculiarly Australian bathroom, very lovable to me—and he showed me my room and I lay down between sheets of awful whiteness and slept my long sleep until morning.

It was a long hot Sunday after, but delicious—a Sunday of visit. I was away from the plantation for a while, far away from the atmosphere of it, in cattle country. And cattle country is such a great relief after crop country. Through the day streamed the ignoble music of America from the gramophone, showering out from the cool shady sitting-room that looked out on the wild Australian road. The earth lay dead and white, a skeleton, beside the black records of songs written in America. It was all jangled, tangled. The records didn't know Australia; they didn't even know America; but I was enchanted. An unnatural world in the making was building itself and superimposing itself upon the past. The Austral-American Age had begun.

In the morning at about ten or eleven, before it grew too fiercely hot, Kelly saddled the white Arab and drove some cattle over to a grazing paddock near by. I watched his superb seat in the saddle, the musical swaying waltz of the body there. His mare leapt a log, and he sat like a centaur; the very veins, you might think, that tossed the blood up his Arab's legs were joined to and tossing the blood up into the rider's heart. Around them, mare and rider, the blue-grey bush hung in the mock dejection of Australia, melancholy for no reason at all. The sun shone, but the leaves drooped, yet the underlying glitter proved it all to be a pose—a helpless pose, like my own sorrow, an inevitable pose; it was Nature's way of fixing the gum-leaves and making them . . . gum-leaves. The man and the horse threaded about over dead logs and branches, taking out the cattle. In the afternoon it grew very hot, and in the heat of the day I lay in the darkened bedroom. The great cruel continent, Australia, masterless, lay outside the window, brooding over itself. And I loved that continent. I longed to be a man and live in dry yellow glittering gum-leafed gunyahs and labour in pitiless heat. When I raised myself from the black-grey earth, all I asked was that which came, a cool wind, like a drink, from the sea, a drink for the thirstiest parts of my body, my armpits and my chest.

I was walking in the dawn, among the barren and dry wattles around their house. I walked quite a long way into the bush, because sometimes in Australia that is the correct thing to do. I had had shocking dreams all night and arose, like Pharaoh, early in the morning to find an interpreter, a Joseph, to ask him the meaning of the dream. A wattle-bird cried harshly from the boughs, "Go back! Go back!"

But I was haunted by Pharaoh. In the morning, I thought, the king sent for Joseph and told him his dream. And Joseph said to the king, "The seven empty ears blasted by the east wind shall be seven years of famine. . . ." That hot Egyptian morning, so like our own Australian summer morning, burnt with a curious light in my mind. On the parched earth round the palace I saw the purple convolvulus growing. I looked and saw a strange scarlet cloud in the east. I listened and heard thunder in the north. "Out of Israel . . . out of Israel," it boomed.

The scarlet cloud grew blood-bright. And I remembered, "Who is this that cometh from Edom, with dyed garments from Bozrah? this that is glorious in his apparel, travelling in the greatness of his strength? . . . Wherefore art thou red in thine apparel, and thy garments like him that treadeth in the winevat?"

It is enough, I said, to be condemned by that voice. It is enough to be haunted, cursed and crushed by one who could utter such words that torment because no man thought them. Crush me then, God, put me out from Thee, for my life is a torment.

As Kelly and I rode along the dry track towards the Cherry-tree Hotel I told him of the thunder and the scarlet cloud at dawn. We glanced at each other, troubled. The two horses, the black and the white, had more in common than we, the riders. They displayed an eagerness of mutual step, and shook their heads so that their bright metal curb-rings made music all the way.

The sun lost the golden morning gentleness and became burning hot and white, then no colour at all, and I was not aware of a sun so much as of a haunting fever that lay over everything.

"We've got to split here," said Kelly, swinging off his mare. "I've got to go on to Bruthen from here, and this is your turn-off for Metung," pointing to a miserable track among the dry brown-purple bracken. I dismounted, and we sat down near a log, rotten with white ants; the earth on which we sat was as dry as though it had been mummified for a thousand years. The horses, streaked with sweat, stood by as we talked, turning their bits over in their green mouths, twitching their ears and staring, startled, at everything that moved slightly on this bitingly hot day. Then we remounted. Kelly cantered off to Bruthen, and I took the back track to Metung. I had gone about three miles through the scrub along that narrow track when it ended among swampy grass of a snake-like, whirling, lashing nature, at a fence below a property that lay in a nightmare, deserted, lonely, blank and awful. The house on the hill! I stared at it. That house was haunted and filled to my youthful mind with tall and fiery men. They might come swarming down on me at any moment. I stared round at myself and my property, at my naked and beautiful arms, shining in the sun, at the black silken horse under me, and the delicate leather of the saddle and the bridle. I dug a frightened heel into the horse's side and fled back the way I had come with a mad heart beating in terror. And found at last the right back track to Metung.

It was night when I arrived home at the baracca. When I tottered down to the office next day, there was a letter from Blue to say that she had landed at Buffalo, and that Charlie Wallaby and his mother had met her. This time her eloquence persuaded me, and I began to make plans to join her, but when I showed the letter to Jim McLachlan he demurred.

"Steve, there's such a lot to do here yet—easily two more pickings off the tea. The men will be working on it until early autumn, and I shall want you here to help until then. By then it will be winter, and I really should advise you to stay here during the winter, because it will be very severe up at Buffalo."

I knew that. When the snow comes over Mount Buffalo, Mount Bogong, Feathertop, and St Bernard a hideous quality comes into the country. I had stayed at Buffalo and knew all about an alpine winter. So I decided to stay with Jim and see the tea-picking through, and let the Bogong take care of itself. This Gippsland with its heat, its most awful loveliness and loneliness and the pure precision known to me as man, the worker, would never return again, I knew. These days said that they would not return again, and I believed them.

A VISION OF CLOUDS

II

THE last hot days of the long summer poured down on the little
hut in the gully; the patriarch-cum-priestess there, having worked
hard among the tea—"two leaves, one bud, two leaves, one bud,
two leaves, one bud"—all the week, and having addressed en-
velopes and taken down letters in fine Pitman and gross Australian shorthand, lay alone at the week-end reading poetry, or
wandered in the bush. One day I took my rifle and went far along
the foreshore to where, in a dead tree, the gut-hawks nested. The
great brown and white tree rose straight from the ground, naked,
appearing to go thousands of feet up into the air; at its very
summit among a claw of dead boughs the hawks were nesting
and feeding their young. I lay at the foot and waited for the parent
birds to come to them. Their approach began far out on the blue
lake, with an absorbed whirling motion, closing in on the tree.
There was mystery, delight, and satisfaction in partaking of the
day and the homecoming of the hawk. Afar they had been killers,
over the paddocks they had ranged as slaughterers, without mercy,
but at the sight of their tawny wings making tilted lights against
the blue sky, a syllable formed between the element and the bird,
a sympathy expressed to me that within sight of the nest the bird
changed, and was no longer the killer but the solicitous parent.
These contrasts had a strange enchantment for me. Between the
wing and the sky and my vision a subtlety was spoken. My heavy
rifle, too, was mysterious—first, in that it tied us all together in
life and death; secondly, in that it couldn't have hit a house at a
hundred yards. There was a fault in the barrel. I aimed for the
breasts of the hawks as long as the bullets lasted. They were heavy-
calibre ·44. I took pleasure in the pain of the report, and the
hawks' tearing one-sided flight.

Up on the hill above the long green crops waved, below the salt
lake tossed froth and sea jetsam over the shore, in the enchanting,

vivid, and immortal blue and white day. The water raved incessantly, softly about us. It complained of us to the rocks and the sand, to the rotten white wood and the tongues of land going out to meet it. The hawk had a piercing whistle that plunged forward in noise, as the hawk plunged forward to its prey. Eight jerking, strong, forward-rushing notes that ended in a wild scream of triumph, eight paces ending in a cruel plunge, eight aeons of threat ending in one second of terror. I imagined it above my head as an enemy while I crouched in the sand. In its desperate haunting scream I bathed myself, waiting to be killed. The poetry of desert and death sang in it. At night, weak from want of food and chilled, I left the hawks' nest and came home to the baracca to eat hot golden cakes and drink black coffee. When I had eaten, I went outside and sang "A' Vucchella" to the dead trees.

The skies grew vaster, bluer, holding the last of the summer in mighty strength, holding on to their clouds, day by day, keeping them in the same pattern from daylight to dark, and even unto the next noon. I rode down by the Tambo one afternoon and saw a cloud rise up, shaped like a gigantic cup, a Grail, with a slender stem, standing on an altar. The colours of the cloud were blue and ivory, and below it, on the more human horizon, there was a redness and many black swans flying. The cup was veiled, shapes flocked about it, entwined in it, and the black swans sang as they flew, the song that sounds like the rusty doors of a dungeon being slowly opened, and from the doors floated the Grail, dragging its priests and priestesses behind it. And when at noon next day I rode along the lakeside, I looked over and saw this same Grail moving towards me on the horizon, but violet and angry with the heat of the day. A veil of darkness and showers came over it, swathed it, and moved with it, and fell on my head in stinging rain. For two days this Grail stood solid in the heavens, wandering in cloud form up and down the Tambo—the huge secret cup of the court of Arthur, that for which Sir Bors and Sir Galahad had ridden and searched for so long.

One day as I sat behind my hut, in the cool black patch there, the gut-hawks flew over, whistling and searching . . . but for what? Together they cried their eight tentative notes, ending in the one sad wild screech of death and aim. "Here, here, this is the place!" they cried above my hut, and fled circling outward. Then from over the horizon came an enormous cloud like a city, teeming with people whose faces, lit with romance and adventure, looked down on me. Their leader, an old patriarch, clad in sheepskin, beckoned to me slowly, turned, beckoned to his people and halted the city before my eyes. For an hour it stayed there, and was gone.

I went into my hut, and on smoky yellow paper wrote of it, as I saw it, a vision of clouds.

A VISION OF CLOUDS

What forms are these, huge, cumbrous, silent, slow?
What garland's this, that for a measured space
Moves on the sky's broad brow? What toil, what woe?
What great incline of limbs? Immortal grace,
Strange family, swift changing cameo . . .
Women and gods and children that with smiles,
Keen downward looks, deep frowns and inward glow
Of sweet emotion beckon and beguile
My tensive eyes . . . Who are ye? From what shore
Embowered in shining laurels do ye turn
Your temple galleon, wreathed with cloudy store
Of holy vase and bowl and rounded urn?
For what strange war do these young men prepare
With shield and spear and coarsest horse-hair plume;
These captains spurring ivory-footed mares
Through endless plains of darkest blue-bell bloom?
This patriarch with silver ram's fleece flung
About his noble loins, and this tall girl
Of pallid mask with thunder-buds among
The cold arrested movement of her curls . . .

The javelin flight of beauty's headlong day
Slackens and ceases, and its great haft gleams
Along the foam in star lands far away.
Fair gods, fair gods, uplift me to these lands!
Teach me the way of wings! But no . . . but no . . .
My strong emotion, grip me with sure hands,
Bend, bend, my rough mortality, my bow
Of arching thought . . . and from the trembling string

Expel the spirit's arrow. It will cleave
The eagle's sea above us, and will fling
Sharp shoulders to the cloud. Adieu, I leave
All flesh that dies, all wounds that give it death,
To follow gods. Remember, he that climbs
With fine impatience, fearlessness, proud breath,
Outlives his fellows and outstrides his times.

As autumn came I grew lonely, remembering the bitter promise that had been made to me as I worked in the maize along the Ovens River, the great cry, "Immortality!" "In Primavera," the earth had said, "immortality shall come to us, and all through the autumn and winter, you shall be satisfied." But all this was ended.

The last picking of the tea had been made; all useless dead bushes had been put roughly through the hoppers and stripped and clipped, dried and packed. Now, after the long rich romantic summer, the earth lay fallow, the plantation deserted, and for only a few days a week did I work in the office. I thrust my feet into black rabbit-skin slippers and sat by my fire of smoking wood all day, as the autumnal rains came, swept over from the lake that led to the sea. There, on the grey tin at the back of the hearth was the ornate signature, "Guiseppe Tuncredi", just as he had written it in springtime, that wandering Italian, who went through the bush singing:

"Comme le rose d'Aprile, le gioie
D'amore son morte per me."

But Guiseppe, who can ever understand it? Not even now can I believe it—that like the rose of April the joy of love is finished, is dead for me. Up on the hill stood the remains of the bark hut, and the blue-white bare framework of the shed next to it, where we had all lived long ago, a jolly company—Blue, Jim, and myself. I stayed away from it. Of what use going there? Why haunt the place that haunted me? I sat before the fire and wrote on the back of the letter from the young Chinese poet who wrote to me.

Each breath I draw is keen with pain; every smell and light and sound runs like an old man's rheumatism through my

58

blood. My very hand aches to the sweetness of the pen. And why? I hear the far Pacific brooding dully along her sliding shores. I hear among the bracken on the hill a bird that cries richly and insistently, "Io . . . Io . . . Io!" Who is it? questions my thought-bereft heart. "Io . . . Io . . . Io!" the hidden mouth responds. Curlew, I've often sought you . . . when I heard your tormenting cry in grassy paddocks, in cool deeps, in drying ferns. There's only one of you, I'll swear. I heard you cry from a dark hill lashed by light showers at midnight, some two years ago. And those that sat with me, then, before the fire, placed their hands before their faces and said, "That is our hearts crying out on a lonely hill." But the curlew continued still its sharp appealing from the night.

While I was in the middle of this passage Eb Coleman came in through the shower, and ducked his head at the low smoke in the baracca.

"Steve, you're a funny sort, you are. 'Struth, you should see yourself. Sitting here at the fire writing—fancy a girl like you living in this shack!"

I looked irate. I loved the baracca. "Is anything wrong at home?"

"No, but a fellow's going down to Melbourne this week, wealthy chap with a car; he's been staying in at our place and going out lake-fishing with Pa. He's passing through Dandenong. Why don't you go home for a while? The tea's finished, isn't it?" Eb rolled a cigarette and stood above me, very tall and fair. "Well?"

"Yes, I'll go, Eb."

"Better chuck some water on the fire. Is this it?" bending to a billy there. "Now she'll smoke. Come on."

Within forty-eight hours I was walking round the red bricks of the flagged court at home in Dandenong. My mother had bought Laurel Lodge, a big two-storeyed brick house, vaguely like a picture I had seen of an old hunting lodge that once belonged to Henry VIII. It stood in the middle of a wide red-brick court, and was dark with ivy. The many rooms rang hollowly underfoot, and the usual mass of plum-trees, now winter shaken, stood around. I walked in on my mother.

"Ah, Madáme! Come va?"

"Steve!" Mia exclaimed in her high, sharp voice. "Such a sur-

59

prise! How Blue would have liked this! She will be sorry she is not here. Up at Kaloramma, you know. I'll make tea for you."

"By Jove," I said, "I've been working among the beastly stuff all year."

"Well, black coffee, then." She took down the percolator.

"No, since you love tea so well, let it be tea."

Mia and I settled in for a fortnight or two of winter, after that first afternoon. I took much persuading to remain at home. Dandenong always appeared contracted to my eyes, used to the miles and miles of Gippsland. I walked round the Lodge and eyed the laurels gloomily. I could not understand how my mother could be bothered living in such a place. Motor cars were passing it every minute; clerks and shop girls went by to their work down in the main street. And next door one could hear the servant saying to her blind old mistress, "The figs will soon be ripe, ma'am." I longed to be back near the Tambo again, and to see Black Mountain and Bruthen and hear the train hoot at Bumberrah.

Mia had placed all our treasures in the right places. On brackets on the walls were my seven rifles and two Service revolvers. There were foxes' skins, wallabies' skins, the skins of eagles and snakes, bandicoots and lizards, jockeys' caps, racing bridles, saddles, powder flasks, bullet and cartridge belts, two battle boomerangs and half a dozen exhibition boomerangs. My drawings and Blue's were pinned to the walls, black-and-white line drawings and delicate wash drawings of a Balkan, Hungarian, Romanian sort. They came of all countries, like us. But it was the religion of the desert that showed in them more plainly than anything. A woman of the Russian steppes stood by herself on a green hill, with her apron flying and waved, far away, to no one. Her clothes haunted me. And in that slight, mournful, waving arm, there was a dream sense, as though she had really lived once, and the waving had happened.

The fortnight stretched out and I ended up by staying all winter at home. Boas Davidson, my mother's brother, came to stay with us for a while. He smoked good cigars, day in and day out, and the house reeked of them. He was an *habitué* of Tattersall's Club, and owned a large racing stable with a fair sprinkling of steeplechasers. It was he who had taken the cavalry remounts to India. He was chockful of anecdotes of Bombay and Calcutta and up-

60

country stations. These Tales from the Hills warmed the Australian winter a little—and, perhaps, brought on an earlier springtime.

When winter was ending I made ready to go back by train to Gippsland. Young, refreshed, poetic, I rushed, I flew, I fevered back to Gippsland . . . along the golden line, the olden line, the steam and dew and iron line, to live the last and loveliest springtime I should ever know. Flushed and splendid for the slaughter I returned, as men go to war, as men burn for their faiths, so went I, burning and blazing along the line to Gippsland. And in the trees the slow and solemn roar of my innocent springtime arose and made melody. I longed to cry out everything in one long tumultuous inky shout. At Sale I made for a carriage smelling of tobacco smoke and talked of racehorses and Gippsland to a Bruthen man all the way to Bairnsdale. Conversation! The excitement of the rapid words, the nearness and interest of men—it was wine to me. I flushed like fruit, my eyes shone. Gods, I lived, lived, lived! The Bruthen man said he supposed me to be about sixteen years of age.

"Sixteen?" I cried. "Too old! I have just been born!"—into happy, sparkling existence.

At Bairnsdale Foley, the mail carrier, a large, handsome, intense man squeezed me into the front of the big Paige car between himself and another big man. To be in Bairnsdale again! To be engulfed in the whirling, curving, backing fleet of cars at the station, to be in good clothes and wild spirits, to see Duleep Singh trailing down Main Street with a pink turban on, to see the crowds at Cook's Corner! Oh, the smooth road, the swift car! Foley fairly hurled the Paige to Johnsonville. We passed everything. I said to Foley, "You're a great driver!"

"Think so?" he answered.

"Yes." He was Helios while it lasted. It was, it had been, great to drive beside that man. He put all his tense energy into his wheel. "Yes, you are Helios. And I am a god, winged, flushed, triumphant. No mortal woe shall sadden me!"

That was the way to start spring! And the season, the spring of 1928, started like that, within itself. Under the trees, the golden capeweed, black-eyed, started out from the earth. Out came the clematis, bearded and white, and the brackens clenched their fists like workmen at the sky. In the rainy blue air a fire sparkled.

61

It came from the white-silver boughs of the eucalyptus, as they tossed their purple-black hair of leaves in the air. They roared, and turned, half turned slowly with the wind. All things half turned to the roaring tune of the spring. Out came the harbinger of spring, drooping speckled little flowers in a shaft of green leaf. The wattle with its throat-catching perfume, its aromatic perfume, was a head of soft powdery golden curls stuck out of every dark place—a gigantic theatrical wig of gold above a silver face, for its leaves were like misty coins. And in damp clay the white heath, the speckled and the red heath, a thought as bitter as death, set in a close heavy comb of blossom along the bough and mixed up with youth in Australia, bitterly and wildly and desperately it bloomed. Bellbirds and wattle-birds clanked and barked all day in the bush; and the creeks, mossy and ferny-faced, laughed in water all day, in the foaming, gurgling, singing, caught-up water of Gippsland, that eddies around in pools and catches on logs and chants through its captivity the song of the sea, a hoarse, roaring song, with a little sad mirth under it all—tears running down the cheeks of a giant who is shouting songs of seas he will travel on when he has left his home and his love. I began to chant poetry at once. First, to the Pacific that rushed white with haste on to the sand at Lakes Entrance.

> God, God, will it never cease,
> The sliding and the roar
> And riding of tremendous seas
> Along tremendous shores?
> There, listen, it comes again!
> The foaming scuffling smother,
> The ponderous heave and the pain
> Of one love dragged from another.
> What is it that shoreward leaps,
> That seaward is strongly hurled,
> On the points of spears, to weep
> The music that haunts the world?
> The mighty brow that tosses
> Its white locks to the stars. . . .
> The tortured thought that crosses
> The shingle of splinter and spar.

God, God, will it never cease?
The sliding and the roar
And riding of tremendous seas
Along tremendous shores?

All night in springtime, as one lay in bed, the huge white and blue seas, the vast Pacific roared and thundered in stifled sorrow up and down the long golden beaches at Lakes Entrance; and beyond Silvershot one could hear it all night, rising in foam and fury and pain against the moon. Often in the night I raised myself in my bed and listened to the cumbrous sad Greek of that which I called *Thalassa*, the sea. Human woe could not touch me, but this sea, this Pacific Ocean, *mare nostrum*, it billowed in white and ponderous sound about my ears, and made me sorrow, I knew not why.

Ma, Primavera . . . but, springtime. . . . The Italians would be back here again. Peppino would come back and play his mouth-organ masterfully to me. I should see Domenic again. But, best of all, Peppino would come back to Metung and sing the Italian songs for us. I polished up my *"A' Vucchella"* and *"O Sole Mio"*. At night, the tree-frogs, the crickets and I croaked it together.

Blue was working on Peechelba Station, the station that Morgan the bushranger had stuck up in the sixties. She wrote to me from up there.

I cannot say when I shall see you both, but, O God, Steve, you'll never feel the break as I have. Perhaps I may see you in spring, the exceptional season that inevitably holds nothing. You say you are not changed, then has the lad's life still further fascination for you? Has the life in the bush, as often planned for, still endured—is it still unforgotten? I am turned trapper now, and the set is laid out after dinner, and I finish before sundown. I set twenty-five traps which belong to my boss, five for water rats, whose skins are valuable, from 2s. 6d. to 5s. each. There is a rabbit bus that comes here, and a nice chap drives it. He buys the rabbits by the bulk, 1s. 6d. a pair large and less if small. Hares, also. I've only caught two hares as yet, three possums and one cat. I let them go. I caught something

63

you would have liked, Steve. A swamp-hawk, like those at
Metung, that used to soar above our down-bent heads. I bought
a pair of rubber boots in Wangaratta a while back, mostly for
going round the traps in the long wet grass. A fox followed
me, the other night, howling.

Down from Bairnsdale, to stay with Eb, came Macca's younger
brother, Alan. Oddly enough, throughout the years he has remained in my mind as an unripe cherry. This little neat fellow,
with his protruding blue eyes, his full pursed lips, straight fair hair,
and tidy way of laughing amusedly, secretly, yet not too secretly,
at someone taller than himself, was attractive to me. I liked him.
"Me and you's going shooting tomorrow," Eb said to him one
evening as we sat round the fire together. "S'pose you haven't
had a shot for ages?"
"Just a few minor explosions at home, when something went
wrong," Alan drawled. "As a matter of fact, Macca took my rifle
with him when he went over to Royle's to stay. Oh, by the way,
Steve, he gave me a letter to give to you." He handed me a large
envelope, which I opened at once.

Stevie, the best and most beloved Stevie, I should so like to
see you. And I want to see you alone. If I come down to Metung
on Sunday night and go along to the old bark hut up at Hardy's
where you and I and Jim and Blue used to be such good company last year, will you be there? I shall do my best to get
down, but if I am not there, write to me, and tell me if you
will marry me. For Stevie, I do love you . . . all suddenly . . .
as Rupert Brooke put it. I want to see you on Sunday night at
the old hut, for the sake of old days, really, and for love of you.
I know you loathe love and marriage, and like Proust try to
reconcile Time and Space to Man, but I really want to marry
you, just as I wanted to last year, and the year before. But you
look down on love and marriage so. That's the poet in you. I
know you love me for friendship's sake and because of time
and place and my red hair, as you've so often said, and my broad
shoulders and the white shirts I wear and my way of looking
mysteriously Celtic and profound and vaguely godlike, but I
want more than that. My one love ever. Remember, Stevie, I

always called you that. My one love ever. And I'm only really happy when I'm with you. Other girls bore me to tears. If I cannot manage to get down to Metung on Sunday, please write and say that you'll be mine or something like that.

Anyhow, I know I shall get you at last, Steve—"spite of the miles and years between us". I know, of course, what your immediate reaction will be. A negative answer. And pages of the most exquisite prose regarding your poetic love of me which is much, much too splendid for our marriage. The ideal. That's you, Steve. And we two, haunters of old bark huts and red fires by night and all things Australian, could be so utterly happy, too. Please be sensible and say yes, instead of sending me pages of love and an undecided no. I know you love me. But will you marry me? I love you dreadfully.

MACCA.

The day changed and swelled about me. I became conscious that my heart was beating, and rapidly. For a long time I had had a letter, a sort of bill of repairs, ready for Macca in the hut. I edged my way out of the room, caught my horse, and rode off to get it, and address it to him, care of Royle, Mossiface.

By the side of the road in the twilight, stood Domenic Olivieri, a short, squat young man from the north of Italy, Alessandria. He had the flat, tranquil, sharp, shrewd face of a Japanese wrestler, and the balance stance of ju-jutsu. Two slanting brown eyes with a deep, fleshy line or two under them. He rubbed his sharp-beaked Dantesque nose when he saw me.

"Well, Steve," he said, in a clipped masterly voice, cold and precise and proud. Domenic thought a lot of himself, and not without reason. An old soldier, he could sing hundreds of the songs of the Alpini, the mountain soldiers, and had the culture of a working man who has travelled. He was now a pea- and bean-grower in Metung.

"Good evening, Domenic. How are the peas getting on? The early ones, I mean. Any chance of picking for a while yet?" I loved to ride along to Domenic's and work for him in the fields. It was like the writing of pure poetry. And since the tea-plantation was being prepared for the next crop with pruning and potash I was at a loose end for the time being.

65

"Well—" he drew his cloth cap sharply down over his eyes; then thrust it up again on top of his head, revealing a white, deeply lined forehead—"well, Steva, it iss not too goot the weathers as yet. Sair iss a very small sample on at present, but I will let you know." He said this last, "I will let you know", in a musical singing way and dropped into the phrase gratefully as though he knew it well, and felt safe in it. "I will tell you what," he added on a rising note, "I would want a bean-sorter next month. If you care for the job, I could give it to you at one pound a day, that is if you have finished work in Jim McLachlan's office. I have a young fellow, Samozarro, staying with me in the hut, and he would take it on, too. What would you say, Steve?"

"I'd like to. Mind you, haven't sorted beans before . . ."

"Oh, 'tis easy. Just a matter of sieving and picking out de best And it wouldn't be hardt, for dey are a good sample. *Buona roba*. Good stuff. Drop in one days and have a look at them, that is the best. In the meantime, I must get home."

"Yes, so must I. *Buona sera, Domenico*."

"Good night," he replied in his strong clear voice. I felt myself to be slight and unimportant as I turned from him, with my romantic appetite and empty intellectual dreams. Here was one who could labour alone and unrecognized for the love of labour and possession.

The twilight seemed green and fertile as I left him, and the memory of the white-flowered peas fluttering at his feet gave me a sense of poetry and purity. I took the letter from the bookshelf in the baracca and rode over to Swanreach to post it. Above the Tambo River the moon wandered through the clouds.

"The wandering river, wandering with the moon," I thought, but no other line would come into my mind to couple it, though I listened and wrenched my brain about in great effort.

I had reached home before I realized that I hadn't promised Macca that I would be at the bark hut on Sunday night. I let it go. But the next night, having brooded and wondered and worried all day, I was by that time in the right mood to write and tell him that I should be there. It was my practice with Macca, when I got a letter from him asking me a commonplace question, to write from nine to ten pages of poetic prose after the style of Keats, Ruskin, or Wilde, and post that, sending the commonplace answer to the commonplace question in a separate envelope. Now I began to write. In the face of Macca's love, I had to strike an attitude, though of course, being a writer and poet, I had fundamentally no feeling about anything save literature and poetry. But in order to be human one must strike an attitude. All day the cuckoo had cried petulantly and monotonously in the bush, and the haunting cry in its circular flight had struck hard to my heart. Now in the ferns by night the curlew cried, "Io! Io! Io!" Ah God, I thought, here it is springtime again, and the lost years haunt me! The time of the curlew, the cuckoo, and the wattle urged me to write. The flames, beautiful and primitive, waved over the black tin walls of the hearth, over the floor, over my earnest young face, with the long shining hair hanging on either side of my cheeks, dropping softly from the temples that beat with intense feeling.

When the letter was finished, I got up and, hunting round in the dark lane for my horse, I found him drooping away from the moon, which he disliked. With clinking bridle and squeaking saddle I was off again to post my letter—through the bush, onto the main road, past Billy Creeker's, Domenic's hut, the hut of Akbarah Khan, and so to Swanreach. On my way back, out of Domenic's hut fire and voices poured in that strange, dramatic way they have of doing in Australia, and Domenic sang out, "Steva, is that you?"

"Yes, Domenic."

"Come here for a moment, will you?"

I edged over to the post-and-rail fence round his hut.

"I wass round the peas today, Steve. I think might be you could tell the boys, if they have finished working the tea for Jim McLachlan, that they could start tomorrow, if they li-ike," he said in a plaintive polite way. "Dey is ready, a few of them for the first pickings. They might get a couple of bags. It is a start, anyway."

"Yes, it is. I'll tell them in the morning, Domenic."

"That will do. Good night."

Next day I lay in bed, shivering with a touch of malaria, drinking pearly absinthe-like quinine in small strong doses. Towards evening the rare sound of trampling feet outside my baracca; a knock on the door, and a cry of, "Hullo, Steve", announced the arrival of Eb. "Came out to see——" said he, sitting on the edge of my bunk.

"What, are you crook? Oh, that malaria of yours. You and Jim McLachlan are always going down to it with that malaria. Well I came out to see if you'd lend me that racehorse of yours for the week-end. Alan wants me to go in with him and stay. I'll look after the animal. Macca's coming home for the week-end, too, so I'd like to go. I could go by car, but there are to be races on at Lucknow and I thought I could enter your Alpini II and try him out in the gallops."

"Very well, Eb. Take Alpini if you want him. And will you take a letter from me to Macca?" I wasn't sure that the others would have reached him, for bush post offices are peculiar things, and letters often lie for weeks in them. So off went my third letter to Macca, whom I was to meet at the bark hut on Sunday night.

Yes, on Sunday night [I wrote in a thick slanting hand] I shall go once again to the bark hut, as you ask. You will be there. You will always be there, shadowy, pallid, calm; your tender face bending over me in the dark, for ever. But I shall stand in the long grass outside the little window and smell once again the dry strange smell of that room. I shall call your name softly once or twice, as I used to do, and you will stir in the silence, and rise up and come towards me, but if you are not there, I shall hear nothing but the thunderous knocking of my own heart. Macca, on Sunday night, remember me.

When I had written the letter, I took my racing bridle off the wall, and wrote along it the name he had called me, the name that the peewits cry along the shores and across the paddocks of golden capeweed in Primavera, in springtime, "Stevie Talaaren". In a fine, slanting, quivering hand the black name stood there. The racer would bear it against his profile all the way into Bairnsdale, and I felt that I had a centaur for an ambassador.

From Friday until Sunday was a long strange period, but at last the hour came. In the darkness I walked up towards the old bark hut. I opened the iron gate we had so often opened together; then there was a long dark track through a damp and lonely gully. Only after showers, when the blue and white sky and the green towers of the gum-trees fell into the pools on the blcak earth, was this place lovely. Then a rough climb up a rusty, hard little hill, a flat space of dead trees haunted by the grey thrush at dawn, and lastly the long, grassy, sloping hill that leads to the hut. The night was moonless; lit by the stars, I saw familiar landmarks—-dead logs we used to avoid, or sometimes stumbled over, the old tree, black and white, by which we used to stand and watch the whirling of the stars. And the log on which we sat on a night of most awful heat and dreadful moonrise. Now all those days were far away, and in the hut, I thought, there is silence, desolation, wreckage, coldness and patches of quiet moonlight, where there should be music, happy love, strong walls, warmth, and eternally loved faces. Agony and sorrow stabbed my heart like spears. Yet I knew the real and perfect joy that comes to one who has kept the faith and loved strongly all the past. I am the ghost, the lonely phantom, the familiar spirit that haunts the house of those I loved long ago. There is happiness in that knowledge, I thought.

Above the hut the sky swam, dark, terrible, gigantic, with stars whirling round in it like small arrows. The wind rushed swiftly and harshly through the desolate branches of tall dead trees, vile, horrible. And now the stars looked down through the roofless rafters; the thick rounded walls of bark lay under my feet; the beds were broken; nettle and ferns were tall on the floor. But the kitchen was untouched. I stood with my back to the door and looked at the log by the long empty fireplace. I remembered the peculiar sense of the heroic in his shoulders, the warm red waves of his hair, and the soft thick white column of his throat. I thought I saw his shadowy outline stir in the dark.

"Macca!"

"Yes, Steve." And Macca rose up from the log and came over to me. He quickly lit a fire in the fireplace and we sat before it as we used to do years before, and talked about the past. Always the past. *Sempre il passato.* I thought of nothing but Time. Time was my passion. And so, in the end, we could not agree to marry, because I wished only to be alone and worship the past for the sake of it, and poetry.

On Monday, Eb returned with Alpini II. I took the bridle from his hands. The black name "Stevie Talaaren" shone in Indian ink on the yellow leather.

"Well, Eb, have a good time?"

"Snifter," said Eb. "I gave your letter to Macca, Steve."

"Yes, I know. I saw him at the bark hut on Sunday night."

"Yes, he said he was going to meet you there. He didn't get home from Bruthen till Sunday. First chance I got was when he went out to the tank outside the tennis court for a drink. I followed him out, and said, 'I've got a letter for you, Mac.' I gave it to him. He looked at it. He was glad to get it. He hung on to it all day. Towards evening he went down to Metung to see you. And I suppose when he asked you to marry him, you turned him down."

"I don't know."

"You don't know?"

"No . . .

> *I only know that you may lie*
> *Day long and watch the Cambridge sky,*
> *And, flower-lulled in sleepy grass,*
> *Hear the cool lapse of hours pass,*
> *Until the centuries blend and blur*
> *In Grantchester, in Grantchester . . ."*

"Brooke, eh? You'll go around quoting that fellow and thinking about him, Steve, until you'll have us all turned into him. And then we'll be all Brooke."

"Yes."

"Or broke."

"Too right."

THE RICH RED-AND-WHITE ZARRO

III

No days were ever like the days I worked for Domenic. I should
have worked for a hundred Rachels if he had been the father. It
was like a voyage to the South Seas mingled with life in a back
street in Naples and in a palace that the sea has broken half to
shingle in Capri. Domenic lived in the hut that a short while
ago had belonged to Karta Singh, but Karta had raised a weird
white tent over himself and gone about the bush buying and selling
bags and vending withered lemons. I met him far in the depths
of the wilderness one hot morning, and holding up a shrunken
lemon, he offered it for sale. Even the heat could not make me buy.

But Domenic, ah, Domenic! The sunlight was there, it was
there, silver and blue, sliding through the air after rain; above his
hut the golden princess gum-trees stood swaying, and the shimmer
of their bodies held the purple-black-red of their hair. To know
Domenic was to know the wind blowing keen against the ragged
walls of the old hut, and from him I knew the roar of the warm
fire he kept burning on his wide hearth all day, even on the hottest
day of summer. It was the most enchanting thing I had ever seen,
this red terrific deep fire burning in the dreadful heat of summer
in the dark hut. Yellow were the ashes there as the breast of the
swamp-hawk is yellow, and rose red were the flames and the
coals. Domenic gave me the swollen bean-bags, leaning back
gaping against the walls, and smouldering within them the red
and shining beans, round, healthy, and fruitful; he placed in my
hands the fine dark sieve through which I might shake them; he
put tins at my side, two, so that the rejects might go sailing down,
pink, chipped like old porcelain platters, and on my right the
fruitful seed would fly down to the vessel that might carry them
into the soil. The tins clanged until they were half full, and then
gave out a soft sound of work being done. I cooked for myself on the
wide romantic fire a billy of red beans and mixed with them

Domenic's butter and tomato sauce. I ate them with bread and drank weak black coffee he had left for me, and ate an apple from the case under his bed. All day long as I slid the counters of the beans to the right and to the left, like a croupier at a baccarat table in Monte Carlo, in the wind-shaken hut, haunted by the organ-voice of the dust that gathered together to the making of men, all day long that indefatigable son of Italy worked in his field, barefoot, hoeing or harrowing. And at dusk, he came home, alert, suave, and genial, and we shared tea together. He placed the loaf before him, Italian-wise, and tore scraps from it. The candle-waxen spaghetti tumbled down into the huge pie-dish, and we ate together by the fire.

Before I set out for his hut one morning I stared down at the speckled mirror that lay on my bed. I saw my round brown and pink face, faintly freckled, lying there; the red lips smiled and the green eyes glittered, and slowly, on each side of my temples, the short red-black hair shone and swung.

"You are nothing but a painted tree," I said to myself. I had given up men's clothes for the springtime and wore my old high-school tunic of navy-blue serge, box-pleated, a white blouse with thin red stripes, and brown sandals. I delighted to put on these clothes each morning; the health of my body filled them and gave them some sort of poetry; and I remembered my schooldays and wished that they were back again.

It was eleven o'clock. I walked through the dewy fern that the sun had not reached on a narrow track from Lake's paddocks to Proust's. The delight of being the first to walk on this track each day was a jealous one with me. I saw the grey dew on the cob-webs, and in the tough green ungrasslike Australian grass I saw the wild violets. The ferns hung before me like the hard backs of black eagles, brown here and there, and I raised them and passed between them. The track was stripped, in a sense, of itself and its contemplation with my coming; and strengthened and intoxicated by content, I moved on. Beside the old fence where Harry Grant, the New Zealander, had had his camp two years ago a short wiry stalk of white heath grew, parentless and alone. I looked back across the paddock of grass and saw a tree swaying a heavy crown of leaves in the resounding sunlight. Between us the mystery of movement and life passed; the tree gave to youth some knowledge, some tormenting power.

"There you stand," I said, "with surging roar and swaying slow half turn, and I know now that you are part of the universe. It was the half turn that startled me into knowing this, my tree. You follow the path of all rounded things and as such, are part of my blood."

The capeweed was thick and grey along the headlands of the paddock through which I walked. The flowers left sweet sticky yellow pollen on my sandals; down blazed the sun, up drifted the perfume of the capeweed, and the top of my head burnt with the heat. I closed one eye and looked through a hair that lay across my face; mosaics of purple, green, and gold lay on it, brooch-shaped. The mystery of light was all about me that morning. From Domenic's hut came a toneless monotonous voice, singing huskily some Italian song in barbarous dialect. The rough, slow drone made me feel sleepy; then my heart beat very quickly and I could scarcely breathe.

I opened the door and the sun smacked the table with a fierce square blow that made the dust rise from the heap of beans lying there, and behind the blood-red beans and the gilt dust sat a tall young Italian dressed in black shirt and trousers, with a thin bright belt about his hips. He was a broad, handsome, sulky-faced youth, with full red lips pursed comically and mournfully, drowsy brown eyes, and a head of thick curling black hair. Generations of oil-eating parents had given his face the most delicate lustre, like an old, old oil painting. Under the eyes this was most noticeable, but so dim, so barely brushed on by hereditary influence, that it gave him just a smoky look of being half hidden behind an oil lamp.

"*Buon' giorno, signor,*" I said politely.

"*Buon' giorno, signorina,*" he replied circumspectly.

"You are Samozarro, I believe," I said, burrowing into the bean bag and filling my sieve with seeds.

"Yes, I come back last night," he said in a hoarse voice, a gloomy voice that suited his black shirt and trousers.

I sat down opposite him and he leant forward at his work. I stared once at the broad white flesh of his chest in the gloom, and began sorting. He rocked himself while he worked, from the hips

F

upward; arms, shoulders, head, rocked soothingly above the beans. It was very hot in the little hut, and sweat came out on his broad white forehead at his double labours.

"What part of Italy do you come from?" I asked, hands and eyes on the beans that slid clanking and banging into our four tins.

"From Naples," he replied in a careless rough voice, rocking himself steadily. A gleam of amusement came into his face at my interest.

"If you come from Naples you should be able to sing."

"Oh, yes," roughly, "I sing all right." In a thick, intoxicated voice he added, "Non't you know this song?" and with an extra violent lurch, he sang in a voice that had no tone whatever,

> "Io sono Napulitano, se no' canto . . . moro!
> (I am a Naples man, if I cannot sing . . . I die!)

"Non't you know it?" He said "Non't" for "Don't" from the moment I met him to the day we parted.

"No, I don't."

He laughed. "You tell me a song."

" 'Sole Mio'?"

"Oh, that's rubbish. I like old songs—'Julia'." He said this name in a marvellously beautiful way, in the true Italian throbbing fashion. "You know that song 'Julia'?" He began on the same monotonous note as he began the other one, and despite the lack of tune the song was beautiful and mournful, because of his rocking white half-seen body, the forward groping hand, large and marble-white, and the down-bent handsome face glowing with youth. Also, the song, to me, sounded of almost incredible antiquity.

> "Julia, mi prese mezza la vita . . .
> La gioia è finita . . . finita per me . . ."

By lunch time, I had decided that he was, despite his rocking, his tunelessness, and his voice, hoarse, imploring and remarkable, part of my existence, and consequently a poet, or part of a poet's diet. I told him that I should like to call him "Amico", since the name Samozarro was very long and seemed to me more Arabian than Italian; I told him that it reminded me of some lost city of

76

Arabia, but he said that it was Italian, and that since it was too long he would like me to call him "Amico".

And deep in the grass or in the trees, the curlew wailed; all day it whistled, "Io . . . Io . . . Io. . . ." It was part of the pulse of the earth; and became unnoticed, until, here and there, in a silence, I found that there was no silence; that all through the springtime there would not be silence while the curlew lived and sang—hurried, passionate, and infinitely mournful—and I was afraid. The face of Samozarro was the clock on which time wrote. I looked up at him, half expecting to see him old. No, still young . . .

At twilight, when the note of the wind had changed in the trees, when it was bowing the trees with a breezy, cold and swishing note, Domenic thrust open the door and came in.

"Well, young man . . . well, young girl, you have met. This is Samozarro, Steva! Samozarro, this is Steva!"

"*Si*," said Samozarro. *Come va?*"

"*Bene*. I call Samozarro 'Amico', Domenic."

"Oh, Amico? That is a good name for him. By Joves, it is cheely tonight, eh? Zarro!" he exclaimed rapidly and sharply to the young fellow, "*Sei tu* . . ." There followed a long, forcible speech in emphatic Italian about work; Zarro spoke quickly and morosely in reply.

The talk ended with Domenic saying loudly and with an air of finality, "*Ah, no, lavoro a contratto e lavoro a giornata sono cose differenti.*" ("Contract labour and day labour are two different things.")

His icy exact Italian struck through the hut and the dramatic air of opera and ancient songs there. "Ah, here is de bread." He was very much the master. "Now for de fire. My word, you peoples don't mind de cold; but I tell you——" stooping to warm his hands, grey, at the embers—"it is going to be hardt frost tonight. It is just my luck; the peas will be spoilt." He rose and his brown, alert eyes in their wrinkles of saffron flesh flashed on us; his fine, mocking mouth was half open, with an aristocratic smile on it of politeness and contempt. As he turned his profile to us, the thin lips were more marked and beautiful as they moved in speaking, and above them the slender hooked nose shone pale.

This Alexandrian from the cold north, a supple man intent on power.

The candle was lit; the water boiled in the great clean billy; in poured the spaghetti, and out it came, steaming and loose, into a pie-dish, from which, with forks only, we ate.

Domenic read Shakespeare throughout the meal, concentrating on the sonnets, the style of which, he said, reminded him very much of Italy's own poet, Dante Alighieri.

I came to work now in the mornings with a different delight. I liked Amico, as I called him, but more than that I enjoyed the poetry he gave to the day. He was a splendid companion, and his instant look upward for me, every morning, gave me happiness. And I grew to think of him as part of the springtime, his husky monotonous voice singing, *"Mamma, mi scritto"*, as I neared the hut. In time, the very word "Mamma" meant springtime to me. We worked earnestly; the tins clattered with the falling beans, and the fire crackled on the hearth. I was no longer alone with the chaste sense of Domenic and solitary enjoyment of my meals. I thought to myself, "I am now like that log I passed this morning." Someone had lit a fire in a great black log that had lain dry for years, shining with charcoal and set with delicate deep moss. And the fire had transfigured the log. From silence and lifelessness it had been transformed into a cavern that glowed with a red that tempted me to walk through it, to devour it, and own it. And it roared softly as I passed, this red—ah, how the colour roared at me, the voice of wood, satisfied, I thought, to be burning, immersed in its own destruction and licking its lips over it, viewing it and partaking of it, thinking, "O glorious death-bed of fire! Ah, how good it is to be destroyed with a living fire! Roar . . . roar . . . roar . . . roar . . . sink into me, eat of me, I am the living fire. I am the matrix from which this earth issued. I am that fire of which the Jews spoke, and which they loved."

At noon, I rose and left the hut, and sat down in the cool shade of a log to rest. The yellow clay of the path stared at me ruggedly, not a sound in the tall scanty bush, with its rich little touches of individuality, twigs against the blue sky, sparse and fine, a purple sarsaparilla plant lying like spilt wine of libation on the dry earth, each tiny flower like a flattened grape. And far over towards the lake someone was burning off and making images in rolling yellow smoke arise from lost crops. The ghost of fertility arose and mourned above the earth, stifled all about it with a hot, sad breath, with a last gasp of fire, and then drifted out to sea, alone. I longed for the smoke, I stared at it with avaricious eyes, and through the glassy heat the wattle-bird cried harshly, "Go back! Go back!"

I went back and sat down to work and stare at Samozarro, who sat in his wide-shouldered and beautiful youth opposite me. In the afternoon I rose and made black coffee for us both on the great red splendour of the hot fire roaring on the hearth. A billy, blackened like an old Spanish canvas, stood to one side, half full of crimson beans, with the creamy, stiff cooked kernels showing. Zarro and I loved our cup of coffee, and the dry sound of the Australian ground wind blowing the fine dust up against the lonely door.

The hut was lined with many fine wooden bunks, the blue sky glowed over it, the young green gum-leaves, red-rimmed, leant over it, with many ancient pictures threading their way through white fibre and green. The Australian sun, fiercely hot, draws all the legendary past out of the earth and imprints it on leaves and sticks and trunks of trees in a richly powerful and impressive fashion. I have often thought that many, many civilizations may have lived on this huge continent before ever the aboriginal came to it. It has always appeared to me, particularly where its earth and trees are concerned, a country of infinite culture.

And all this while that I was working with Zarro I had a feeling of great sorrow, for I felt that these days would never return again. And I stared at Zarro hour after hour, thinking, "Someday, Amico, I shall not see you again. In the years that lie ahead, you will grow old, and die, and I shall not see you again."

One night, at twilight, I stood on the white road with Samozarro. Far across from us, the dark bush rose up and from it shone one star, *"una stella"*. And I heard the silver laughter of a fox in the blue-black starlit bush. The infinite sadness and stillness of the white road in the night, half sweet with early dew, was under our feet.

"Some day, Amico, this road will be empty of us, we shall not be here. This little white road that we love, we are traitors to it, and shall leave it, and all these trees about us will mourn, for we shall not be here, and no man, Amico, could love these as I love them."

What was I saying? Zarro didn't know, anyway. It was all Greek to him. The owl flew over our heads. *"Quorrk . . . quorrk!"* The liquid cry tortured me. Perhaps the selfsame owl that used to fly overhead when Jim and Blue and I walked these same roads two years ago. And now, all that was ended. Always that futile cry to Fate, because it was ended, the jolly company, the night sky, the stars and the mopoke with its Minerva moan—throaty, Greek, and powerful, secret in the night.

"Addio, addio, Amico."

"Addio, Steva, addio."

The next day it was blowing and showering heavily as I rode up to Domenic's hut to work. I had no need to thrust open the door; the wind pushed me in. Around the table sat a large company. The fire was burning high and red, the room was thick with the blue ghosts of tobacco smoke and smelt of Chianti. Domenic, home from the paddocks for the wet day, was overseeing the sorting. And Samozarro and I had been reinforced by two seraphs from another world, Angelo and Gabriello. These two ancients crouched over their beans, singing monotonously. I knew Angelo well, for I had often driven him away from my hut with a rifle when he became quarrelsome. He was a tiny fellow with dirty clothes, a crumpled hat, and a wizened brown face that was spiteful and keen. The wrinkles radiated from his nose and spread out widely at his ears; he rarely looked up, and when he did it was hurriedly and from under his hat and his eyebrows, in a simian manner. His fellow seraph, Gabriello, was a little dreaming man, with a black moustache; he scraped at it now and then with his finger and thumb, and sighed tiredly, as though he were tired of serving it. He, too, was wrinkled and hid the wrinkles under a greasy cap. They spoke a barbarous dialect, difficult to understand. To me it always seemed as though they had come from some hole out of the Italian earth, that their education had been taken in hand early by a college of frogs, who had then passed them on to a nest of serpents for finish.

Samozarro appeared like an Adonis beside them; Domenic looked like Dante. I stared at the faded blue back of Gabriello's trousers with the black buckles and straps and sat down unhappily to sort. Above the red rattle of beans Angelo's voice sometimes rose in song. As the hours and the days went past I heard the songs so often that I learnt them all off by heart. The first was *"Il Presidente"*. And it must have gone back into antiquity. I placed the first version of it somewhere about the ninth century. It was the type of song that comes out every year. Beginning with a melancholy

Tinkety-tong . . . tinkety-tong . . . tinkety-tong . . .

in imitation of bells ringing, Angelo howled mournfully:

> *"Un giorno un' donna gridè,*
> *O, il Presidente!*
> *Domani, mio figlio va via*
> *Alla ghigliottina*
> *O, il Presidente!*
> *Tinkety-tong . . . tinkety-tong!"*

Angelo also sang a long and sprightly ditty, beginning:

> *"Caterinella, Caterinella, non te piace la mia buona roba."*

And then he reverted to *"Il Presidente"*, and tobacco smoke rose high in the room. How the fire blazed and the rain spat down wrathfully into the wide fireplace! The mournful song and the splash of beans into the tin made me feel sorrowful. I couldn't see anything funny about Angelo and Garbriello at all.

But a fine day after rain, with the rapid Australian wind blowing all over the country, great miles of bright blue-gum before it and their white and brilliant branches and the many golden flowers of the continent flying in showers through the successive waves of the wind, made me happier. And at lunchtime various discussions used to arise in the hut, just as they arise over the tables in the city. On the question of military salutes, for instance, Angelo and Gabriello could not agree.

"When I was conscripted for the five years' service," said Angelo, "I was stationed up in the Alps. In my day one got very poor clothes in the military. It was perishing cold. And the food was not very good. Also there was not much to drink. Always the eternal *Bacia-mi-subito*. Dost thou remember it, Gabriello, my dear? Dost thou remember it? So weak, too, that it had to be supported into the mouth of the glass. No tea, such as here, hot and strong. Ah!" He began to sing absently his bell-like "Tinkety-tong, tinkety-tong".

Gabriello, who smelt faintly of olives, grunted and, raising his hand from his bread, stroked his Kaiserian moustache farther up into his eyes, leaving birdlike crumbs sitting on it whitely. "*E vero, davvero!*" said he.

"And so, one day, when the *capitano* ordered me to my duties, I said, '*Signor capitano, si*', and saluted smartly." Angelo touched the visor of his cap with his fingers, rattling his heels together as he sat.

Gabriello started violently; some ancient military pride stirred in him. "*Che?* You couldn't salute like that! Who ever heard of the captain of an alpine regiment being saluted so? Remember, Angelo, my dear, remember truly! It was like this that we saluted!" Gabriello arose and placed his flattened hand to his temple, and his duck feet spread out like a couple of fans before him.

"*Ah, ma che!* No!" Angelo glared at his mate in contempt. "No, you have worms in your head. We touched the cap—how else would they wear out, and have to be replaced? You know we were told to wear things out as rapidly as possible. Officers made great profits out of bringing in over-stocks and selling them to friends. I handed in one cap ten times to my *capitano*, and when the new stocks arrived he handed it back to me. 'Here is your new cap, Angelo *mio caro*,' he says. 'Through transit it is a bit worn and soiled, but the weather will soon clean it. Get to work and assist it.' So with boots, too. One was encouraged to kick the other fellow as often as one could. I was the best French boxer in our *regimento*. The French box with their booted feet."

He rose and turned his back to Gabriello, who rose enthusiastically with him, crying, "And I, well, you shall see!"

With his back to Angelo, he drove in a mighty kick that knocked the dust out of the angel's trousers. Angelo retorted with a smart crack to Gabriello's shin. There was a brief, startled howl of agony. A vicious "*Dio mio!*" through clenched teeth and Kaiserian moustache and Gabriello's toe disappeared into remote regions of Angelo that bellowed and writhed.

"Nothing, nothing . . . *ma che, niente*," Angelo muttered, turning his eyes back and, rushing forward, he kicked out long from the thigh, turning flexibly as he reached his mark.

"*Basta!*" shrieked Gabriello. "You are *maestro!*" And he sat down to cough and belch. But he rose swiftly, crying, "*Ancora, il capitano domando questo saluto.*" ("Yet, the captain demands this form of salute.") And with his hand to his temple, he rapped his feet together and sat down. "I say no more."

"*Impossible, O obstinate!*" shouted Angelo. "The *capitano* demands this salute," and he touched the visor of his cap, rattled his heels and sat down vehemently—on nothing. Samozarro had thoughtfully removed his chair while he had been talking. Angelo fell on his back in the dust. Rising, muttering, he plunged at Gabriello and, seizing him by the whiskers, rolled him in the dust. Their precious sorted beans fell over them, and good samples and bad mingled as the two old *alpini* squirmed together in a new campaign. "*O, il Presidente, tinkety-tong, tinkety-tong!*" we sang.

The day Angelo discussed a murder in theory was one of lashing rain and flying wind. I ate my lunch and read Henry Lawson, deaf to the argument and murmured complaints under my nose.

"Listen," whispered Zarro, "that silly old man———" indicating Angelo—"is telling Gabriello how he was going to kill his wife."

"I can't hear anything."

"No, he sees you listening; you look your book and listen." I bent down to Lawson again and let words swim in front of my eyes.

" 'All right, all right, kill me, kill me,' " said Angelo, squeaking to imitate a woman's voice. "And she insulted me. 'It is a wonder I haven't died long ago, seeing such a face in front of me every day,' said she. At this, I struck her."

"But a man shouldn't kill his wife." Gabriello nursed his moustache upwards to his eyes wearily, and stared at a fly on his hand.

"What? When she nearly killed me?" retorted Angelo. "She used to hit me on the head with a stick every night."

"No?" cried Gabriello incredulously.

"Yes . . . hit me on the head . . . like *this!*" He picked up a solid stick from the fireplace and smacked Gabriello across the dome with it.

Gabriello winced. His eyes watered, but he said nothing. He, too, grabbed a stick and, spitting on his hands, aimed well with his eye.

"What? Like *this*?" he cried, rapping Angelo over one ear.

It must have hurt, but Angelo scarcely trembled; his eyes rolled a little, and his ears lay back, quivering, but he raised his stick and said happily, pleasantly, "No, no, like *this*!" Crack! Right on Gabriello's nose.

"Aha!" exclaimed Gabriello, with his feathers flying. "Aha," said he dizzily, "I see—like *this*?" Bang! Thud! Angelo lay across the table with his face in the beans, completely outed.

"*Ahimè!*" cried Gabriello. "*Povero amico mio* . . . Angelo, my good old friend, why did you play husband and wife with me, *mio caro*? I, too, have been long married. Ah, it is experience that tells." And throwing some cold water over Angelo, he went on with his work.

The wife-killer raised his head after some time, and stared at us giddily.

"Aha," we said playfully, "what a week-end you have had! What wine! Oh, you have been in the money all right, Angelo; you've swigged it this week-end."

"I think I go my plice," said Angelo sadly and staggered off to his hut.

But it was the warp in the woof or the weft in the warp that parted them. And weft and warp were in the precious woollen scarf that Angelo had brought out from Italy with him, as a parting gift from his daughter. The wool was thin with grease and the scarf was lanky with use, but Angelo loved it. There was an odd sort of beauty about it, the work of a peasant woman who relied, not on imagination, but on patterns handed down through the ages. The design was one of square white flowers on a yellow background. The flowers, of course, looked as though they had been dipped in tar by this time, but here and there one could see that it had once been a fresh, lovely thing. A tape was sewn to it, and it dangled from a nail on the wall. At night, Angelo would rise, wrap it round his throat, and with a muttered, "*Buona notte, tutti*", off he would stroll home.

84

Gabriello, living farther off, departed earlier.

One day Zarro saw a strand waving from the scarf; it had begun to disintegrate, and only the grease from Angelo's neck kept it together. The wool had changed one greasy-backed owner for another when it left the sheep and came to Angelo. Zarro tied the strand firmly to Gabriello's knapsack. At twilight the angel of the trumpet, sensing that the hour had come, lifted his knapsack and swung it over his shoulder. The wool ran a little way out of the scarf, deserting it basely for this new owner.

"*Buona notte, tutti,*" said Gabriello mildly.

"*Buona notte,*" we cried anxiously, staring at Angelo and praying that he wouldn't turn and see the wool from the scarf pulling on the knapsack on Gabriello's shoulder. He grunted.

"Gabriello," said he, half turning.

"Angelo," I said in alarm, letting a sieve of beans fall down his back, and pushing him half over with the weight of them, "*perdonami, è pesante.*"

Angelo swore, blinded by dust and beans.

"Good night, good night, good night, dear Gabriello," we chanted. "*Addio, per sempre.*"

And off into the dark went the angel of the last day, with the wool tied firmly to his knapsack. Sitting and sorting, engaging Angelo in conversations old and new, begging him to again raise that Caruso-like voice and enchant us with the aria of "Tinketytong", we watched the scarf with glistening eyes. Row by row, as it hung by its tape on the nail, it fled from our sight, through the open door. Now and then it dragged and seemed to meditate in some glade afar, or, as if caught on a protruding spur, it pulled irritably, tugged, and then confidently went on, for the road to Gabriello's hut was as straight as a die from Domenic's. Towards the last, one must confess, it wavered, perhaps sad to leave the ancient mould. But, with a last tug of triumphant emancipation, it was off, leaving only the tape hanging and waving dismally from the nail.

"Ah, Gabriello is at home," we said aloud, and laughed.

"I, myself, must go," grumbled Angelo, rising. One hand went out to the nail to take down the scarf. "My scarf, where is my precious scarf?" cried the nondescript angel, hunting behind the

85

bean-bags. "I hung it here—well, here is the tape. Who has taken it? That vile Gabriello, perhaps? But no, here is the tape."

"And here a little of the wool, too, *Angelo mio*," we said solicitously, picking up the tail end from the threshold. For here the last of the thread had fainted and could go no farther.

"*Dio mio!*" shouted Angelo. "What is this? Where does it go to? Wait, I shall take it in my hand, I shall take it and follow. Ah, I perceive now! I know where I shall find it." Thrusting his cap on his head, he rushed off into the dark on the track of Gabriello, along the line of the wool. And what they said to each other in the small hut that night, and what they did to each other, no man knows. No more came they to sort the beans within the hut; no more chanted Angelo the song of "*Il Presidente*". But silently they left town, and I saw them as I rode behind them slowly, one hot day, with the black Australian flies lying thick on their backs and floating in billions round the unwashed heads, like dark halos.

And so in the hut there was peace again and poetry.

The beans were almost all finished. Domenic didn't bother to put anyone else on. We reckoned up our averages for the day and told him that within a week we should be finished.

"It is just as well," he said, "for the peas will soon be ready to pick. They are a nice sample. And the prices is goot—twenty-five shillings a bag. This will go down, of course, and at the end of the season I will not be able to get five shillings a bag for them."

It was good to know that the peas were not yet ready. The romantic slowness of them made the season rich and strong with a myriad fluttering green wings. The white drag of their roots under the earth held on to the days and kept them back among us, those beloved days that will return no more. I loafed along in a great wave of time, waiting to see the familiar forms of the Italians loom along the road to Metung, for each pea-picking all the Italians I knew came back to Metung to work. And Macca came back with them sometimes, to help his uncle with his harvest.

I rarely saw Jim McLachlan these days. He was busy preparing the tea-plantation for his next crop, which was to be sown in late August or September or early October. And sometimes August in Australia is a huge, cyclonic summer month such as it was when Zarro and I sorted the beans for Domenic. And then follows a bitter green September; these two months are full of summery indecisions and do not know what to do. But October brings the true summer and there is then no further escape. Therefore, after working for Domenic through a warm August that swam in a haze of liquid heat and glittering gum-leaves and golden cape-weed, I came to the house of the Buccaneers in cold September weather. The white and long hospitable table was spread under the window and the large family dined there in peace and happiness. They were always glad to see me. While we were sitting at the table one night there was a knock at the door and in came Peppino.

"Ah, Peppino, mio caro . . . ah, mio caro, ah, amico mio, sono biato. Sono in cielo quando ti vedo. Sono mezzo-matto di gioia, vecchio amico mio." One can think and say in Italian what one can never say in English. But to see Peppino! What bliss! Blue and I called him, "Nostro fratello . . . fratello nostro." Our brother. We and the people of Metung loved him. He was remarkably handsome; an oval Spanish ivory face with unusually noble lines in it. His hair was like black grapes; he was as ornate as Beardsley's illustration for Oscar Wilde's Salome; and his thick creamy eyelids were in a heavy Greek slant from the temple down. But he wore this beautiful mask of a face with such a splendid unconsciousness of it, that one was all the more struck by it. And he had a throat, thick, white, strong and rotund at the base, that Caruso might have envied. His expression usually, was one of timidity and anxiety when asked anything in English; but when he had replied, as he thought, satisfactorily, he ran his finger round the inside of a very stiff white collar and laughed merrily and happily. The English language was torture where Peppino was concerned. His brown eyes glowed fiercely. Licking his dry lips, after his torrent of English greetings, he sat listening to us talking.

"Peppino!" cried everyone. "What a long time since we last saw you! Where have you been?"

In a soft, hurried voice, he said, "Oh, I been come fram Mossiface on dis mai baike." Fascinating caricature of very good English which one could listen to for hours. "Long taime I no see you. Work too hard all de taime."

"Making big money, eh, Pep?" said Edgar.

Peppino bent his head appealingly. "Oh, no, no much money,

justa work. I live wid mai countrymen, three mai countrymen, in a liddle plice, not so big as dis room." He looked about it, appealingly, too.

"Blue would have liked to have seen you, Peppino," I remarked. Peppino loved Blue. He thought she was a splendid violinist.

"Where Blue working?" he said imperatively, something starting to attention in him. "At Buffalo?"

"Yes, at Buffalo."

"Oh, dis long way off, ay?"

"One hundred and sixty-three miles, to be precise."

"What, what, you say?" he looked admirably surprised. "Oh, too far for me for walk I tink." And he looked to the younger members of the family to support his jest. "Peas soon start pickings here, I tink. I am come for ask Mr Royal, if he give me job. He say, 'Start soon as you like.' I go back my plice and tell mai countrymen, 'You come too quick. Mr Royal, he give you job.' Dey not been Metung, before. O, yes, one, Benedett', he been here . . . he been here before. You remember Benedett', Steve? Yes. But the others they not seen Metung before dis. They play too much music all the time. But very nice, good fellows."

Peppino laughed, and then suddenly looked grave and kind. The black glistening curls hung over his ivory brow and his white teeth shone. His beautiful eyes were set on such a slant and his red lips were so brilliant above white teeth when he smiled that he looked over-handsome, except for the innocent, good, kind expression that revealed him to be sincere and an honest man of steady principles. And he was all this. In repose, his face became quite sad and resigned and timid and dejected.

I said, "Blue would like to hear you sing 'O Sole Mio', once more, and that lovely song, 'Gigolette'."

"You tell her come Metung, and I sing too quick," he murmured earnestly. "Where Macca and Jim now?"

"Macca is working at Mossiface."

"At Mossiface? I no see him there."

"He is working for his uncle. And Jim has married a widow woman with five children, and is wood-cutting somewhere along the Nicholson, or driving a taxi in Melbourne." No one quite knew where Jim was.

"Peppino, it will be a good Primavera, do you think?" I said.

"*Davvero.* Plenty music, plenty dancing. You wait, I come soon with these my countrymen, and we play *la musica* all night."

"It is September now, Peppino. Soon all springtime will be in full flood here in Gippsland. During all August I worked with Samozarro for Domenic Olivieri, *per scegliere i fagioli.* The beans were bright vermilion and all through the long hot days of August, Peppino, we sorted and sang. For Zarro comes from Naples and can sing all the old canzones of that city. And the great fire of yellow and white wood burnt and roared on the hearth of Domenic, and sang in unison with the broad and mile-long wind of early spring, which rose whirling and thundering outside the hut. *Mio caro,* I shall never forget this August that has just passed. *Non posso scordare!* Never again, Peppino *mio,* will such an August live on the face of this earth; there will be other Augusts, but none such as this with its heavy, melancholy, fiery winds and brilliant singing sunlight. All this August I have been happy, Peppino. And now it is gone. What, I wonder will the true Primavera, this September and October, bring for me? More, I suppose, immortal beauty and sorrow that it should die at last. What will it bring, to sting with sorrow the heart of the world, Peppino, *vecchio compare mio?*"

"Steva, I shall come from Bruthen with my friends and too much music, and this will be a Primavera to remember. *L'ultima Primavera.* The last springtime."

"Well, then, when at last you come with your friends, seek out my baracca and visit me there. It is not far from Royal's, down on Jim McLachlan's tea-plantation, on the foreshore nearly. You can come over on a dry and grassy back track from Royal's right to my door. I shall not be working for Jim McLachlan until fairly late in the hot weather, round about Christmas. I have promised to weigh up and overseer generally for Domenic during the pea-picking, and when the pea-picking is over, I have promised Leonardo della Vergine that I will go down and do his accounts for him and overseer for him when his beans are ready. He will have many men working for him then."

"*Bene.*"

"Do you still play the mouth-organ, Peppino?"

"*Si . . . i!* I get a new one for come Metung, and I play all day and all night." Pep dragged the collar away from his full throat and got ready to start. He had two great songs, *"O Sole Mio"* and "Gigolette", which he rolled out sonorously.

"When you come, Peppino, to Metung, springtime will have begun," I said.

Remembering his kind and handsome face, I went back to the baracca, comforted, and wrote:

> *Proud years, proud years, ye shall not crush me down!*
> *I'll keep my conqueror's flush, my inner song. . . .*
> *Carry my shield unshattered through the town*
> *Of Heaven, in clear ecstasy, so long*
> *While in the thicket throbs the thrush's heart*
> *Melodiously, while yet the greenest leaves*
> *Press softly to the fern that keenly starts*
> *Up from the darkening marl, and each day heaves*
> *Exclamatory hands toward a space*
> *Of blue above its head. . . . While these things breathe*
> *I, too, shall breathe, nor ever turn to chase*
> *The cloudy runner with his cloudy wreath.*

One day I stood beside Domenic Olivieri on the headlands of his green pea crop.

"Coming on well," I said. "Sorry, Domenico, that the men didn't turn up that day to pick. They had been busy with the tea. Did you get anything?"

"Oh, one or two bags, not much; just a run-over, you see," he said severely.

"And what about the bean-sorting? Is it entirely over?"

"Well, Steve, if you have nothing to do, I will tell you what. I have some bags of very special seed I should like you and Zarro to re-sort. They have already been sorted, but I should like you two to go over them again. I will give you a good price for them. They are *buona roba* . . . good stuff. And when the peas are ready I will put you on as overseer for the pickings. How will that do?"

"*Troppo buona* . . . too good. But I was going to mention, Domenic, that Edgar Buccaneer—you know him?"

"Oh yes."

"He wanted me to take a turn on the nets with them tomorrow. They are working short-handed and expect a big haul. I shall not be hauling, of course; they just want me to pull the fish out of the nets. I thought it would be a good chance to learn and earn, as it were. What do you think?"

"Please yourself. As you like. It is good money. Then you could start on the foll-*ow*ing day." I smiled at the delicious "foll-*ow*ing".

"Yes, that's right. *Addio*, Domenic."

"Good-bye."

"I think you have the most living hair I have ever seen on anyone's head," said the Black Serpent, as we sat in the fishing smack, watching father and son putting out the long net. "In the hot sunlight, Steve, your hair glitters red, and then green and purple and brown and black. I have never seen such hair before. It is like the wing of a lowrie."

"My hair to me," I said, "has always been a thing of most strange purpose. It lives a curious life of its own. It is immortal and will be forever, I suppose, like myself."

"I cannot ever imagine you dying, Steve."

"Nor can I," said I firmly. "Not even my hair."

In a dotted half-moon, Eb and his father worked the dinghy across the straight blue water. Eb stood guard over his end, while his father rowed with his back to the net, which slipped noiselessly over the roller, then came in long, graceful, brown-armed sweeps towards the shore, again. I raised my head and stared at him. Cork by cork the net dropped, and against the blue sky, the cold afternoon-lit sea, the pattern was fantastic and Asiatic. Drawing his boat up on the beach Edgar slipped the net-hook over the hook on his strong canvas netting belt. Eb slipped his over, too; they shouted vaguely to each other and leant back slowly. Soon, as though they were tugging the dark misty tangle of a woman's hair, the net came to them; fold on fold lay beside them on the sand. We sat by, under the quivering canvas and the mast, watching. At last, the net gleamed a little, then it leapt, it struggled and jumped, it rose up from the sand and flopped back again, exhausted. Eb gave a long whistle from afar.

"Hi there, yarr-r-rum, yarr-r-rum!" cried the Buccaneer, in imitation of aboriginal talk.

We could hear the harsh insect-like breaking of scaly bodies against each other.

G

"What a catch!" said Edgar's wife. "You'll have your work cut out, Steve."

In the boat, late that night, I cut my work out. I had sat there from early afternoon until eleven o'clock picking fish out of the nets. The afternoon had drowsed into a peach hue; a bloom came on the waters; and quietly the boats of the rival fishermen, the Neumanns, slipped up alongside, to net after us in the generous place.

Their boats chugged quietly past with the sails up, needlessly, leaning over the heads of the tall men, and above the rhyme of the chugging came the voices.

"Good catch! Hope the prices keep up!"

And Edgar, with the jocose guilt he felt when he had got in ahead of another man and done well, shouted modestly, "Ah, the sight of this will bring 'em down all right."

In the moonlight, with raw bleeding fingers, I took the last fish out of the nets, and the engine was kicked over and we staggered off home to a huge tea of meat, vegetables, pudding and cakes.

But now that there was a time between things growing I decided to be conscience-stricken by my brief apostasy from the One Love, the sense of Time. I took to wandering up to the bark hut at night to pay, to suffer for what I thought was my faithlessness to things past and passing. On that hill stood a half-dozen enormous dead trees, white and dry. When I leant against them they had a sweet, parched odour, faintly like the hide of a horse, but more mysterious, smelling of sun and wind and rain; they made me thirsty. I ran my lips along their split white sides, and under the hands they felt like silk, so long had the wind flowed round them and the sun glowed on them. Stroking them, I stared upward at the stars. The heavens appeared to be whirling with a livid light; the stars pierced me and fought against me, without kindliness.

"The stars in their courses fought against Sisera," I murmured.

On that hill everything was related to me, but fiercely and savagely. The cruel heavens, by some trick of my eyes or sorrow, were emptier here than anywhere else on earth; an empty whirling cruelty, a maelstrom of stars shone and dragged my vision into the depths. What could the years hold for me now? What lay ahead?

With the mind of a logician I attempted to deduce my fate; by relating the past to the present I tried to discover the future. It was not, I knew, in my power. But perhaps, somewhere among my letters, my writings, my poetry, a part of the whole lay below my eyes, in a jigsaw puzzle only waiting to be assembled by Time. My exaggeration of life, through the repeated exercise of poetry, which removed me from reality, made me dissatisfied with everything and everyone, save the Ideal.

What lay ahead? The way of least resistance, I feared, because I was fighting so fiercely against it, with such strength, with a will that would not last. I made too much noise about it. Had I been able to lie passive, evil might have passed me. It was my struggle that would attract the attention of my destiny.

And yet I could not be passive; ever curious, I longed to see what would happen. If I had said, calmly, satisfiedly, "I don't want anything to happen. Let me go on, year after year, in this village, working and secretly writing, content with the practice of that art", it would have been so. Nothing would have happened. But I had to feed my art on diverse food. I had not the reasoning power of a man, whose summing up of his kind is based on humanity. Mine was based on femininity, and femininity must be fed with emotion and passion, the lesser things bringing pain in the backwash.

On the back of a long letter from the young Chinese poet I wrote:

Last night the thought of world sorrow recurred again. Evidently I've not drawn much benefit from love. Despite the years and the days between, the clear memory of Mackinnon penetrates like a sure spear the warding shields. He has destroyed for me the whirling beauty of the starry sky. I watched it too often with him. Whenever I stand upon that hill and gaze upon and upward at the milky constellations teeming among the thin dead trees, I mourn with awful sorrow, with dreadful impotency. I desire to create for myself another Mackinnon, with his white sad face turned moonward. Whenever I pass that tree I remember the night and his white lips. Assure me that I shall forget, and perhaps I'll start afresh! But yet, to forget is most horrible also; in truth, in very truth, I don't know what I am writing. My head and brain are alike slow and mute with the clogging of heavy tears unshed. Indeed, indeed, Cynara, I have been faithful to thee, in my fashion. Nevertheless, I do not wish to live other than in this way, dedicated to the years.

And through the pages the words of the young Chinese poet came faintly, reversed, lying like threads of cotton, above my thick upright hand. His writing was like a frail broken stream running between dreadful banks of sheer black jet. And when I turned the page over to read what he had written, my writing stood behind his like broken stones.

There was his translation of one of the loveliest poems in all Chinese literature:

OO-LING

The careless gallants of Oo-ling,
Ride forth, caparisoned in Spring,
With silver saddles, horses white
And dainty garments fluttering.

Soon, in the golden market places
They crush the flowers with heed-
    less paces,
And drink in ardent wine the eyes
Of Tartar girls with merry faces.

Below it he had written:

Alas, would that I, too, could ride forth in springtime down the soft green hills of Oo-Ling, with the gallants there. See, how the small blue sky shines in the first wet winds of spring, and the red earth is carven into little idols under the silver hooves of their horses. And down in the market places the great flowers are lying on the ancient grey stone of the floor. . . .

I decided to write to my mother and beg her to come up to Gippsland and stay with me. For the year was beginning to make

94

beautiful all the earth and I felt that I must share it with her, and renew the life in her once more.

Cara madre, I've been sitting before a huge fire in my baracca, eating cakes and honey and drinking black coffee and reading your last letter. I suppose I shall have to go over to work soon, but I need not hurry. I am still sorting beans with Samozarro, since the tea-plantation is lying dormant below on the foreshore. But what about coming up soon for a couple of weeks? The land is lovelier than a bride. The purple flowers about the lake will soon be in bloom, and the perfume of the waxen pittosporum fills the air. Why not come and stay awhile with me? Just two weeks, madre mia. Please don't refuse, for I shall be so busy after spring with the tea down at Jim McLachlan's. I can arrange a day when you could come. The great bush is lonely; it is full of ghosts, and I cry continually, "Oh, where are my comrades? Why have we deserted each other?" "For the best, for the best, for the best!" as the jays cry in the deserted orchard. This may be the last springtime I shall ever spend in Metung. I shall make it an echo of that first September I spent here. Once more I'll go again to all the familiar places . . . the lonely hut . . . the lake shore and the bush tracks. Sometimes, as I am going to work in the morning, I pass the hill and the old hut. In the clear morning, in the bright day, I am filled with agony. Oh, if I could turn the years back! I am sick with memory.

IL PANUCCI

IV

IL PANUCCI! The very name runs through the being as swiftly and powerfully as did the name of Endymion run through the soul of Keats. And when I think of Il Panucci, and when I remember him, I remember again the flashing and brilliant Australian year of 1928, surely the continent's most burning and splendid year, when the earth was a great brown page across which the sun wrote the green poems of the spring, and the blue poetry of the summer. For in Australia the spring is green, but the summer is blue, thousands of miles of blue set on yellow clay, by reason of the heat of the blue-gums and their million leaves that are like red-lacquered eyes set keenly over the huge land.

And Il Panucci was lord of the spring and summer, and is lord of it yet, and shall be in the remembrance of it for ever.

The hut of Karta Singh was made royal by the coming of Panucci . . . and all down the hot roads and through the secret and dry aromatic back tracks, the music of Panucci wandered as though within his mandolin and guitar were all the little cities of ancient Italy. All over Gippsland was the soul of Panucci spread in music, for he was the greatest genius of music that I have ever met. The whiter roads of all Gippsland remember him; the dry grey fence outside the hut of Karta Singh protrudes a strange Greek charactery because of him, for Panucci was like a Graeco-Latin satyr or faun to look upon.

And when he came to Metung the whole season swept like a ballet into the most lovely and romantic movement of all time, into, at last, L'Après-midi d'un faune. Yes, the foaming blue and white skirts of the sea frothed out and were joined to the male strength of the glazed and hot blue-gums, and to the classic glory of the Australian clay underfoot, and in a wild passion of beauty, so did the entire earth dance L'Après-midi d'un faune.

Only the earth, the sea and the sky could do this in Australia, for it is that sort of country. Neither man nor maid could swing into ballet there, because of summer indolence and the weight of heavy Grecian years, and shame that we no more are Greek; because of all this, our spirit flies into the earth about us, and a vast ballet of passion is performed for us by the continent.

And in the night, when in the dark heavens the white stars shone, it was down the pastoral roads of ancient Italy, wandered into Australian ways, that Il Panucci came striding, mandolin lying like the pearls of Cleopatra across his breast, gleaming dull and soft in the evening light. So did he make tremendous melody with the lost pearls of the great Egyptian, and had she listened she might have heard many *"canzone Romane antiche"*. For Panucci played the Cicala music that the Romans listened to in Cleopatra's day, a music exceedingly delicate and intricate, elusive, and never to be pinned down.

And by the lake, along the foreshore, when Panucci walked there at night, the slow waters moved white-lipped towards him from shore to shore and murmured there, like lions that remembered songs heard in darkest antiquity when the world was young. The green phosphorescence of the waters grew pallid and deep and stirred and churned in diving plunges of sound. So did Panucci walk, with the lost pearls of Cleopatra swinging in eternal music across his breast.

Si, mi ricordo Il Panucci!

I came to meet Il Panucci while I was still sorting beans with Samozarro for Domenic. The springtime was still with us, and outside the dry door the hot grey earth cracked open with the small fine wither peculiar to it in Victoria. The gum-trees tossed in a dead delirium against the hard and bright wind from the sea, that was white and swift with salt and delicious as wine against the mouth at midday.

In the little garden before the hut of Karta Singh a few plants grew, seeming in this dry land to be things of infinitely rich and magnificent genius. To tell you the truth, so dry was Victoria in those years that the sight of any sort of growing vegetable in the bush was as good as a great Rembrandt in the Melbourne Art Gallery; it had the same rich quality of splendid oils. The hut of Karta Singh was poised on a long dry hill, with the white mail road running down in front of it, harsh and sandy, and on one side saplings full of picturesque leaves, and on the other the long grassy paddocks of Billy Creeker, who had bright gilt hair and a dusty face that sparkled like a far-off star. And it was in this hut, sorting the crimson beans, that I waited down the days for something to happen, for someone to come along and change the entire face of things.

"I shall loaf from now on until the peas are ready," I said to Samozarro, sliding the red beans under my fingers with the professional speed and subtlety of a croupier. There was a feeling of dissipation and abandon in the air, the revolutionary feeling of being free, a false sense of turning employer, myself, or casting off the yoke of the employer. "I shall ride everywhere."

"You shall ride everywhere, Steva?"

"Si. And, Amico, you shall buy a hack and ride with me, all over the countryside. But you would have to dress like an Australian."

And Samozarro who was singing dolorously, "*Mamma mi ha scritto*", and rocking over the last of his beans, said, "How you mean, dress like an Australian?"

"Riding kit . . . and broad-brimmed felt hat."

"I have a topee here." Zarro reached up to a hook and pulled down a stained helmet and clapped it down on his handsome Mark Antonyish head, and his great Italian face glowed like a rose under it.

"*Ti piace, Steva?*"

"*È bello!*"

"*Allora* . . . I shall buy a hack."

"Ah no, you won't, Samozarro *mio*. For you don't love the land. That is the first thing one must do. Or you must love stock. Here in Australia there are words on the hills for those who can read. That is the divine Australian language. The language of Italy is written, too, on those far-away plains, misty, bearing a purple bloom seen behind the shoulders of Christs and saints, behind those who are crucified and those who are glorified. But in Italy the lover of this language didn't buy a horse, he bought paint and brushes and wrote the language down on canvas. The Australian buys a horse and rides towards the words written on the hills. What does all this sound like to you, Samozarro?"

"*Parole di Dante.*"

"So, as I said, you will never buy a hack. And happily the language of both Australia and Italy is hidden from you, the divine language of its earth. And why should it not be? For you are the language; you are Italy, putting forth that bloom, that far-away fascination, purple-dark like the plains and golden-soft like the hills. I have come, racially, to the end of my tether. There can never be, among my children, if I should ever have children, another *me*. For I have felt it all. They will be impatient and turn to other lands and back again to the Greeks. I have given to Australia all the love that is possible. For beyond a certain point, love ceases to be noble and becomes merely fulsome. Imagine, Amico, had the children of Dante been still writing *Convito* and *Commedia* to Beatrice this day, what a boring repetition! How we should have laughed at them!"

"Steva, you have too much *conoscere* for me," said Zarro bewilderedly.

Domenic strode in, uncoiling the scarf from his throat and pitching his cap on the table.

"Well, young woman. Well, young man. How goes the beans? I think to myself that you will be gone when I come home, Steve, and I would have to take a walk over with your cheque. I will make it out now, before you go. Remember to come over in a week's time to see me about the overseeing of the pickers for the peas."

He sat down and wrote in his cheque-book in a round hand, over which the crosses for the *t*'s slashed very sharply, weighing the roundness to the ground, like a hard sharp nature pulling at a generous one and influencing it definitely.

I was standing by the table, my work finished, staring down at the hands of Samozarro moving among the red beans; across the table the kerosene lamp spread its fire and the candle muttered and waved its head of flame, as the warm wind came in through the open door. The trees outside hissed in the night. Over my arm I carried a racing bridle and saddle; the metal glittered brightly, and the leather shone. Domenic sat over his cheque-book.

Three men came to the door, softly, through the dust. Under their arms and across their chests they carried guitars—two of them, the third carried a mandolin with a pearly front.

"*Buona notte!*" exclaimed the tallest in the voice of the born linguist.

"*Buona notte!*" added his companions in rumbling basses.

"*Buona notte!*" replied Domenic. "*Dove andate, gentiluomini?*"

"*Alla casa in Metung,*" answered he of the good voice, "*per suonare la musica.*"

"*Suona per noi, per favore,*" said Domenic, leaning back in his chair and smiling at us.

"*Con piacere,*" responded the other. He held his mandolin before him in playing position; the others shifted their guitars more slowly across their chests, and their fingers hung poised above the strings. They looked at him with an expectant expression.

"*Il valzer!*" he exclaimed with a masterful, sharp stare at them. "*Suona!*"

At the word all the fingers struck the strings at once. The leader, with long white delicate hands, led with music such as I never heard before. It rang incessantly, wildly, deliriously, above everything, in cadences and codas, gipsy-like, compelling, and maddening. It was music flying, escaping . . . defiant and beautiful . . . rushing away from whoever tried to hold it. And below the waltz the two guitars throbbed sullenly, boomed sullenly, hollowly and sadly. But the mandolin—oh, how it played! It was like a heart gone mad and beating itself to death, swiftly and inevitably.

Domenic stood up beside me; his satanic face peered over the edge of his greatcoat. He said softly, "Ah, that is the best waltz in all Italy."

When it was ended, the leader said briefly, "*Marche!*" at the same time breaking into the swift measure of this march, which to me sounded like the wind haunting an empty house and wailing for its demon lover.

And while they spun rapid fingers among the strings, the players gazed quietly round, with far-away and wandering glances . . . into the fire, across to me, holding my saddle and bridle, to Domenic, who regarded them deeply, and to Samozarro, seated on the bed, at the back of the table full of crimson beans, smoking moodily and gazing at the lantern. He had never looked so handsome, with his broad flushed face, cleft-chinned, with a faint glimmer of eyes and ivory brow under a dark cloudy coronal of soft hair.

As for me, I knew nothing save the music. I saw nothing save music. For the first time in my life I forgot man as he stood before me. Rapt in music, I stood dreaming. It stopped; Domenic threw yellow and red apples to the players; they caught them and began to eat with strong white teeth. When they went I followed them out, with the young Australian who had been standing behind them.

"I'm taking them over to my aunt's place," he explained. "Aren't they wonderful players?"

"Who are they, Jeff?"

"Oh, one of them you ought to know. He was here in Metung with Peppino Nicholas last year. You know Steve, don't you, Benedetto?" he said to one of the Italians on the outside of the group.

"*Si*," he replied.

"*Ah, Benedetto! Salute! Come va!* Who has made such a fine musician out of you?"

"*Ah, come sta, Steva?* Yes, I can play now. Panucci . . . Il Panucci can teach one anything," said Benedetto, turning towards the tall, scholarly-looking young man beside him. He had the pale, satirical, amused face of a faun, clear, pure, devoted to the arts. He was exceedingly slim, and graceful, with the remote bearing of a student, and the decided appearance of a clerical worker.

"Panucci! Il Panucci! What a romantic name, there is genius in it," I said. "It is a splendid name for a musician. Can you speak English, *signor?*"

And the first remark he ever made to me is still fresh in my mind, coming mockingly through the starlit Australian night, on the clay hill outside the hut of Domenic.

"*Parlo poco e comprendo pochissimo!*" cried Panucci, striding away down the long white road with his companions. "I speak little and comprehend less!" Soon he was gone; presently the bantering sound of his mandolin came back to me. I stood on the road alone . . . the wanderers had gone, making music with wild defiant fingers as they went . . . letting rags of melody float back to me. Gay beggars!

And I went home, too. . . .

Ah, Poetry, let me loose my blood in you. I cannot forget the music. With a seagull's quill I wrote:

The magic flute of Poetry hath been
Against my lips all day. I have not seen
Sunrise or setting . . .

The seagull's quill fell out of my hand and flew seaward, and the paper went back to the tree again, and I sat dreaming, dreaming, while all the lovely sounds of the night before came to my mind. Surely rich words would come to me some day, rich, mystical, and enviable! Words to torture and enchant men for ever! Surely, with me, they would share this trance of thought; surely this was the only sleep man could have, his slumber in poetry. Surely poetry and music were all. Worship of them must bring its due reward. I shall serve this god and none other.

Then thunderously, almost hideously, came the great cry from the book of my people, striking hard at me, warning me with a cruelty that made me shudder, "Thou shalt have no other gods before me . . . for I the Lord thy God am a jealous God."

Only Jehovah could have uttered that. It was a mountain speaking. It was Time declaring itself. Then He still lived? Well, since Thou art, what dost Thou demand of me, O God? Is not poetry Thy pleasure? No, no, that is not His pleasure. His pleasure is my humiliation, my destruction, my abnegation and utter self-sacrifice. He has set me aside to suffer and find ecstasy in my suffering. He has set for my Promised Land the fabulous country of death, which lies beyond the mountains of fantasy. No, I will not. I shall stay among men and love them and be loved.

Why dost Thou pursue me? Who am I, O Lord, that Thou shouldst set Thine heart upon my sorrow? Who am I that Thou shouldst desire me to stand with Thee when my heart is with man? What is Thy will of me? Between me and man Thou placest Thine hand, and strongly movest against us. Why am I not suffered to love? Why must I wander on for ever and alone—for that, I feel, is Thine implacable will?

Here in the wilderness I struggled with God as wildly and vehemently as any prophet of ancient days. I fought against the Lord. I turned towards my own happiness. It was acceptable to Him, I felt, that I fled from Him . . . outward, downward towards man.

However, after many cups of black coffee, Arabian sweet and

Italian weak, and some dozen hot golden cakes from Jim Mc-Lachlan's larder, I felt more or less independent of the Deity, save as a kindly and disinterested provider.

When Domenic's peas were ready for picking I began work as his overseer. This was not exactly a glorious job, but it pleased me. I had to weigh up and sew up the bags and load them on the truck, after labelling and consigning them to the buyers in Melbourne, and drive the truck down to the jetty to catch the *J. C. Dahlsen* on her up-lake trip. The crop was in a hollow, near a bed of broad beans. The smell of the pearl and black flowers entered my nostrils and filled my brain with thoughts of all lands that would forever be like that, of a soil that would be perfumed, of roads, that trodden on, would press forth odours.

Down the sultry morning of spring and the deep blue-green paddock came little Peppino, very smart in his blue serge suit and dangling ornaments of green tin and gold. For he was a walking aviary when abroad, and wore all the tin and metal ornaments his mother sent him from Italy. These *"uccellini"* as he called them, swarmed over his chest like medals. Doves, hens, eagles, and ducks clustered over him, as if he had been a bag of mixed mash. And in his pockets the pious fellow carried pictures of St Paolo being beheaded, St Lucia being impaled, St Sebastiano being delivered, and St Agostino running away and leaving his mother standing on a long, lonely shore with her hands to her eyes, and the Saint's little boyish figure with short tunic fluttering against an old dark sea.

"Fu un' diavolo quand' era giovane!" Peppino said seriously of St Agostino.

There he was coming down the hill, unchanged. It was the first time I had seen him in daylight for two years.

"Steva . . . come va?"

"Bene, e voi, Peppino?"

"Non ce male."

"Peppino. Dio mio, I have met Il Panucci!"

"Cosa pensa di lui?"

"Panucci? O, il genio. Candidly, I think he is the most remarkable man I have ever met. He is to work for McLachlan as chemist this year, industrial chemist or analytical, I forget which. He is a great musician in his way, and a cleverly spoken man."

"*Si*, Panucci is very clever. We all like him. *Lui, mangia la musica*. He reads and studies music while he eats and drinks, while he sleeps, while he dresses; *tutto il tempo, mangia la musica*; many books he has, and he reads them through all day and all night and practises till all hours in the morning. And he is expert in his knowledge of old Italian and Greek history. He knows all the old gods and heroes by name, quite well."

"I should like to hear him play again, Pep."

"Yes? Well, one night I bring him down with the others to play. You will like that? Well, Steva, sorry, but I must go now. I go Metung——" a phrase that sounded most beautiful from Peppino—"for get some *mangiare*." Yes, the entire blue-green warm way to Metung, the great road and the splendid sea, rose up in soft billows of sound then.

"*Si, Steva, vi vedrò domani, se possibile. Addio.*"

In one day, we cut out the small paddock. And on my way home I called in at the house of Billy Creeker, the short poetish looking man, with blue eyes and a great head of dusty golden hair, for whom I had worked two years ago.

"Well, Steve me lad?" Billy always called me "Steve me lad", or "Steve me boy".

"Mr Creeker," with scrupulous politeness, "when may I start the bean-sorting for you? We've just cut out Domenic's bottom paddock, and the rest of the crop is still a long way off ready. And Domenic told me you wanted me to sort. Samozarro and I, he said."

"Well, Steve me boy," pushing his hat off the mane of hair, "the beans are down there in Domenic's old hut." A hut that a man had lived in was called his for months after he'd gone, was called his until someone else had lived in it and had gone, and then it was called after him. "And you could start when you like. Tomorrow? How'd that suit you?"

"Oh, not tomorrow. I've just finished on a big crop. I'd like a day off, to think work over. You know."

And Billy Creeker, who was as idle and fantastic as I was, understood well.

"All right, day after tomorrow. Or day after that. I don't know. Just ride over one morning and start on them, Steve."

I stayed for tea with Billy and his family that night. He was a widower, and his children ruled the house, which had a happy, haphazard sort of wildness about it. The kitchen was bare of everything except a table and a few chairs. There wasn't the faintest sign of its being a home; the grate of the stove was choked with blackened papers; a tin of melon jam stood on the table, a couple of big loaves of white bread stood beside it, and the eldest girl was giving the rest of the family a sharp-tongued lecture on the villainy of robbing the nest of her hen. She had banked on getting the eggs, and the others had got in first and cooked them for breakfast while she was out.

"Now then, now then, Molly, that's enough," Billy exclaimed amiably and weakly from time to time. "She'll lay tomorrow again, won't she, Steve me boy? Have a cup of tea, Steve? Damned if I can see a clean cup around."

"And there isn't one," exclaimed the daughter sharply. "I'll root one out of somewhere. Here, get up, Fanny, you're sitting on the cups."

And Fanny, who was red-haired and extraordinarily like John Keats's Fanny Brawne, got up from the old couch and there were the cups.

"Now where's the tea-pot?" said Molly. "It was on the stove a minute ago. Jeff, where's the tea-pot?"

"I put it under the couch," said Jeffrey from his room, sounding muffled, as if he had a stud in his mouth.

There it was. I had a cup. I loved the place. It was young, vigorous and careless. It was a children's house and, in a way strange to imagine, it was so innocent. The man, their father, contributed nothing to it in the way of subtlety, for men are not subtle, and they don't think much of houses. It was naked and clean of the influences of a grown woman, and that, strange to say, was lovely, and yet vaguely dangerous. Women burrow into a house; they make fungus-like growths of consciousness come into it, by their habit of cultivation . . . for along with the flowers come the weeds and gradually impoverished soil.

But here, dash it all, said the house, nothing grows but weeds of an honest likeable sort, and there's no chance of the ground being impoverished for it's never used. The weeds grow up in their season and die in their season, and enrich the ground. The wind whistled in the bare rooms, the feet trod heavily on the bare boards, and it would have distressed a womanly woman terribly to have sat there and watched tea being served, or rather flung, to the children. But they were used to it. A housekeeper would have worried them. They had one for a few years, but cast her forth. They were all battlers, sharp as needles and rough as bags.

"Have you heard the musicians, the Italians that came over with Peppino from Bruthen?" asked Billy. "My word, Steve me boy, that Panucci can play, eh?"

"Clever fellow," I agreed, eating bread and melon jam, soft white bread covered with square lumps of melon, and drinking cups of warm sweet tea. There was something heroic in dining here, at this long bare table, among such a vivid, ragged, knightly crew.

I stood next day on the hill of white stones overlooking the hut, and flung the stones down, one by one, to make a neat fireplace in place of the old one, which was burnt out. I was determined that my mother should come up and stay with me. Peppino came along dressed in his best, with the tin aviary swinging over his chest.

"Hey, what you doing?" he called out, dodging away from the coming shower of rocks.

"Come up here, millionaire," I replied, "and help me throw some stones down to make my hut beautiful. This is my furniture."

He stood beside me on the hill and he shied the stones down.

"Peppino, *la mia madre* is coming up to stay with me soon, I think."

He looked delighted, and grinned from ear to ear. "Yes? Your mother is coming to stay with you! I am very glad. Dear little woman, your *madre*. I like to see her again. Tonight I bring my friends down to the Buccaneer's to play music. Why not you come?"

"Why not?" I said. "Call for me at twilight and we shall go down together."

"No, I must go with my friends; they not been this plice before."

"Ah, that's true. I'll go alone."

Peppino departed, and I continued to cast the first stone unto the last and make a hearth that Francis Ledwidge would have broomed out with joy on an Irish June morning to the odours of daphne and red rose. And then I went inside to write and tell *madre mia* about this hearth of the gods. But alas, when she heard that it was but stones cast as it were from Connaught of the Kings, she turned the entire trip down, and lived on in solitary luxury at Laurel Lodge.

Carefully dressed in a blue serge suit, with a tussore shirt of thick creamy hue and college tie, a brier-rose in my buttonhole and all the bloom of youth burning like a pink and green and silver fire through my blood, I went down through the spring evening to the house of Edgar Buccaneer. I took the long white road through the dark bush, curve by curve, back track and sounding foreshore, till its serpent depths of dust ended at a long red-golden cliff.

I could hear the music before I climbed the track along the cliff to where the house stood among blackwood wattles, young gum saplings, and many flowers and island fruit-trees—the high, ringing thrum of the mandolin above the guitars. The sitting-room was crammed with people; all the children were there, and Edgar and his wife, and Peppino and his Italians, and other men and women. The three musicians sat on the couch together, under the window. Panucci in their midst. Now one could see exactly what he looked like. That starlight night had been deceptive.

The music stopped just as I came in. He stared at me with a whimsical, mocking look, the look he had for everyone, then he spoke sharply to Benedetto, who began clumsily to retune his guitar. Panucci, dissatisfied, took it from him, bent above it, tuning rapidly and talking more rapidly. Yes, one could see what he was like, exactly.

He was clerkly looking, tall, thin, and stooped, and his pale round face, sharp-toothed, wide-mouthed, with thin lips, had a faint colour in the cheeks. His nose was up-tilted and long, elfin and mocking. The whole bearing of the man was of one who bore the load of mockery, humour, passion, eagerness, and tolerance. Hair, unlike any hair I had ever seen before, fell in long dry crinkled waves over his forehead. But the man, the musician, and the elf danced in the eyes, the brown eyes with the faint blue smoke of his race blowing through them. These eyes danced, snapped, and laughed all the time he was playing with a vigorous, humorous delight, so that they enchanted more than the music. Brimming over with merriment, they stared from face to face. But a note only had to go wrong, and a frown appeared, and there was stern whisper of *"Piano . . . più piano . . ."* or *"più forte. . . . Assai!"* And the brown in the eyes was lost, as the whites turned towards the accompanist. There will never be another Panucci.

Marches, waltzes, songs, anthems, hymns, and country dances were hammered out on the strings all night. It was waste of time to sit still to it, I thought, but yet it was so strange, rapid, and intricate that one wouldn't know what sort of dance to tread to it. So there we sat, enchanted and tortured, the children with open mouths, and the adults eager but with troubled hearts, their bodies thrashed into life but forbidden to move, because our Australian feet and hearts were shy and couldn't dance to music like this, the delirious cadences of the tarantella.

Edgar Buccaneer, however, who had a touch of German blood in him, and felt, perhaps, the memory of the dances they hold at the wine festivals along the Rhine, only waited to catch some one else's eye, and he would sing out with a wild note and stamp his feet loudly. As for me, my mind was dancing and that was enough for me. And no one was as strongly caught in it, as I was. For me, it was fatal, and drew me down, unknown, into the depths; for me, it spread webs in the years and made me dissatisfied with my life; for me, it had a demon power and thrust me down into Hades, into insatiable longing for ancient Italy and for the days before the Italians, the satyr-haunted days of ancient Rome. Yes, that night love of Italy struck deep roots into me and began to put out poisonous and possessive leaves.

I got up and followed the Black Serpent into the kitchen to watch her preparing the supper. Leaning over the table, I said, "Well, this is music." It was still ringing in the next room. "That Panucci——"

"He is looking at you too often, Steve. Remember the colour line!"

"Let him cross it, if he will," I said carelessly.

We laughed. In fact, I thought Panucci saw nothing and heard nothing but music, and I was quite right. The music stopped when the supper was brought in; and I heard the shrill, sweet voice of Panucci again. It was vigorous and full of staccato exclamations, and eager, so eager and impulsive. His lack of knowledge of English deprived us of his genius. In his own tongue he spoke quietly, masterfully and in good expressive Italian, but English

111

made him more elfin than he was. In his eagerness to talk he would take hold of any word and throw it about, allied to the most grotesque grammar. As he regarded us all with his humorous and mocking eyes we couldn't criticize him, for his whole attitude, playing or sitting silent with the mandolin across his knees, was, "Isn't this comical? Am I not comical to be sitting here, making such ridiculous sounds and feeling pleased about it, and aren't you comical to be sitting there, amused by those sounds? This makes me laugh inwardly until I could burst; I am really splitting my sides at the comicality of it all." For he regarded his music, in the main, in spite of his ardent study of it, as being vain and comical.

As I walked home along the lakeside with the four men, under the stars and the moon, they played old, old songs of Italy in the dark. The dramatic threat of showers came from the sea that roared incessantly over the sand-dunes six miles away. But the lake murmured that it would be fine again. Bruno and Benedetto strummed their guitars, and Panucci, looking towards the horizon, sang:

> *"La luna parla in cielo,*
> *Una stella ancora brilla ..."*

> ("*The moon speaks in the sky,*
> *One star again brilliant ...*")

And together, Panucci and I looked towards the star that hung over the sea. What does one take from such nights? What does one remember? The dark group walking beside me? There is nothing in that. That is the social group; that is man in company. The music? No, I have forgotten it. Only three things remain, then, the great sky, with the stars and moon shining among white clouds, the two lines of poetry, and the directive forces that the poetry and the earth exerted on me. And that is destiny. *"La forza del destino."*

And, looking back, that is all that remains to any man. And there is always the wish to have contended with it and brought it to bear on life in a different fashion.

The shower fell among us, all thick white and splashed with

112

hues from the blue and white and green deep sea; it was like thick white paint falling across the trees in the night, and, laughing, we parted. The guitars were put into their bags and the voices of the musicians died away in the scrub at the turn-off.

Peppino came with me and took my hand. So, stumbling through the dark and the rain, we walked to the hut, singing, "Santa Lucia" . . .

> "Tui sei l'impero, dell'armonia . . .
> Santa Lucia . . .
> Santa Lucia . . ."

The bush wept around us, white tears that we could see; they lay on our clothes, and ahead lay sleep, deep sleep and long, all night, and all the next day, if that next day proved to be wet; and the whole world held for me, and I knew it, nothing better. Those were the riches allotted me, and never rejected.

"I will go to Italy! I will go to Italy!" I cried next day in my letter to my mother. "But first, *madre mia*, you must come to Metung and hear the music that draws me there. You must, I beg . . . demand. Shut up the house and the suitcase. The heath is sparkling on the hillside in chequered bloom, red, white, and rose." But all day a name rang in my mind, a grieving name, of one who grieved. Why should it come to mind? But, imploring my mother to come to me, this name came instead of her . . . and I made of it a song.

NIOBE

> Niobe, though, alas, I have not known
> From Grecian leaves, thine olden golden tale . . .
> Still is thy name a volume thick, alone.
> I know that thou wast fair . . . that thou wast pale.
> Niobe, pale word that was the moan
> Of helmed heroes. . . . Yea, thou dost appear
> White as the moon at morn, a smooth sad stone,
> A snowy urn, a sealèd vase of tears.

This song I hung up on the wall where the thick smoke from the fire could blow against it, and give it ancient yellow hues, so

113

that it might appear as old as the Greek writings and as like to the Grecian contours of the land in its approaching hot, Hellenic summer as did the twisted trees in the marsh beyond the hut.

Samozarro and I started to sort beans for Billy Creeker that week. The cool, rusty shed was half filled with bags, and on the table the sieves and heaps of bright-red beans lay before us. Once more the tins rattled as we slid our piles of seed right and left. And again we rocked and sang. No more for me was there enchantment in "Julia", or in "Mamma". I had heard greater music.

At night we walked home together over the neglected paddocks covered with red sorrel and passed by the machinery that Billy Creeker had given over to the hand of rain and wind, and under a cloak of pretentious rust and mould they were slowly beating them back into the earth again.

But at the end of the week Domenic wanted Samozarro to work for him again, and I was left alone to finish the sorting. After school the children came down to the hut and talked to me. And I was happy in that cool dusty red shed on the edge of the grassy hill. Above it the clouds, huge gods, toiled slowly with some invisible load above the far-off sea, or they sat in splendid removed thought, with down-bent heads and idle hands. Their great curved bodies gleamed, and they were more alive to me than the faces I turned to once again, to Molly Creeker, as I took from her hand a cup of tea and drank it, standing face to face with my unreal world of clouds. In some distant apple orchard I heard the jays singing with swinging jovial voices, "For the best . . . for the best . . . for the best . . . oho!" And I was happy, for springtime was in her prime, her lovely prime, and the big trees were pallid and naked, flung up into the blue air like the fair bodies of women, and as I rode or walked over the lacy hills of golden capeweed I sang the song I had made:

> "What? Is all vanished for ever and ever?
> Yea, lover and loved do silently sever.
> And the shape of Beauty? No, never, never!
> That still awaits the high endeavour."

And every beautiful morning of the days I worked for Billy

Creeker I saddled my black horse and came galloping to the gate, a Cyclone gate; the racer seemed to know it, and without waiting for me to open it would burst straight through frame, wire, and catch, with a strong silken breasting movement, full of black grandeur, as though we had both been gods; and winged. It was springtime and Alpini, grass-fed, was as light and dangerous as foam under the saddle; uphill and down he would gallop, white-mouthed, red-eyed and with fire burning the day from his centaur nostrils.

Eb Coleman rode the racehorse as the ancient Greeks used to ride them. He would vault on to him, without saddle or bridle, and thrusting his long white fingers into the horse's nostrils, to swing him to either right or left, up over the golden cliffs, swarmingly, and squat, man and horse would go in bright and strenuous power. I rode like this occasionally, but the horse finished up like a streaming black and white fountain in the heat. And I preferred a light racing exercise pad to that form of horsemanship.

Domenic gave me a small black and tan and white dog named Figaro. Whether he was named after the big Italian newspaper *Il Figaro* or after the Barber of Seville I do not know. But to the chiming chanting tune of

> *"Figaro qui . . . Figaro qua . . .*
> *Figaro giu . . . Figaro, su . . .*
> *Sono il factotum della città . . .*
> *Sono il factotum della città . . ."*

the little dog romped across the landscape of Primavera and charmed us all with his gaiety, and his appetite for everything under the sun, while Domenic stood in the grey rain and sang tarantellas to him as he, dappled and pied, danced about his heels.

On the warm dry afternoon I finished the beans all the children came down, and Billy came down himself, too, his face like fallen afternoon, gilded with the royal dust of Australia, his eyes tired with the smoke of burning off, and his hair hanging in a weary sparkling fashion from under his wide military hat. All old soldiers on the land in Victoria wear their hats into a sort of military shape, as he did, a faint sort of curve up on one side, and where their badge of the Australian Imperial Forces used to shine, with

115

its rising sun, well, the sun itself must supply the emblem and shine there. The tea-cups had been brought down and stood on the table. Enough for us all, and for Peppino, who had called in to help me finish and to walk home with me. He was not yet working.

Up and down outside the hut Jeff, the eldest boy, struggled past with the plough. A rough trample of feet, the shaking of bits and chains, the rough whirring wheels and sliding foot of the plough breaking past over damp soil, and the stagger of Jeff as he held on to the handle and the reins.

We laughed as we heard him crying out as some strong man in his agony cries out for his love, "Bonny! *Bonny!*" and immediately after, in great despair, "*You* lousy ole dorg, I'll give yer the *father* of a hiding!"

Over the tea-cups and the chutney sandwiches, I spoke of Blue.

"Well, I had a letter from Blue yesterday. She is going to be married soon."

"To the same fellow, Steve me boy?" asked Billy.

"Yes." Blue and Keith Wilson had been going to get married for over two years now. They had gone to high school together, and had been practically engaged there. "Blue is different. You remember her? A handsome girl in boy's clothes—well, she has a different side, you know, to all that. What drawings she can do! I can't explain them. Also, as you know, she plays the violin well. She has humour and love of beauty; she mimes like an actor; she is more clear-sighted than I am, far more independent. And what is strange is that she would rather wander the world with me than do any other thing. But I dissuade her. I wish to be alone. Poets always wish to be alone." And I stared at Peppino, the lovely Latin face, the black mole under the brown eyes, and the well-shaped head held high under the soft confusion of black shining hair. That day Peppino looked utterly Spanish. To my mind, behind him bellowed the hot yellow sandy silk-decorated arena where the bulls shone like black jewels and the pools of green shade curved out to meet the toreador and matador. One is very near to unconsciousness at a bullfight. There one could lose either memory, or money, or any other thing. "Also, to be alone, is good for the soul."

"Has anyone a soul, Steve me boy?" asked Billy Creeker.

"That is an Australian reply. The Australian is sceptical and jests his soul away from him. Here, in this country, we are all humorists. That doesn't satisfy me. I am not that. I am in search of my soul."

"Not me," said Billy. "I wouldn't like to go seriously into a search for truth in a hard dry country like Australia, Steve me lad. Why, the other night I had an awful dream. I thought——" he told it jokingly—"well, Steve me boy, there I was lying in bed, and I looks up at the roof. By Jingo, what do you think happened? The whole ceiling turned into a devil with a green face and red eyes; he looked down on me and howled laughing. 'Now I've got you, now I've got you, Billy me boy,' said he, and the walls on each side of the bed turned into hands the size of this hut, and they squeezed me and the bed between them into pulp; and all the time I'm looking up, Steve me boy, you see, and staring into the red eyes of this devil. And he's roaring and laughing above me. I woke up in a sweat, I can tell you. So I say, lad, if those are the things you see on the road when you're looking for your soul, I'll do without one."

"And you survived the pulping, Billy?"

"An Australian'd survive anything, Steve me boy," said Billy. But his uneasy voice told me that he lived on the edge of something. "Yes, Steve," he went on, "under the joke of the Australian can lie such terrible things, and then each man in the bush goes down to the pit, laden with hell and never having said a word about it. And that, to some, is worse than anything. Better to get roaring drunk and tell it all than let the bush triumph and life triumph and take your hell with you. But you'll get nothing out of the Australian. Humorous, dry, independent, sarcastic, sentimental, and yet well balanced, he goes his way. The Australian has a duty to his country, the duty of dignified patience and the power to suffer, with his own God, for the sake of the very sun that beats and blasts its way through his brain, in great noble dumb blows, thunderous with power, and out of respect for the loved brown continent that he has walked upon, his earth, his native earth. The Australian, in the face of great odds, works, icy and unafraid, silent and contemptuous, yet dreadfully happy that he had lived . . . a *man* . . . and suffered as a man should, to the last day of his life. Only a lonely spirit in yourself guesses and struggles in a fury of anger at his battling . . . and I long for a manifestation of passion, for a womanly emotion to reveal the race as I want it to be revealed, Steve!"

As for me, all I said before this revelation, was, awkwardly, "Your nerves are in bad shape; you may need a holiday or a rest." And I subsided meekly into my own Australianisms of putting to the side, as dangerous, all the subconscious things.

Peppino, not understanding what we were talking about, deeply inhaled and exhaled cigarette smoke in the precise and sophisticated manner of the Continental. I felt sleepy with the loveliness of that afternoon . . . and I dreamt upon it.

"Steve!" cried Billy Creeker, lightly, yet painfully:

"The poetry of earth is ceasing never—"

"What?" I laughed, awoke, and sorted the last of the beans into the tin. "What? John Keats now!"

"Your face as you were looking downward reminded me of Keats for a moment, Steve. I often wonder if you were Keats. You may have been. Sometimes, looking at you, I could swear you were John Keats."

"What?" I felt shocked and saddened. I had a very high opinion of Keats. "O Gods, never! Don't say that." Keats? Half asleep, I thought, Was I? Was I? Oh, no, it was incredible. But the suggestion enchanted me, for to be like him would have been a light thing, a pleasure, an awayness from myself. I slipped in and out of the thought as I pleased.

I was happy as I walked home with Peppino. He swung his long dark cloak over one shoulder *à la toreador,* and with what an extravagant swagger he walked! To be walking in this great romantic pastoral of Primavera across the fields of late afternoon with Peppino was far lovelier than walking with kings.

We were great poets and great lovers in those days, we Australians, we Italians. On each other's faces we stared with a sad eagerness, a lyric sorrow, a strange joy and melancholy. Something told us all that we should never see each other again.

"Peppino, have some *mangiare* with me tonight, and let us play some music. You say you left your gramophone and records in my hut as you passed?"

118

"*Si, Steva,*" he said subduedly.
"*Cosa pensa, Peppino?*"
"*Niente, Steva.*"

Still thinking of nothing, he sat and ate hot cakes with me and drank black coffee by the side of the fire in the baracca. Outside was the spring evening, sultry, stifling with odours, atmosphere, and time and life; there was no end to one's power over earth; one merely breathed and the earth burnt like fire and gigantic shapes of terrible grandeur moved over it; and that which lay in the rose-red evening was of the gods and unutterable and unknown. It was youth and health and toil out in the open under the wide sky.

While the Italian baritone sang "The Last Song" Peppino looked across at me, calmly and quietly; from within himself and beyond himself came the sense of race and far-off Italy, still thinking of her wandering and working, *figlio,* her beloved son. And outside the walls of the house of his first love, the Italian mourns in "*L'Ultima Canzone*", and clutches the climbing vines with desperate hands while he sings:

"*Man detto che demani, Nina andrà sposa . . .*"

A fascinating dark record with a black-and-gold label raced rapidly round on the gramophone with this old song on it. It was a song that hung tilted a little, like the earth. One sensed that it came from somewhere up under the Italian Alps; in some black village there they told him that his love was to wed another, and the song spun down over the valleys and plains and across beds of flowers until at last it landed at the feet of the old friends of the *contadini* from whom it had started in the Alps. For most clearly to mind came the picture in the mountains of a large empty room, with forms along the wall, and the peasants sat on those forms, stamping their feet on the floor and softly tapping their hands to the pastoral chant of the opening, which went:

"*Durdula . . . durdula . . . durdula . . .*"

A rhythm that sounded as old as the earth. And from the north of Italy to the south, down went the vast Olympic runner of the song, carrying the wild flame of his love bright and clear, like a

119

blue star, down into the south, to some old large room there, where awaited the Greek chorus of yet another group of *contadini* or peasants, holding the thread of the *canzone*.

> *"They tell me that tomorrow, Nina, you will marry,*
> *And, my God, I sing to you again the last song.*
> *On the high plains and in the brutal valley,*
> *Oh, how many times have I sung and resung it to you!*
> *O Nina, remember! O flower degraded!*
> *The kisses I gave you . . .*
> *Nina, remember the kisses I gave you, oh, ardently."*

How broad and ivory-pale Peppino's face looked as he turned to me! The fire burnt up on the hearth. And one by one we played the Italian records; from the white sad face of each Latin singer arose the loud, sweet, sure voice in piercing Italian; those masters of the language, bringing image after image of Italia to my mind. The room filled with wave upon wave of music and was heated by it. It became choked up with the Italian language, and when one opened the door to let the words away, in stamped the white words of the Australian stars.

Blue wrote to me:

A thousand thanks, Steve, for the foreshore flowers. Oh my God, I long to be with you on these fine moonlit nights, to wander along the foreshore in the company of you and Peppino and his music and song. Alas, alas, I long to see you and exchange reminiscences and tales of many happenings.

Haven't any new clothes and don't intend to get any; will get a horse when I come to you and riding kits galore . . . and that will do. Dash clothes! Want to live; want to laugh and make merry once again in your company. Do you think you could welcome the sailor, Blue Peter?

And across the back of the letter, I wrote in secret, to myself:

Look! Even when my body's very old, and thought has to be slowly searched for; even then, when on a thunderous day I look out, as I looked out just now, and see above the hills and the trees on the hill, the approaching summit of the ranges of rain, and hear my senses say inwardly, "Ah, no work today"— even then I shall know the tremors of liberty, the knowledge, keen in me, that the rest of the day may be spent in eating, in drinking, in hearing a great singer's heart crying, in the learning of a lovely language, in the romance of a great speaking author, in the tireless imagery of the gods of poetry. When one feels that music and language return the passion we give to them, that, that is all. There is no more life than that . . . for me. After all, to be loved, as we love . . . is not that everything? Who was it that cried once, "Lauré, Lauré, I am young and my plate is empty! When will my two great desires, to be loved and to be famous, be granted?"

One afternoon Peppino came along to tell me that he and Benedetto and Bruno were to start work for Jim McLachlan, planting out the small tea-plants that Jim had in their thousands in his large potting sheds. These were to be put into shallow holes in the prepared soil and carefully watered until they came to sturdy independence. The old crop would be ready to pick by February, when the earth was at its worst and deepest, dustiest stage. Tea-picking under such conditions can be a torturing job. The earth has to be kept very loose round the plants, and the dust is fine and irritating. The bushes have a strange effect on the soil; they dry it out very rapidly and thoroughly, since they absorb an enormous amount of moisture. The official advice is, "Two leaves and a bud", and on a supervised plantation the Government sees that this rule is strictly adhered to; but on a small experimental plot such as Jim's there was no need to be particular, seeing that he grew for a Chinese buyer who was a close friend of his. We picked all over the bush, usually selecting, of course, the largest and best-shaped leaves, and Jim, who had his own way of drying them, slid them from the drying sheds into the sun and from the sun into the drying sheds. Peppino said that he thought he would have enough work to do there to keep him going until the sugar-beet was ready to cut in Maffra. "On this place I will store away tea," said Peppino, "and in Maffra I will get a lot of sugar." He saw himself making a profit out of the year ahead.

121

I was glad that Pep was going to work for McLachlan. All down the blue and white day the sun shone in the gales equinoctial, for it was still springtime, and the year was young. This meant red fires on the dusty hearth, heath in the dark places of the earth, and always the fierce loud wind bursting open doors and windows and blowing the dust about in eternal and happy holiday. Peppino and I sat down in the hut and made black coffee and ate golden cakes while the records were played.

Tinkling airily from the top of a steep hill, rang the bells of Trieste, with a mad merry abandon, and in the close dark streets, rich with flags, with fresco and design, the trumpets blew gaily and shrilly. And the singer, robust and brave, sang:

> "*Sulle spiaggie, sulle spiaggie di Trieste*
> *Suono e chiama di San Giusto la campana!*
> *L'alma dolce della madre non lontana,*
> *Lei rispose, 'Libertà!'* "

The contrast between the little jewel-like city of Trieste, with its medieval turrets and towers, its one long street full of noblemen, riding slender steeds under the blossoming banners and flags of festa, and the borders of Italy, seen with faint white towers standing still from earth to heaven, was indescribable. One could hear the little bells faintly responding, "*Liberta!*" That thing which is sweetest of all. That for which all things must be endured.

In that hut, surrounded by the ringing Italian music, I imagined my life to be aesthetic and full of poetry; I, like Panucci, *mangio la musica*. I cleansed myself with music; I became Italian song; all day, I sang, all day I dreamt of Italy. I was full-poisoned and aching with the draught. The purple flowers blossomed along the foreshore; the red bells of some rough flower, yellow-tipped, as if fresh from the fires of spring, blossomed there, and I walked, singing with Peppino through them, while the lake waters returned to the shore. Such days made one hungry to live for ever; even to get up in the morning and hear the songs again, that was enough. And every night and every morning Peppino came along to see me, and when he came we played music.

Work was hurried over; night was sought. All I waited for was the soft rustle of Peppino's feet over the grass to the sound always of "*Estudiantina*", that Madridesque melody. For as soon as I played that at night I heard Peppino come over the grass in the darkness, with another collection of Italian songs gathered from Panucci.

"Il Panucci told me to tell you that some day soon he would come along and see you," he said, "and bring more songs of Italy with him; and he would listen with you to Caruso and Chamlee singing, and all the rest of the singers."

And I said, "Let him come when he will. I want Panucci to see this place and sit and talk to me about *il passato d'Italia*." The thought of plunging into Italy's history and becoming myself the most ardent of Italians made me feel thick with turgid poetry. But I said to myself, "I am an Australian; I have a country lovelier and more mystical in its droughts, its rains, its teeming springtime with the hint of coming poverty of earth in summer, than any other." And picking up an old letter, I wrote on the back of it:

What? Is it the long road again? I suppose so. My body walking between dripping sodden trees in a midnight of rain; the track shining like grey wet moonlight before me. Peppino, I shall remember you, too keenly, too keenly. When Caruso sings I want to throw defiantly off the long brown arms of my country and fly at once to Italy. What harm would that do, I wonder, if I were to live there and mingle my blood with the race? But . . . my country . . . my country, Australia, and all the associations strong in me! I know the smoky glamour of your fallen afternoons; I know where in privy and enchanted places the spring's earliest deep-vermilion heath grows. I know, too, where her palest heath grows, between its dark, dark leaves, like a pallid girl in the clutches of a swarthy robber. And what a honeyed weight the tea-tree bears, murmurous with golden inhabitants.

Ah, frozen breath of spring, sweet wild flowers . . .

My country, my country, I cannot give you alien blood.

No, it is ended. I must stay in Australia, and be for ever Australian. More beautiful, more strange, richer to the heart than the beautiful strange words of the alien singer, is the thought of Gippsland and her old traditions. Mother Country give me back, give me back again, the lost days; the past.

I

And in all circling wings of wattle, tea-tree and red and white and rose heath, the blue-green form of the Australian bush arose, laden with royal smoke funereal, as arose in heaven mighty Hector, leaving the Trojan fields and ascending to the gods.

Over the page Blue was mourning for her Promised Land, for the light in her darkness.

No lover, Steve, could love you so wholly and purely as I do. You used to say once, that I was most fortunate. You say so now? How can that be so? Where and how am I most fortunate? Where is my best friend? Where is the only mate I ever wanted? There you are, with the smell of the sea about you, and the yellow sand in your hair and music and gladness in your heart as you swing along the road on your burning black racehorse. You used to interest yourself in me once; you were *my* friend, *mine* only, my tutor, my guide, my sympathizer. You brought me up, lifted me from the mud with your splendid thoughts. Under the mud . . . under the mud! What's the use of lifting me out, when you don't want me? It's like the wanton destruction of a flower or the picking of fruit when you have no hunger. Take me under your care again. Will you?

And I had replied with the evasions of poetry:

Enchanted adventurer, where is your old arrogance? Where is the confidence that once so splendidly upheld you? You are sad; all the others are sad. Their letters read sadly. They perish. And you perish . . . and why? Oh, remember, remember the Promised Land. That cloudy gleaming pinnacled mass, the white shining shoulders of fair temples in far cities . . . lost Carcassonne, pillaged Troy, Zion aghast and long-sought Samarkand.

And that was all the sympathy Blue got from me. Gently, but heroically, with poetry and blinding prose, I thrust her off. For I loved to be free. I am guilty, was the undertone of these letters; I am guiltily merging my soul with the soul of Italy and working my own destruction, racially. I am engaged in intoxicating myself with the wines of song and poetry. You are the noonday; you are the voice crying out from the housetops that which is being whispered in the closet. Away with you! I might quite well have sung in tune to far away Samozarro:

"*Io sono Australiano, se non scrivo . . . muro.*"
(I am Australian; if I cannot write, I die.)

For when Blue was with me, there was neither the time nor the true inclination to write. She liked to keep me working, and distrusted the long silences that meant I was lost in study.

Back to Domenic's for the pea-picking came the Bulmer family. They had been picking for him in the previous year. After a few days of sorting beans for Billy Creeker, I had to go again to Domenic's to weigh up and bag up *i piselli*, as he called them. And there stood the Bulmer family, young Vere and Eric and their father. The boys had both been electrical engineers in Melbourne, but the wanderlust struck them when their mother died, and they and their father did nothing but travel all over Australia, doing anything at all. They were pale-faced, short, sturdy youths with thick Dutch sort of features, and were given to wearing black engineers' shirts and soft black wide-brimmed hats of the American sombrero type, under which their fair hair glistened and shone in the sun. And their father was a very superior sort of man, who had had a good schooling once upon a time, but thought nothing of it. "The ole codger", the boys called him. It had a fascinating, fishy sound about it.

Mr Bulmer greeted me with his usual superb air of superiority. He always spoke in set and measured terms. His eyes protruded, shining wetly. I wondered how it was that they could stand out so far, and the moisture not run off. Yellow whiskers like old straw stuck out from under his nose. In the paddock he always wore a bowler hat.

"As in my office in Collins Street, Steve," he said to me firmly, "so in Domenic's paddocks in Gippsland. The bun hat, Steve, the pillar and foundation of our great British Empire."

Always calmly immersed in his own importance, he knelt among the peas, giving me a strong feeling that he should have had his roll-top desk and morning mail carried out into the paddocks with him, and a neat stenographer to stand by and take a letter from

125

him now and then. But he picked solidly, staring down at the crop with a dignified, self-satisfied smile, a little beery and drowsy. He appeared to be talking to some one in his mind, or was he addressing the peas?

"Yes," he appeared to be saying, "there you lie, flat and cold, you peas. I'm moving above you, full of genius and respectability. How clever I am! That pleases me. Just clever, that's all. I couldn't avoid it. Born like that. Tra-la-la, life is strange; I am modest. It's just as well. I want to smile all day as I pick you, because you are so stupid and I am so brilliant."

As he passed the headland where I sat on horseback watching the stooped pickers, he said suddenly and pompously, "Persistent plodding permanently prosecuted produces prosperity," and he smiled down at the peas, secretly, and his eyes and moustache twitched. "We are going down to the village tomorrow, Steve. You might care to accompany us. For the purpose of volition, Mr Proust has generously lent us his equipage, the buggy and the steed thereof. We shall look forward to your gracing us with your company. At ten in the morning. We shall call for you." Bowing, he crawled past me, because there were not many peas on his row, and, as if we had really parted until the morrow, for the rest of the day he coldly avoided me.

At ten next morning I was ready, and the equipage rushed up to my door in a cloud of dust. Vere and Eric hung on to the sides of the buggy and the splashboard. Mr Bulmer, "the ole codger", sat upright in a spinsterish fashion in front. The reins were gripped between his hands in a peculiar fashion, a frigid, timid, simpering grip.

"I am exactly imitating Mrs Proust," he explained. "She very kindly demonstrated to me the exact way she held the reins. It seems that the steed will not respond to any other grip. One pulls with a certain timidity from time to time on the reins. This timidity is pleasing to the animal; it responds . . . as you will see."

He waited until I got in; he pulled like a parson taking the last cake from the dish at a church fair, and we were thrust forth by the impetus of the horse's jerk. Down the steep, very steep hill we rolled with the dust flying, but on the uphill our pace was dragging and stiff. It took us almost half an hour to ascend a small rise; the steed sweated and toiled, but our ascent was painfully slow.

"The mechanism of the equipage is at fault, apparently," said Mr Bulmer. "Vere, you might descend and assist us. Eric, when Vere's strength fails, assist him too."

Vere got down and laid his broad shoulder to the wheel. Our progress was painful, and a moody depressing silence fell upon us. Presently, at the top of the hill, Vere sang out, apparently to Eric, to whom he addressed all his remarks, "Perhaps if the ole codger was to take his foot off the brake . . ."

"Great Heavens!" cried Mr Bulmer, drawing his foot up off the brake and almost under his chin. "I completely forgot to take my foot off the brake when we started off!" With a dry whirr, the brake sprang up; the carriage leapt forward like an arrow from the bow, almost on top of the horse, and we flew down the hill, leaving the oracle prostrate on the roadway. And in this way came down to Metung.

But now the month was growing warmer, and my inward eye kept roving over crop after crop, in a delighted and deliberate fashion; like a huge Cyclops I sat alone in my hut and dreamt over the fields. Away down on the foreshore, meaning gold for me at last, Peppino was busy planting out the new species of Japanese tea that McLachlan had imported from Japan. Far up on the hill, on a rain-loved slope, Domenic was lingeringly preparing the crumbling soil for that most delightful of episodes, the late summer beans, which when they were come to full growth shook and shuddered in black shadow over the Chinese earth of Australia—for sometimes the earth there is very Asiatic. Struck full in its brown face by Eastern weather and Oriental summers, it could scarcely be otherwise. And in the hut, on the grassy kangaroo-haunted hill, Billy Creeker's vermilion beans still waited for the return of the sorters, while his green pea crop down below rose in white crests along the furrows. Far over in another paddock he had an extraordinary crop that Samozarro and I had gone over in the winter past, or rather, the early spring. Zarro had sung his two great melodies there, the unforgettable songs in English that he told me he prized with all his heart and soul. One was a thing of fire and fury, beginning,

I meeta you whena the moon shine, dirra Louise.

127

And the other was a thing of strange texture; he sang it *più forte*, and held it to be one of the gems of the English language. It had one solid verse that outsoared all genius, and that verse went thus:

Very well, in the tin for no man!

Sung in a high key and with many florid fragments of music still adhering to it, chanted in the best Neapolitan, that song held one and raised the hopes to heaven. "Very well, in the tin for no man!" I would not ask him what it meant. I dare not. Never should I sully such melody. But I remembered the paddock and the crop because of the song. The remembered fields were therefore ripening with crops and soon, what with peas, and tea, and bean-seed and beanlands, both before and after Christmas, one would be able to make plenty of money. When the earth began to dry and grow warm and deep underfoot, I wrote a poem called "Apostasia".

I take no heed, nor count now, the earth's swift bronzing graces,
For I have left her utterly; yea, alone in her own wide lands.
Fairer to me now, are the fair, false faces
And the clamour of voices and clinging of hands.
And Poetry ... which her voice is ...
Has curdled in my veins.
It's in laughter and song that my choice is
With my hands on the bridle-reins ...
But, earth, I'll return again!

During the long, long springtime, there had been nothing but Italian music and the long roads and my sunburnt arms and hands Australian, and the torrents of flowers all along the foreshore; but now summer was coming, and Peppino grew sad and moody and truly Calabrese with the shadow of heat falling over him.

"By the way," I said to him, "I want you to write out the words of 'Gigolette' for me, *mio caro*. Here is the paper ... pen ... ink. Off you go."

Peppino took hold of them with a frightened stare. "*Mia cara*, I not too good for write songs."

"But you sing this song all day, you know the words. Why not write them?"

"More different to sing a song than to write words," said he.

"Italian must be an extraordinary language, then," I replied. "You can sing it, but you can't write it."

I left him alone; he sat down and struggled with the ink and paper and at the end of an hour and a half had nearly covered a page with Italian of the most Assyrian sort I have ever seen. A language that looked as old as Time, but scarcely Italian as we know it. It seemed to me that he had drawn on depths in himself of almost incredible antiquity, and out of those depths had arisen a dark midnight-blue room, with a large black ebony table standing under a window there; through the window shone a moon as white as Troy; and the corners of the place were crowded with gouts of mercury and slabs of dreadful drug, like big soft stacks of opium, shining gently in the face of the Trojan moon. The room was crowded with tall white-limbed young men, some in armour, like Hector and Paris and Ajax. And they were gathered about the beautiful dancer, Gigolette, who stood on the black table and danced to them there. They bent forward and stared upon her as she danced; and some set fine glass and crystal goblets there at her feet, that she might overturn them with the lightness of the dance, the spilt wine running red from the table of ebony. I looked at the page of old writing and coveted it, a wonderful song, a more wonderful episode, tragic, doom-filled, fraught with the weight of awful Time. What it meant I did not know.

Peppino said desperately, "*Mia cara*, I think I take this over to Panucci and he will write it for me."

But just at this moment came Il Panucci lightly to the door. He wore grey clothes, a grey tweed cap, and carried a finely chased shot-gun.

"Steva," he cried in his high voice, "you got many rabbits here?"

I thought of Omar and that bird in the *Rubáiyát* crying in high piping Pehlevi, for "Wine! Wine! Wine!" Il Panucci spoke in high piping Pehlevi all the time. I had never heard such an extraordinary voice before.

"Rabbits? At twilight, from this door, I often see twenty feeding on the short green grass. But you must wait until twilight."

"I shall play the music if you please," he said calmly, and sat down in front of the gramophone.

"Peppino has just written out the words for me of 'Gigolette' in Italian. I try to read them, but I cannot. If I let you look at them, would you help me to understand them?"

"Yes, I will try."

I brought the page. Panucci looked down on it, and laughed to himself tenderly.

"O Peppino, Peppino," he murmured in Italian, "I have seen spiders write a better Italian than this in the morning."

Peppino smoked moodily and, muttering something about having to attend to the plantation, disappeared up over the hill, and Panucci and I were left to wrestle with his rendering of "Gigolette".

"Steva," said Il Panucci, "I shall correct Peppino's words for the song 'Gigolette'." Pencil in hand, he went over them. "There is an error here, in the commencement. *Guarda, l'errore!* Peppino writes '*suonmanteaciel*' for '*si ammanta il ciel*'. And, *Dio*, the extraordinary length of this last word, written, as you see, '*vadansiancorpermi*'...." He divided the tangle up neatly with strong strokes of the pen. "It is really '*va danza ancor per me*'—'go and dance again for me'. But it is such an old song, this, very difficult to translate. You lose the meaning in translation. Truly, it is possibly as old as Troy. I have read that it had something to do with the Roman occupation of Gaul, for the city of Paris is referred to— '*Parigi è nostra . . . tutta nostra . . . la cittа!*' 'Paris is our . . . all ours . . . the city!' Myself, I think it was first sung in Ilium by the Trojans or the Greeks, with reference to Paris, Prince of Troy, and finally it came to Rome and the soldiers of Caesar sang it to celebrate the taking of Paris."

The heat glaze began to rise and quiver through the room in bronze; the roof drummed with waves of flecked burning iron; the lights on it were like the scales of fish. I glanced round at the beloved brown walls, the tropical roof, and the poetic blue brand on it: LYSAGHT'S QUEEN'S HEAD: SPECIAL FLAT. Every hut in Australia bears this brand. And Spanish paintings, like torn-off shadows of some one's genius, hung about the wall. "*La Baracca*," I said aloud. " '*Los Borrachos*'," said Panucci, "is the name of a painting by Velazquez—'The Wine-drinkers'. Green and rust in it, and thin glasses and round white shoulders. A paddock picture, Steve. *Una pittore della campagna*. But it has not the same meaning as *la baracca*, the barracks or hut."

130

At midday I lit the grey fire on the hearth; it was like setting fire to the earth with poetry. The tea-tree that I brought in had been dried by the hot Australian sun and bleached by the hard Australian rains to silver lightness. The slender, stiff, costly branches bounced on the hearth, and I set the red flame of the match to them, and saw the swift fire run through them with a short crackling roar. I made tea, and Panucci and I dined on boiled eggs and olive oil, of which I kept a good stock. He read the close print of the books, and I wrote while I ate, and in this way it was soon into the magic afternoon. I ran over odd scraps of writing—this, that, the other. When did I write this?

I went out into the night, sad, sick, and walked through the damp grass to the school. I stepped into the schoolroom; I felt the shining, slipping wood of the beloved cabinet beneath my hand. I picked up the grooved records, smelt them, held them, ran my fingers around them. Here, in a black prison, was the loved "*Rêve de Jeunesse*" imprisoned. Oh, I wanted, wanted to hear the violin, wailing, murmuring melodiously my ever recurring trouble.

The Dream of Youth! Alas, what is the dream of youth but to be free, for ever free, for ever young, and for ever engaged in writing of great poetry and prose and in the living of great adventure? Without that dream I shall die.

But it was the day that was dying. The long slow Australian day of learning and of music.

"Steva," exclaimed Panucci suddenly, producing a small red Italian-English dictionary, "why don't you Australian people speak in the language that is written in this book? I showed this book to Mrs Buccaneer, where we were playing music the other night. I said to her, 'If you would only speak as it is written in this dictionary, I should be able to understand you very perfectly.' Like all Australians, she uses too many diminutive *parole*—words. I cannot understand."

"Yes, that's true, Panucci. Your speech approximates the Latin roots in our dictionaries. I listen to you and hear what is really only a superior and more ornate English."

"Now, Steva!" exclaimed Panucci, on fire with genius, and quite imagining that through the agency of the dictionary he had completely caught, trapped, and pinned down for alien use for ever the wily English language. "Now, Steva, let us let the old languages go, and see what we can do with this new *lingua*." Staring fixedly at the all-saving ruby-red volume, he began, as though on the edge of most awful danger, and with rapidly turning pages whirring swiftly through his mind, faster than ever his fingers could turn them to seek the right word, "A-a-a-ah . . . *allora* . . . Steva . . . listen! Give my thoughts consideration, and you will, with delight, I hope, comprehend the totality of my phrases." He flapped the pages over in search of more matter. Turning to me, but buried in the book, he continued, "Now I find the English language intelligible because intimately related to the Italian. If what you tell me is true, why does not the population use the language as written in this *en-cheek-clo-pad-ee-a*?"

I backed away at the sound of that word. "What? Panucci? What?" I felt like getting out of the hut before it was too late.

"The book, Steva, the book. This." He held the title page out to me.

"Oh, encyclopaedia," I said, relieved. I laughed at the quaint insect-like length of the word. "No, it would be too grandiose. The beauty of English lies in its simplicity. Large words are too cumbersome and slow."

"I comprehend. I take this encyclopaedia and tonight when visiting, shall speak from it, and demand that the English person respond from it."

"You'll be knocked out tomorrow, if you do. And don't bring it out at supper-time, or the other fellow will have all the cakes and you won't get any."

But Panucci really was a very serious student, far more than I could ever be, and had little or no time for cakes. How laughable we were, the two students, bending together over the books of grammar in the smoky hut, brushing the flies from our faces and hands as we discovered points of interest and words in common between our languages.

"The flies are very bad," I remarked angrily.

Panucci stared at me. "Steva, what does this mean—The flies are very bad'? *Cattivo*? Wicked? Robbers? *O che cosa*?"

"It means that they are about in too many numbers."

"And is that bad, Steva?"

"No, Panucci . . . it is crook." Sometimes I deserted the lyric tongue of Latium and fell down at ease among the many diminutive *parole* that I had promised faithfully to evade. Panucci, however, was without fatigue.

"Ah, Steva," said he, "*la lingua! Nostra passione mutua!* Inform me, now, in regard to the psychology of the Australian and the cultural movement here."

He sounded like those little camera-laden Japanese officers who used to wander up and down the Block in Melbourne, in the days when I worked at a commercial-art studio there. Groups of them would follow and photograph, most politely, the beautiful Melbourne girls against that entrancingly lovely background of spring golden wattle, boronia from Fern Tree Gully, and daphne from Berwick or Cranbourne—those charmingly polite and subtle olive-skinned Japanese officers, with the sense of their large, dangerous, explosive fleet behind them in the sea-road, beflagged, signalling to all nations and heaven, on mysterious mission to Australia; and beyond, rising up within them and within me, their old and strange and awful nation, their teeming millions living, threatening, and their teeming billions dead, their divine ancestors, and repellant and cold and like chilling shadows, their Emperor-God, the Son of Heaven.

But now, from the Block to the bush, from the commercial-art studio to the tea-plantation, the cuckoo called me back with the mellow peal of its long, long notes, ending in a soft, shattering fountain of scorn, the mixture of melancholy and scorn that was so sweet to a native heart.

"When we come to Australia," Panucci went on, "the only book we can get hold of except *Il Popolo d'Italia*, the local newspaper, is *La Piccola Guida*. A dreadful volume. Here it is." The unfortunate dragged it forth, and recited its content or discontent. " 'I have a large family. Give me work. I am honest. I had a headache. I have influennaz . . .' "

"Alas, Panucci, I have seen too many of these pitfalls in literature."

"They are *inutili*, Steva! No reference is made such as, 'I have a mind; I have an intellect; I possess a strong passion for music and art and literature'," complained Panucci. "Ignorance of languages

133

resembles the different heats in different latitudes—the small difference makes one race black, another white. Through our ignorance of English, we Italians are, as it were, aboriginal to you, and you are anthropophagi to us . . ."

"If I had to speak Italian daily I, too, should get rather dark. To my mind, English clears the brain, whereas, Italian chokes it up."

We drank black coffee and smoked cigarettes. I dragged more yellow paper out of my desk and found a poem I had begun to a tree, a sapling that had grown in front of our old home in Walker Street, Dandenong. I thought of that little house, like broken Japanese jade, lying under the white and odorous and over-rich wings of fifteen towering plum-trees. The wide vermilion yard about it was set in bricks of a jewel-like rubiness, of fierce purples and stream greens and river browns. From the purple jacaranda-haunted garden across the road, from the deep ferny coolness there, came incessantly and painfully, at the rising of the summer sun every morning, the loud clamorous throaty Persian cry of the blue peacock. Hour-long its strident voice rose in warning over the secret wall about the great house. The blue peacock! The jewel-crowned, brilliant-headed peacock, crying day-long, "That jackeroo . . . that jackeroo . . . that jackeroo!"

This great voice split vision from the sun, and one saw white miles of dry station grass; a long, long fence of split hardwood that stretched for miles; a small boundary-rider's hut in the corner under a quandong-tree, with its red lanterns burning. There, lithely swinging as his horse swung under him, nervous and tumultuous with the heat of the wide brown western plains, before the peacock's eyes rode the lost young jackeroo. A brown young man, who'd lost his English fair skin, but not altogether his sense of being English. We often spoke of him at home, and wondered if he lived.

"Hear that peacock today, Steve," my mother used to say to me. "Heavens, doesn't it ring through your brain? Hour after hour—'That jackeroo! That jackeroo!'"

And, busy in the writing of poetry, I would return, "I wish to goodness they'd find him, or that he'd turn up, and the peacock would stop!" I said to her one day, "Was there ever a jackeroo lost

134

on any of the stations we were on? Or did ever a rich young Englishman come? I was so young, I don't remember."

"Well," said my mother reminiscently, "oddly enough, there *was* a rich young Englishman on one of the stations. I can't think of his name. The Honourable Someone-or-other—I forget now. Anyway, a young girl came to stay there, very beautiful, but moody and spoilt. She and the Englishman disliked each other at once. They argued and squabbled incessantly. And the weather was dreadful. Frightfully hot. One afternoon, when everyone had retired for a siesta, the young man came walking down the corridor—it was a long, airy, cool red-carpeted corridor, right through the big homestead—and as he passed the girl's door she came out, and she had a small revolver in her hand. And she shot the young man, and he fell down on the red carpet with a bullet in him."

"Heaven!"

"What a to-do there was! She said it had gone off accidentally. They took the Englishman to hospital, and he recovered. I don't know what became of him afterwards. I wish I could remember his name. I will some day."

But she never did. She died without remembering it, and I am still in the dark as to who was the jackeroo, and who was the mysterious Englishman. But whenever I remember the old house in Walker Street I remember them also, with the writhing-limbed woodbine at the gate, and the wide coarse Egyptian flax on which I printed the story of a journey to Mecca by a small and poet-haunted man centuries ago. It was before this gate that I used to stand, summer after summer, chanting with the modern English poets:

"Lord Rameses of Egypt sighed
  Because a summer evening passed . . ."

and

"Roses are beauty, but I never see
  Those blood drops from the burning heart of June
  Glowing like thought upon the living tree . . ."

Our roof was loaded with golden roses; perfumes that would have broken the heart of the world hid robber-like in the many

135

petals. Mauve lilac bloomed under. But alone, in the front of the house, stood a day-white, night-black sapling that rustled in leafy Greek down the blue night. This was the tree I had written of in the unfinished poem that I now read over in the Gippsland hut.

> In the days before you were tall, young tree;
> Before your black head was crowned,
> Years ere my tears ran hot from me,
> Aeons ere my head was downed . . .
> I saw the wind touch you, before it touched me,
> And we both responded with sound.
> I smelt a black ship and the soak of a sea,
> I saw a white foam on the ground . . .

I wrote steadily, while the last of the afternoon surged slowly along, and while Il Panucci read and listened to Caruso.

The day was done. Grey shadows had come now into the hut, and the dust of the continent that I loved shivered and shuddered across the floor. The long day that I had wished might last for ever, the day of poetry, the dream of youth, the million-textured things that filled the air and could not be said. The brown earth breathed the sun back into the faces of the coming stars. It was almost evening.

A winter's coldness came into the hour; Panucci stood facing the tan walls, reading my lightly printed poems there. In the twilight I stood with him, too, reading, while above a rosy, pearly quivering glow made an intoxicating half-light of the heavens, from the blue-heaving, trembling, and voluptuous sea, to the curved and dry-grassed earth. . . .

A medieval poem, this, or perhaps it might have been written by some young Roman or Greek soldier who had come over to Britain with the armies of the imperial Caesars.

GRAVE'S FRINGE

> Alas, to be grown over by the grasses
> Of many a Lover's grave . . . to lie limb-twisted,
> In bramblie pits, a-mouldering unwisted
> By any, save the wild bird as she passes.
> Between the kissing knees a gaunt spear leaning

Heavily on the brow that August's greening.
 'Tis the mortal end of Youth . . . poor Youth, expending
His meagre hours from winter unto spring,
Remembering all his days, and never ending,
Withouten pain in the remembering.
 Alas, to watch the moon at noon come hither
And go . . . without a fragile name to give her.
Nor any little song to recompense
The bitter loss of brief magnificence.
Dreaming of naught but sobs, and with sobs shaking
The crimson budders to an early waking.

"This poem is like Italy of the Renaissance," remarked Panucci.

"No, it is English, very early English."

"And this?" moving towards the poem "Niobe".

"This Greek!" I stood by the door in the half-light, looking up the dark-green gully. Panucci moved over towards the door, and leant against it. Over his shoulder one could see the tall white trees, with charcoal scars on their sides. The split silken wood gave out weather odours when the days were hot. The branches shook with a heavy feeling in the blue air, dead-white huge hands, sensitive, soft, belonging to some race as old as the earth.

"Steva," cried Panucci to me with a lightning look, "*tu sei una diva!*"

"A goddess? I? Ah, no, I should fear to be a goddess."

"Then . . . a god!" cried Panucci.

"Panucci, I should not like to be a god. For gods suffer, and I, I do not like suffering. But if such were my unhappy fate, I should like to be Pan, who lived in a little hut, with a pot of herbs and a hunting dog and a heap of ancient jewels to keep him company. *Your* name Panucci, *mio caro*," I said suddenly. "What does it mean?"

Panucci laughed, and said, "You will never believe. It is so apropos. It means this—*Pan*, the wood-god Pan, and *ucci*, a contracted form of *Uccilegon*, or Trojan. Or precisely, 'Pan-Trojan' or 'Trojan-Pan'."

"What a strange coincidence!"

"*Si.* My family, the Panucci, or Panuccilegon, are supposed to have come from Troy in the beginning, a very old family."

"I think you are very Greek to look at, with that fine delicate faun face of yours, Panucci, and yet Roman, too."

It was now growing dark about the hut.

"Ah, here are the rabbits!" exclaimed Panucci. "*Silenzio!*" He crept to the door and stood there. The rabbits, about twenty of them, in a thick furry mob, stopped feeding. Panucci remained perfectly still. Raising his gun slowly, he aimed it steadily at the rabbits, who showed to him, amusingly enough, one frozen, statue-bronze curved thigh apiece, as though they wished to convey to him the fact that they, too, were Greek. Panucci fired twice. The rabbits fled. None were slain. I laughed.

"Steva," said Panucci again, "you, *davvero*, a god. The god of rabbits. Next springtime I promise to meet you here in Gippsland and dictate to you a book, telling all about your life as a god in ancient Italy."

"Steva is the name of a saint, not a god," I said.

Panucci said lightly, "*Buona notte.*"

"Or in English," I said happily, "notta bunnie!"

"*Davvero!*"

He departed with the *en-cheek-clo-pad-ee-a*, to speak from it verbatim in the longest words procurable, and so astonish the natives of the village with his profound English. And I returned to the lonely hut again, to brew more black coffee with golden foam on it, and to read and write until it was time to go to bed. A rattling, scaly, writhing noise along the rafters assured me that I had plenty of company in the way of a large black snake, which had been drawn to the place by the sound of music and loud voices. The Australian black snake cannot resist music.

Next day was Sunday, lovely, blissful, blessed, excitable bush Sunday. A strange blue deadness like a long stratum of ossified mind hanging over it in the afternoon. I sat writing to my mother.

Cara mia madre,

It is Sunday, as you will note by the dust lying heavily on the page of this letter; dust lies more heavily on Sunday than on any other day. All yesterday and a quarter of today I have been searching through old books and papers, rattling about in the bins of love tales and romances. The best book of the million was *The Princess of Ultima Thule*, and it came from the

138

Mechanics' Institute in Haunted Stream. How on earth it managed to get up here to anywhere near me, I cannot imagine. Not entirely unexpected, however, do you know? For so many years I've listened to your most fascinating stories of the old days at Haunted Stream, that mysterious gold-mining town, that I feel with my patient listening and embellishing of your tales I've drawn this dearly loved book to me. Haunted Stream! If only you knew, or could guess, or feel, what that name means to me! A strong sad stroke of sorrow and desolation arises in me at the name, and I shudder, I know not why. I see it now as it stood in the eighties, in the light of the moon. The wide white road, faintly yellowed at night, deeply carved by day, with dark bush on either side, and the wide-roofed Mechanics' Institute standing at the side of the road. A desolate spot, God knows. A few houses scattered about, and up the road, the store, and down the road, the boarding-house. Haunted Stream. A haunted village, the place of the lost, the town of ghosts.

Yes, if one could go back forty years tonight and stand in the bright lights of the Mechanics' Institute at Haunted Stream, and see Montague, the dashing Englishman, again. With what grace he crosses his legs at the piano; with what an air of devilry he pushes the boxer back from the brow, Haunted Stream's noblest brow, and after a few careless racy trills, settles down to a steady hour or two of playing.

The readers are flipping over and over the weekly paper's pages; the dancers are slipping and gyrating about the floor— the institute being a mixture of library and dance-hall, card-room and all else. The ladies are preparing a fascinating supper in that charming wooded spot known as "the ante-room". If only I had courage I should ride down to Haunted Stream, or up to Haunted Stream, and go by sad familiar ways there and mourn for the past. The eyes itch for the mixed and radiant colours of the romantic. No, not the romantic, the excitable. A bushranger . . . a runaway train. . . . No, not even that. No, no. A good dinner. There, dash it, I've sneezed twice and blown my eyebrows off into the next paddock.

I got the bullets for my new rifle. To shoot out of your own new rifle is wonderful, proud, magnificent. I never fire at anything but targets, but the great thunderous explosion at my ear,

139

and the recoil of the gun as it goes off, and the jagged star that rips its way into the tin of the target, gladden the heart. And then those very beautiful and precise mathematics entered into when target-shooting over large sheets of water or across lake undulations. I am writing with a sea-gull's quill, broke my pen on a mosquito's shin a month ago. The flowers along the foreshore are dying now. In spring the earth there expressed its mood in white clematis and soft purple abundance of some flower I do not know. I shall keep the volume called *The Princess of Ultima Thule* until I come home again. That which was silver once in Haunted Stream shall surely be gold in Dandenong. By the way, Haunted Stream's true name as a township is Sterling. I suppose you knew that? I have often wondered if there are any silver mines there, or possibly new and precious metals bearing strange names, to charm men.

An Australian thrush, delicately grey with an English seventeenth-century greyness, clear and smooth, and dark streaks like the strokes from the charcoal of an artist of genius across his side, landed on the roof, casting behind him a great wall of leaf and dark shower, and in a voice exactly like Caruso's sang with a note of the most awful and impressive richness a long stave of song. Such singing I have never heard before, nor have I heard it since. How he had come by this magic note I did not know. One would truly have imagined that my poem "A Vision of Clouds" had been true, and that directly above me lived Greek heroes and warriors, gods who had the power, and the goodness now and then, to rain down their great minds in incidents of power and beauty, and to put into the throats of birds such as these melodies and ballads of the most glorious beauty. Like the family in the fairytale, I ran outside to see this magic bird, but it fled at the sight of me, and I heard it singing far up the gully.

Damask-cheeked, faintly whiskered, after a late night of playing music to the Australians, Panucci came to my hut at noon. When he took off his cap his hair looked moist and black, and a sweet smell came from it. He sat with me on the seat before the fire and stretched his long legs in their neat trousers and socks and shoes out in front of him.

"Here is your book. It is not *utile*, Steva. I took it out, and said to them, 'Here, why do you not speak the language in this book? Then I will comprehend.' But they said it was not *utile*, too difficult. *Inutile . . . troppo difficile*."

"I told you they'd say that. Don't you remember?" I replied.

"In the night . . . no matter about the book and the language . . . in the night I remembered a Neapolitan song. I wish I could hear it today."

"What is the name?"

" '*Cor' Ingrato*' . . . 'Ungrateful Heart'. Ah Steva, when I was a soldier in Italy, I was transferred with my regimento to Naples. Steva!" he buried his head in his hands. "Ah, the dialect of that city, *caro dialetto di' Napuli*. If a girl spoke to you, so expressive and sad were her words, that you must cry. And when the tears came into your eyes, she said to you, '*Comme quannere?*' Not the pure Italian, '*Perchè piangere?*'—'Why do you cry?' You see? But such a delicious distortion of it, '*Comme . . . comm-mme,*' " he murmured softly, " '*Comm-mme quannere?*' The streets of Naples are long, miles long, and filled like a circus with colour, cripples, books, song-writers, and musicians. With bootblacks and tumblers, with jewellers and freaks. It would take one day to walk along a street. One entire day. For at the beginning you must have your shoes cleaned. And if you refused? The bootblacks of Naples are cunning. They will spit cigarette tobacco on your shoes as you pass; *per forza*, one must have the shoes cleaned, then. Beside you stands the song-writer. 'Tell me truly, *signor capitano,*' he says, 'what is the name of your *amore*?' Ah, but Steva, in *dolce Napulitanesi*—oh, the sweet tongue of Naples! He says——" and Panucci murmured in his hurried remembering and was in an unsharable and profound ecstasy—" '*Dimme, di verita, il nome del' tuo amore, signor capitano!*' Even if you are a serious man and have no lover, you can say, 'Beatrice', and anyhow that will gain you the most splendid song. Yes, in a few moments he has made the song, written the music through it, and hands it to you, singing it, and playing it on the mandolin. *Ah, Napule . . . ah, come bella . . . come bella!*"

"And this song?"

"*Che canzone?* Which song?"

" '*Cor' Ingrato*.' "

"Ah, *'Cor' Ingrato'*! Yes, Enrico Caruso sings this, like no one else in the world. Give me paper, pen, ink. I shall write the words in the dialect of Naples and show you the difference, the sense of ruin in it, as compared with pure Italian."

He wrote rapidly in a strong, upright hand, each word ending with a back-curled tail, like the sting of the scorpion recoiling over its spine.

"And what do the words mean in English, Panucci?" I asked when he had finished.

"I tell you . . ." And the telling took all afternoon; it was more like a problem in Euclid than a love song, and was explained by words scrawled on the walls and diagrams drawn on the dust of the floor. For it took us back to Dante and down to India and Egypt where the gipsies come from. At last it was written out in English, the song, "Ungrateful Heart", to the woman, Catari.

> *Catari . . . Catari . . . why do you talk love words to me?*
> *Why do you speak in my heart?*
> *You torment me, Catari!*
> *Don't you forget that I gave you my heart, Catari.*
> *Don't you forget.*
>
> *Catari . . . Catari . . . you are a true gipsy.*
> *You have for all a spasm of love.*
> *You torment me; look at my life.*
> *My blood is wasted; you stay, a far-away love,*
> *Heart, ungrateful heart . . .*
> *You torment my life.*
> *All the past can return no more.*

The song fell on my mind and hurt me. I stared at Panucci with his fine features, great brown eyes and flushed face, singing it before me. And I loved Naples. There was no spiritual freshness about the song; it could not manage to get outside love, but it had a sadness, the eternal sadness of Latin love. For all the women in Latin love songs are false. And so coldly and terrifically cruel. And it is always, inescapably, in the street, out on the pavements, their love. In practically every Latin love song that I have heard the man stands in the grey and naked street, face to face with his love.

And in the harsh face of the day she repudiates him. Then he sings—old songs, terribly old. All pulsing with words like "blood" and "heart", "my life", "waste"—love. Yes, faintly butcher-like, fleshy and sensual. But it was not to any woman that Panucci spoke, but to a city, to his Naples. Why must the flesh be in all Italian love songs? And why such frightfully false women? There was no sense of

> *I did but see her passing by,*
> *And yet I love her till I die.*

Twilight fell on the grass, and Peppino trod over her sweet-smelling body. Panucci gave us good night, and went sedately away, humming, "Catari . . ."

And Peppino sat down, and drawing my head against his broad breast sang to me in his full rich voice:

> *"Piccolo, amore, piccola mia primavera . . ."*
> ("My little love, my little springtime . . .")

A song I loved dearly. In the darkness I said, "Peppino, tell me a fairytale."

"What is that? *Che cosa è?*"

"Well, a *romanza d' una sirena*. Yet *sirena* is an awful word for a fairy."

"Ah, you mean *fata*."

"I don't like that. It's too heavy and Eastern. Let us have the awful wet *sirena*, then."

Peppino tore his hair out silently and sweated in the effort to think of a fairytale.

"A long time ago there was a village. In that village there was *a fontana*, called Fontechiara."

"The clear fountain?"

"*Si*. All the *ragazze* wash their clothes in this Fontechiara; all day, with soap and scrubbing brush, they work at this fountain. They sing like nightingales and drink wine and laugh, and the water runs in long streams out of the fountain. One young man, *un pittore*, a painter, came sometimes to this *fontana* to wash his dress. He came by moonlight to wash, and when he stood by the

143

fontana to make his dress clean, up from the water leapt a great *sirena*, all young, with red hair and a red mouth."

"A grey *sirena?*"

"Grey-bodied like marble or a statue. She caught the *pittore* by the hand and pulled him down into the deep *fontana* with her. But he screamed, and all the people of the village ran out and pulled him out of the water and out of the hands of the *sirena*. And he was sick for a long, long time."

"And so, *addio alla sirena*."

"*Sì*. No more *romanza di sirena* . . . too much trouble in my head for tell." And Peppino breathed heavily and stared at the troubled whiteness of a patch of moonlight just inside the door.

The moon costs nothing, at first glance; but she is most costly, in the end, to youth, to lovers. She is, in fact, the dearest and the most distorting light in the world. What I looked like to Peppino, and what Peppino looked like to me, was dictated by the moon.

"Peppino, tonight you look so beautiful . . ."

"*E tu, Steva, tu sei gloriosa*."

"I have never seen such curls, and your eyes glitter back there in the dark. Now that you are leaning your head against the wall and out of the moonlight, I cannot see your face at all. So it appears that you have no flesh, and that you are the eyes of the universe, soft and beseeching . . . beseeching life for what?"

His long slender white hands shone in the night.

"That murderous Australian moon! Surely the Italian moon is not like it.

"*And this same moon that stared in Caesar's eyes* . . ."

Sick with the white, long, silent gaze of the moon, we stood at the dark door. A flood of yellowness glowed like fire and lava in my mind; where did it come from; what did it portend? I saw a dark wood, small leaves, sharp and dry, and unknown images surrounded slowly that dry yellow fire, and I shuddered and was glad to see Peppino go. In the cold rough bed among harsh blankets I slept all night, gladly by myself. And in the morning the sun, he and I, the light from my face shining into the light from his . . . and like old friends, the bracken outside by the door, now very tall; last night had made it grow, I thought. It had lost the furry boots of youth and was furrowed with ribbed lines of leather. I lit the fire, drank cocoa, and ate cakes.

Then, while the night was still clear in my mind, I wrote, "How can my heart be faithful, my spirit unfaltering to this lost Grail? Italy, I desire you! How may I take the Famagustan boats of iron and come at last to you, *O Italia verde?*"

From the dead tree outside the hut, the naked steely laugh of the kookaburra, enormous, shouting, and supernatural, poured, wave upon wave, echo upon echo . . . the day bulging and bursting in the throat of the bird, and sweeping upon me pitilessly.

Through it, I was writing rapidly, "Why cannot I take ship and go to Italia? My hot blood is in my lips . . ."

"*Acka . . . acka . . . acka . . .*" rang the laugh.

"The past has never been . . . has faded . . . become blotted . . . unwanted . . ."

"*Hoo-hoo-acka . . . acka . . . acka . . .*"

"The one true light, the quasi-spiritual love, the fair-haired youth of my own country, is a cold thought to dwell on, impenetrable as his own Black Mountain . . ."

"*Quarr . . . quarr . . . acka . . . hoo-hoo-acka . . . quarr . . . quarr . . .*"

"Italy . . . *Italia* . . . the loved territory of your face; there is a place on your green *campagna* that I know, a pressure keen, strong and articulate. My blood wastes, wastes, wastes, as it will always be wasted. There will be other countries, but only one *Italia.*"

I threw myself down on my bunk. The cool mattress was filled with coconut fibre; I pulled strands of it languidly out of a hole that ran down the stripes, and wondered why Jim McLachlan didn't put in a big patch of coconuts, and go in for copra. He had some palms up at the house, and made a few jars of coconut oil out of the copra obtained from the nuts. His Chinese cook put a couple of drops of this into pancake and cake mixtures, and the taste was unforgettable, I thought.

But from the bunk, all that the eyes, yearning for cold green things, could see was . . .

> *Only the harsh brown bracken shaking*
> *Under the weight of the sun;*

Only the dry earth crackling and breaking
As though earth and man were one.

It was a dry and brilliant day, that on which I went into Bairnsdale in the *J. C. Dahlsen* to see the Clerk of Courts. Jim McLachlan had departed for Melbourne, and had asked me to undertake the trip to settle some matter of business for him. All along the lake the dry white grass blew into the purple-blue water, and the ghosts of Ultima Thule arose in me, and cast their spears of glittering bronze along the shore, crying out the name of that place sought by poets and sad heroes, Ultima Thule.

"Ultima Thule . . . thulamus . . . thulamus . . . the last marriage chamber," said the tall slant-eyed stoker to me, knotting his piece of cotton waste round his throat, like the scarf of an Oxford blue. "The last marriage chamber. These two lovers, lost and flying before all men, as before the hurricane, the whirlwind, and finding in the copper Celtic isles their resting place, in the bleached isles of the Hebrides, the places of the dead white rushes, and the broken bleached and canting Viking ships—Thule, Ultima Thule. All men have sought, hound-like, to run to earth these two golden foxes. Why? I do not know."

The tall stoker, whose name was Heydon, had been for years up in Roebuck Bay, near Darwin, with pearling luggers and shark fleets, and had worked with Kingsford Smith, the great aviator, the imperishably glorious. Heydon knew all the things that men on pearling luggers should know, and was a veritable art gallery with his hundreds of pictures of the Northern Territory and its coast.

But still along the bleached reedy shore stood the snowy pelican and the slender silken screen crane, immobile waders in the blue floods of these Chinese smeared lakes. In Bairnsdale, down by the Mitchell River, I found the Court dreaming among the leaves, and in the time-haunted room that had a ghostly carpet of chalk on its wooden floors the Clerk of the Courts rang up Mr Dunbar, who had once been a business associate of Jim McLachlan's in the tea line. And he came bustling down, a jovial-looking short man with a great sense of the Levant about him.

"And how's Jim getting along down there?" he said. "Still pulling up the bushes and running them through the hoppers as he used to do? Tell him not to put so much aniline in it. McLachlan is a terror for loading tea, isn't he?"

I said he was.

"And what do you do?"

"Oh, I help around the place generally, you know."

"I suppose you pull up the bushes with Jim, too?" said Mr Dunbar. "The last packet he sent me, or rather the last box, left leaves in the tea-pot half an inch across, and one stem was about a quarter of an inch around. I suppose you make chicory out of the roots of the bushes."

"We make everything short of wages out of the bushes, Mr Dunbar."

"That's McLachlan for you. And where's this affidavit he wants signing, and what's it about? I though Mr Campbell could attend to that."

"I thought I ought to get you to witness it, Mr Dunbar," said Mr Campbell. "I heard that you were up in Omeo on a similar business . . ."

"Yes, quite right, came down relevant to the Spicer case." He signed his name boldly. "Like witnessing my own signature as writer of affidavits. Oh, it's nothing. Charmed and pleased to be able to help any of the Davidsons. You're one of the Davidsons, aren't you? Thought so. And of course, one just *has* to help McLachlan. Good afternoon."

And Mr Dunbar, who was utterly of the eighties, and hadn't altered in his way since those gay days, dashed off.

I caught the *Gippsland* home, and became acquainted with the mate of the S.S. *Burrabogie*. This redoubtable and romantic vessel was known to us as "Old Three Sticks". She always stood far out, preferring a straight blue sea-road that was absolutely stiff with tide of some sort; the S.S. *Burrabogie* had the air of a boat that preferred roads to seas. She was long, and a bright brown, and an inextricable mass of square boxy-looking hatches fore and aft gave her the look of a furniture shop. Three shining tan sticks shooting straight up in the air from her mysterious deck gave her her nickname. She carried tea, wattle-bark, hides, fish, sunflower seed, peanuts, oil and sealed oil-gas, and rock petroleum—all the fruits of our local industry, for our district was rich in oil bores, and we had them spouting shale-oil and petroleum from every pore, with

147

an attendant mass of bore-gas which was useful when canned. I envied, therefore, the mate of the *Burrabogie*, and told him so. I told him what a romantic ship she was to me, and how I longed to know her crew and her captain.

"What's the captain like?" I said.

"Ah, he's a real character."

In a dreaming voice, as if the old cargo-boat had been a glass of wine, the smell of which held him drunken while he talked, he said, "Yes, you should come with us next week to Sale and back, with wattle-bark. As you say, it's a strange old boat."

"I knew that."

"Well, the captain . . . he's odd, you know. He ought never to have been a seaman, that man. He won't wear a cap, you see, not the sort of cap that they usually wear on board, a regulation officer's cap." He paused to enjoy my wonder, and slipping his fat hand under his belt, lifted it up and down across his stomach.

"And what does he wear, if he doesn't wear a captain's cap?"

"A bowler. Yes, always a bowler hat; running round on the deck, giving orders or at the wheel, he always wears that bowler hat. When we come in sight of land, or port rather, he runs below and puts on his braided cap—that's for ports of call. He explains it to us like this, that the *Burrabogie* is a sort of business, not a ship. She is only a ship when she calls at ports. And he is only a captain then. Other times, he's a business-man, and so he wears the bowler hat."

"Well, at a distance, you know, the *Burrabogie* does look like a very busy store, and then at other times it looks like a very dead store. Nothing doing. You carry a lot of sugar from Maffra, don't you?"

"Oh yes, and tea from down Calulu way, and around here, and hides and tallow and oil and all sorts."

"Well, I suppose its mixed cargo makes him think it's more of a business than a ship. But she looks great standing far out, silent and tan and tenuous, with a strange hint of having something to do with Joseph Conrad. There's such a fragility about her; and then, being long and low, she's got an islandish appearance."

The mate looked at the water luxuriously, with a green thickness in his eyes. They sparkled in the black hollows of his eyelids, and his full lips smiled dreamily.

"Yes, she's a great old boat, the *Burrabogie*. Sometimes the captain sings old songs. Sea songs. I'm the mate, of course. There's only the rest of the crew, and they're always coming and going. We move along slowly, you know. Up and down the lakes and rivers—you ought to come with us, and watch the captain wear his hat out, and run up and down changing from bowler to braid."

"I will, one day," I said. And the wind moved the thin spars of the *Gippsland* above and the horizon retreated in lilac mist; the dredge lumbered by, belching black smoke; pelicans stirred on their little lonely lands and all the blue of the lake and the sky was in my blood. "Ah," I thought, "why cannot I live for ever?"

The mate of the *Gippsland* came along for'ard. "Y' see this chap you're talking to? He never works."

The mate of the *Burrabogie* grinned pleasantly, and his green eyes shone. He stared across to the pelican-white shore, to the purple oil of the sea, to the wine-brown wind that drifted inshore.

"No, he never works. He just hangs around on that old lugger of his and never does a tap. He and the captain are tarred with the same brush. Neither of them like work."

"But he's colourful, there's something about him. He doesn't need to work. And if his captain wears a bowler hat, then why should either work? Their ship is fantasy and their life fantastic, too."

The mate of the *Burrabogie* said, "Oh, I work now and again. I just hang around and think, though, most of the time. I often wonder what the name 'Burrabogie' means. It's aboriginal. Sometimes the captain puts a tent up on deck and sleeps in it at night," he said airily.

We had left the river mouth and were travelling fast across deep blue-brown water of an Asiatic tint to Cunningham, where we were to pick up a small cargo of guano and nacre. Cunningham was an ideal place for such stuff, and another man up from the islands, having settled there, like Jim McLachlan, kept up the old island tradition. Seagulls in their thousands, and as many pelicans and swans and ducks of all sorts to match, kept this guano-gatherer busy all year, and there was enough shell about to use as a form of nacre. The guano was loaded down into the hold, nearly choking us all with its cutting white dust. The mates tied thick black silk handkerchiefs round their mouths, and warned

149

the passengers down below. Me they allowed to stay up on deck, masked, while the treated guano poured down in its diabolical whiteness. I thought to myself, and I said to the mate of the *Burrabogie*, "Guano's one thing I wouldn't touch."

"Ah, you get used to it," said the mate.

The mate of the *Burrabogie* influenced me strongly. Do you know, when I looked into the delicate chipped mirror hanging up in my hut next day I saw how animated I was by his spirit? I remembered his eyes, shining like green water far down in the dark pits of his eyelids, and his lips curled lovingly about every word he spoke. His lazy stare was restful, but he looked with the sharpness of light into one's eyes and lips as he spoke. And his body was bulky with the ponderous travel of the *Burrabogie*, and light and dark like those remote thick water growths over whose wavering bodies the boat passed, rippling, day and night. A thick green-eyed growth of the sea. Yet I liked the man. Not every man can look at another as he could, with that dangerous, frank, affectionate stare which cannot stop at the natural barrier of the eyes, but threatens to pour over and over wherever it lands. I was aware of him, because he was aware of himself. A man actively working forgets his starving sensuality and creates about himself an air of clean absorption. Not so with our mate. He rarely worked. Yet he fascinated. All idlers do. For an hour my receptive mind felt as his felt; my life throbbed as keenly as his. For the years of the *Burrabogie*, its long telling years, went on within the mate of the ship.

THE CRIMSON CAMELLIAS

V

ONE November day Panucci and I sat together again in the baracca. Down near the faded blue of the lake, in the hot, dusty earth, the tea-plants with their sharp, serrated leaves spread and darkened. They would be ready for the main pick-over in January, the hottest month of the year, but Panucci and the rest were going over them from time to time. The wide plain-edged Japanese variety, with its dark-green faintly rubbery leaf and stem, was doing very well in this alien earth; at evening after rain a very beautiful perfume arose from it, and something very interesting in the way of blend was expected from it.

The heat in this early November weather was terrific. On a red-hot axe-head outside on the burning earth, Panucci and I fried two eggs, and saw, with concern, a number of small birds falling from the dead trees, faint with heat. But this torridity aroused in me only the most enormous love of Australia. I liked her to blaze with dreadful blind heat and smash down most awful rays of light on to me. The great continent is at her dramatic best in hot weather. Inside the baracca the walls cracked and buckled with pent thunder, and there was not a breath of air. The shade of the hut was like widths of deep-brown crumbling irritating earth, and warm, living, sweating limbs of bushes and trees of all sorts added to the humidity about us. We took our axe-fried eggs within and ate them, laughing, with sauce and oil and green salad.

"*Experimentia docet,*" we said.

The memory of that hut! The poem-saturated place, the golden walls and the dark, the Grecian tea-tree marsh just behind it, with one white topee swirling day and night in all weathers, on a short broken staff of tea-tree. I loved the look of that topee. It was an idol, a god, to me—the great god of the British Empire. I remember the day I set it there.

"Here's another topee for you, Steve," Jim had said, handing over a large white specimen of the sort beloved of Gordon in the Sudan, the British Empire in India, and Secret Service men in the East. "This was a swanky helmet once. I bought it down in the islands and used to wear it there. It was much admired, but tropical mildew set in. See if you can whiten it. Sun and air might do something for it."

So I took it home and, going out into the dark, cool, poem-coloured marsh, I broke down with a burst of sap and a yellow splitting splendour of torn wood and papyrus bark a thick young tea-tree, and on the snapped and bristling end I set "the dragon white, the luminous, the serpent-haunted" topee, to whirl like the turban of the preacher, Ecclesiastes, morn, noon and night, among the purple and white frozen tongues and furry hides of the wild violets. The ancient days gradually washed it white, and the sun and the moon and the wind gave it a grandeur inexpressible. And this solar helmet spinning and flying on its living axis, gave to my days a gubernatorial nobility, and a strong sense of the mighty and omnipotent people to whom I belonged. To me the British race had never seemed so great, so rich and strong and chivalrous, as in that year. The white topee was the eternal symbol of the white man as it swung back and forth under the Australian sun, and coldly and most lonely under the Aurora Australis, the pink and subtly thunderous Aurora Australis, and the blanched craters of the slow-moving moon.

In the hot hut Panucci jawed away in Italian in his absent-minded, flickering-eyed, studious fashion, and I took one of the four rifles down from the wall and began to run the cleaner, soaked with oil, through the barrel, and rub up the silver tip on the fore and rear sights. And I took out my boxes of bullets and counted them, and refilled my belt, in case we decided to go shooting in the early evening. Books on Greek and Roman mythology lay scattered about the room, and large sheets of paper on which Panucci wrote out arias from the operas and old folksongs for his own peculiar pleasure rather than mine. He loved them so ardently that one sensed he could have comfortably sat for days writing them out. He made a list of records that he insisted I should buy.

"What?" I said, staring down at it. " 'La Vita è un Inferno'? 'Life is a Hell of Unhappiness'? Ah, I must have that one, Panucci *mio*."

"*Si, la vita è un inferno all' infelice*," answered Panucci. "What else is it but that? I do not like life, but I love music."

"On Monday, Panucci," I said, "I am riding into Bairnsdale. The Wilsons at Lucknow have written asking me to stay. Perhaps I might be able to buy some records in Bairnsdale, and bring them back with me."

"Steva," shrieked Panucci with all the enthusiasm in the world, "do please buy some records. You see this list I have made for you? Take it with you! And, Steva, do not stay very long, but come back, *presto . . . subito!*" Had he been able to do so, he would have packed me off, there and then to Bairnsdale to buy the arias and be back before nightfall.

While he studied his music and listened to Caruso I took out a fine sheet of soft paper and began to write on it a poem to "*Los Borrachos*", the painting by Velazquez. And what was there that was Spanish here? Only the dry ground, and two or three of those bony horses that always seem to me to be the Spanish kings as they meander, foreleg thrust forth, long sea-crested manes quivering to right and left as they feed, with the delicate geometry of the brown starved hip-bone square against all skies. I wrote my poem and read it over. Then I gave it to Panucci to read. "*Il vero Espagnolo*," he said. The true Spanish? It wasn't, but I longed to write it out in the free and easy Spanish written hundreds of years ago.

LOS BORRACHOS

O golden drinkers underneath the vine,
A soft dark matron with a dusky brood,
Youths and old men, who smell of Spanish wine,
Whose lips are drowsed and reddened by its blood.
In bright cool water from this earthen jar
I drink to the deity who, underneath the bough,
Sits with the gaze of one who sees afar
A wilder wine, the while upon the brow
Of a kneeling youth he binds the vine's soft hands
And takes unto himself the worship of those two
Who stare into his face. An old man stands
Respectfully beyond, and as he doffs

155

His wide black hat obscures himself in awe;
His old friend at his lowly gesture scoffs,
And pours wet purple on the earth's dry floor.
And see, beside him, one with icy hair,
Whose saffron mantle grows on him like grass,
Holds to the god a glass of golden air,
Through which the bubbles like small planets pass.
And there are two who sit with genial eyes
Beside the god, and with old roguery
Neglect the god and bowl and Spanish skies
And through the aeons wish to look on me.
And where are these? And whence has gone their toil?
To what brown furrow garlanded with weeds,
Returned the youth who kneels upon the soil?
And that young soldier whose romantic deeds
Lie stained upon the dagger at his side,
Whence did he wander when the wine had flown,
And the god had gone and the vine had died?
Or did the drinkers go and leave the god alone? . . .

O sunburnt fringe of summer indolence,
O blessed age of grape and mouth and dust,
Resting before me in kind magnificence,
I, who am subject to the lords that rust.
Again in cool water from the earthern jar,
I drink to the deity underneath the grape,
And in the water's darkness see a star
And hear a cry from the vessel's beaded gape.
Or is it my own breath that comes to me
Sculptured by the cool hands of the bowl,
And whiter and softer than Aphrodite
Enters the echoing gallery of my soul.

In the morning light we strolled up the fern hill, Panucci gesticulating and brushing the flies away from his long shapely nose, and I holding out my hand for the paper he was writing on as he walked.

"You get, if you can, Steva, 'Questa o Quella' . . . ah, the music of that is beautiful!" He hummed it to himself. "Or, 'La forza del

Destino' or '*Cor' Ingrato*'. Get any of these. Wait, Steva, wait—there is one you must get! This one, Steva, you must get . . . *se possible*. It is called '*Ombra mai fu*'. A *largo*. *Uno largo*. Steva, this is the most powerful piece of music of all. Get '*Ombra mai fu*', please Steva!"

"What does '*Ombra mai fu*' mean?"

Panucci, walking lithe and light beside me, reading over absorbedly that which he had written, trod down the faintly Highland bracken and said across a world of half rain, half dew and all sunshine, " '*Ombra mai fu*' means 'He never was shadowed'."

"He never was shadowed," I said mistily, thinking, "He must have been a criminal, but one who was protected from the police and detectives."

"No, no," said impatient Panucci, who had caught the inflection and, having once been in the police force, knew what I meant. "Not that, Steva. This means that he was never in shadow . . . never unhappy . . . never shadowed by sorrow or pain."

"Oh, and who was he, Panucci? A writer?"

"No, no, some one in opera. You read about it some day and find out all about him."

"So . . . he never was shadowed; never was unhappy?"

"Never, never. *Ombra mai fu*. He never was shadowed."

The slight pain this gave in the lovely day passed when I got on the road to Bairnsdale. Over the punt and away, cantering lightly over the wettish sandy roads with the blue-black shadows of the slender gum-trees pencilled on them.

Ah, but I was lonely; the great Australian loneliness, that old disease of mine, swept over me, making my blood slow and painful along my veins. I was lonely and I was unloved. And worse, far ahead into the future my soul struggled and saw no end of it, no end for ever to my thirst for love. Because, you see, I really didn't want to be loved. Not at all. What I really wanted was to be a man, and free for ever to write and think and dream. I had the utmost contempt for love, and a very real fear of it—"the beastly second best". I would rather have wandered the earth and written for ever than bothered about love. However, love is valuable if one wants to attitudinize when life is empty. One can strike attitudes when one would be better employed in striking matches.

157

The brisk gravel and sand under my feet spun away and away into eternity. Here the bush was grey; here it was dead and tall; here grass, brown and short, lay behind fences; here lonely houses among feathery wattles held their sorrows and joys from me. I turned off and cantered down the back track I had ridden along earlier in the year, towards Sarsfield. I thought, "Yes, today I shall inflict pain on myself to feel some sort of life within. I am strange. One would think that I was walking about dead, for I am utterly without feeling for anything or anyone. I walk about with a stone-dead face and form; my head is like a huge brassy planet veiled in cloud."

> Deep in the shady sadness of a vale,
> Far sunken from the healthy breath of morn,
> Far from the fiery noon, and eve's one star,
> Sat grey-hair'd Saturn, quiet as a stone. . . .

To be able to sit like that, aeon after aeon in the shades, feeling only the impact of light from sun and moon, and earth, that was all. To Hades with emotions of all sorts! I loathed the feeling of life in them. But can one go to a party in that state? I have tried. White-faced, immobile, calm, silent, I have sat at parties as Saturn, brassy planet and god, with golden-haired Thea, of the great majestic height, by me, one great hand set upon my shoulder, and her ringing voice saying, "Saturn, look up!—though wherefore . . ."

Actually, of course, it was one of the guests at the party who, stiffened by my immobility, approached and begged me to live, lest all perish about me. Instead of a hand outstretched to take cakes, I felt that I should have been able to press a button and see a winch rise slowly up from myself to grasp with a crane the edibles and crush them into the inferno of my body. Not often did I go as Saturn to a party. They didn't want to see me twice. No, one must act if one wants to be popular, alas!

As I passed the old orchard I saw a group of youths hoeing the grey soil; the clink of their hoes striking the huge clods came to me musically. A youth to a row, moving towards me steadily, with the hoe rising and falling, making a little dust like smoke in the afternoon. Behind them stood the long white offices of the orchard, which exported nearly all its fruit to Berlin, Hamburg, and Liverpool. And a young red-haired clerk stood at the door watching the men with hoes. It was Macca.

The day struck me hideously, and I trembled; yes, it is true. The day wheeled about and struck me, every part of it; light and form and substance was my enemy and weakened me. The sight of Macca always shocked and terrified me with a great whirling sense of strain, as though he didn't live on the earth at all, and was only the solid projected mental image of God, flung to the earth and moving over it. That red hair was so much a part of light. Only a part of light was he to me, and in some strange aloof way he was glad of it. One felt that he loved his aloofness and treasured it and did not want to be on the earth or belong to any woman ever, for ever. And since the night at the hut, and my refusal there, and his quarrel with me and his words of hatred on leaving, I had bitterly repented and wished to see him again, for now I felt that I loved him. Really I didn't, but he was so aloof and I was so dead that I was glad of this chance to inject some life into the proceedings, the grim proceedings called Life. I saw him through a haze of mingled terror and hope. I wanted him to utterly forgive me. For months I had waited to see him, I had hoped to see him, and now, after the long ride, the hopelessness and the lonely sorrow, he stood before me—"I, the lone worshipper".

I dismounted and flung the bridle over the post of the fence. I walked through the gate; the clods, once I was in the paddock, became gigantic and formidable. I picked my way through them slowly, and the unrich, grey, and sick earth repelled me; it told me what I already knew, I think, that it was hopeless. The youths looked up, saw me, looked down and worked feverishly, the dust rising from their hoes, gilded by the sinking sun. I walked in a nightmare towards Macca. I stood by his side, in silence, at the office door. I trembled, panted, and was weak with my agony of mind, one half of me; the other half was still that dazed dreaming man making a long road in Algiers in days of terrible heat, and saying within, "O God, when this is all over, at last, and one can rest! I've not heart for it; it's not for me; I wasn't made for it. I was made to wander and work; I've not heart for bothering about man. Give me countries and roads and the hell of toil rather than the hell of man. The folly of it! Oh, I'm tired, a million aeons tired, and still down a thousand years pursuing this One True Light, this man with the burning head. Curse him, I'm tired of him!"

But no, the framework of things dictate worship of man. Right! Let's get it over! For two long months I had waited for this moment, and at the end of my despair all I could utter was the word Panucci found so laughable—"Well."

"Well, Mackinnon?" Out of my depths, my well of sorrow and loneliness, I rose in humour of a sort. "I'm the man that sunk the first oil-well in Abadan."

"Well, Steve?" said he, from his own cool depths.

"I'm a trespasser, I know," I went on. "But it's someone else's land, so you can't put me off."

He stared at the youths hoeing the bitter earth. "I see you've still got the same green eyes," he said.

"I'm mad Carew, still," I replied, "and stole them from the little yellow god; ill fortune accompanies such thefts. And you, Macca, have you forgotten the little fires we used to make round the foreshore in that far-off springtime?"

He stared at me, coilingly. "I'm afraid, Steve, that of those dead fires only the cold ashes remain."

"And the messages you wrote on stones for me, Macca? And hid away under green leaves by the lake?"

"The rain has washed the words out of my mind, Steve."

"Ah, Macca, what can I say?"

Macca looked very firm about something. "I don't know what you can say, Steve, but at least *I* can say this. A few months ago I went all the way down to Metung to ask you to marry me. You calmly turned me down, and now you come along here, with your Oscar Wilde and John Keats accents, asking me to remember the past and sorrow with you over our long-lost love. It's time you got a bit of sense, and found out what you really wanted in life, beside wanting to be the first man to sink oil-wells in Abadan."

"And what would that be?"

Macca said he was dashed if he knew. "What are you sorrowing about, anyhow? I'm still here, you're still here, and you're young and a poet. What ever's wrong with you?"

"What can I say? For two months or more now I have waited to see you, and now delight clamours in my blood so strongly that

I am only aware that I am with you. Do you remember Jim, Macca, and Blue, and the old days? Do you remember the bark hut?"

Macca said earnestly that he did. He also said that he remembered that I had turned him down in that same hut.

"The book of fairytales you gave me? The book of poems . . . 'Why art thou silent?' "

"Why am I silent? Ah, Steve, I think I ought to go out and buy you a jewelled necklace to make you forget that book of poems. Although, God knows, you wouldn't like a jewelled necklace. Don't you ever, Steve, think of anything but poetry and literature?"

"No, beyond literature there is nothing."

"Dear, dear, dear!" exclaimed Macca. "Distressing, really." The sun sank steadily towards the darkening trees. "Righto," he sang out to the youths, "you can knock off now!" They came up with their hoes, which he locked away in a shed. Then he locked the office and his own quarters and said, "I have to go in home tonight to Lucknow. All the hotel proprietors in Bairnsdale are giving a dance in the Town Hall and I am going to be there. The wife of the proprietor of the Albion is an old friend of mother's, and I am going over to Hadfields' to pick a big bunch of dark-red camellias for her frock, or for her to carry. They are still flowering there, even so late in the season. And why am I silent, Steve? Ah, but that was Wordsworth who asked that question, Steve. It was asked in England, where they answer. In Australia no answer is made by man or land. Well, my motor-bike is out of commission at present, so I shall have to ride Emma, Ack Emma, the good old grid, over to Hadfields'." He drew towards him his bicycle, which was leaning against the fence, its delicate wire wheels burning in the sunlight, and I took the bridle of the racer and held it over my shoulder, and he with his hands on the handles of the bicycle, walked beside me. The wheels and pedals whirred softly and the horse's feet sank deeply into the white soil of the Sarsfield flat.

We came to the old house. "I must pluck the red camellias here, Steve."

"For me?" I cried, staring at his red-gold hair and blue eyes, as he walked through the old gate of Hadfields'.

Suavely, gently, he said, "No, Steve . . . I told you, for a woman's evening frock. She is going to dance with me tonight. The frock

161

is black, and I have promised her the camellias—the reddest, the darkest—for her shoulders."

"But, dash it, you said they were for a friend of your mother's," I said.

"True, Steve, true," said Macca gracefully, "but then, my mother has so many friends."

I forgot my pain, for I was with him; hypnotized by the pleasure of his presence, I could endure all, I thought. For ever, I thought, as I watched him moving round the tree, for ever I am part of you, as you are part of Gippsland. How slowly he moved, choosing and refusing the cool crimson lips the dark tree offered him, just as he refused mine. But, of course, I had refused his in the first place. And these flowers would lie on the white shoulders of another woman, and all night she would dance with him, and all night he would look at her, and I, the poet, would go home to my lonely hut. I thought to myself, "I shall remember this hour and this old house with its garden for ever." Macca stood behind the dark-green, shining tree, snapping off camellias in silence.

"Ah, Macca, take one for me," I said. "One for me, too. Let me be part of the night and the woman and the dance; let me be part of the passion and the sorrow, for I am so alone. Give me a camellia, too, so when I sit alone in the hut I may imagine that the music and the light of the hall is about me." I almost added, "Though really, being utterly Byronic in my habits and outlook, I should rather be dead than dance in the local town hall." But one doesn't say that in Australia, ever. So I continued in the "our heroine" strain, "Let me imagine that the dancers are circling about me, and I, among them, am desired and befriended. Oh, if I have a camellia, it will hurt more, but I shall throw myself over the hurt and be wounded until I cannot feel anything any more." Plastic surgery and anaesthesia had nothing on me when I got flat out to it. "Oh, the past, the past haunts me!" A choked de Balzac. "The days, the days of sorrow . . . well, what can one say? Soon you will be going away from me into your evening, a night of pleasure and love, but for me, alas, it is dark and desolate."

We stood together on the dusty road, and the still fiery sun shone hotly on us, the slow Australian sun, reluctant to leave the earth. He gave me a dark-red camellia.

"Here you are, Steve."

Staring at those in his hand, and seeing them on the shoulders of the woman, I cried, "I love you . . . I love you!"

Oh, to be able to say that to him, after the years of saying it to myself! What that meant . . . to let those words that had grown to be inhuman torment to me fall in some sort of human kindness on the ears of the one I loved.

Macca was silent. His lips moved and then, with his eyes on the flowers, he replied, "I'm sorry, Steve, I can't return it. If I had loved you still I'd have come for you long ago."

And there, at last, on the bitter, barren earth, I stood and heard the answer that my mind had known for long, but had not believed. But in the intoxication of the moment I was not hurt, for he was with me. That was all. I felt no sorrow, I knew no pain in that hour. Only the grandeur of being thrust out into my desert, only the power of being flung back to regain power, for on I must press, for forward I must go and carry him off by the force of my soul and the peculiarity of my love.

"Then be my comrade, love me as a friend. You surely cannot mean to cut me out of your life for ever. What harm can I do you? Stay with me, counsel me, for I am lonely. Only you can sustain me. Think——" under a large, crowded gospel-tent, vivid with lights—"here is one human soul pleading with you, begging you to save it from—who knows what? Ahead of me lie the dreadful years, and if you desert me, what will become of me? I am lonely and afraid, I am tempted on all sides. If you would only write and sustain my love of you by kindly friendship. It is all I ask. And I will live alone in my hut for ever and by the thought of you I shall be nourished. On your friendship I shall rest my head and by the cool waters of your kindness my loneliness shall be ended."

By now the late afternoon, the brown earth and crimson camellias had grown inextricably mingled, and Mackinnon listened in the dream that was his youth.

"Friendship . . . letters . . . a visit to see you now and then? Is it so much to ask? I shall respect your wishes and understand you—that you cannot love me . . . but why, then . . . why did you say it, long ago? What is this love?"

. "You told me at Metung that night that you would never marry. I refuse to keep on hanging around you, Steve, if you won't marry me. You care for little else but the past and poetry."

"Perhaps that is so."

"I found with you, Steve, that the moment you got my love you flung it back in my face. That is the type of being you are."

And since, unfortunately, this was absolutely true, I was silent.

"You are better without love; you don't want love; what you want is work, and plenty of it. There are thousands like you in this world. They don't want love; they want work."

"I know. I admit it. Then what lies ahead for me? For you and me? Yes, we are caught as of old. I see it. You are the wheel from which I am flung off, and the momentum of God . . . and I, what happens to me? I go flying off through space now, into my hell, and you, where do you go? Ah, the years will tell us, and cruelly, Macca."

"I shall write to you," he said calmly, watching the sun.

"You mean that? You mean it truly?"

"Yes. And I shall come down and spend one long day with you —perhaps on New Year's Day. Yes, we shall sit together and walk together as we used to do, Steve, for one day, and then, after that, I'll write to you from wherever I am. And keep you from loneliness."

"That is enough. I am rewarded a thousand times over. It is enough." I felt I had the energy, having been promised this, to run the entire race, though as dead as stones, into a full flight of burning immortality. I flung the fire of genius over all things; empires arose mighty in a moment, and there and then standing in the dust of Gippsland before Hadfields' scarlet-camellia'd gate, the twentieth century arose and blossomed as no century has ever blossomed before.

He came out of the garden and stood with me on the road. "And now I must go, Steve, before the flowers wither . . ."

"Before we grow old, standing here on this road, Macca, and are dead."

"I have to go home and be cleaned and ready for the dance by eight o'clock, you see, Steve."

"And I have to go back to the baracca, and be cleaned and ready for the ghosts of the past. At eight o'clock, when the moonlight is falling noiselessly on the floor, the ghosts of the past will come. One has your voice, one has your features, and they cry softly, 'Stevie . . . Stevie Talaaren . . . ' "

"And what does Stevie Talaaren mean?"

"The hard earth."

"And that really is you, Steve. The hard earth."

"It is a good thing to be."

"All this talk of the past, the ghosts, the moon, the loneliness and grief . . ."

"Under it all, Macca, the hard earth."

"Poor, poor Steve," he said softly; with the same softness, as though he had no wish to awaken me from my dream, he put his foot to the pedal of the bicycle and, with that half-flying, half-ballet movement of mounting, he said, "Good-bye, Steve", and was gone.

But you must not think that I was stricken by this. Ah no, drunken with hope, with the sight of him, and with my own obstinate feeling that I should make myself purely feminine and want him, and win him, I rode after him, watching him for as long as he stayed within sight, and then I went into Bairnsdale and bought two records without glancing at them, and great bags of fruit, fresh-smelling and sweet. I piled them on the altar of myself, and rode back to Wilsons' with them. For I needed company that night. I broke in on them, flushed, triumphant, entangled with moods and feelings of great victory to come, immortal poet and lover; with these feelings I came to them in the high green kitchen, the shadowed room, and put the fruit before them, and ate with them, and talked with them in the language of Gippsland.

As for them, what could they understand of me? I was of a different race. I spoke wildly and vividly, not feeling anything of what I said. I made for the future plans that I would never carry out; I embellished the country with my fantasy and made for them stories that enchanted them and told them with a fire that made me more drunken than ever. Gigantically strong and healthy, tormentedly virgin, snowy with virginity and powerful with it, I leant above their table and held them by power of my virginity and my poetry until late in the night.

I stayed with them all night, and went into Bairnsdale next morning with Rita, Kelly's sister, and bought the record "Cor' Ingrato" for Panucci. In the afternoon I skimmed, galloping, round the sandy curve that opens the road from Bairnsdale to Metung, a well-worn, faintly classic curve, and fast through the afternoon and evening rode home. Still drunken with hope and despair, I sang as I rode swiftly and wildly through the bush. In the grassy lane Peppino stood waiting for me.

"*Mia cara.*" Gently he helped me to dismount, and in the moonlight his white face shone. In your black coat, Peppino, I thought, you look like a medieval knight, and indeed, for chivalry, you are one—but you are not Mackinnon.

"*Mia cara.*" Yes, to the hut, then, and let us talk.

The moon shone that night over the rounded fields as though all the lost poets of all time still wandered lost about the world in a great radiance of death. As we opened the wooden gate onto Jim McLachlan's property I looked back, and saw in a lonely paddock one tree standing curled and rich and cloudlike against blue heaven and whiter cloud. A significant tree.

"I have a record, Peppino—'Cor' Ingrato'. Let us light the fire and play it together."

Or was it a ghost with me that night, and did I play it alone, "*Cor' Ingrato*", "Ungrateful Heart"? But now, as never before, I wrote.

Yet the day dawned over me, and I must work, crouched low on the silver soil, hot and poor as it was, hoeing round the silent shiver of the Japanese tea-bushes, sick for want of sleep. Through hours of tired agony I worked over the leaf, replying to the Cubans in a faint sleepy voice, greeting Jim McLachlan politely when he arrived. And all the while I longed to sleep, to forget . . . that counter with oblivion that the gods provide. And all day the refrain in my ears was, "*Tutto passato non ritorna chiù.* The past will never return."

"Steve!" Jim stood over me, looking down out of his white face with its crown of fire; one felt that one would do anything for such a glorious face, even if lying in deepest death. "I want you to take some letters for me."

"Jim, when I'm dead with the way of life I like to get on to the earth and keep close to it; I'm Antaeus the Second; I can draw immortality from her. Must I crawl into that office and type today?"

"I'll make you a hot cup of Chinese tea, or, if you'd rather have it, green tea, Steve, and you'll feel better. Why must you go out again tonight when you're so awfully tired?"

But I love to look back and think of the wild, white, silver-dry light that shone over the soil that hot day in November 1928, when the year was dying. The day died all about us like a huge, tough old Australian politician of the days of King O'Malley. A great silver face shone, and in the bearded gully the swish of wind and sun. Deep dry sand underfoot and sparse tea-bushes. And the awful death of the day, spectacular and most clamorous with death. Age all about us, and eyes that stared, and the old aboriginal log-like form of the country swooning towards the year's end. And above all I was so enchanted with my own dreadful sense of dying; momently, within and without, I perished, and I was delighted; there was no sensation in me, no thought, no feeling or remembrance of anything under the sun, and the inward death that was like the drinking of wine and the eating of slow sweet foods was life in itself; and there was no end to me. I was life, flowing gigantic and hideous out of God; and God, that day, was merciless; but the silver sand there, the long day of the desert, the hard sense of Algeria and its most harsh miles and ways of poetry, fire-laden to the horizon's brim.

At night Peppino called for me, to take me to the Buccaneer's house so that we might hear the musicians again. Savage with sleeplessness, laughing with it, bitter with it, I entered the house. The music rained from the other room, wild and sweet and urgent, and my life and genius danced to it in hopelessness. I stood beside the Black Serpent; her plump hands buttered scones and put jam between rich cakes.

Watching the hands, I said, "I saw him when I was in Bairnsdale. I saw him. I spoke with him."

"Steve, tell me."

"There is nothing to tell."

"Steve, when Macca came down to ask you to marry him, you didn't want him. Why do you bother any more?"

"It's that beastly red hair of his. It torments me. I keep thinking of a word. Ur. The ancient city of Ur. And do you know, I don't want the man at all; it's the city that I want. Ur of the Chaldees. And I mourn for that city as though I had lived in it when it was royallest. And I just want to be in Ur again, that city of the jewelled streets, that city of the handsomest men on earth. The sons of Ur were all copper-haired, and against the flowery mosaic of the city

167

walls these heads flamed in splendour above their white faces."

"And there is nothing to tell?"

"There is nothing to tell."

"I think I'll have a talk to Edgar and see if he can get Macca down for the Christmas holidays. I know for a fact that Macca loves you. But it is you who are so strange, Steve. No man wants to settle down to marriage with a woman who does nothing but sorrow because Ur of the Chaldees has not been rebuilt. A man wants a woman who can cook."

"Marriage and cooking do not matter beside the rebuilding of Ur. Still, if you wish, you may ask Edgar to see Macca."

We looked through the door into the room where the music rang with passion and conceit, rang with ardour and mockery; we stared at Panucci's eyes, glimmering with laughter and self-mockery; he raised them to us, and smiled with his gentle, firmly pressed lips, his tight smile repressing all his mirth. And his soft brown eyes turned away from us and stared absently, ashamedly, on some one else.

Peppino knelt, one knee, beside the chair of Edgar Buccaneer, and his curls streamed down over his brow. His face looked dark against a very white collar. Panucci always wore brown shirts that gave his face a peachlike bloom.

The night ended and the rain came, and I had time to write more and yet more prose. I had time to build up my life. In the wet day against the fire of buddha wood, white and thick and dry, I wrote:

When I spoke with Mackinnon on that rare day of enchantment, my brain felt slow, awkward, not subtle. I understand now, how strongly learning and learned company sustain men. I see now that in the brain is the essence of our immortality. My brain, my brain, be to me, lover, home and food. Even if all things fail, brain, I shall have *you*. Last night, when in the dark wood, I saw the pale face of Peppino, then did I know the sorrow of life, the stillness of it. For a sad courage lay along the flat line of his lips and a muted peace and melancholy was in the thick pallid angle of his eyes. I love Australia. I have wept painful tears for it, the painful tears of purity. Many miles in the heat of an Australian summer I rode and returned again, along the dry road at noon, an endless quest ended. Myself, since this country is the only one you love, since this youth is the one star along your skies . . . follow him . . . follow him. . . . No sailor can steer for stars apart. . . .

But it was night, the fire was flickering and performing great black antics on the walls; the grass outside rustled, and Peppino came to the door.

"*Mia cara*."

My writing lay on the ground in the dust, saying, "Peppino must go."

"Peppino."

"*Si, mia cara?*" so gently, softly, and kindly.

No, no, I could not bother him. As for him, his eyes grew larger and flashed, as they say—or, as I say, filled with white light—as he stared at me. But he was not unhappy.

"If we could be together for ever, Peppino, *amico mio*, listening to the voice of the great singers! Down all time, I think, I could sit here, writing and staring at the burning red log in my mind, and then, through the great voice of music hear your beloved footsteps over the summer grass, and see your white face at the door, and hear your voice, saying, '*Buona notte*'. But I'm forgetting, here's a letter McLachlan asked me to give you. It came in the night's mail."

He opened it and read it slowly. His face grew dark and dreadfully enraged.

"*Diamine!*" he exclaimed.

And then I saw that most remarkable thing about which so much has been written and conjectured—the fit of Italian rage. In Australia it is a thing spoken of with awe, and to those who have witnessed it the profanation of temples is as nothing compared to this baring of the Italian soul.

A muscular contraction of rage passed all over his sinewy little body. "*Mia cara*, don't you say anything to me. I am too sick." I put my hand on his, for I was afraid. "Le' me alone." He bowed his head between his knees and stared at the floor, muttering to himself; the sheets of paper from the letter lay below him. They held it all . . . they held it all. He ground his hand into his hair and pulled out curls and twists of black hair and flung them over

169

the floor and the writing on the letter. Fascinated, I saw the paper slowly darken as he pulled and flung curl after curl on it.

"Steva, don't you speak to me, please. I am too sick. I am go my plice." An enormous darkness was building up between us, shot through with my great interest in what was happening.

"But what on earth is it, Peppino?" I thought that it must be some terrific love affair in which he had engaged and failed. A woman, glad, tired, surfeited with power, putting her faith in some tragic destiny that tore them apart. Some vision of minor faults, seen or believed now that he and this love of his were apart. He had trusted and had faith in her, and she had perhaps betrayed it.

"I go now, Steve. I see you tomorrow. You not ask me anything. I will not tell."

His feet rustled away over the grass, and I stood holding on to the tin fireplace and staring, glaring down into the fire that danced with weary red limbs on the hearth. Ah, but, Peppino, I thought, there is bed . . . there is sleep . . . don't fret over women and their love . . . there is always sleep. And I turned into its breast and lay there, alone in the bush, dreaming, dreaming, drowsily curling and uncurling on the bosom of Sleep, my one love ever, after all.

In Metung, in that hut, one could lie thinking of all the shades of the days that one had walked about the beloved land. Nothing mattered, save that the sun rose each day in awful heat and turned the earth about within itself, as the earth turned the sun about within itself. Only planets matter in Australia; people don't. Sometimes the brown grass was dark and frizzled with heat, then it lay flat and pale with it; and the lake was as thick as pale-blue paint, with fine oils in it. Oh, to dip a brush in that and paint landscapes from shore to shore! All manners of lights and heats came out of the shoreline, and thunder strode the earth, remote, slow and reluctant to clothe himself in cloud and fall as humble rain, grey and silent over the land. And heat forced us all to drift about as its slaves from place to place, greeting each other in holiday for ever.

I went into the village for the mail, and walked with Edgar Buccaneer up the dry hill. On one side was the old post-and-rail fence, parched, yearning to drink in rain. In Australia this great need is dominant; everything thirsts. The eyes stir, refuse to rest as they see these signs, for the thirst of the land smites deeply into them.

The grey clouds swept over us; Edgar dragged thoughtfully on his fair and salt-showered moustache and the thick ring on his finger stood out against his reddish cheek and the earth. Twilight seemed to be over us and we, it appeared, were walking in a dream. In the village behind us men and women were coming away from the small post office, where the mail had been sorted and given out; they drove away with their letters into the bush once more. It was disturbing and sad to see them as they passed, some reading, others whistling since no letters had come, and they were anxious to talk with others and had excitable complaints to make about the crops and the weather.

Edgar said in a low grumbling voice, "I shall do my best to get Macca down here for the fishing, but, remember, it depends on you . . . then . . ."

"Yes, yes," I said.

"Won't hang around being turned down for ever."

"No."

They were both of them absolutely determined to get me married. On my marriage the fate of civilization seemed to rest. Great slow massive moves were made about it, as though I had been an elephant or a god. And I hated marriage. But, no, marriage it must be, according to both. And Macca it must be. Because of his red hair. In Langham's Italian-English dictionary I had found "*Macca*: much".

Quite true. That is precisely what he was. Much. And really, I didn't want much. I liked to love Macca in a platonic sort of way; I liked to write to him and about him interminably, sensuously, intellectually, praisefully, sentimentally, romantically, in every fashion of prose and poetry possible. The world turned about him, to my mind aesthetically. Marriage would ruin it all. Marriage would disgrace the whole thing.

Edgar and I kept our twilight conspiracy, half thought, half spoken. His wife eyed us over the well-spread table, with its Eve of St Agnes custards, in which red jellies gleamed and yellow cakes lay soft and crumbling; she smiled and touched me as I passed.

I lay awake all night, listening to the sad heavy roar of the

171

M

sea over the sand dunes. I gave myself up to it, and lay in that
weight of water and struck the shore with it.

> *"God, God, will it never cease,*
> *The sliding and the roar*
> *And riding of tremendous seas*
> *Along tremendous shores?"*

And all along the sides of the bush morning it roared, as I rode
back to the hut to begin working. The earth was dry with a desperate note of dryness, and artificial, stagey with drought; the air
was fevered, and my skin and the hide of the horse, they were
hot at this early hour of the morning. It was not yet seven, but the
sun, which had barely left the earth, had raced back again to throw
yet more heat into the summer; it worked on the Australian earth
without ceasing. Broad patches of brown shadow and atmosphere
and colour broke and burst from apparently nowhere at all, and
gave the ground the look of a magnificent book, with myself and
the black jade racehorse, red-nostrilled, white-eyed, tan-saddled and
golden-girthed standing, quivering with heat and life, in the
middle of it.

Down the brown hill came Peppino and Panucci, talking very,
very seriously in Italian. They drew up, under my stirrup, and I
looked down into the two faces. Peppino's eyes were red with lack
of sleep; in his drab coat and short dusty trousers he looked an
inhuman bundle of pitiable helplessness, ineffectual and vulnerable. Panucci's eyes brimmed over with mocking merriment, as
he watched us meet.

"Hullo, Peppino."

"Good morning, Steve," subduedly. And Peppino's large brown
eyes stared into mine with a desperate long glance.

Panucci smiled consumingly and looked away, almost withering
the trees with his repressed laughter. He was delighted; nothing
could touch him. He did not know love, except for two things,
music and Italy. I felt angry with him and wondered what Peppino's trouble really was.

"I come tomorrow and see you, Stef'," said Peppino. "I want
talk with you."

"Very well, Pep. Good-bye." A sad, dusty, dry meeting, with,

172

as it were, tears to moisten the earth. I felt disgust at being a woman, and a witness of the sorrows of men.

I rode down the long eastern stretch of the plantation with its warm white feeling dust until I reached Jim McLachlan, who was busy with a field thermometer, trying out the heat of the sheds.

In the broken, lackadaisical rhythm of sorrow I said to the red god, "What's wrong with Peppino? Do you know?"

"Yes. There's a woman in the case. He told me he'd be leaving shortly and going on to Maffra to work on the sugar. I'm sorry. I think he's such a nice chap."

"Yes, life's rotten."

"Oh, he'll get over it. Nothing much to it. Very commonplace affair."

"Glad to hear it. I thought there were exceedingly high ideals involved."

"Oh dear, no. Steve, you look tired yourself. You need a holiday."

"Ah well, there's always that trip to the Alps, you know."

I left Jim moving about the drying shed, with its complex apparatus, in that capable and experienced way of his—white, lonely, eternally a bachelor, young and very handsome in his linen shirt and cord breeches and helmet, the wide shoulders, strong arms, the pale metallic mouth, the down-dreaming eyes. He kept the secrets of the trade solely to himself, and for all his handsome looks and gracious manners would not allow any questions to be asked. The Italian overseer and chemist with whom Panucci worked were permitted some little licence, but McLachlan preferred to do it all himself. But, since in those days I lived in a dream that precluded and excluded interest in tea and its processing, what did I care? I knew that he doped it a lot with aniline blue and a few other expensive chemicals and drugs to darken it and give it flavour, and all I cared for was that he *did* dope it, for green tea is the nearest thing to chaff I have ever tasted, and there is no doubt about it; it is in the drying and doping that tea is made.

I went over to the office and filled in the hours by lightly and very delicately typing a long letter to Blue:

Maker of mosaics, you have comforted an old warrior; your fair words have compensated and softened the pain of lost battles.

173

I have fought hard to retain romantic territory, and I have failed. I have relinquished my hold, abdicated, and from afar I see the retreating mass of blended colours, the tossing plumes and the mingled tumultuous musics of the lovely rank and file and column. Perhaps it was from this army that you dropped out and sat for a while by me on some never to be known roadside. My mate, my friend, thinker in colour, rare colour, shape and form, fragile mind that creates so delicate fragility . . . we should never have emerged from the land of Faerie. Some day, after the long quest is ended, in disappointment and negation, I shall say to Myself—for Grizzlebeard and the Sailor and the Poet will have been dead long ago—I will return again over the fantastic farrago and say, "Out of all these, who loved me most? Who was most akin to me?" And it will be the Sailor, Blue Peter. Macca is the strong, pure, unwavering love of the imagination, to me. He is poetry, or the chill mysterious source of poetry. I brought home the camellia he gave me and pressed it into the white hands of a book of fairy tales, *The Princess of Ultima Thule*. I said to him, "Mackinnon, dear mate, dear youth, if I shouldn't see again ever the beloved form that's you; when you come to the last island I shall be there. We are young; death seems a thousand thoughts away . . . nevertheless, sometimes I hear, from that last isle of the horizons,

> *"The sliding and the roar*
> *And riding of tremendous seas*
> *Along tremendous shores.*

"The visions of faerie, of giants and their huge castles, of witches and fiery wizards, of enchanted princesses, and great rose-trees, haunt me ever. I know that I am immortal. I feel keenly my immortality. Mortality shadows me, saddens me. It is the water in the wine of my life. I cannot tell you how often come to me, ecstatic shapes, dim beginnings of lovely adventurings to come." Place this camellia's outer heart, Blue, among my letters from Macca.

But the crimson-locked McLachlan came in for afternoon tea, and I broke out of the enchanted places and made it for him in

174

one of the delicate Japanese tea-pots he used. And while he ate and drank and smoked I stared with adoration at my hero and determined to write great books and greater poetry before his altar —this golden Celt, this pure and luminous rim of the Greek horizon with its columns of glassy, classical endless fire.

Peppino was waiting for me down at my place that evening; I heard the voice of the Italian tenors pealing out as I came striding down the ferny hill. Peppino, pale and cool in white singlet and navy trousers, was bending above the Decca, winding the handle rapidly.

"*Buon' sera, Steva,* I came to see you . . . *umpo.* I am going soon to Maffra; one *l'ultima notte* at the house of the Buccaneer with the Panucci and Benedett', and I go to Maff' for work among the sugar."

"By the gods, Pep, I am glad I am not going to work among sugar in the days of such great heat."

"*Si . . . troppo caldo.*"

"Yes, the boss told me that you were leaving us. Ah, well, I don't know how long I shall be here myself. I am overdue at Leonardo's, and I expect to hear from him soon, asking me to go down. After that, there is quite a bit to do among the tea, for Jim—but then, I don't know what to do. This Christmas will be dull, I think."

Now when the deep pink rose of evening made luminous all heaven, and the strong silver wind of afternoon still blew in a wide mask of romance and sea-blue pain across the brown grass of the earth, at that hour when all heaven seemed full of dark lines, wide shafts of dramatic meaning, and narrow streaks of splendour, Panucci came lightly and smilingly to the door.

"*Buona sera, Steva . . . buona sera, Peppino.*"

"Ah," I said suddenly, "I had forgotten." And I went over to a shelf and took down from it one of the records I had bought in Bairnsdale and quite forgotten.

"Ah, what is this?" Panucci cried, delighted, holding out his hand for the precious disk.

The wide black record whirred and rocked and spun a long powerful song of sheer machine before the searching needle found that quavering black shaky stammer that was the broken, drum-like beginning of *Il Prologo.* In my soul a long obstructed gallery

175

opened its rounded doors, and the black stammer of the Prologue and the drooping pink rose of evening that from its blue jar dropped, fled fast within it, and there, from a long, long distance, a man's voice began to speak.

Presently, the singer was crying out, in a clear, firm, remembering voice, tinged strongly with truth, sorrow and positiveness:

> "*Un nido di memorie in fondo all' animo,*
> *Cantav' ancora . . .*"

"Tomorrow night, for the last time," said Panucci, "we play at the Buccaneer's."

"I go to Maffra," said Peppino, "and my records I leave with Steva."

He had made all this warm springtime and summer one long flood of beauty and poetry with his animated and happy friendship; he and Panucci and Samozarro had given the entire year an incommunicable richness, and one felt that generations to come would lean on the columns of their souls and become impassioned by the thought of the lives we had led among the forests of lilac and white blossoms shaking, sea-sodden, on the foreshore, and the robber-red honeyed heath and the voices of the great Italian singers.

A long hot day had passed. We were now walking through the ferns at the back of the road; we were on the deep white road itself, silently ploughing through the dust, like camels through a desert. And there, the moon, moving against the unmoving trees, and in the night, no breeze, only the fanatical glitter of the enormous stars, haggard with the heat. That night we were tired, the music was slower, and thicker, for the strings were troubled by the heat, and the unnatural moonlight, like the light of a dream, murdered all our lightness. The house was full of company talking in high clear voices, like parrots crying in the bush, voices that were full of colour and mockery. And a horrid glaze withered the face of the moon.

When he was tired of playing, Panucci produced a tweed cap, and claimed that it held the absolute elixir of immortal life and beauty inside it. He consented to let it be tried out. We were all to stand in a ring round the room, and let him count up to twenty.

The person in whose hand the cap was when "twenty" was called out was to raise the cap and rub it hastily over the face. From behind this tweed ocean, claimed Panucci, would arise a face more beautiful than Venus, in the case of a female, and, in the case of a man, Adonis himself would be outdone. The cap, he said, came from Adelphi in Greece and was made of a cloth that was one of the wonders of the world.

The cap went from hand to hand, to the accompaniment of chanted numbers and powerful incantations in Italian, which helped a lot, and we all waited enviously to greet the new Venus or Adonis of this age. When it came to the hands of the prettiest girl in the room Panucci called out "Twenty!" The lovely creature raised it to her face and gave her entire visage a good hard rub, all over. Then she lowered the cap, and we stood staring at her jet-black face with a good deal of interest and various emotions that ended in howls of laughter. For Panucci had plastered the inside of that cap with black, moist shoe-polish. The friends and relatives of the black Venus withdrew to various corners of the room and thought things over and stared at us with antagonistic eyes, but we played on through the hours undeterred, until the youths went forth into the night to fill the pies and savouries with soot. Panucci deftly arranged it so that they got those, too, and what with their black-faced girl friend and themselves chewing pastry cases full of soot, the night grew dark indeed, and there was a sense of retaliation imminent. Panucci turned his head uneasily from side to side under their glances. At last he rose.

"*Andiamo*," he said sharply to us. "Let us go", and we and our beauty mask for glorious ladies and handsome men departed in peace into the night.

On the way home he made some half-angry, half-contemptuous comment on the house, and said wearily, "*Non mi vedi più*"—but hurriedly, so that I should not hear, for he knew that I loved to go to the place and be happy among men and women now and again.

And when he came to the long hill, when he saw on each side of him in the deathly antipodean moonlight the long post-and-rail fence going up the hill, he flung his hands out and stood under the drooping silent gum-trees, and cried in a voice like far-away fire, "*Ah, nostalgia per l'Italia!*"

"Ah, nostalgia for Italy!" The saddest cry I have ever heard in

177

all my life. Heartbroken, alien, savage, utterly Latin, such a dreadful sweeping cruel cry against this Australia. One felt that he loathed Australia, that he felt it to be raw, young, and devoid of culture.

"I was at university in Italy," he said suddenly, addressing it to Peppino and Benedetto. He and they became deeply and terribly Italian and I, I felt like the sad dry Australian earth by them. Groups of all the young intellectuals, the university students he had known in Italy seemed to rise luminous against the night and sorrow for him.

"Panucci, Panucci," I said, moving over to him, "you condemn me. I feel that I have evoked that cry in you. *Perdonami*, friend, if I have contributed anything to your unhappiness."

"No, Steva . . . no. But often *nostalgia* comes to me. Among the Australians I laugh and play, and give my music, but with a sense of uselessness, for I am aware that I am not contributing to the life of my own country. Had I played tonight in Italy, I should have been participating in the love, the passions, the marriage and the birth of Italians. That is what it is to be part of Italy; for centuries the musician has drawn those wages, as men and women loved, mated and bore children. The musician drew it all out of them, and moulded the limbs of future Italians. But here . . . but here . . . who is for me?"

The heat of the night was dreadful; it was an olive-green heat in a blue night. We wandered along the moonlit road slowly, for it was too hot to go home to bed to even try to sleep.

"And again——" and the others murmured swiftly their agreement with him—"in Italy . . . look at all the places of amusement there are, and the many millions of people, and the voice of music ringing for ever all over *cara Italia*. Opera, circus, playhouse, stage, Roman games, Greek amphitheatre—alas, what is here——" he laughed—"but bush!"

We had ascended the hill. I took his long white hands in mine and stared down at them.

"Hands like moonlight," I said to him in Italian, "but an older and deeper moonlight than ours. It has become accustomed to looking on civilization, that moon."

"*Ah, nostalgia per l'Italia,*" he sighed, taking his hands away from mine, and walking away with his companions.

Peppino and I, left alone in the silent bush, walked together, close side by side. We spoke no word, but in a space on the hill top among rough and broken ferns, where the moon shone with a horrid and eternal light, I turned to look at him, as though we had been buried, swamped in dark and deep seas all through our walk in the bush, and now a wave had carried us high up against sky.

There shone the face I loved, heart-shaped, ivory, gentle, with waves of blue-black hair lying thick and crisp on the broad brow, and the perfect mouth close shut, the dilated nostrils with their arrowlike pride below eyes glittering calmly, fulfilled with the surfeit of passion and its control, the delicious and exquisite control that springs from virtue and respect. And this white mask bent to me in the moonlight, and the great head of waving hair eclipsed my face, as Peppino said, "*Ahimè, mia cara*, I wish I had not to leave you, for you and I are good friends. But I must go."

As for me, since the hot night was cooling towards this, the dawn, I knew one thing only, love of and longing for sleep. Drowsily assuring Peppino of my undying affection and friendship even unto death, I made for my bed and the oblivion of dreams.

The going of Peppino, then, to Maffra and the glorious days were encouraging me to stay at home. Once more I was alone; I luxuriated in it, for Peppino had been so often with me, had loved every moment he spent with me and made heavy demands on my time, insisting on taking me with him and Panucci all over the place. The tea was still in its youthful stages. There was a long period of idleness ahead. I saw the beans growing, too, and they looked so lovely after a night of rain with their wide black hat-like shadows lying on the wet earth, that I felt I must work among them, when they were ready. Whenever I passed the fields, I looked in and said to them, to the cocked ears of the flowers, black and grey and white and pearl-hued, "Take it easy, friends. I am happy; I am young; grow slowly."

Peppino had left all his music with me; day flowed into day, and the hut was full of Italian songs; I drank cups of coffee and ate cakes, wrote, dreamt, made poetry and slept. And out in the bush the birds with long-drawn ruminative cries made for me pools of moisture in this dry land. For me, the birds were nothing but wandering waterfalls, creeks and pools, rivers and billabongs clad in feathers that were only developments of leaves, and in their breasts bubbled eternally the few drops of that element under the shelter of the foliage over their hearts.

For company I had the white topee, belonging to the island planter. It still hung on the piece of tea-tree at the back of the grove, and the wind whirled it round all day, and it grew white and smooth. Every morning I came to look at this white dome and please myself with its contours and devise stories of its beginnings and adventures on the head of the planter.

Luxuriously, sorrowfully, I wrote to Blue, asking her for drawings of the afternoon and the camellia-tree, and she, out of the heat, sent back one full of bloodlike reds, trees full of the night of the camellia, and women embracing like shadows on the ground, shadows of leaves on the ground about it.

Dreaming that I was sending with this the beauty of Blue's face, and the thin far-off songs of her violin, I wrote to Macca, giving the drawing and in the letter striving to say:

Macca, when you entered Hadfields' garden on that amber afternoon, to break camellias for the dress of a princess—yes, please, not an innkeeper's wife—that's absolutely insupportable in a fairytale . . . well, I leant over the old gate and I said to Myself, "O heart, immortalize this lovely moment in some word or song or colour; watch that completely absorbed youth as he hovers about the garden, the enchanted garden, choosing and refusing the crimson lips the dark tree offers him. He is the chill mysterious source of legend and poetry; in some peculiar, incommunicable way, he is Australia . . . and Monaro. When you were very young, Myself, how many times have you heard of the Svensons who used to bring down from the hills cavalry remounts that were shipped across the dark water to India. And here before you, is the cream of Gippsland, somehow turned sour, distorted, gone awry. Interested more in the new plum shade for topcoats than in the visible loved spirit of his highlands and lowlands. Myself, whenever you pass a great log smouldering redly with a murmurous inward roar, in the fallen afternoon, of whom else could you think but Mackinnon, for red, the oldest, kingliest colour in the world, burns sometimes in the bronze of his hair. Myself, after much travail and pain . . . after abiding with robbers in dark forests, after servitude to princes and apprenticeship to witches, you have discovered, at last, little Kay, little Kay, in the palace of the Snow Queen."

"Call to him . . . call to him!"

And my heart cried, "Little Kay, little Kay, return again!"

But the camellias were crying too, and their fine voices were louder. He never turned in answer.

I wish I were a youth. I could be a faithful mate to you for ever, and with you wax passionate over plum topcoats and the symmetrical lines of Bairnsdale's females. *Dio*, I go alone.

This drawing is "Fallen Afternoon", that afternoon. The camellia you gave me deserted its promise of immortality and died. I pressed it into the white hands of a book of fairytales and broke the wine-glass that held it.

Awkwardly, sadly, mingling him with Blue, taking from letters that I had written to her the words that would not come, as though neither people even existed except in my imagination, I tried to write, day after day. But at last, hopeless, I took up another of my Chinese poet's letters and thickly wrote across the back:

I cannot write to him. I have tried . . . and cannot. My pen halts and each written word comes slowly forth, saying, "We are going to the dead. No man reads us. There is no man there." Perhaps, O God, every letter I write removes him from me. I strive to maintain a balanced humour, a kindly distance . . . alas, my sorrow must show at every turn; my belief in life plays at laughter with stiff limbs. No, better send him the drawings without the accompanying letter. In some sort he is the editor of my heart, for to him I must send the poetry of it. The knowledge that I must leave this land he lives in is horrible, unbearable, insupportable. The farther I withdraw from him, the more my sorrow will grow; the stronger my illusions will be. He has said, "It is hopeless. My heart is immune, now. I love no one."

Yet does my mind go slowly back again, along and along those golden days, those olden days. I love . . . what do I love? More than man, more than lost hope of happiness, more than the future . . . the sweet, ungraspable, the individual, the past. Ah, there are so many pasts . . . and all, all unlike each other. The illusion is strong in me, "If I can reclaim his love again, in some sort I shall reclaim the lost years."

THE SEA WIND

VI

DECEMBER! Ah, here it was at last! The very height of summer, summer at the zenith. *Estate*, in Italian, summer. White paddocks, my lord the drought king of all Australia. Among the thin dry blades of grass a great fever shone, and the trees drooped more heavily than ever. Skies as blue as the atlas seas of coastal Australia, day after day of stiff blue skies and stiff white clouds creaming up, thunder-tinged, but nothing more. Floods of silver fire poured across the dead hot paddocks, as the mirage mounted from its round secret altar in the middle of the field and spun itself and its devotees across the earth.

Stiffened and paralysed by the great heat, we lay about in the shade; after eleven o'clock, McLachlan said, there must be no more work done, in case of sunstroke or fevers. In thin white sleeveless shirts and shorts and sun-helmets we sat talking slowly and refraining from drinking too much water, and laying off food for hours on end. Sometimes we thought of getting up and going for a swim in the blue lake, but the sun spat at us savagely when we strode half out into it, so we relapsed into the shadows and ran our idle hands over the hot soil. McLachlan, with the blue-black shadow of his topee quivering over his beautiful eyes, stood in the big garden, running a fine mist of water over his tropical plants, but the sight was hurtful to the imaginative, for the burnt-out land for miles about, at the sight of that water, seemed to leap up on yellow paws, and a huge eye within the earth drank up the moisture savagely. And in one's mind so many sad dry little wild flowers longed for a drop of the false rain. Jim told me that I must stay up at his residence as much as possible and that I was to keep out of the sun during the hours when it is a hideous lion, speechless with rage, brazen-clawed, blind and black with devilry and pitiless to white flesh. Blue, red, and silver flashes struck from the stony paths down to the point where the lake lay in a pale-azure oily posture, sending long suave ripples in to the shore, and under heaven listening to the rolling reeling heat of the enormous sun of Australia.

But a letter arrived, white, fine-lined, with the windy misty blue mistral rising at high noon to haunt me and draw me down at last, down Kalimna way, down Calulu way, down Nungurner way.

It was from Leonardo della Vergine.

Cara Steva,

Vi scrivo poche righe per dirvi che ieri ho cominciato il raccolto dei fagioli, raccolto che promette molto bene.

Mi fareste un immenso piacere se poteste venire ad aiutarmi per due o tre giorni.

Rispondete se vi è possibile e non temete ch'io sarò segreto a vostro riguardo.

Constima vi saluto

Cordialmente vostro amico

LEONARDO.

"I am off," I said to Jim, "as rapidly as the poet princes of Arabia. Down to Kalimna, deep into Calulu, and steeply into the fern heart of Nungurner I go, for Leonardo has called. He has started picking the beans and he wants my help with his letters and accounts. And anyhow, Jim, he has such a lovely big windy veranda where the breeze blows cold all day, and big rooms full of all sorts of treasures."

"I should wait till the rain comes. Too hot at present."

"We shall see." Within two days Leonardo was at Jim's door, begging to see me; in his arms he held green branches of cherry, pink and white with surprising fruit.

"Steva, these I grow for you under a box." I believed him and took the delicate *cigliege* from his boiling hands. Many other spiced gifts, too, he had brought and gave to me. Then he drew me aside and pointed across the long dry yellow miles of paddock, to where, against a silver fence stood a darkish creature. "*Questo cavallo, Steva, per te.* This horse, Steva, I give to you. This glorious *cavallo* you must ride and keep. This horse gallop like the wind, *come il vento.* When you come to my place soon, ride this horse down

186

and let me see you come fast to my house with your red scarf flying. *O Steva adorata!*"

Jim picked up his binoculars and trained them on the animal from the window. "Oh, it's that black stallion of yours, Leonardo. Gracious, do you think he would be safe to ride? He used to belong to Hunter down at Calulu, I remember. They brought him over from New South Wales with them, and he's rather a character."

"This horse not named Caractacus, Signor McLachlan, this horse named Inferno. He is quiet . . . good . . . kind. When you approach him he lifts up his eyes and sighs gently. He knows all that you are thinking. He, too, would like to go riding if you want to go riding. He will help you undo the halter sometimes; he will pull with you when you are tightening the girth; he will almost lift you into the saddle with his teeth."

"Ah," murmured Jim, "I've heard about those lifting teeth of his."

"He s-scratches and tears up the ground so eager is he to be off," thus Leonardo. "He opens all the gates you have before you, and if they cannot be opened, he——"

"Crashes through them, or scrapes you off in his fury to get them ajar, or jumps over them without warning and leaves you on the hard track with a split skull," said Jim. "Ah, yes, I've heard all about Inferno. He's got a great reputation down at Calulu. And is he supposed to be a Christmas present for poor little Steve here?"

"*Si*, Signor Jim." And Leonardo departed in high dudgeon. But the black stallion he left behind at the fence. I left him thus all night.

Next day I went over slowly and curiously to have a look at the gift horse. Far down the bleached lane against the stark wooden fence he stood with black head bent and massive body absolutely mad with energy. He looked very deathly to me, a lethal dose of horseflesh. He was not tied with a halter, but stood stock still in hobbles. Leonardo expected me to reach down and untie those hobbles and ride Inferno down to his place on the morrow, but I had no more idea of doing so than of flying in the air. I came back to Jim's place and told him so.

"I'll send my man over to untie the hobbles," Jim said. "But I think you should ride down to Leonardo's on your own horse, if you really intend to go."

So next morning I started out on my own horse, through the miles of scrub that lay between McLachlan's and Leonardo's, grey-green dogwood in thick white bushy flower. I thought of *caro* Peppino and wondered when he would write, and I remembered Macca, and the sad-sounding poems of Adam Lindsay Gordon came to my mind, down Calulu way.

Behind me lay the lakes and our early days there, when we were happy together and young and there was no end to life, the green about us on the olive earth, and the blue above us in noble heavens. And with Gordon I said:

> *"The skies were fairer and shores were firmer—*
> *The blue sea over the bright sand rolled;*
> *Babble and prattle, and ripple and murmur,*
> *Sheen of silver and glamour of gold. . . ."*

Down at Lakes Entrance, Banjo Paterson was writing while I rode, and adding yet more honours to Australian letters. I cantered down to Calulu, singing *"Cor' Ingrato"*:

> *"Cor', cor' ingrato,*
> *Ma turmiente vita mia . . ."*

A few wallabies and kangaroos rushed their valuable red-brown coats off into the wilderness as I approached, *en opéra*, with the grey armour slipping off Rosinante, as on some days I called the horse. Or Bucephalus, or Pegasus. The solid white stony moon stayed fast over Ajalon and I rode on. There was, after I had cantered down a long hill, one hill yet to go, and a straight run past Richard Shepherd's place. Sometimes the exquisite Richard was standing at his gate or his door, an amazing marble statue come out of the blue-grey dim bush, a male Galatea sprung so beautiful life there; a tall Kit Marlowe still singing melodiously, and asking all England sonorously and masterfully:

> *"Was this the face that launched a thousand ships,*
> *And burnt the topless towers of Ilium?"*

I always called him Kit Marlowe, that old, old name, rank with all the gigantic life that teemed in the lost back streets of London in the sixteenth century. Splendid dry wilderness that was Calulu, its book of verse was this Marlowe, the shepherd; its jug of wine was the enormous open breast of the sea, the white thunder-voiced Pacific, seen jade-green one day, with a huge tilt of wave, as high as a house, cream-blue in colour, trembling for a long, long moment, far out. . .

The marble-white one stood at his gate this morning staring at the great cracks in the equatorial earth. I said, "Good morning."

"Good morning." He had a very cold, reserved voice, an icy face but very handsome, classically so.

"And what was your last poem, Marlowe-Shepherd-Marlowe?"

"Oh, this, only", handing over a purple page with the poem written on it in delicate white ink.

> But Beauty is the red fox of the world,
> Hunted to earth by the horns and hounds of Time;
> They say that auburn Helen was down hurled
> By warrior shields and swords dipped in old rime,
> That Paris by dark Scamander buried deep,
> Murmurs for ever in his uneasy sleep,
> That Ilium's walls still warmed by red flames stand
> Looking toward Tenedos, where the sand
> Burns lilac far within the thickets grey
> Where gold-armed Greeks lay laughing all one day,
> And, setting warm lips upon their bright shields' rim,
> Chattered of Paris. "O, to Hades with him!
> And with all those whose locks for love are curled,
> And those who swear that wars and death are crime,
> For Beauty is the red fox of the world,
> Hunted to earth by the horns and hounds of Time."

"That's very beautiful, I think," I replied, handing it back to the poet.

"If I'm like Marlowe to look at, as you say," he explained, "I may as well write poetry."

"True." I rode on; not far ahead lay the great tip of the sea, the green, the clamorous, casting up the alpine wave of ice and snow far into the air. There was a sense of thunder in the horizon, and perhaps rain might be soon coming to bring brilliant hues from Asia to lie on the springy ferns down at Calulu that were netted in dry and split clay.

In the bright light of the full blue thunderous midday, behind a rich grey netting fence, strong-stretched, iron-hard, something ran . . . something terrible in its power . . . red-nostrilled, moonlight-eyed, with black thick outstretched throat, the most formidable stallion I have ever seen. He was in a mood of excessive anger and stared at me viciously, dangerously, savagely, then with a thin scream of hate and impatience, he fled, royal, shining and huge, into the impassive blue-gums with their blood-red branches, red as madrepore.

The next peculiar outpost of the past lay ahead, and it was really worth remembering. Two brothers, wealthy sheep-farmers, had a large property, which, to be seen to its best advantage, needed a very wet day. So I had first come upon it—pouring rain, sodden skies, thunder cracking the horizons apart with fork, sheet, and chain lightning, mud to a depth of six feet or more, slush and puddles everywhere, ditches lying open to all comers, hail and half-snow falling into one's face, hat, trench-boots, binocular case, sword-sheath, service-revolver holster and rifle barrel—ah, now, now we are nearing Journey's End.

We are there. This is no traditional home of two rich sheep-farmers—my God, what is this? I rode past, stunned. For these two brothers didn't live in a house at all; they lived in dug-outs! With regulation army trenches lying in front of them, and sandbagged areas rising in ramparts to the right and left.

On this day of rain and storm the two sheep-breeders were standing at ease before their dug-outs, field-glasses to their eyes, scanning me as though I had been the entire German Army. A large trench-mortar, bought apparently from the military authorities, stood with a black and searching nose on a stand before the door of one dug-out. The two brothers, tall, aristocratic, striking, stood together at the door of the main dug-out, togged out in complete trench outfit, down to the trench-boots. The rain fell white and thick and strong; the brethren stared at me, expectantly, as though they thought I was their officer-commanding, straying from this lost war of theirs, or Napoleon riding home alone from Moscow in the most profound melancholy. I stared back at them, and cut them a smart salute; they sprang to life and cut me a couple in return; after which I rode on, thinking that, being utterly English, we should spend the rest of our lives cutting each other. I had met them again, though, at Leonardo's, and they had promised to one day tell me why they lived thus in the midst of their riches. On this hot day I rode past the imitation Marne, or Somme, or Ypres, and hoped that the two troglodytes would be present when I reached the home of the virginal one.

Through the gate and down past a stupefyingly fertile garden of cucumbers, tomatoes, and lettuces, I rode, and to the door of Leonardo. You would have thought that the two great geniuses of Italy were meeting, for our ceremonious greetings were heavy with the centuries.

"Benvenuto . . . Benvenuto . . ." cried Leonardo. "But, Steva, the horse I gave thee—where is it?"

"Cellini . . . Cellini . . ." I responded happily. "*Amico mio*, I have been so long away that you have forgotten my name! *Ahimè*, this will never do. Who ever on this earth could forget Benvenuto Cellini? Am I not still the greatest gold- and silver-smith in all Italia? *Si*." Curse the horse! I wished that he would forget the sullen brute.

Leonardo bowed and agreed with me.

"And thou, Leonardo, art thou not still Italy's finest painter, her greatest engineer, her most gifted musician, poet, writer, sculptor in marble and maker of aeroplanes? *Credimi, credimi!* Thou, Leonardo, the favourite of popes, cardinals, kings, and princes!" Curse the horse, I thought. "It foundered, O Leonardo," I said soothingly.

"*Davvero, davvero, Stevano!*" Leonardo agreed with me in whatever I said. He was stout and rugged and rosy and knew no more about art than the river-rat running round his amiable doors, but I took him to my heart as artist and brother. "*Tu sei Benvenuto Cellini, senza dubbio*, welcome, welcome, welcome." The doors were flung wide open, the wine-flasks swinging by straw handles from the glowing walls were taken down and opened, and across the red depths we saluted each other. Rotund and compact, in from the long brown fields, came Leonardo's man, Gennaio, or January.

"But the horse I gave thee, it foundered . . . how?" worried Leonardo.

"Aha," said I, "the old friend of Napoleon salutes him once

191

more. General January, my best friend when I struck Moscow at the same time as someone else did. *Et tu, Gennaio? Come va?* The horse died," I said hastily to Leonardo.

Gennaio had never had the pleasure of meeting me before, and looked rather stunned.

"*Chi? Chi? Chi è questa?*" he exclaimed to Leonardo. "Who is this?"

"It is *Monsieur l'Empereur!*"

Leonardo, stunned, was thinking of the horse. "Dead? Dead? So soon?"

I rose up, wine-glass in hand, with one lock of red-black hair lying over my green eyes and my golden face glittering with fire. "Yes, I slew it."

"It is *uno spirito diabolico*," howled Gennaio, and he rushed from the room, crying, "A diabolical spirit is in the house with us! Bring the priest and the holy water and exorcise it! If he slew the horse, what of us?"

Leonardo and I fled after the flying month and caught it just as it was about to tread on the tame water-rat, and handed it the vegetables for the evening meal to prepare; and by the time General January had toiled through the potatoes and beans he was normal again. The blue sea outside the mistral windows kept filling the darkening room with daylight, with east lights, north lights, and south lights, until the last light from the west, all flag crimson, came square by square into us, when the fire began to glow more vividly, and Leonardo cast on the wide table green grape-vines and grapes themselves and many things to eat. Wine did we drink and had rich cakes to eat and Italian dishes of caviare and tunny fish. This most delicious fish, sharply salted and well flavoured, Leonardo served with clever oil salads. And the caviare we ate with our top-hats on, and no man said us nay. At night, with guitars, we thrummed and sang . . .

"*O dolce Napule, O sole beato,*
Con me sorridere volle il creato."

I was awake early next morning, down Calulu way where the bright banter of sea and shore make an ultramarine hue come darkly into the tide by noon. The sun in my room found a Watteau shimmer all over the place, for Leonardo had had this room decorated for me, especially, so that I might stay there whenever I liked. From somewhere in the city he had bought up yards of ancient watered silk, deep cream, with shifting patterns of pink, green, and brown-yellow, and the hangings and quilts and curtains were all of this.

Gennaio was sent in with my breakfast; soon afterwards I rose and rode round the property with Leonardo. He always insisted on showing me the place whenever I came down to visit him. We rode round the sheep; they were luxuriant with silver fleece; we took the tea in our stride, and Leonardo was suppliant with many questions regarding McLachlan's secrets of tea-blending, but I could tell him nothing.

Suddenly a large green-black snake about six feet in length shot out its hole right under the feet of our horses. Leonardo yelled out for Gennaio, and his man came running from some corner of the farm to see what was wrong.

"Serpe! Serpe!" exclaimed Leonardo. The beautiful reptile lay on the dry earth, hissing from its open mouth and showing a mouth full of compound teeth and a long forked yellow tongue, which darted back and forth with machine-like precision. And its small, flat-looking eye, like the dead eye of the white silken crane in a Chinese tapestry my mother had at home, held the landscape about it, the gem-like crops and the sun moving, cloud-surrounded, through the windy sky—all this one could see in the small flat eye of the black snake. Gennaio departed with it in a box, bent on sending it somewhere where it would be both a source of interest and profit, and Leonardo and I kept on with our inspection of the farm and the tea-plantation. He had a small crop put in, very healthy looking. Oddly enough, his leaf had a very South African look about it, a totally different type of tea-plant to McLachlan's. I climbed up a slight hill and stood on top where a reedy pool held a little water and looked down on the plantation and the farm. On a slope of rich volcanic hill, seven men were working among the beans.

"I fagioli," said Leonardo proudly. The beans.

While we sat on horseback watching them, one of the seven flung down his hoe and made for a large gum-tree with a deep pool of dust under it. We were interested to see what he would do next. Taking a small book out of his pocket, he carefully opened it at a particular page that appeared to have diagrams on it. This book he set up against a stone, and then, rapidly removing his shorts, he stood before us in a pair of neat bathing briefs. Still staring earnestly at the book, he took a sort of short dive into the dust and lying flat on his face began to do a form of Australian trudgen stroke, or crawl, in the soil under the tree. Strange strokes I had never seen before, swift squirming lurches to left and right, while his legs worked up and down with such vigour that they made the dust rise like a cyclone about him. He was hidden from all eyes within a few seconds, and we stood and stared upon this local dust-storm of some magnitude under the trees.

"*Cosa fa?*" I questioned Leonardo. "What is he doing?"

"Oh," said Leonardo with obvious pride and delight, "He *squeem* . . ."

"What?"

"He make for squeem . . . in water . . . like-a this . . . like-a that . . ." and he nearly knocked me off my horse with his whirling arms.

"Oh, you mean swim?"

"*Si, si* . . . swim. Oh, this young fellow very good squeemer. He squeem all the time like this, every day."

"In the dust here, under this tree?"

"Yes, yes, he like this more better than water, but he squeem well in water, too."

The swimmer kept his eye fixed on the small book with its diagrams, and apparently obeyed its instructions faithfully. Talk about Grantchester and Rupert Brooke, and the shade of George Gordon, Lord Byron . . .

> Still in the dawnlit waters cool,
> His ghostly Lordship swims his pool
> And tries the strokes, essays the tricks,
> Long learnt on Hellespont, or Styx.

Here, seemed to be some lost part of him, essaying another sort of trick, in thick dust under the gum-trees. I drew near and stared down at the volume, *Learn to Swim in Twenty-one Lessons: A Manual Issued by the Education Department of Victoria*. The

194

swimmer, a fair-haired young man, looked up and saw me. I raised my eyebrows and he raised himself from the dust.

"This is strange, *signor*," I said.

"I am sorry, *signorina*, I have to do this; it is a matter of form."

"Form is the word," I replied, "with a good hearty accent on it, too."

He put on his shorts again and said, "If you care for a swim after I am finished work, *signorina*, I shall be down on the beach in front of Leonardo's waiting for you."

"Will you be taking that book into the water with you?" I asked.

"Oh yes," very seriously.

"I shall be there, and, Leonardo——"

"*Si, Stevano?*"

"If you would be good enough to put out in your launch and hold the book over the side for the young man to read while he swims, all will be well."

"I shall do that, Steva," Leonardo assured me.

"And, *signor*, does the book advise you always to practise in the dust?"

"*Si, signorina*," emphatically.

"What? Let me have a look at that book." I took it from him and read the indicated paragraph. " 'Lie down in just the lightest of swimming trunks . . . lie down in just the same position as indicated on the chart . . .' Not dust," I explained through shrieks of laughter. "No, no, not dust—*just!*"

"Just? Just?" repeated the swimmer. "What does 'just' mean?"

"*E giusto . . . giusto . . . exacto . . .*"

"Oh, not dust like dirt here under this tree?" His face fell nearly to the ground. "I show it to Leonardo; he say, 'just' mean dirt. 'Lie in it!' Leonardo say. I thought it was because of being *più securo* . . . more safe."

"No, no, just a way of making you do exactly as the manual says."

"Oh, good. And then one day I see little birds swimming in the dust, like that, and I thought perhaps it was the Australian style of swimming."

"Those birds weren't swimming; they were cleaning their feathers."

"Oh . . . thanks, thanks, *signorina*." And back to his work went the swimmer.

"He's a nice-looking boy," I said. "What's his name?"

"Nino Nuvola."

"Oh, Nino Cloud."

Leonardo and I rode away down to the house again and Gennaio began to prepare our lunch. In the large *forno*, or white oven outside in the garden, the hot bread was baking for the meal; a kind of tamale was cooking on the fire. Leonardo loved these, and so did I. He ate them at all hours, dripping with red sauce and peppers.

In the late afternoon Nino and Leonardo and I went swimming in the flat tide; the swimmer left his manual behind and did quite well. We spent the next day in a *festa*. Gennaio set the table to the tune of guitars. The day was hot and brilliant against the sea and sky, and all the ends of the world in immortal weather were gathered there. Towards noon there was a knock on the door, and a tall, thin man poked his head round and inquired, "*Con permesso?*"

"*Si, si!*" exclaimed Vergine.

The tall one slowly insinuated his form into the room and bowed to us.

"This is Vita Cherinuova," said our host. "*Sedete, sedete.*"

"My name," said the thin man significantly, "means 'big snake'. Yesterday, Leonardo, you caught a big snake?"

"*Si.*"

"But I am the sort of snake no one ever catches."

"*Sedete, sedete*," implored Vergine politely.

And in English, too, Vita Cherinuova was begged to sit down, sit down, for not every day does one see a big snake sitting on a chair. Out in the garden near the glazed-breathed, whitewashed oven the real snake rattled away harshly in its box. Vita Cherinuova was a remarkable-looking man; he had the air of one who had travelled all over the world, and so he had. For a snake he had certainly wriggled around a good bit.

Slowly he sipped his red wine, and the yellow tongue of the snake outside seemed to be twisted all through his soul; one could almost see the hues of it sticking out through his tweed clothes. We listened hour-long to him as he wandered, before our eyes, over

196

Austria, whence he had drawn the haggard faces of all the people of Vienna, by the subtle look of him, and through France, the hard iron black industrial part of it, and over into the rioting Germany that was, once.

Again there was a knock at the door; this time it was one of the English brothers who lived in that sandbagged, trench-mortared sheep farm across the way—Frank Foster, a tall aristocratic man of about sixty years of age. Delicate, nervous, sensitively quivering all over, he spoke a uniquely proud, deliberate English, and one watched his mouth absorbedly, seeing the phrases forming there with masterful precision. He had just come from Judge Box's, he told us, and the judge had said that he might be over later on in the afternoon, to share the *festa* with us. On hearing this, Leonardo arose in haste and set Gennaio to work to make tamales by the dozen, to bring out the special bottles of Chianti and every cake and sweetmeat in the house.

I had met the judge before; he had retired from the bench in Melbourne and come to live along a creek called Box's Creek; before that it was known to us as the Argosy Creek, and before that as Conrad's Creek, but Judge Box sank all these names and called it after himself. He spent half of his days in his big carpentering shed, sawing, hammering, chiselling and planing. And day in and day out he wore no other dress than that worn by the great Oscar Wilde, knee-breeches and black silk stockings. And that in the Australian bush. It meant that he was devoted to and loved Oscar Wilde more than any other writer living or dead. And he believed Wilde to be as innocent as a babe unborn of any crime under the sun.

Frank Foster said, "Judge Box has lent me a superb book called *Pomp and Pageantry*." In my mind, I saw the judge, flinging it, as it were, at his friend, with the remark, "Only rubbish compared to Wilde, but take it where you will and talk about it—might help the writer a bit."

Frank Foster didn't really tell us what the book was about; he stood off it and flung adjectives to it and around it, embellishing it and London modern society as he did so. It was, one felt, rather precarious to talk about in its actuality. But through his long talk with Leonardo, one heard the Oxford boom, from time to time, of *Pomp and Pageantry*. Wool was mentioned and fleeces rolled out

197

from the mouths of men, but fell clinging at last to *Pomp and Pageantry*. Tea-plants clung to the hot soil and quivered under the assault of the name, and oil sprang hot and gaseous from shale bores to the tune of *Pomp and Pageantry*.

From the purple-grey water, among the salty mangroves far out, arose the mistral—for to my mind that beautiful name should be given only to the sea wind, the cool salt wind of afternoon; it is by some strange error that men have come to use it otherwise. And to me that wind was filled with the golden sand from the shores of France, the vivid yellow and tan of those beaches, with their sun-baked thousands of bathers rising and walking down to the water's edge to swim. Here only the lonely seagulls cried and rose on wavering wings looking downward. It was now afternoon and at the door stood Tomaso, Judge Box's man, saying that his master had arrived.

Vergine ran out into the hot sunlight to bring him in, and we all sat in decorous silence while the judge ate and drank. He was very short and slender, with a white, delicate face and hot-tempered eyes and an exceedingly irascible manner. He sat among us, exactly as he did in the court in Melbourne. We felt very afraid of him; he had such an air of judicial authority about him that we literally trembled before him. He was not interested in us at all, however, but sat there in a large chair, in his black silk, and began, after a while, to speak to Frank Foster of Oscar Wilde. If Wilde had been alive he would certainly have felt himself vindicated and his innocence established that day.

He quoted *Salome* in French and English and it sounded like an intricate and beautiful night arising from the grave to the stars. But both men were obviously so great that we fell silent before them and listened to their talk of books and writers, until at last they rose to go.

The days that followed spumed up from the lake like foam with *dolce far niente*; on the old typewriter in Leonardo's office, which overlooked the water, I wrote all his letters, mostly to agents in Melbourne. The name only of one I remember now, an agent named Silk. I wrote to him in an equal fashion. Then there was a dispute about a fence—"*la fensa*", as Leonardo called it. The trouble over *la fensa* was long and complicated; it needed a good deal of thought, and we had many consultations about it. Vergine

198

talked and gesticulated and sat down, carving walking sticks while I worked. Down the long hall, on either side, stood bottle after bottle of Chianti. The men were shearing now in the big shed and fleece was flying flower-like all over the ground.

Just before sunset Leonardo and I went walking across from shore to shore on the point, where the wind blew its loneliest and withered grass grew; behind us the unforgotten and beloved sun of my country, slowly going down, red and huge and blown on by the last wind of the day; behind us in the curling pasture, as grey as themselves, fed Grecian-looking sheep, still remembering Jason when all others had forgotten. Strongly blew the inscrutable wind, tentatively sparkled the last red light of the sun, broken into gold, and the sheep tugged at the beloved grass, the hair of the continent . . . ah, very Greek it was, as though a thousand years ago, one had walked this same earth with one like Vergine; and when he spoke through the classic atmosphere his very remark was pure poetry; it rose like clouds from the earth and ascended to heaven.

"Buona anno per la lana. A good year for wool."

And year after year, following this benediction, it has remained a good year for wool. Then did the sun sink and the earth grow cool and we departed.

The younger of the Foster brothers came along to see us and dine with us. He was animated and vivid in his manners and speech, and spoke both Italian and English. Sitting tall and brown at the table, he proceeded to tell us about the dug-outs. "Why do we live in dug-outs? Why do we have sandbag fortifications about our place? Why do we sport a trench-mortar? We even have duckboards—why? Well, I shall tell you. More wine, Vergine, you will need it, for this is a short but extraordinary story."

Punk, or sea-wood, was flung on to the fire until it rose in green, red and purple flame. In those parts such timber was known as nothing but punk, for it was light and empty. As it burnt more wine was poured out, hot tamales served, and a fitting shower fell outside, and beat at the window to get in and listen with us to the story of Picardy, or wherever it was that the dug-outs had come from.

"Those dug-outs of ours," said Bill Foster, "have little to do with the Great War, through which we passed some years ago. They have to do with a lost young staff-officer, a jacaranda-tree, casuarina-trees, a pandanus, a steamer, and a large field-gun. And they have to do with that part of France known as Picardy. About 1899 or 1900 something happened between Germany and Great Britain which the brass hats and red tabs kept to themselves, strictly, very strictly, for there is no public record of it, to this day. The Kaiser decided to make a little move through Belgium to Paris. The British military authorities got wind of it, and moved at once. With all possible secrecy they sent a force over at once into Picardy; my brother and I were among them; we did nothing but very small significant things. A very long, deep trench was dug, miles long, in the yellow and red clay; sandbag ramparts were built up, very high; long-range guns were planted where they would reach the spot; headquarters was established at a town behind the lines, right among the best *estaminets* in case of embarrassment, and we sat down behind our long-range guns and waited for the enemy.

"They came; they saw; and we conquered. A week of our artillery, and German staff-officers and English staff-officers met and talked it over. And then, next thing, it *was* over. All save for one young man, the son of a titled man in England. He was missing, the sole and only one. We searched for him everywhere, unavailingly. He never turned up. But we knew him well, and he had a premonition that he would go out to it, some day, and be lost, and he said to us, 'It'll be loss of memory. So, wherever you wander, if you build up a place to live in, make it as much like this dug-out and these trenches of ours as you can, and what with pontoons and duckboards and trench-mortars and sandbags, I'll remember something. And I've a feeling it ought to be in Gippsland, Australia, because in the *London News* nowadays they're always advertising Elliman's Liniment, with this ghastly dry Gippsland, Australia, as an advertising background, and I've a feeling that I'll some day land in that horrid place, with complete lack of memory. It would be like death, but if I saw your place all rigged out like these trenches I really would remember in a sort of a way, or feel some sense of life in me. So, if ever you two ever happen to gravitate out to that particular Aceldama, remember me, and get a place near the road as much like this trench in Picardy, as possible. And plant casuarina- and jacaranda-trees about it, and I shall remember.'"

"And did he ever come?" I asked.

"Sometimes we think he did, and took one look at the awful mad mixture and fled cured without calling in on us to make us remember him. Its just something that we do, half for his sake and now, almost entirely for our own. Because we like living that way now. It's picturesque, picaresque, and Picardesque." Bill Foster laughed.

Was this story true? It seemed unlikely, to say the least of it, but there was some subtle shade of feeling about it that haunted me for a long while after, and whenever I passed the dug-outs I almost thought I saw that British Army and that German Army of the years before the Great War marching slowly through green grass and yellow clay to where howitzers stood line on line, waiting and holding off death.

We came home to lunch one day to find a little Italian sitting on the floor of the kitchen playing jacks. Standing above him, we watched the skilful throwing of the knuckle bones, as he herded them into the hollow of his hands. Finally he rose and said, *"Buon' di!"*

"Buon' di. What are you doing, *signor?"*

"I do not know," he replied in Italian. "I cannot speak English, so I do not know what I am doing." Pointing to the jacks, he said, "What you call these things in English?"

"Jacks."

"Ah, jacks."

"What is your name?"

"Salvatore Punchinello." He was very small and dark, with a twisted brown face, sharp teeth and full lips; over his shoulder hung a wine-flask of leather, from a long strap. And in his hand he carried a square tin box covered with rawhide. This he opened and began to eat from a farrago of roast meat and oil therein. We looked at the unappetizing abomination, which seemed vaguely familiar to me, I didn't know why.

"And what is that, Salvatore?" we asked.

"That," he said, "is roast fox. *Volpe.*"

Dio! I remembered David Garnett's book, *Lady into Fox,* and

201

hoped that Salvatore wouldn't turn into a fox before our eyes and be off to the music of horns and hounds.

Leonardo departed hastily, saying, "Scusami, I womit." And, far out in the garden, he did.

Gennaio called in all the dogs at once. At the sight of Punchinello devouring the remains of their mortal enemy they rushed forward and barked him out of the kitchen and far away. We saw no more of him, this eater of foxes, with his white jacks and his leather flask of wine. He was like an old medieval painting, crude, strong, harsh, and evil. I imagined him going fast night and day in the pursuit of the red-hided foxes and slaying them and devouring them in all the forests that lay about the sea.

Leonardo took to making biltong shortly after this, for the cooking of his eternal chili *con carne*. Strips of raw meat were hung out on a big wire frame in the frying sunlight to dry. The frame looked like the cage of a magpie having all its birthdays at once, when he had finished. He managed to get most of the meat into biltong before sundown; a mob of interested blowflies, however, beat him to it with part of it, and he made moan accordingly.

The biltong was stored away in large casks in the pantry, and it was grey-brown in colour and not uninteresting to look at. The eating of it provided us with much hard labour, and it seemed that there was only one thing to do, and that was to make a set of teeth from a cross-cut saw and attack the dried meat with that. Since it would soon be Christmas time Leonardo got to work then and pickled a barrel full of beans, cucumbers, and onions, and a great appetizer that was. Men staggered from his table after a hearty meal and called him, not Vergine, but Vinegar.

All this was as nothing to me. I walked the shores of the lake, and remembered Macca, the red-gold. The thought of him was so pleasant. We are worshippers of images, even unto death. We must have an image to worship, even when love is past, and marriage and all else. Now down Calulu's shores I walked in the summer night. Beside me Nino, the Cloud, strode along with his fair arms gleaming in the dark, and a wristwatch throbbing luminously against the sea.

For lack of something better to do, I was quoting Brooke's "Waikiki":

"And dark scents whisper; and dim waves creep to me,
  Gleam like a woman's hair, stretch out, and rise;
  And new stars burn into the ancient skies,
  Over the murmurous soft Hawaiian sea.

"And I recall, lose, grasp, forget again,
  And still remember, a tale I have heard, or known,
  An empty tale, of idleness and pain,
  Of two that loved—or did not love—and one
  Whose perplexed heart did evil foolishly,
  A long while since, and by some other sea."

And into Italian translating it roughly for the sake of Nino, he who was like those same soft Hawaiian seas and the ancient skies of Hawaii. The small words of English could not find rest or imagery in the long pedantic Italian.

"Ah, the night, the night," murmured Nino. God, the pain of hearing the living voice of man against the darkness!

And then there was that poem that reminded me of Macca, written by Brooke between South Kensington and Makaweli in 1913, dear "Mutability".

Dear, we know only that we sigh, kiss, smile;
  Each kiss lasts but the kissing; and grief goes over;
  Love has no habitation but the heart.
  Poor straws! on the dark flood we catch awhile,
  Cling, and are borne into the night apart.
  The laugh dies with the lips, "Love" with the lover.

Looking down on the floating straws that are men and women and their love, I was only glad to see the morning again, for at night I fret for the sorrow of life. This glorious sun that rises clean of all human form, a thing of the gods, and heedless of all things save the earth to which it vibrates, that soon burns away sorrow for man and woman and love. The very grass that grows is greater, alas.

I went out riding without a saddle to bring in fourteen or fifteen head of horses for Gennaio to take to the forge and shoe. When

o

I leapt onto the horse's naked back it seemed the spirit of Argentina and Mexico sprang up out of the earth and rode with me, too. This dry yellow wind that blew down here at Calulu, I loved it to swing about me like breathing imagery. Over impassive soil I rode and found the horses in a torrid corner of a paddock. Lunging in amongst them, I sent them startled and brown, black and white, galloping down to the stockyard. God, one could live for ever among the silken hues of their downward piston-stamping hooves! Bitter moment when it would be ended—I longed to become part of death, if death were the endless stamping of horses and their nobility.

I was running them into the stockyard when, in their very lustrous midst, my horse rolled sideways, and I fell headlong among and under the yellow ivory hooves of the galloping mob. They swerved aside and I escaped without a touch from them. And after a deathlessly glorious moment that I wished could have gone on for ever, I stood up, remounted, and got the bronze-angled equine warriors into the yard.

While I stood bemused with poetry in the lion days of the virgin, as I called the time I spend at Leonardo's, there came to me a letter from Peppino who stayed in the sweet harbours of sugar at Maffra.

"*Cara Steva, tu sei, credo, in mezzo a tanti uomini*·. . ." Written in bright-red ink, this looked haunted and weird, but such a sounding phrase! Of what power and significant magnificence! I strode around for days afterward, along the blue froth of the shore, over the copper earth, the bronzed grass, the withering-Grecian weed, crying, "*Tu sei in mezzo a tanti uomini*. You are among many men."

Yes, I was among many men and many waters, and a thousand suns and moons of my delight. Let the sun glare down on the white ovens, and the black snakes listen for me as I strode over their cavernous homes in the earth, and the dry curled sheep cry out for evermore for the lost golden fleece that the gods in the beginning promised them; it was nothing to me. I was with Leonardo della Vergine, and to be with him was to be with all archaic Italy. Once more did we labour through the enchanted days in the blue and white, black, clear gardens of the *Decameron*; and through those sultry nights live again; for the virgin spent one

204

part of the day in work, and the other part in drinking red wine and in the telling of tales like Boccaccio's, but with a purity and passion unknown to that unfortunate, whose stories in the original Italian were probably so beautiful and full of genius that *Madre Italia* destroyed them and substituted those we shrink from now ... with a scornful glance along four hundred years to some of us, and a cry of, "*A basta! Indegno a!* Enough ... unworthy!" The name Boccaccio means "one with a big mouth"; and Italy closed that mouth so that we could not hear all of what was said of the secret century, that summer of fever, long ago.

I did not bother to answer Peppino's letter, for on days when I was not working I was out riding with Leonardo, our horses striking notes of wine from the little glasses that the sand of the sea has not yet made, nor the spuming north-westers blown. Or with Nino I plunged, with a furious white slamming slap, from the jetty of the virgin, deep into the phosphorus. How it gilded one's limbs by night, and sped along the blood in fire. With the summer-ecstatic fish we slid in and out along the murmuring depths, our joined hands slipping and sliding apart. And the golden hair of Nino forced forth flames like planets.

Therefore Peppino wrote again, fearing that I had abandoned him, that an enemy had turned me against him.

Dear Steva,

Sono molto in pensiero per il tuo silenzio, e temo d'essere abbandonato!

Forse hai ricevuto qualche lettera da un mio nemico che t'ha persuasa a lasciarmi.

Sono infinitamente addolorato; due lettere t'ho scritto e da te nulla!

Sono triste assai, pazienza.

PEPPINO.

Enchanted by this cry of sorrow, I spent days happier and richer than ever. These two letters, in my hands, rapidly wrinkled until to me they looked like bank-notes worth thousands of pounds.

On afternoons like amber, when there was a salty loneliness to all things, and through the rooms drifted the grass wind, with its long, sad, droning cry, Vita Cherinuova would come into the room where I was working over the virgin's accounts, carrying a bag of pale-pink bean seed, which he would put down with the dark canvas fine sieve, the beloved of the Spanish school of painters, and begin to sort and sing.

Against the noise of water and the crisp rolling voice of the shore, his song rose out of some red-velveted opera house of Rome:

> *"Fronde teneri e belle,*
> *Del mio platano amato,*
> *Per voi, risplendo il fato."*

Remembering then the rattling thunder of the Prologue from Pagliacci, in those rose-pink heavens about my hut—ah, my hut!—I asked Vita if he would sing that, and on the guitar he strummed the accompaniment.

"A word," sang Vita, "allow me!

> *"Sweet ladies and gentlemen,*
> *I pray you hear why I alone appear.*
> *I am the Prologue.*
> *Our author loves the custom of the prologue to his story.*
> *And as he would revive for you the ancient glory,*
> *He sends me to speak before you. . . ."*

At this point we heard a loud cry or two from outside and, staring across the paddocks through a side window, saw Gennaio standing on a small hill, on the other side of which stood the hut of Vita.

"Ah!" exclaimed Vita. "There is that Gennaio. He wants me to do some dirty work for him. I can't see him, can you? If he notices you, pull those flowers out of the vase and hold them to your face and pretend to be a tree."

"What? Inside the house?"

"Nothing would surprise him."

Vita sang on, entranced by his own melodious voice:

> *"But not to prate as once of old*
> *That the tears of the actors are false, unreal,*
> *That his sighs and cries of pain is told,*
> *He has no heart to feel."*

Vita stopped for a moment. "That's like me. I have not heart to feel. Not one thing in this whole world could make me move in a hurry, or give me any feeling of agitation."

"*Tu sei fortunato, O Vita.*" But Vita was prologuing again:

> "*No, no! Our author tonight a chapter will borrow from life,*
> *With its laughter and sorrow.*
> *Is not the actor a man with a heart like you?*"

"By Jove," I said, looking out of the window at Gennaio, "there's some acting going on out on that hill with Gennaio! He is an actor, a man with a heart like I don't know what. Gods, now he's jumping up and down and howling with awful agony. Now Leonardo's joined him, and they're both jumping up and down and shrieking . . ."

> "*So 'tis for men that our author has written . . .*"

Wilder shrieking and leaping upon the hill by the twain.

> "*And the story he tells you is true.*"

I thought privately that Leonardo and Gennaio must have something to tell Vita that was true, too, but no, he wouldn't stir. He had just reached the *bell'aria* part, "*Un Nido di Memorie*"—"A Nest of Tender Memories".

> "*A song of tender memories*
> *Deep in his listening heart one day was ringing,*
> *And then with a trembling hand he wrote it.*
> *And he marked the time with sighs and tears.*"

Leonardo had got an old horse- or cow-bell now, and was ringing it hard on the hill.

"He has been at me for days to clean out the stables," said Vita obstinately. "Let him roar." And Vita himself roared:

> "*Come then! Here on the stage you shall behold us*
> *in human fashion,*
> *And see the sad fruits of love and passion.*
> *Hearts that weep and languish and bitter*
> *laughter . . .*"

Gennaio and Leonardo, running up and down the hill frantically, were by this time weeping and languishing and their bitter laughter could be heard a mile off. I stared and stared and Vita sang on:

"*Ah think, then, sweet people, when you gaze ...*"

And *were* they gazing? Ah, they gazed all right!

"*Look on us!*"

The infuriated pair did, too!

> "*Clad in motley and our tinsel,*
> *Ours are human hearts beating with passion.*
> *We are men like you for gladness and sorrow,*
> *Tis the same broad heaven above us ...*"

Behind the two men beating with passion and jumping with either gladness or sorrow on the hill I saw—what? *Cielo!* What did I see?

"Vita ... Vita ... !"

> "*The same lonely world before us,*
> *Will ye then hear the story?*
> *How it unfolds itself, surely and certain?*"

"Vita, my God! It is your hut. It is afire! For heaven's sake run, run, and help put it out. Your clothes, your best clothes, Vita!"

"*Dio mio!*" howled Pagliacci, springing up, shrieking, running, leaping, the last great lines forgotten, for he vanished among them.

> "*Come then ... ring up the curtain!*"

Vita rung it up, twisted himself in it, fell in it, rolled around in it, and departed wrapped up in it, to save his motley and his tinsel, for the same lonely world lay before us and he would have to face it dressed in bags if the hut wasn't saved.

Up rose columns of blue, yellow, and white smoke, red flame and the smell of burning raiment. Vita scampered over the hill and when he got to Leonardo, the virgin and his servant marked the actor with sighs and trembling hearts and ringing memories, and the three sweet people toiled to save the hut and the best clothes of Vita Cherinuova. And for long after there was no more unpopular song in Calulu than the Prologue to Pagliacci.

Day after glorious day passed against a fine screen of drying biltong, green beans pickling, sheep's cheese maturing into marble, and drying plains and *mare nostrum*, our sea, sending her long blue stormy spears sliding searchingly inland.

It was like part of the life of Théophile Gautier on the Great Blue Desert.

> *"Existence sublime!*
> *Bercés par notre nid,*
> *Nous vivons sur l'abîme*
> *Au sein de l'infini;*
> *Des flots, rasant la cime,*
> *Dans le grand désert bleu*
> *Nous marchons avec Dieu!"*

Always swimming in splendour before my eyes was that poem of his, the beloved "*Les Matelots*"; the blue-capped sailors, toiling, came to mind, and through it all surged the *Burrabogie*, passing us weekly on her trip down to Melbourne laden with tea, sugar, oil and wattle-bark. Entranced with the chart-line straightness of the foam she trailed, I thought the whole world might be placed on the level current of a blue-lined page of paper and sent to Macca as a letter, that noon and grand blue desert and red camellias might be one.

Dear Mackinnon, dear mate,

I am now down staying with the virgin, the lion-yellow virgin, and his vinous house is open to me and to all strangers. Here do we drink and live like Bacchus decorous and work much under the sun or in cool windy rooms against the clouds of silver fleece; for the virgin has a custom of storing his wool as it is sheared in all the rooms, in bales as fine as veils, through which the delicate glimpse of the mask of the fleece may be seen in bearded beauty. Blue tides flow through the windows, bright fleeces shine like the sun in the rooms, and the wine dances in the flasks along the walls. On the hearth, the ruby fire glows all day under the black frying-pans of Murillo, for we have built for ourselves a new Morocco here, and a fresh school of art have we raised from the dust.

But I shall be leaving the virgin soon, and coming back again from Calulu to McLachlan's. I hear that you will be down towards Christmas for the fishing, that slow heavy white period of power when the lakes are silver with sacrifice. I shall see you soon, then, Macca, I hope, for down here, the year and the crops are both waning. And I have a feeling that I shall not be in the Lakes district next Christmas.

The account-books of the virgin were all balanced and laid out ready for him in the coming year, 1929; I gave him, with McLachlan's permission, the names and addresses of the agents in Melbourne from whom he could buy special tea-plants that they imported from the Islands or the East; and I left a fine flavour of culture and Calulu in the mouths of the Melbourne buyers, and kept them wondering for months and years afterwards who was the writer of the intoxicating prose about crops and fleeces down along the Lakes.

"And soon, O Vergine," I said to him, "I must go from your house to that of Signor McLachlan's, for the tea will be ready for picking, and he will be busy."

The virgin turned pale and almost fell to the floor with shock and misery. I was his life, his stay; he had grown to feel that he could not live without me.

"Ahimè . . . ahimè, Steva," he said, "how shall I live . . . senza di te. Stay, O Steva, and make the days happy!"

"Alas, Leonardo," I answered, "great is my delight with you; I am at peace in your house, but the pressure of the years carries me onward. I shall remember your house forever, with the great light of the sun blanching it white against the aboriginal grey earth, and whenever I hear the songs of Italy ricorderŏ il mio amico buono, della Vergine. But, behold, in his field stands a red-haired prince of China, waiting for me to return and set the white net of my hand on the green seas of the tea."

"Fa la festa, fa la festa," cried the virgin to Gennaio, "and set on the table the green Chianti, biltong, pickles, and all the fruits

210

and the most sweet grapes that Steva may feast before she goes from us."

Redly the wine we drank poured out into the sun, into the day, and at last, by virtue of it, I was seeing a double virgin, a far stranger coin than a treble noble or an obvious obolus, and I called Leonardo "da Vinci", in that strong and positive voice which I harbour within my soul, and which, if it rang out clear, might send the bricks falling from the walls of the enchanting Jericho called the past. And I could have sworn that he was da Vinci, for a moment. But still, outside near the cavernous stifled hot voice of the oven, the black snake shuddered in its cage. Gennaio, the month of January, and Leonardo, the virgin, had taken it to their hearts and were teaching it to dance the schottische to the liquid lyrics of their guitars. Saluting them suitably, I left them to their new profession, and rode home along the white silty road from Calulu to Metung. I had had a happy time with *tanti uomini*.

Slowly I rode home from Leonardo's, carrying bundles of dainties from the feast we had had, a little of everything save a slice of the black snake. I had as much biltong on board as I could comfortably carry and a flask of wine to bear the cargo of *pasta* and *dolce* down. The bush was long, lonely, and dogwooded for miles; for the benefit of those who are strangers to this tree, I shall describe it as being of a dolorous hue, a sad dull green, wistful, straight. The leaves are many and feathery light, and the broad cream-white blossom, which is too individual to really be a blossom, is just a sort of crumbly excrescence, which smells most deliciously after rain.

At the side of the road stood a deserted home, which was a sort of guest-house frequented by the hundreds of red wallabies and kangaroos who lived just up the gully and over the range. I rode in off the road to have a look at them. There they were, two or three hundred of them, standing in worn red woolly-looking hides, calmly feeding just outside the door, or musing over the few flowers in the front garden. Under the rich, cumbrous peach-tree a large number stood picking peaches and holding them in their long black-nailed paws to their mouths and eating them slowly and thoughtfully. They heard the horse, looked up and saw me, and ate on; a few scampered off up the dry gully, but the rest remained outside their little home, in which they appeared to take a very real interest and to which, apparently, they were much attached. I stared for a long while at their dull-red moth-eaten hides, much worn as though they had rubbed up against gum-trees a lot, and at last rode on, thinking that if the virgin had seen them he would have bound them all to an apprenticeship with him, to learn some trade or other.

I heard a threatening rattle ahead, and saw Jeff Creeker coming along the shale track with a young light draught mare in between the shafts of a spring-cart, which was full of turnips. He stopped to have a yarn with me.

"Where are you taking the turnips to, Jeff?"

"Ah, down to young Shepherd's place, Steve."

"By Jove," I said, "there's a big mob of wallabies in that old deserted place of Auburn Fiddler's." I forgot to mention that for some time a red-haired youth of an exceedingly romantic and poetic appearance had lived in the old house and played the violin night and day. We called him Auburn Fiddler, and he was now down in Melbourne, still playing his music and holding audiences spellbound with his bow. It was he who had encour-aged the wild life to the old house in the first place.

Jeff said that he'd like to go in and have a look at them, and I watched him with a loving interest as he turned the turnip-filled cart into the garden. Then there was a howl from Jeff and a species of delighted shriek from the starving marsupials as they rushed down on the cart as though Jeff had been a fruit hawker they had waited for month after month in the dry bush. Bagging half a dozen juicy turnips apiece, they rushed off into the bush with them, their round heavy fur tails thumping the hollow earth with a frightening, dramatic, drumming sound.

Jeff stood up in the cart and hallooed and cooeed to them and, being what they were, real Australian bush animals, they turned and stared at him curiously.

"If you wait a moment or two," yelled Jeff, "I'll throw in a pound of salt and a tin billy to boil the turnips in!" But the red shadows fled.

I laughed a lot over this, and rode off, while Jeff rattled away down to Calulu to see young Shepherd about the lawless conduct of the local fauna. A few yards farther on someone—Frank Bond, I think it was—had cleared, in a most dry and dusty and fascinating manner, about three-quarters of an acre of virgin soil, and he had a stylish crop of late peas burning and bleaching there under the dominating sun. The pods had burnt to a rather beautiful blue-green with a dent and a weave in the pattern of them, and the small acre had a great flood of spiritual beauty about it, sorrowfully incommunicable. The deep rusty dust of a burn-off was sunk like a dry vat of fire in the corner of the paddock.

Up the dry hill of a thousand Egypts, where sand whirled with the cruelty of knives, I rode and at last drew level with the hut of Domenic, standing alone in deep white dust. From within came the steady chant of Samozarro, so I dismounted and strolled over to lose a couple of thousand at his roulette wheel. There stood his sieve on dark edge, and the pink chips, the bean seed, which the golden croupier slipped and slid under his agile hands, lay all over the table.

"*Ancora . . . assortisci i fagioli . . . !*" I exclaimed. "Still dost thou sort the beans!"

"*Si,*" returned the slumbrous Neapolitan. "*Si, Steva. Come va?*"

I was so happy to see Samozarro again. I smiled at him, remembering those nostalgic golden days in Primavera, when I had walked through the grey-leafed capeweed along the headlands, seeing the bees lift themselves out of their irritable night's half-angry, half-sweet slumber on the black, dewy, oily pillows of the flowers; white heath, the glory of Victoria, in honeyed combs rose out of the earth, and those August and September mornings lay lustrous over all the earth. And against the windy revolving roar of the cream and white gum-trees I had walked until I came near the hut where Zarro worked, and within it I could hear his thick Neapolitan voice singing in drugged syllables. . . .

"Sing again the song of '*Mamma*'," I begged him.

His wide white breast shining in his black silk shirt, he leant forward, rocking himself steadily under the thick crown of his hair while he began to sing the sad, droning song.

> "*Mamma, mi ha scritto una lettera ancora,*
> *Dicendo c'ognora si strugge per me.*
> *Fiamma che vampa, uccida, divora,*
> *La fiamma che ancora si strugge per me.*

"Donna, donna, ce tu sei nata per farmi soffrir?
Donna, donna, tu mi farai morir."

"Mamma, I write you a letter again,
Saying that that which desires me still struggles
for me.
The Flame that vamps, murders and devours,
The flame that again struggles for me.

"Woman, woman, why were you born to cause
me suffering?
Woman, woman, you will make me die!"

Zarro rose and put the coffee billy on the low ash-covered coals. When it was hot he poured the thin sweet liquid into cups and we sat and drank and talked over old days. I stared round the hut; in the old days when Macca and Blue and Jim and I had lived hereabouts and Karta Singh owned the place, he had it lined with stringy-bark bunks, with a flashing-eyed Mohammedan in every one of them, talking in wild high voices, while he, sitting on a low stool, made johnny-cakes and read the Koran aloud. I thought, "I must write and tell Blue of this." The wind still rang around the walls in lonely, melancholy cries; the salt and the blue of the lake still surged up from the shores through the gum-leaves, the brown paddocks and the fern, to the very door.

Domenic trod solidly through the sultry evening in to us, and greeted me.

"Ah, Steve," he said in the crisp frosty Florentine voice that he invariably spoke in, "you are here? Where have you been lately? I was thinking the other day, 'I have not seen her about now for some time.' But I have been so busy myself with the crops that I had no time to bother if you were at home over at your place or not."

"I have been down at Leonardo's place, working for him, and feasting there, in company with him and Gennaio, Nino Nuvola, Vita Cherinuova and some others."

"Ah, with Leonardo. He is a character, that one."

Domenic took down his edition of Shakespeare, opened it at *Corialanus*, and, sitting down at the table, lit the lamp and began to eat his tea while he read the play.

There was suddenly a slight sound outside and I said nervously, "I hope that is not my horse rolling in your paddock, Domenic. I left it tied up at the sliprails, but it might have slipped the bridle off and walked in."

Domenic said, "My goodness, I have a young crop of wheat out there, too!"

He and I rushed out, to see the horse rolling all over the crop in the half twilight of the warm summer evening. But there was such a certain grace and beauty about the dark shape against the legions of tiny green shoots and the one dead white gum-tree against the sky that Domenic was tolerant. He took hold of the bridle and pulled the horse to its feet, and led it back over the paddock with its hind feet sinking deeply into the dark soft soil.

"Oh, it doesn't matter at all, really, I was going to log-roll the wheat this week anyhow." He had a peculiar custom, brought from Italy, of rolling a heavy log over the field of wheat when it was only a few inches in height. He maintained that this strengthened it.

For some reason or other this night stayed with me for years, the thought of the sloping warm paddock of wheat an inch or so in height, seen green in the darkness, the verdant uniforms of the hosts of the dragon-harvest. And Domenic and I walking together over it, dragging the horse behind us. He had little to tell me; nothing had happened while I was away down at Calulu. His peas were finished; he had a few beans to pick; Zarro, as I could see, was sorting out the last of the bean-seed. It was the same all over Metung. He had seen Jim McLachlan and he had told him that his tea-bushes, which had been having a regular pick-over ever since early spring, were now nearing the full swing of the season. Because of the hot summer, the leaf was very dark, but good, full of fragrance of the bush and smelling heavenly, Domenic told me, in the big crushes.

The best picking of tea is in September, if the nights are cold and the days hot, especially if the plants have been pruned in a warm August that has brought them on very rapidly. The spring leaf is the most delicate of all, though the summer variety— "Thunder-buds" or "Thunder-tips", as they are called—have a powerful genius in them and an unforgettable flavour. The September leaf is called either "Frost Stiff" or "Frost Mask" or "Trancèd

Dew", because of the flavour that the frost gives it, ineffable. And then there is the variety known as "First Part of Afternoon", then, "Second Part of Afternoon Strong". All these names come in, as a matter of course, with the teas from Asia. They inhale Australia into themselves and give it out again in cups of splendid tea.

It was now getting on into the night. I stood at the door of the hut and looked in. Under the mineral circle of the kerosene lamp, the big white hands of Zarro moved rapidly among the baccarat beans as he slid them back and forth. He began to sing "*Mamma*" again.

> "*Fiamma che vampa, uccida, divora,*
> *La fiamma che ancora si strugge per me.*"

—those two strong chanting lines like a fast express bouncing in strength and purpose on the rails all through the night.

Zarro had a head like that of a statue of Mark Antony in the Louvre—pallid, big, good-natured, with a soft cloud of fine dark waving hair—that face of his turned a little towards Egypt, over his shoulder hearing the murmur from far off of the gold and whirling afternoon dust that was the legions of Caesar. Perhaps Mark Antony had sung this self-same song, late at night in his tent on the Nile, when he had thought over Cleopatra and the intrigue that had brought him so far from Rome. And sung it with the same slow, passionate, set satisfaction, thinking, "The strength in that song, the life in it! What does it matter if one *does* go down, engulfed in the flame, the dreadful ardour of it, the savage power of seeing oneself destroyed only to arise again?"

> "*Fiamma, che vampa, uccide, divora . . .*"

The song wrapped us all about in flame. I rode off with long sheets of fire sliding softly over me, and from the sliprails cried out, "*Buona notte!*"

"*Buona notte!*" was the reply.

Taking the back track, I rode on under the stars. To the left the same mopoke called as it had called for years now, against the white dew on the dark breathing leaves. At last I came with a sigh of relief to McLachlan's home. In every square room the

216

electric lights shone, the billiard table seen through the window had the silken curtains swaying over it, blown hither and thither by the beloved Australian night wind. The long lights shone steadily on the big tennis court and the tropical plants, the path was curvingly covered with purple jacaranda blossoms. I went up the white steps and opened the billiard-room door. "Anyone home?" I said.

"Ah, that's Steve!" cried Jim's delighted voice. "Do come in, Steve!" He was in a little room off the billiard-room, writing at his desk. His red hair shone like fire under the milder electric light. "How did you get on down at Leonardo's? I looked after your gift horse for you. My man went over and brought it back with him. I do wish you had seen his face when he took the hobbles off Inferno! Such hobbles! I'm keeping them as a trophy. Leonardo must have got one of his Italians to make them. They're made of wood. Have a look at them." He handed me a pair of hobbles such as I have never seen before.

"My gosh!" I said. "Are they hobbles?"

"They are." There was a small piece of old broad leather, with blocks and bangles of wood let into it. Neatly carved on one large block of wood were the words, "*Resto contento*". That fiend of a horse resting content in the blazing sun, with a pair of wooden hobbles tearing pieces off his hocks!

"By Jove," I said, "if someone put those wooden anklets on me, with 'Stay contented' on them, and left me to stand in the sun for a day, I'd feel as happy as Inferno looked. And what did the *cavallo* do when the hobbles were taken off?"

"He kicked my man over a five-foot fence," said Jim happily, "knocked over two cows, sprained the leg of my mare, trod half a dozen pet rabbits into the dust, broke the door of the stable and made a rush for the poultry yard, strode straight through it, and came out with half a dozen white Leghorn roosters clinging to his back in a transport of ecstasy at having got a free ride. But eventually he quietened down and he is out grazing in the home paddock at the back of the stockyard, if you want to go and have a look at him."

"Ah, any time will do," I said hastily, thinking that in the dark I mightn't be able to tell one end from the other. "And what about the tea, Jim? What time do we start plucking, picking,

217

harvesting, crushing and packing? I feel like having a go at it, after my holiday down at the virgin's."

"What's *his* crop like?" asked Jim interestedly.

"Ah well, he's got very little new stuff in, you know. Just the same old bushes he's had for years now."

"Oh, that broad-leafed early green Japanese Unomi stuff that I sold him? How's it making?"

"Oh, it's too high. I told him that. He hates pruning, you know. And he's got his soil too wet. He has the pumping engine going for four hours every day now—though mostly on some Shein-cocadu he got from the importers in Melbourne. A short, golden-coloured bush, with a great glitter on it."

"Oh, that stuff! I grew it a couple of times, but I wouldn't take it on again. Not enough flavour in it. I had a tea-taster working for me in the islands and he developed dreadful stomach trouble through tasting Sheincocadu. First case I've ever known of sickness caused by tea-tasting. And what does he reckon the yield will be per acre?"

"One thousand pounds per acre of made tea."

"Rubbish!" said Jim.

"Well, one thousand pounds per acre of rubbish, then."

"More like it. Have a drink!"

We drank. The dark Bogong moths came into the room and knocked against the lights and huddled in a heap behind the door. They crawled and hung delicately on Jim's white topee on the wall, and stuck to his books and coat.

"Well, now, regarding my crop," said Jim. "I've had the pickers going over it from springtime onward. We've been processing it as we went. This will be the last and full picking for the summer. I want you to give a hand generally, as usual, Steve."

"Righto."

"Peppino helped plant out a new plantation before he left for Maffra, and it's coming on well. We'll be picking over the old bushes next week if you care to come along. My correspondence is mounting up, too. I want you to attend to that."

"Right. I'll be over." I thought to myself, "As soon as I can get rid of the typing and accounts, I'll dash out into the dust and get hold of some of those old bushes and pick with the genius of an ancient Chinese poet-prince for the glory of the gods and the immortality of man." If there was one thing I loved it was to pick old tea-bushes of their leaves. There was a sonnet of old days in China written on each leaf. As soon as you got into the plantation where the Chinese tea-plants were growing, the rich embroidered atmosphere of courtly ancient China came over you like a huge bejewelled sun in the heavens and spread antiquity everywhere. Jim stared at me, smiling.

"And I suppose," he said, "that we shall have our usual ton of poems from the Chinese after the picking?"

"Yes," I said.

"After last tea-picking," he remarked, "you wrote a set of very lovely little Chinese poems which I admired. I still have a copy of the one I liked best in my desk here." He took it out, and read it aloud to me:

> *"The Emperor's ladies sway like fans*
> *Moved slowly to and fro,*
> *Across the broken Stairs of Han,*
> *Where only Concubines may go.*
>
> *"And when they mock the spotted Shrike,*
> *And titter at the Gallants dozing,*
> *Their laughter and their cries sound like*
> *The rattle of the fan-sticks closing."*

McLachlan stared down at the poem and the frail wash drawing beside it. Outside in the night, under the small white stars, the purple jacaranda blossoms were falling slowly and driftingly; in the trees about the house the green tree-frogs were singing delicately and precisely on sharp notes. The tame geckos that Jim kept in the garden were perched up high against the stars, too, in the tropical trees, exclaiming from time to time, in their monotonous lizard voices, "Gecko! Gecko! Gecko!"

The long Australian night! The heavy silent rising of the planets and the oily blue lip of the lake striking the shore and rolling away in splendour to the stars, and catching fire from them in its moment of apostasia, the white divided flames of the stars. And now clouds as heavy and white as marble, looking as though they only needed a chisel and some heavenly Michelangelo to strike them into form and send careering across heaven an army of solid snowy horsemen. The sky was full of pools of blue, of varying depths, and the rising moon stayed roundly awhile in each characteristic place and renewed herself, time, race, and passion of literature, in the depths.

I awoke next morning in the long ringing melody of consciousness that was the beginning of the day in my own place. Through the tropical slits along the top of the walls, the sun shone wine-red, quivering with the dreadful weight of the coming midday, and with wind-shaken bushes outside. Far out, among the dead trees, the gut-hawks screamed to Isis; by this I knew that the lake would be a hot pale blue all day, with long dark streaks on it; from the wattle-trees the wattle-bird cried out harshly, "Go back! Go back!"—as though I had come out from London by aeroplane in 1900 instead of being respectably and lovingly born from maternal limbs. "Go back! Go back!"

Ah, there is no going back . . . ever! Remember that, immortal bird! But still, sensing that the day was going to be very hot, I did wish suddenly with all my heart and soul that I had been a gay remittance man with a very good family at home, to whom I could pack and take a train and be in cool England and away from this awful heat, and the flies and slow hours. Still . . . I arose, as remittance men arise, in my white pyjamas, and staggered round the hut to the sound of Caruso's piercing tenor, in search of cool water to take away the spin of McLachlan's fierce wines. As those same men do, I walked out into the midday sun, and jumped forty feet into the air when I hit the burning earth with my tender sole. Then I dashed into shelter again and fell, stupefied with the heat, back into my bunk. A large frilled lizard, which I kept as a pet, had decided that I was up for the day, and lay coyly curled up on the bed; we met and, after a rough embrace of a hurried sort, parted with a howl of horror. The frilled party did not, of course, howl, but hissed bad-temperedly. I stuck my sun-helmet on, and went away off down the flat dry ecstatic track to the lonely foreshore.

The water looked much as Streeton used to see it in those thick, oily canvases of his, rich flake and wave and twist of outstanding blue and white. A seaboard as dry and desolate as that along the Dead Sea seemed to be craving for the touch of a living foot. The small stones and the large were of every colour under the sun, as though some palace under the sea had been broken up by storms and spilt along the sand. Large dark crabs stood in the warm golden shallows, and with one upraised arm saluted tentatively, and twitched all over, as though tugged by an earthquake far out at sea. Their clawed feet made small swiftly filling holes in the clear sand with its soft bloom of dust.

I stayed all day at the sea, and at night went down to the Buccaneer's, blazing with sunburn and salt. It was quite late when I got there, and all the children were in bed; the Black Serpent sat alone in the kitchen, reading the Melbourne *Sun Pictorial*; flashes of Swanston Street, Collins Street, and Flinders Street leapt to me from the sheets, like fish from the waters. Suddenly I felt tired of this part of Victoria, for it fed the implacable city.

"By Jove, I'm going over the Alps after Christmas," I thought. "I'm tired of this heat."

Aloud I said, "Where's Pa?"

"Oh, he's out fishing, Steve, with Macca and Jim."

"Oh, is Macca down from Bairnsdale?"

"Yes, he came down last night with Eb." Up rose the image of him, and all his "duds", as he used to call them—Black Watch plaid shirts and wide black sombreros—there was his pale face, his reddish hair, his wrist with the golden down on it, his lazy pleasant fact, his implacable secret self.

"And what's he got to say?"

"Oh, nothing much. His brother Reg is home again from Mildura."

"Did you tell him that I was going over the Alps after I'd finished out at McLachlan's?"

"I did."

"What'd he say?"

"Nothing—or 'Oh, is she?' or something like that."

I tried to break out of a grip like death that held me down, I tried to draw myself up like a man in a book, and spring out of the book, and say, "Ah well, I'm going to Malaya with a civil engineer, as assistant on a dredge." Or, "I'm going up to Papua to work on the rubber plantations"—anything, anything rather than be a

221

woman. For women don't work, really. My idea of life is to be about six feet in height, with enough strength to lift half a ton without effort, and the next idea is to get a lot of hard work to do, either in Malaya or New Guinea, and go and do it.

Anyway, I did say, aloud, "I wish to God, I could get a job in Malaya or New Guinea and go up there and work for years! I hate this sort of life."

This sort of talk always exasperated Edgar's wife. She stiffened, grew cold and quiet, and lifted the *Sun* so that it slanted like a roof that would let tons of rain slide down it very swiftly, and said slowly, "Oh, you don't know what you want!"—with a sort of wide-world force, so that you knew that if you travelled all over the face of the earth, you would still get the same answer. And that made me laugh suddenly, because in the face of everyone that's the only thing one can do.

"Yes, I do know what I want. I'd like a cup of tea with you."

And she laughed and liked me again, for she was the most charming woman I have ever known, and I hated to see her unhappy.

When I had talked about Calulu and she had given me all the news of the village in her marvellous fashion (for she could talk as well as Gorky or Chekhov could write), she said, "And are you going to stay the night, and see Macca?"

"God forbid! Tell him that I have gone to the East on a couple of administrative cadres, and that I shall not see him for at least ten or twenty years. Tell him that I expect to return as young and immortal as when I left, and that I shall expect him to remain the same."

"And you are really going, Steve, after Christmas?"

"I am. Yes, as soon as I've finished out at Jim's place, I'm going to ride over the Alps."

"Something might happen to you."

"Let us hope," I said disgustedly, "that something does."

"And you won't stay and wait till Mac comes home? They'll be in by midnight or about half past one."

"No, thanks. Give him my love. I'm off out to the ranch again. Jim wants me to start with him next week, so I'll rest till then."

Off I went, down the hill in the dark, holding on to the gum-trees that stood short and slippery-leafed on the high golden cliff above the white-voiced lake with its wide blue body stretching from the point to Silvershot. At the foot of the cliff I halted, and listened to the stuttering engines of the approaching motor-boats. They ceased, and the boats approached the small jetty with the water surging quietly about them. I heard Macca's voice. He was in one of those boats. I cannot tell . . . I cannot think for sorrow, remembering that night. *Le temps retrouvé.* Time recaptured. That was all.

The wind blew coldly along the shore in a grey world, in the night world. I stood listening. I desired to die. I turned to the trees and became absorbed in passionate sorrow. Great coldness overcame me, and futility. The years were passing. Soon I should not see him any more. Macca was to me the symbol of man in the year 1928 in Australia, and that symbol, and man as he was, they were both flying from me. Men who were young at that time were in the melting-pot; theirs was to be a short youth only, for more than the years pressed on them. In those days so many were being born that they loaded the young with premature age, and hurried them onward that they might find a place for themselves. Hating change of any sort, I saw Macca and his kind changing before me and new men coming along of another age, and new songs to take the place of those they sang.

OVER THE ALPS

VII

WITH wide white flashes of light along the Lakes, Christmas 1928 came to us, and all I remember of it is having a hot rich dinner at the Buccaneer's. Grandfather Buccaneer waited for hours for this dinner, and while it was being prepared and cooked he strode up and down, up and down the wide dry veranda round the house, dressed in a white linen suit of a very old-fashioned cut. The long tails flew out in the cold strong wind that blew round the place, and whenever I came to stand outside on the cliff and look down into the water at the mob of yachts I saw also Grandfather's white linen coat-tails flying like the sails of a racing keeler.

A few days afterwards, in the New Year, 1929, I got into my field kit, clapped my white topee on my head, and sauntered down the hill to help with the tea-picking. Jim had some two hundred acres in, all told, but it was a six-acre plantation of Chinese tea, Royal Peking, that he told us to go over. Grasping my numbered basket, I slung it well behind me, like the harp of the Minstrel Boy, and, getting myself into a suitable frame of mind, Tenth Dynasty, Ming vase, white crane, golden reeds, blue water, and flower-embroidered dark-blue silk, I laid hold of the antique bush and began to pluck to the tune of:

> *The careless gallants of Ooling,*
> *Ride forth caparisoned in spring,*
> *With silver saddles, horses white*
> *And dainty garments fluttering . . .*

I took about an hour to fill the long basket the Italians had made of willows and wattle-bark, in the same shape as those of Chinese reeds that Jim had brought with him from his place in the islands. When it was filled I took it over to the shed, where the leaves were tipped in with those of the others into the tray of the truck that would take them up to the drying shed where they

227

would go into the tats. The tats were large grey tin trays with sharp, open, tormenting corners for ventilation, placed on high three-tiered shelves in the drying shed with its long polar-ridged thermometer. Then after drying, the leaves were taken out and put through the rotary rollers to get the characteristic twist. At other times Jim would give the dried leaves another richer baking under the sun outside, and put them through the machinery and break them up. Before they were sieved he mixed packets of very fine dark-blue powder with them. It came from China and had a beautiful smell and no name on the packet at all. When all had been graded and sieved by the Chinese and Italians and Cubans, the tea was packed in wooden boxes and the truck took the consignment down to the wharf below the plantation, to wait for the *Gippsland* or the *J. C. Dahlsen* to take them away.

Panucci was at work in the chemistry section of the place, and wore a long white coat over his navy-blue suit. Dark, slender, faintly flushed, smiling, he stood over glass retorts, all day busily working; through the window I could see the delicate outline of his face and long wavy hair. He had parted from music for the time being, and was silent, and not often to be met to talk to, for his interest in his work was intense.

As for me, I cared for nothing but the summer, the golden body of it spread hotly over the earth, smelling of dry grass, reeking of cracked soil, as though the ground were filled with jars, vases, and sherds. On the hill, the tea-bushes shone glossily from the red, cream, and purple ground, in which like phoenix-trees they grew, and while I picked, I spoke or sang aloud old Chinese songs and legends. I chanted the story of Wang Shuh and the Red Cloud herb, and the blue boy who rose from the mountain pool on the back of a red carp and rode through the stormy clouds, while I tossed the moonlit dark leaves of the tea into my harp basket, and the pickers chimed in at the end of every verse, with the musical refrain of *"Lo-ti! Lo-ti! Lo-ti!"*

The blue and purple mists of afternoon rose from the lake and the white sand on the shore; the silver wattle shook and trembled there, and clouds like white ivory surged in summits above us, shaped like Chinese poets and gods. This was the way to pluck tea; there is no way to compare with this style of approach to the sacred bushes. Twenty of us there were, moving slowly as the shadow of the sun up the field, laying first one hand and then the other, all gilded royal with the sun, on the leaf; our white topees stood out like white oil-paint against the green leaf and the palette red, the fiery cream and Japanese purple of the earth. The frail baskets lying along our backs were full of the singing leaves, and they were grey like an old stone temple in the north of China.

We took a row apiece and worked up it, returning on the row next to it. Now and again we came on a patch that was interesting, for into it had drifted all the varieties of tea-bush that McLachlan had, and a square-leafed, fine-feathered, pale-green species of mixed Japanese, Darjeeling, and Chinese variety was produced. But the bushes are rough and hurt the hands a good deal, and in spite of its poetry, tea-plucking grows monotonous. After rain, the red earth was like a hideous quagmire underfoot and picking was prickly and unpleasant, but the smell of the bushes was very sweet and individual. And the factory was flooded with the perfume as the hoppers crushed the raw leaf up. The days passed in the tea-paddocks uneventfully save for one remarkable incident, characteristic of the Australian bush, which is a peculiar place.

One afternoon two strange men broke out of the jungle of blue-gum and fern that grew high about and sprang into the midst of us, with a loud halloo of a peremptory sort. We had never seen such men before and stared at them in awe. Both of them were clad in morning-suits, of a highly British sort, and on their heads they wore black silk toppers. With their white hands resting claw-like on their walking-sticks they stood and returned our gaze.

"Who are you?" the overseer said finally. He advanced a couple of steps towards them.

"Keep off . . . stand back!" They waved him back with their sticks. "No farther. Taboo! Taboo!"

"Well, but who are you?" I asked, coming forward, too.

The rest of the pickers stopped and listened, ready to advance and have a close look at them.

"We are British statesmen," said the taller of the two, leaning on his cane and surveying us loftily, "on holiday in Australia, and

229

interested in the tea-planting industry. If this plantation appeals to us, we shall have no hesitation in financing it."

"It belongs to Mr McLachlan, a tea-planter from Malaya," said the insulted overseer, "and he doesn't want you to finance it, no matter if you are British statesmen."

"We come from Downing Street," exclaimed the equally insulted statesmen. "From London, my man; we want to invest money in colonial enterprises."

The overseer walked rapidly towards the elegantly garbed top-hatted pair, whose spats were sunk deep in the dust, and he let out a howl of rage and fury.

"What the hell have you two been doing with my pots of black paint?" he screeched, tearing the top-hat from one of the heads of the London investors, and rubbing his hands rapidly up and down the object, which left large black streaks of house-paint all over his fingers. Then he rubbed the black tail-coat of the other statesman; off came the paint in handfuls. The two Downing Streeters turned tail and rushed off into the bracken with flying tails, as the overseer called the dogs.

The wanderers must have strolled into the repair shop and given all their miserable ragged garments a good thick coating of paint, and pulled their hats tall, into high round crowns, which they stiffened with paint, and with the stuff still wet and shining they had come over to impress us with their wealth and importance.

We went back to our picking and left the overseer to grumble about the loss of a tin or two of good black paint until it was time to go over to the office and have afternoon tea. As we sat in the shade, drinking our tea, now and then from the bracken fern around the plantation came a faint nervous tremble and shake, as though our two British statesmen were still resting within and timidly hoping that all would go well, but the dogs were flung into the breach with such vindictiveness that soon the twain departed and the bracken was quiet again. I went over afterwards to have a look at the deserted nest that they had left behind, and you could have painted a house with the pool of paint they had been sitting in.

It was a yellow canvas we wandered through, not the earth; and fiery red was the soil underfoot, when it was not hard yellow also; in the big paddock next to us tall, oily-green barley grew right down to the edge of the cliff, limp and swooning with the heat, and out of it all day rose skylarks, singing of the blue coral seas of Baiae. Whenever I saw the skylarks, whenever I heard them sing, I thought of poor Shelley, over whom so much darkness lies.

On the beach, the dry stone- and shell-covered foreshore, the silver wattle flashed and darkened, white to grey, grey to white, like a great light, for the sake of Joseph Conrad and his pale painted boat that smashed up in delicate foam and fire along some such coast as this. In tall cream, golden, and silver gum-trees half-way down the high cliffs gut-hawks and sparrow-hawks screamed: "Isis, Isis! Horus, Horus!" all day. Farther up, along the dry dusty road that led into the plantation, stood the little tea factory, rattling like an old donkey-engine with its thumping machinery. The unforgettable, sweet, indescribable perfume of the crushed tea-leaves invaded the place; it is a smell that makes one feel unutterably sad, haunted, tormented with a despairing longing for some unknown land, some country of the mind, and it remains to torture for long years after. It is, of course, the magic power of the East, of old Asia. And I would go, walking through the tea-bushes, striding down the dry dust and fallen leaves, with a singular, mellow, serious, white-faced Englishman in my mind, from whose mouth seemed to issue these words of Kipling's against a yellow, empire-girt heaven, bronze with swords and the giant will of the British Empire, imperative, masterful, saying:

> "Oh, East is East, and West is West, and never the twain
>   shall meet,
> Till Earth and Sky stand presently at God's great Judg-
>   ment Seat . . ."

Over and over, saying this, thinking it, until the words seemed to rule the world and were as gigantic as Fate, and as forceful as the years. I longed, in those days, to see something as magnificent as a day when Earth and Sky would stand at God's great Judgment Seat.

McLachlan's small office, shining brown, redolent of the East, in the morning when all Asia seemed to come sweeping in on a monsoon breeze and there was thunder hiding in blue rich luxuriance among the laurel-green tea-bushes; and strange tropical insects paid us short interesting visits, while from Japan came swimming in their thousands, wave on wave, the purple Japanese shrimps from out the yellow seas. Along the shore stalked the plovers, who would, within a few short months, be off on that beloved annual long flight of theirs to Russia. My heart ached; I longed to be going with them. Yet I did not wish to leave the Lakes district. I wanted to stay about it for ever, watching wave after wave of sun and weather yellowing the earth. Sometimes I wished that I could be, perhaps, a bronze statue, lost and hidden in the ground, rather than to go from the place I loved. To be that, and remain for imperishable ages in the same beloved soil. To have murmuring over and about me, like undulating fire and air, that last great ode of Horace:

> "Exegi monumentum aere perennius
> regalique situ pyramidum altius,
> quod non imber edax, non Aquilo impotens
> possit diruere aut innumerabilis
> annorum series et fuga temporum."

The village reminded me of some old silver citadel in ancient Persia, to which, one dry white afternoon, came some thousands of bearded and beardless dark Persian warriors, carrying the sharp half-moon of their scimitars curved on their thighs, and gained the sharp-hilled city after a long fierce fight. And how should I be able to endure the giving up of Thalassa, the sea, for the indescribable alps?

Still, much as I loved my country, sometimes, I felt an impatience of it, and wanted every town to bear Greek names, as old as Theocritus. Into this idea I put all my genius as a real-estate agent and town-planner. I would turn into a ball of fire with the heat and energy of the thought and roll rapidly and blindly over and through the district, taking away the English names and giving back the Greek, building the white forts of those days everywhere in the bush, and square grey stone farm houses.

"Wouldn't take long," I used to say, marching ravenously over the country in my mind and uprooting the Australian weatherboard and galvanized-iron-roofed houses, not to mention the galvanized inhabitants. Down went the signposts on the road, but

I left the fences standing, struck them with lightning that convulsed them into the most splendidly and intricately worked wire of ancient Greek sort that you could find.

I took the youths from the fields and smote their ploughs into ringing thin melodious copper and clad them with the mail of soldiers, and sent them carrying the Roman eagle and the Greek palladium from town to town, giving back to the bush what it had lost, the broken wandering golden sunlight of brazen arms carried across the country by professional soldiers. And all those lost temples to be raised, white column by column, to our unforgotten gods. The Australian bush is so empty; all it needs is a marble quarry every few miles or so, and out of that one could raise anything except the wind or cash to keep going on.

And then, up and down the lakes and rivers, I wanted to see the old Greek biremes and triremes running, whether on oil, gas, electricity or hot water, I didn't care, as long as they ran. Wool for cargo, and tea, sugar, hides, wattle-bark and oil; and the purple Japanese shrimps could sit in a large tank on the foreshore and sweat purple for us and we could send that down to Melbourne, too, and sell it to dyers.

"And then," said Jim, "you'd get sick of that . . . and what then?"

"Oh, just let them stand, and mix them up a bit. The old and the new."

"What? The Japanese shrimps in the tank?"

Laughter, more brimming cups of green tea, or red, and a complete lack of interest in the entire subject, at last.

There was a good deal of veranda-farming done round about, talking over crops past and present, while the loaded soda siphon stood behind the talk with its sultry cloud of capsule and its strong sharp shower of soda-water. McLachlan's veranda was a favourite meeting place and the tables on it were laden with books, whisky, and cards. In the sitting room beyond stood the black grand piano, to which McLachlan gravitated to play to us now and then. The lacquered gold of its down-turned forest of fallen harps gleamed in the shadows and glittered in the sun.

Looking back over the season, I remembered Zarro and his rich muttering voice that had made the Primavera so lovely, and Panucci whose mandolin had been like a pearled heart beating in

233

passionate music down the nights and days, Peppino to whom I had sent one dark-red rose wrapped in manuscript, and Leonardo, the virgin, whose crimson, ancient, faint-lined *fagioli* letter I loved and should keep for long years. What would happen to us all, at last?

Over the Alps, for me. I decided to go into Bairnsdale and get some riding kit tailored for the trip. The tailor, a tall, distinguished-looking man, was consulted on the question of riding kit for the Alps. What could he suggest? He replied staidly that he was but a year out from a minor part of Bond Street, with an adjacent view of Savile Row, and didn't know what I meant by the Australian Alps. What were they? And where were they?

They were a large body of mountains, I told him, lying some long miles from here.

"Is there snow on them?"—taking out an expensive book full of the latest Swiss alpine fashions for strolling up the Jungfrau and Matterhorn.

"Not in the summer."

"What is on them, then?"

"Daisies, alpine daisies, bachelor's buttons and alpine moths, very large."

"Very large moths?"

"Yes."

"You will not need to wear anything with wool in it, then."

"I am riding over the Alps, not camping in them."

"Oh."

"Perhaps," I remarked, "since there are bachelor's buttons growing there, I shall not need buttons on my clothes."

The adjacent view of Savile Row grew faint, but the Bond Street shop-front still shone, a little.

"Why not khaki shorts, with a shirt to match?"

"Yes, I'll take a couple of pairs of shorts and a shirt or two," I said.

"That will be from one of the shops down the street," said Bond Street, coldly.

I eyed him gloomily. "I shall still, after having committed that crime," I said, "need something more than shorts, for it is a long ride and I am doing it on an exercise pad." I said this in an obscure and defiant way to show the London tailor what we Australians could do with things, creatively, when we tried.

"I thought," said he, "that an exercise pad was a book for writing in. I never heard of anyone riding over alps on an exercise pad before."

"Oh, this is a thin saddle used for exercising race-horses. Jockeys ride on them every morning before breakfast."

Down came a volume full of the latest rider's kit for Ascot, pages shining with silk caps, thin blouses, and skin-tight breeches fluttered across my vision.

"No, no! It's a one-man affair. No one on the field, bar one."

"What about a pair of Bedford cords, then?"

"I've got a pair already."

"Well, jodhpurs?"

"No, no. Too much like India—attract the heat, bring over all the Indian complaints about the place, worsen the malaria, bring on the Calcutta cough, the Bombay backache, the hill-station headache, and Lahore legs. No good."

The man from Bond Street eyed me gloomily and inwardly loathed Australia. Finally, "Well, what about a divided skirt?"

"Well, what about it?"

We whatted about it for a while.

"I think it would be very sensible."

"Not appropriate, not appropriate," I said smartly. "Now, if I were riding over the Dividing Range, there'd be some sense in it. No good for the Alps, at all."

"The Dividing Range? Where is that?" He seemed to look a little brighter at the very mention of the name. Was there actually in this accursed dry country, something in the nature of a cut, or a sartorial term?

"The Great Dividing Range," I said with all the accuracy I could think of, "runs from . . . er . . . Victoria into New South Wales. I saw it one night from the top of Fern Tree Gully. It is the most horridly lonely thing I have ever seen in my life. You should go there towards evening in autumn and stare across at the Great Dividing Range. Dark red, gum-tree covered, morbid, far away, lonely, more solitary than the moon or a dark star, stretching from the Victorian wilderness into the sadder bush of New South Wales. You'll never want to make another divided skirt again."

Finally we agreed on a pair of Bedford cords of a sublime cut, to go with either golf socks, leggings, or riding boots. My cousin

Clive Davidson had given me half a dozen pairs of grey, brown, and khaki golf socks with Scotch College tops of cardinal, gold, and royal blue, cardinal, to match the sweater and tie. I felt that, wearing these under the breeches, I should be able, collecting all the remarks and retorts encountered along the road, to get a degree in chemistry.

Then, I went down the street to Grose, the saddler, and from the dim, cool shop full of wrinkled golden hides bought enough leather, two sheepskins, to make a pair of American cowboy's chaps, for wearing over my slacks or breeches, if necessary.

I intended to take Eb's staghound, Micolo, over with me, on account of his size and the fact that he was a good traveller. It was a long way for a dog to travel, but I thought he could do it, if his feet did not get sore. Australian drovers, however, make boots for their dogs to wear on overland trips, so I bought four boots from Grose, who made these articles of footwear for canines by cutting out and reinforcing a strong piece of leather and threading a band of buckled leather through slots in it. These little boots were very comfortable to wear and saved the dogs' feet. When I had added a blue-and-grey checked Mexican shirt, a leather water-bottle, and a box of ·44s, I went off home, to get ready for the trip.

One day I rode over to Bruthen to find out if there was a back track from there up to the foot of the Alps, which would save me from having to go near my relations at Tambo Crossing or Ensay. For I thought, "If I go anywhere near them, and say that I'm going to ride over the Alps, they'll stop me, or raise the hair on my head with tales of fatal rides that ended in plunges to death from the top of the highest peak, and they'll want me to leave the horse there and go over with them by car. Dreadful! What an age! I insist on riding over, and I won't be stopped. However, I'll just dash over to Bruthen and see about that back track I've heard old-timers talk about." There was supposed to be one so steep that you crossed the same creek twenty-seven times. I thought that by the time you'd crossed it as often as that you ought to be somewhere near the Alps, or even in the vicinity of Mount Everest.

It was a hot, thundery day over at Bruthen; I rode along under the big bridge until I came to the first hotel. I was dressed in male clothes; I walked into the bar. A long, sad Australian of the half-city, half-bush, Percy Lindsay bookmaker's bagholder-clerk type stood at the bar, steadily imbibing a syrupy sort of beer; beside him stood a racehorse-owner sort of man, accompanied by his jockey and trainer. They stared at me, and I stared at them—hard stare, cool stare. They relapsed into their drinks and interests. I was nothing. I rejoiced in such moments, but wondered how long it would last.

In a deep bass voice that almost shook the roof off, I ordered a ginger ale. Alas! An electric effect. It shot into their consciousness that I couldn't be all I was supposed to be.

I said to the barman, "Is there a back track round here that leads to the foot of the Alps?"

The barman said he didn't know, and he asked the owner; the owner asked the trainer, the trainer asked the jockey, and then they all asked the sad gent. He didn't know. So they all asked me.

I said, casually, "Ah yes, I believe there is now I come to think of it. It starts about six or eight miles from here, just off Thunderbolt Creek and it goes away to the back of Stirling, Tambo Crossing, and Omeo, right to Cobungra, almost." At such a moment, you want to have in your pocket a false beard and moustache of an iron-grey sort; then you can clap these on and say carelessly, "When I was a young feller in 1881 we used to ride along that track after shorthorns."

"Oh, there is a track, eh?" said the trio. "Well, who wanted to know? What's it all about?"

"Well, this young feller here," said the barman pointing to me, "came in and wanted to know if there *was* such a track."

"Well, there is," they said all together. "So what?"

No one knew.

"But you want to go up along the road to Tambo Crossing; that's the best way, of course," said the owner. "The Davidsons have a hotel up there."

"Yes," I remarked bleakly.

"You're the image of Clive Davidson," observed the owner. "Are you his cousin, or what?"

"Just his cousin."

"Well, why don't you get Clive to run you over in the car? Better than riding."

"But think of the publicity," I said. "Person rides over Alps, etcetera."

"If you was a woman," said the sad gent gloomily, "be something in it. Good publicity stunt for a woman. Nothing much for a young feller like you; lots of them ride over every week or so to feed salt out to the cattle they've got up there on Bogong."

I was sorry now that I hadn't entered as a woman, but we all lunched together and they wanted to know what the ride was all about. I said it wasn't about anything. I was just going to ride over the Alps, that was all. But they all followed me out into the stables afterwards, and after looking over the horse and reckoning it was too light for the trip, and the saddle too thin, they got about me in a worried emotional huddle and begged me again to tell them what it was all about. Why, precisely, was I going to ride over the Alps?

"By God," I howled at last, "I'll tell you what it's all about! It's so I can get away from you blanky bores, who lie all over me beerily and worry about me and weep over me and want to shelter and shield me as though I were a cursed god on whom the fate of the entire race depended."

I thought that would insult them and they'd loathe me and leave me. But no; cloyingly they clung, and offered to drive me over, get me rides, buy petrol—anything, so that my precious being should not be insulted by the ordinary things of life.

"Don't go. Take my tip. Don't do it. Anything might happen. Take our tip."

I held out my hand, but got nothing. So I didn't take their tip, after all. Drawing myself away from them, at last, as though they had been a huge kind, emotional cradle of fatherly kindness that held me in the one place and didn't want me to shift or move for myself, I rode off, leaving them weeping and worrying in a tender fashion reminiscent of the Mock Turtle singing and moaning on the beach.

"A great kid!" they chanted from afar. "You're a great kid. Wouldn't like to see anything happen to you."

I eyed them sullenly and rode away.

It was the same with Edgar Buccaneer, when the trip was talked about. Edgar swore that the bush was full of carpet snakes that lay along the trees and did a trapeze act from them. He reckoned that one of the cheapest ways of getting down to Melbourne, according to local carpet snakes, was to lie concealed in a snow-gum until an innocent traveller came along. Then the reptile swung down out of his perch and, changing rapidly into a carpet bag, got into the traveller's grip and refused to be put down until they all stood in Collins Street.

Then, of course, we had the dingoes. Edgar said that the fiercest dingoes in Australia camped in the Alps, and that they would tear a man from his horse and go through his pockets in such a businesslike way that only his outstanding bills were left in his possession when he came to himself.

"Only one way to keep them off," said Edgar. "Get hold of a chip of wood, tie it on a string, and ride over dragging the chip behind you."

"Not on the shoulder, as according to literature?"

"No, behind you, behind you!"

"Why a chip?"

Edgar didn't know. But then, as he pointed out, neither did the dingo; that kept him guessing.

One afternoon I went down the hill through the bracken towards my baracca. After a very light shower of summer rain the dry grass had softened and smelt like sad wet straw. I heard from the hut the long pealing tenor of Caruso, and I knew that Panucci must be sitting there, playing the records that Peppino had left me.

Yes, it was he. There he sat, with his brown cap beside him on the seat; he was dressed in a brown shooting suit, of the pleated-back Continental sort. His peculiar smile of dimples, moonlight teeth, white hands, rose flush and Dante Gabriel Rosetti hair, outfloating in small wiry dry waves, flashed over me.

"Ah, Steve . . . you are going away soon?"

"Yes, Panucci . . . *sopra la montagna* . . . *l'alpe.*"

"I will look after these records of Peppino's for him, while you are away. When will you be back again? Next year?"

"*Non so.* I don't know." Staring at all my stuff in the hut, I thought, "It'll be safe here. Jim will look after it for me."

I went outside and took the white topee off the broken tea-tree, at last. All summer the symbol of the Governor in residence had swung and whirled from the flagstaff below the hill. It was well blanched now, and had a most romantic air about it. The agony of nostalgia went through me as I stared at it, and remembered

239

old days of work in the paddocks, long days under the sun. I hung it up on the wall above the rifles and double-barrels. I was leaving them behind, too. My revolver in its holster I took. I had a flat saddle-bag into which I packed a pair of pyjamas, a clean shirt, and a few other things. But I was travelling light. Once down on the other side I could buy what I wanted. Suddenly I felt exhilarated by the thought of the long ride ahead. I wondered what I should see along the road, and what adventures would come to me.

I said to Panucci, "I shall miss you, and our talks about the mythology of Italy and ancient Greece." I looked at him, and wished I could tell him all that he meant to me. "I hope when I return, Panucci, that you will be here, too. For I want to see you again. I wish I were Benedetto or Pep so that I could go away with all of you, and be one of the band of players, with guitar and mandolin. If I could play with the genius with which you play, Panucci, how utterly happy I should be! I envy you, *mio caro*, I envy you!"

"I shall be here, Steva, with new books and songs and instruments. No matter if it is two years before you return again——"

"And it may be that."

"—I shall see you. I shall return here again, for I love this place. Just as you love it, so too do I."

"As for me, I leave this place next Wednesday to go over. My sister, Blue, will be waiting for me on the other side. I shall see her, and many others that I know—but, Panucci, I shall be changed. I shall not be as you know me now."

"Changed, Steva? How?"

"When I am alone and away from my sister, I live the life of one in a book, devoted to literature, music, friendship and many pleasures, and I have the feeling of being immortal, of having always been, of never having been recently a child, or even young; the feeling of eternal age is about me, and I love it. And I am what I wish to be, at will. But when I am with my sister, she, who remembers me, can say, 'When you were young . . . I remember you when you were small'—even as I remember her. And I do not ever want to have been young, although my youth was such a lovely time. But I loathe and fear the first of it, dreadful black-outs in time and space, when I don't remember even having been alive, and then journeys like concussions all over New South Wales and

Queensland. I feel like making a long sad melodious moan in Greek about all this, and appealing to God regarding my beginnings."

"*Bisogna cominciare tutti,*" remarked Panucci sententiously. "We must all begin, all of us."

"And to be born does not appeal to me. When they begin to talk about my extreme youth, I wish to rise up and say in a perfectly level and dignified fashion, 'I was forty-four years of age, and the compleat Englishman, the night I landed here on you, dash it all! And if you don't believe it, here is my hat-box with my best silk top-hat in it, still bearing the Bond Street mark of the makers. Here's my morning suit, here's my lounge suit, and there under the couch, with the cat sitting on top of them, are my spats.' "

"And do you ever say this, Steva?"

"Oh, sometimes. But you see, the trouble is, I haven't got my baggage with me, Panucci. If I still had the top-hat I should be right. No, *mio caro*, there is only one way for an extraordinary character like me to have been born, and that is for me to walk in on a nice family on a dark night, with letters of introduction and the best part of six months' remittance in cheques. And I should say in a most stately manner, after I had put down my luggage, 'Pardon me . . . I am Born. Spell it anyway you like—Bourne, Burn, Air-borne, Bohun—but Born I am, and to you! Yes, I am Bourne, and you, if the gods will it, are made.' But truly, Panucci *mio*," I said, "I must tell you about the day I was 'born'.

"It came about in this way. There was nothing; I was not. Then there was a huge blackness far away off in the earth and sky, and in this far-away blackness, which was a certain length of time, part of me was like a star. I came to myself in a buggy, at Minildra, in the Australian bush, sitting between a man and woman. I was Oscar Wilde, or I had recently been him. A sad white veil of melancholy drifted about me like my lost soul. 'There goes the devil's bargain!' Above me, immense in Heaven, stood the figure of Almighty God—He whom I knew also in old days as Apollo, the glorious. Even in that dreadful hour, arising I knew not how, from darkness, I knew and saw His immortal frame, and saw and heard issuing from Him the great, blinding, grave words, written in the air about me, and proceeding into my mind from His: '*You* have been born before. You have never been born before. You will be born again. You will never be born again.'

"What does such a term of negation mean in the Greek? What does it mean in the equation of the mind? It is the riddle of life. I do not know what to make of it. Perhaps the Almighty is jesting with me, and there is no need for all this wisdom. I have always been. Far before me, into Time and Space, He flung these words. I stared down at my body clothed in black silk, at my knee-breeches and silk stockings, and, being only partly conscious, could not speak. I made a great struggle to be once more, and at once, the always brilliant Oscar Wilde, beloved of London, or known of London, for the astonishing genius of his swift recoveries from the most severe attacks of Fate or man. But I could not. Yet, I fancied I had done so, for I turned with the half-sublime, godlike air I always affected, to the right, my head inclining to the right, and staring into the awful loneliness of the painted-looking Australian bush, the coarse blue-gums, the coarse yellow dry earth. All these, looking like a vast savage picture to be thrust forward to influence Australian and world art for an age, stunned me.

"At the same time the thought formed in my mind, 'What a magnificent country to colonize!' as though I had brought to the surface some other part of myself, some ancient Greek or Roman emperor who had visited the country at the time when it was known as Nothus, or a man of perhaps the time of Macquarie.

"I became conscious then, of sitting in this buggy between a man and a woman. At the same time I had a sense of being out driving with my mother, Lady Wilde, and some Princess. I saw the green linen driving skirt of the Princess quite plainly, also, with his right foot on the step of the royal vehicle, was the house detective employed to care for us, dressed in a black suit and a Homburg hat. But this picture melted as I stared at the face of the man driving the buggy. It was very stern and severe and harsh; he was a short man with a large head and a small brown moustache. I felt that he was to be my father. I regret to say I did not like him at first glance, though in after years I came to love him well. I sat in the buggy between him and the woman. She looked to me faintly like my mother, Lady Wilde, having a rugged sort of nose. While I sat staring at her I heard her say, as though we had just come home from the nursing-home, to her husband, 'I put your clean socks in the drawer.' A house rose up before me on the left side of the road, some miles on, with a chest of drawers in the bedroom, and in the drawer, which opened before my eyes, a pair of socks were lying, neatly folded into each other. I wondered how I had come to be in this buggy.

"Then I saw a form of picture-show flash above my head, together with a luggage rack with green wire on it, and in the rack reposed a very large old leather portmanteau. Even at that awful moment it gave a touch of comedy to the entire scene. Had it borne the label of 'Victoria: The Brighton Line' I am sure I should have been capable of exclaiming, '*The handbag!*' It looked as though it were full of manuscripts. I stared at the picture above my head to my left. In it I saw myself in London. I had dyed my hair. I was sitting in a flat opposite a sallow-faced man, a doctor, and I was huddled in my chair, mad with worry and fear. The flat was either in Regent Street, or above St James's Park. This man and I sat in our chairs, leather chairs, button-studded. He spoke seriously to me, in a hypnotic voice, and I felt myself faint with fear before him, I ran my hand over my brow and pushed my short curling hair back from it. He told me something—I cannot remember what it was—and I shuddered with fear. It was something to do with mob feeling against me. I had to leave London at once. It was a dreadfully hot day in London; the sun was like a white or yellow glass bottle that has burst with hideous heat. I left this man's flat and rushed down in a cab or taxi, with a friend, to Tilbury to catch the *Ophir*, bound for Australia. We were late; I remember the dreadful rush up the gangway. London was seething and roaring in the heat of a summer afternoon behind us. The big liner stood above us, with its hot wooden deck, and its memories of the recently crowded troopships off to South Africa loaded with white-helmeted and felt-hatted moustached men off to the Boer War.

"Handing my ticket to the uniformed official at the gangway was my last memory of London, my last first memory. My next memory as I sat in the buggy between the man and the woman, was of an old-fashioned plane of the sort the Wright Brothers used to build soaring above us. I felt as though I had fallen straight from that plane into the vacant seat in the buggy and knocked its occupants unconscious with shock. I didn't know where I was. I just kept looking round and looking round in agony, with the awful feeling that I was going to go out to it for years in a moment. I would have given a million pounds at that moment to have seen anyone who knew me. And just then, to my horror, I saw the white ribbons fluttering from a baby's bonnet, and staring at them, saw a baby sitting on the woman's knee. The ribbons appeared to me to be waving out against a cold chill windy afternoon, and I exclaimed with the most dreadful despair and horror possible, '*Heavens! I'm the baby!*' I at once collapsed into deepest unconsciousness, while the horse moved on with us through the bush of Minildra. I awoke from this state some time afterwards to find myself leaning over the pram of a dark, sad-looking little girl. But I collapsed again into black oblivion. I woke up again at Killeen's station, in a small schoolroom alone with a governess who was giving me a reading lesson. And I went on from oblivion to oblivion for years, without a chance to explain."

"And, Steva, did you really come to your family in this way at the beginning?" asked Panucci.

A mood of red fire and fury came over me and I said, "I do not know," and then a mood of dreadful sorrow fell upon me, and I said in a low, sad, hopeless voice, "Life is the most dreadful thing under the sun, *mio caro*."

"*Si,*" returned Panucci, seriously, "*la vita è un inferno all' infelice.*"

"It is true," I repeated. "Life is a hell of unhappiness."

"*Davvero.*"

"It is best, therefore, not to want to know anything. *Tutto è la volontà di Dio*. All is the will of God."

However, I loathe unhappiness, myself, and Panucci hated it, too. What is there to be sad about, anyhow?

"Come on," I said, "let's go over and see Jim McLachlan; it is nearly evening, and he will give us some tea." We shut the door of the hut, and on it left a brief notice, "*Ritornero in cinquanta anni*", which means, I think, "Back in fifty years".

Skirting the plantation, we looked over the lonely paddocks where the bushes stood resting after the season; only large shining leaves were left. We had made a good job of them, the lot of us. The tea-factory was silent, and the drying sheds closed. Through the side gate at Jim's place we went, and trod loudly on the wide veranda with scraping feet. Our hero was sitting down to his early tea, and we fell on his shoulder with joy at the sight of the loaded table.

"Sit down both of you and have something to eat. So you're going to leave us on Wednesday next, Steve? The alpine ride, eh?"

"Jim, if you were my rich uncle I would never leave you."

Jim said, "Well, I told you not to go, and I have said to you repeatedly, 'My home is yours, Steve, for as long as you like.' But she's restless," he said to Panucci, "and young, and wants to wander all over the place."

"Yes, that's true. I feel melancholy if I don't keep travelling about."

"Youth," said Jim.

Around the room big Chinese vases full of tropical flowers sent out clouds of warm perfume; Chinese prints on the walls, books in shelves, and sea miles through the wide windows. We ladled whipped cream and ice-cream over our papaw, passion-fruit, and banana salad, while Jim poured out our tea. There he sat, broad-shouldered, red-haired, handsome, looking on us with a happy expression of having lived well alone.

"And do you think you'll be back next year, Steve, for the tea-plucking?"

"I don't know. I'll try, but I mightn't be back until the year after."

"Ah well, I shall still be here, and Panucci will be back, too."

"I told her so," said Panucci.

"But I want to come back. Even the thought of losing one Primavera here, is unhappy."

"Well, personally, I don't think you will be able to stay there too long," Jim said, "because that horse of yours is a lowlander and used to a warm winter. When the snow starts to get thick on Bogong, Bernard, Feathertop and Hotham, he will lose condition and you'll have to bring him back again to the lowlands."

"But he'll do well all summer there, because the grass is green for so many months—in fact, all summer. It doesn't dry up as it does here. Ah well, if the winter's too much for him, I'll be back."

Going to the foreshore window, I stared along the beach in the far white foam of twilight that came to the sea there, and the sound of the waters rolling and murmuring below made my heart

245

ache. Why must I go so far away from it all? And when I came back again, what would have happened? This shore, this back beach that I loved so well—it always made me think of a little beach that lies just up from a village somewhere in the Islands. "I shall travel until I find that place some day," I thought. I wanted to stare at it, and the wrecks of ships there; perhaps a book would drift up on a tide, a full tide, and I should open it and read, at last, the immortal tale of the Islands, in the name of Tusitala, who wrote best of all.

Benedetto came in then, to find Panucci. They both began to play a sort of last serenata, trembling, light, sad, bantering, romantic, like some white Italian in the blue and crimson twilight of Italy saying farewell to a crumbling city by the sea.

> *"Addio, mia bella Napule, addio, addio!*
> *Addio, cara memoria, addio, addio, addio!"*

That hurtful music of Naples, the heart-breaking, bantering strings that do not care, and this sad mortal heart that cares too much. A face stared outward from a book on the table, a face cursed and caught in an ancient coin of the city, with agonized eyes staring down all time into the face of negation, thinking savagely, "This day I lived that man might live, this day that I stamped on my mind with all my power—I shall forget it." That bitter face, listening like my own to the delicate strumming of those strings, the waters rushing across the shores. Beside him on the silver coin was a lyre and a bronze vase like those that stood about the room, into which Jim McLachlan had put the red roses of summer.

Perhaps in the hearts of all of us lies Italy, but it hurts too much to have it revived.

And this life of ours, with a voice like the sea, now flooding forward full of power to live, and then timorously withdrawing and not wishing to live at all, as Gordon sings:

> *A little season of love and laughter,*
> *Of light and life, and pleasure and pain,*
> *And a horror of outer darkness after,*
> *And dust returneth to dust again.*

But yet of what a giant immortal, rich, and eternal form he speaks in that verse of his, the body that, once under the earth, can dream down the aeons and arise when it likes! Something just thrust into the dust to load it with legend and romance, that which is careless of death, and will be for ever.

> *Under the sea or the soil (what matter?*
> *The sea and the soil are under the sun),*
> *As in the former days in the latter,*
> *The sleeping or waking is known of none . . .*

I couldn't think that Adam Lindsay Gordon wrote this anywhere else but around the Gippsland Lakes. On very hot days when I wandered in my tropical delirium, I used to have a form of literary collision within me, wherein I had Marcus Clarke fixed not only as Henry Lawson, but as Adam Lindsay Gordon as well, and the entire entity had lived and written somewhere round these lakes in the late nineties. But Gordon turns alone to the sea again, mourning, chanting, promising, writing as a man writes who can do all things and do them with power and splendour. For Gordon strides into the sea with wonderful power and beauty, and depth after depth, as you follow him, through all deaths, he still keeps his genius clear for the sea, and runs her amber lines and hollows into your blood and his own for ever. No man ever mastered the sea as he did, or gave it such magnitude. I felt jealous of these lines, and thought they ought to have been written about Lakes Entrance and the great seas down there:

> *In your hollow backs, or your high arched manes.*
> *I would ride as never a man has ridden,*
> *In your sleepy, swirling surges hidden,*
> *To gulfs foreshadowed through straits forbidden,*
> *Where no light wearies and no love wanes.*

One day I had ridden down to Lakes Entrance, wanting to call on Banjo Paterson and ask him all about Gordon. It was a long, lonely ride through the bush, such a deep, dry, dusty road. At high noon I called at a house, like a dream, a dead sad nightmare, to see if I could get water for my horse. A pool-green house in a pool-green bush, with logs lying about it; a little girl came to the door and took me down to the real pool that sent its shadows and reflections over the place; it was a small scummy tarn, rich with creamy soft green scum, and I scooped a little of it aside and the horse drank. In the slow moving dust of afternoon I remounted and rode away, leaving behind me the lonely little bush child and, seeing her, I was glad that I was grown up and able to get out into the world.

There were oil-bores all along the last part of the road to Lakes Entrance; among the dry yellow shale hills with the down-hanging sad gum-leaves the bores poured out oil and gas. Mary Capes, one of the girls I knew there, a cousin of the Buccaneer's, was going to marry the manager of the oil-boring company and go back with him to America. Her magnificent engagement ring blazed on her finger as she turned the plough on the headlands of her father's farm. Alpha of the Plough. Mary Capes lived as I lived, on the land.

But down below me lay Lakes Entrance, like hundreds of soft yellow pancakes lying in the blue wine of the sea, that wine which the students of Montmartre used to drink a century ago. The yellowest, most golden, creamiest beach I had ever seen. And frothing and roaring and springing up in spume and spray and thunder around these pancakes and the blue wine was the open sea, rushing in to beat in terrific rage and poetic beauty against the shore. High up in the air, in big white towers, hung the storm balls and baskets, which told by their different heights what lay ahead in the way of trouble on a very rough sea, that ocean which roared night and day, in huge billows under the moon, and the white and green rising towers of fury by day. I stared down and halted my horse. So beautiful were the sea and the shore that I didn't want to go near Lakes Entrance itself. The very thought of shops and houses in such a spot was sad.

But a long thin man approached me as I sat on horseback staring down at the pancakes and the blue wine.

"Have you got a match?" he said

I took a box out of my blue flannel shirt pocket and gave him it. He very slowly extracted one, and said, "What's your name, young fellow?"

"My name is Steven," I said.

"And have you ridden down to have a look at the Lakes Entrance?"

"Yes. Do you know Banjo Paterson, by the way?"

"Yes, very well. But he's down in Melbourne at present."

"I wanted to see him about Gordon," I said. "Adam Lindsay Gordon." But he was away from home. So I turned my horse round and rode back the way I came.

It was night now at McLachlan's and the stars shone. We spent this last evening together listening to the songs of Italy, and at midnight I said good-bye to him. I stayed at the Buccaneer's for the week-end, and on the Wednesday morning I was up early; all my preparations for departure were complete. In the stockyard Alpini II stood shining, as black as Lucifer in the morning sunlight, with bright-brown leather pad and tan web girth; his brown-and-white bridle made a silvery sound as he shook his head. It was a glorious morning. I waited until I heard the mail-car hoot as it rounded the bend of the road beside the blue lake; I heard the *Gippsland's* siren hoot in answer as the big brilliant leaden-painted boat rounded the point; and in my mind I heard the loud lonely whistle of the train at Bumberrah; all three coincided at ten in the morning there. Then I brought the horse out of the yard and led him heavily like a black cameo down the golden cliff against the ultramarine water. Micolo followed me slowly. Edgar's wife stood on the wide grey veranda to wave me good-bye.

And what did I think of? Of what was I most conscious really as I rode away? Only of the drought, the dry grass, the dry road, the hard blue heavens above, and the rolling, strangely dry-looking miles of dark-blue water, foam-lined, that were the Lakes. I had the miles and years before me. I was glad to go and see new country, new colours and shades of earth. Within two or three days I should be right under Mount Buffalo, where the mountain streams rushed gurgling into the Ovens River and gave out pouring green miles of grass. I was glad for Alpini's sake that we were going. I looked back at the turn of the flat spinning sandy road and waved to the little Kirghiz figure on the long grey veranda, then with one last look from bronze haft to blue and white shaft end of the long romantic Lakes, I rounded the corner and rode slowly in the hot morning, past Dr Woods's, below Bond's, and uphill athwart Johnson's to Creeker's turn-off. I stopped there, and looked across the acres of slowly growing wide-eared beans, that to themselves held tremblingly the black shadows of long-lost

249

showers. My heart ached for the poor little plants, soft, gentle and deep, that longed for rain, and that on their slender tiny feet stood probing the stern earth for moisture, long day after day, and pattering in stifled tongues as the tall hot glassy thunder winds strode through the rows, beautiful with gathered images of cloud, but not bent on bringing rain. Alien among the beans, stood the lonely little tea-plantation, the dark, polished and desolate stranger to Australia.

There it lay, dark green on the yellow hill; moving up and down it were half a dozen Italians, looking over the bushes to see if there would be another picking before autumn. Ah, the feeling of that last nostalgic, frail, tired look-over; the worn weariness of the bushes quivered in my soul. McLachlan stood near the little tea factory watching them. His white suit and white topee gleamed in the hard bright morning sun. The white topee! I saw down the years, from Khartoum to Calulu, the long line of solar helmets and the great minds dreaming in their cool curve, and out of their dreams making an empire. And joining themselves to that line I saw our own dreams, and the toil we had given out of ourselves through this great ideal summer, the Australian summer that we had shared together and that now was ended. I thought of all the years I had given to Metung, and of Jim, and Blue, and Peppino, and Panucci, and the hard agony of life burnt in me with a great white fire, as once more with all of them I trod the bush track again to Creeker's turn-off. Once more, in my mind, I saw them walking before me like ghosts, talking in the half-sad, half-hopeful voice of humanity, the utterly kind simplicity of the great Australians, that strange gentle child-like emptiness of theirs, a people who loved the bush and work and old huts and few possessions, these silent peaceful poets of the earth. With one last sad tired look over the sunburnt head of Gippsland and deep into the fiery blue eyes of it, the sea, I touched with my shoe the black slumber of the racehorse into the bright angry fire of life, and, remembering deeply within itself some set goal of long, long ago, it set out with long striding strong impatient steps to carry me towards the far-off Australian Alps. The black-and-white staghound ran ahead, and Gippsland fell behind.

Also in SIRIUS PAPERBACKS
THE PEA-PICKERS
by Eve Langley

Eve Langley's unforgettable story of brimming youth and of survival in the Australian landscape: Steve and Blue are two girls who dress as men, who work as itinerant workers for the Italian farmers of Gippsland and who love and laugh all the way through the Australian Alps...

``The Pea-Pickers is a marvellous book — one of our literature's most memorable attempts to capture the essence of life in Australia."
MARK MACLEOD
SYDNEY MORNING HERALD

"There is no doubt The Pea-Pickers will retain its own individual niche in Australian Literature."
RUTH LESLEY,
CANBERRA TIMES

"Its poetry and humour bursts with vitality and with good things so abundant that it demands to be savoured."
IAN MAIR,
THE AGE

"It has the dew on it. It contributes something fresh in Australian literature. It is rare. I think it will be cherished."
FRANK DALBY DAVISON

"It is so beautiful and so original . . . We really have nothing else in Australian literature quite like it . . . It is the best evocation of the Australian landscape that has ever been done."
DOUGLAS STEWART

A STATE OF SIEGE
by Janet Frame

After the death of her invalid mother, Malfred Signal, a New Zealand art teacher, leaves her birthplace in the south for a beach cottage on a sub-tropical island in the north. She hopes to be alone. But the solitude she has sought mocks her with echoes of her past, when, one stormy night, an intruder pounds ceaselessly and inexplicably on her door . . .

Janet Frame was born in Dunedin, New Zealand in 1924. Apart from her highly acclaimed three-volume autobiography she has written eleven novels and has been awarded the New Zealand Literary Award for Non-Fiction, the prestigious James Wattie Book of the Year Award (1983 and 1985) and also the Fiction prize of the New Zealand Book Awards.

"She has shown, so quietly, a mastery of the English language which dazzles one beyond ordinary praise . . ."
NAOMI MITCHINSON

"Her fragmented visions are true nightmares, raising authentic goose-pimples upon the skin."
NEW YORK TIMES

". . . She is a giant among prose writers in English. It is impossible to call yourself well-read if you have not yet discovered Janet Frame."
STEPHANIE DOWRICK,
SYDNEY MORNING HERALD